POWER REDEEMED

WILD HERITANCE, BOOK 3

S. LYNN HELTON

Power Redeemed is a work of fiction.
Names, characters, places, organizations, and events are either products of the author's imagination or are used fictitiously. Any resemblance to actual persons, living or dead, organizations, events, or locales is entirely coincidental.

Copyright © 2020 S. Lynn Helton
Cover by R. M. Helton

ISBN (Paperback): 978-1-7326763-8-1
ISBN (Ebook): 978-1-7326763-9-8

Scripturio Books
www.ScripturioBooks.com
24.04.05

DEDICATION

To Mom and Dad, *with love.*

ACKNOWLEDGMENTS

A big thank you to
Bekah, Elaine, Mark, Rena, and Vickie
for all your terrific suggestions for improvements,
and for catching all those gotchas
before they got me!

CHAPTER 1

Something seized Namid's arm. It yanked at her, but she stood frozen.

"Run!"

She should be... what was she supposed to be doing? Something important. She knew that much.

But for some reason, she could not seem to think of what it could be. The haziness that shrouded her thoughts and the buzzing in her ears would not clear. She had been....

The coronation?

She fought to pull her thoughts together through the haze. Disjointed images flashed before her and flitted away again.

Memories.

The ruins of the city of Rhadanthus and a faintly glowing sword, shattered. Three towers, a wall enclosing them. A book with a red cover, a devastated village, green-yellow flames at a temple complex. Gods who weren't really.

Yokana, her mother, handing the crown of the Monarch to Talorisin, her brother, after they all knew that

Levil, husband and father, had died.

Her mother placing the crown on Tal's head.

A boy and girl fidgeting, dressed in fine clothes for some important event.

Namid shook her head. Or thought she did. Why couldn't she think?

She couldn't stay. She needed to leave.

Familiar Power swept across her. The magic coursed through the great hall where the Monarch typically held court, today festooned with lavish decorations and scented with rich, rare spices for the coronation.

"Namid!"

Someone shook her. She needed to pay attention. Needed to….

And the haziness shredded enough to let Namid focus on her surroundings and try to make sense of what she saw.

Two translucent figures stood in the center of the hall – a man and a woman dressed in rich clothes, both with light-colored hair and skin. Their heads reached the ceiling, a full two floors above.

She knew them. Belaraketh and Ilenii, the sibling 'gods'.

They stood there, their eyes not focused on the people gathered in the room.

Namid remembered… they had appeared right after Tal was crowned Monarch.

"Some kind of semblance," Aahmes had murmured in her ear.

And Ilenii had said, "People of the Six Realms, we bring warning to you. Two monsters lurk in your midst, plotting harm. They seem like people, these two dangerous Power-users who are spreading lies, who seek to tear down the gods and bring destruction."

Namid remembered this, but seemed to be reliving it, her thoughts sluggish under the weight of everyone's somewhat dazed regard, quickly turning hostile.

Two new images had formed at the so-called gods' feet:

Aahmes and Namid.

"These are the two," Belaraketh said. "Do not tolerate their presence. Reach out to us, to our temples, if you see them. Help us hunt them down and foil their vile plots."

The haze and lethargy that had engulfed her snapped, swept away by a cool wave of Wild Power from Aahmes. Namid exchanged a horrified look with him as realization crashed into her.

The courtiers and guards assembled for Tal's coronation as Monarch this day—those who did not know her personally—wore expressions that ranged from worried and angry to outright hostile. They eased closer, as if to surround her and Aahmes and yet afraid at the same time to approach them.

Yokana shook Namid's arm with surprising strength then clutched Aahmes'.

"You have to go!" she insisted.

"But…" Namid protested. She looked at the people gathered on the dais. Tal and his family stood near the front. Haeith stood guard behind them, with the guards Ordra and Krendl nearby. Mehratar the Healer stood beyond them, in the front row of those gathered to witness the ceremony. Enric and Cameni stood near him. All of them were dressed in fine silks for the coronation and all wore expressions that urged her to go.

"Run!" Yokana shoved Aahmes and Namid toward the family's door at the back of the dais.

As she shook off the last of the haziness in her thoughts, Namid grasped Aahmes' hand and they fled.

~ ~ ~

Aahmes and Namid slowed when they reached a deserted side corridor. With almost everyone in the citadel at the coronation, servants included, they had encountered only one roaming guard. They easily evaded his attention.

"We should head to the hidden passages," Namid said.

"What was that back there?" Aahmes said at the same time.

They shared a quick laugh and Aahmes nodded.

"Hide first, then talk," he said, and they crept through a couple of the servants' corridors to the nearest opening to the passages, hidden in one of the storerooms. At the back wall, Aahmes pressed on one of the panels with one hand at shoulder height and the other at his knee. A small lever popped out next to his lower hand. He gave it a sharp upward tug, then pressed it back into place. A thigh-high panel snapped open to his left. He pushed it further open and crawled through, heedless of the fine clothes he wore.

With a frown, Namid gathered the skirt of her fancy dress the best she could and crawled after him. He helped pull her trailing skirt into the narrow passage and closed the door behind her. Enough light leaked through narrow, random cracks in the walls to let them see.

"I remember a spot up ahead where there's no chance we'll be overheard," Namid whispered.

Aahmes nodded and kept his voice as quiet as hers. "Won't we have to crawl most of the way there? Going to be hard on your dress."

Namid chuckled, with the tiniest hint of unease. "I'm not worried about it. It's nice enough, but—"

"Not your preference, I know." He grinned at her, then scrunched around to lead the way.

As they crept further into the hidden passages of the citadel, the cracks in the walls grew fewer and smaller. They each drew on a little of their Power to create a small glowing orb to light their way.

Close to a quarter candle-mark later, they reached the spot Namid had remembered. And she had cursed her dress under her breath almost the entire time. The passage opened into a small room-like section, with three other openings that led out. Here they were able to stand.

Namid made a half-hearted swipe at the dirt on her blue gown and examined a long tear on the right side, then shrugged.

Aahmes watched her and smiled when she looked at him. She had to return his smile. He had a smudge on the side of his face, not too obvious on his red-brown skin. And his shoulder-length black hair had come loose from the queue he had tied at the nape of his neck for the coronation. He had dust in his hair.

Namid brushed her hand back over her own hair; before they ventured into the hidden passages, it had been braided and curled in an elaborate style for the ceremony. She tried to smooth a loose strand out of her face and wondered how dusty she was. Aahmes' smile widened.

"Yeah, pretty much a mess," he said.

"Thanks," she muttered. "But also my thanks for breaking through that haze the 'gods' put around me back there."

"Haze?" Aahmes said. "I didn't see that. But I saw you frozen. Held in place, it looked like. And you didn't seem to be fighting it. Good thing the Wild Power cut through whatever they were doing."

"It didn't affect you? What they were doing?"

"Didn't affect me the same. I felt extremely tired, had trouble keeping my eyes open. After several breaths-of-time, I realized something was wrong since I slept well enough last night. So I called Wild Power, and whatever it was snapped."

Namid slid down the wall to sit on the dusty floor.

"Back to living under a glamour, I suppose," she said.

Aahmes slid down next to her and shook his head. "I tried to place one on us as we ran through the halls. That Power we've felt before is there again, or one like it, the one that previously prevented glamours in the citadel and Kilaadi."

Namid gave him a surprised look. "So then it *wasn't* Andrin who placed it." She pictured the Dark Priest turned advisor to the Monarch, now dead. "I could see him capable."

5

Aahmes nodded. "And he might have. But I'm almost certain this one, at least, is from the so-called gods."

"Great. So we get to skulk in the hidden passages of the citadel. Again."

"I doubt we'll find anything here to help us deal with Ilenii and Belaraketh."

"True. I just wish we could find that book from Wesh's tower. Maybe there's something in there that would be useful. Where could Odasoro have stashed it that we can't find it? Wish he was here to ask." She fought off the wave of grief that washed over her at the reminder of the troubadour's death.

"Who would've thought he'd hide the book so well that a couple of Rhadanthus' famed Shadowers can't even find it."

"I don't know that I'd say famed," Namid muttered. "And I agree that staying here isn't likely to help. But where can we go that *will* help?"

Aahmes shrugged. "How about we figure that out after we grab what we can and get ourselves someplace better?"

Namid nodded as they both stood. "I've got the door to my rooms secured with Power. Should be safe enough to make a quick stop. Get my blades, better clothes for this sort of thing."

Aahmes leaned close with an intent look. "Too bad, really. You are stunning in that dress."

Namid smiled and gave him a lingering kiss.

After the kiss went on longer than she had intended, she pulled away with a wish that she did not have to. "Gear, clothes, maybe some food, too," she said. She looked around at the four openings.

"Now which way will be fastest to my rooms?"

~ ~ ~

Dressed in nondescript hats, gray tunics and trousers, and worn-looking boots, Aahmes and Namid stepped out of the small alley in which they had concealed themselves for close to a half candle-mark to observe the comings and goings in the city. At least no one seemed actively looking for them. In case that might change, Namid placed a veneer around them of belonging and being unremarkable.

They carried a single pack each as they strolled along the street, keeping their pace to the same as the others who were out in the midday summer heat.

"Find an inn to stay at for a couple of days?" Aahmes murmured to her.

Namid looked at the people they passed, and unease crawled down her back. As they moved further down the street, she and Aahmes drew longer looks from everyone. She checked the veneer – it was rapidly fraying.

"Problem," she whispered, and Aahmes nodded.

They turned into a side street, smaller and with fewer people. And heard the sound of heavy boots coming toward them.

A quick look around showed them several people in the street pointing to them. Others backed away and a few ran away entirely.

Namid turned into the first alley they came to and they broke into a run. They managed to duck through a couple of adjoining alleys before the owners of the boots— guards, most likely—got close enough to catch sight of them.

Aahmes shoved his arms through the handles of his pack so it clung to his back, then climbed the closest wall. Namid followed his example and in a breath-of-time, they both lay flat on the slightly sloping rooftop.

Namid tried to place a veneer over them that they were nothing more than an irregularity on the roof, but it slipped away from her. Even when she drew Wild Power.

Namid clasped Aahmes' hand then spoke to him through thought-speech.

~Can't hold a veneer now, either.~

So they scuttled away from the edge and huddled in the

7

shadow of an actual irregularity.

~We're going to need to completely change our appearances,~ Aahmes said the same way after they clasped hands again. *~I could wish we had all the Shadowers' resources here. Would make it so much easier.~*

Namid grinned. *~I've a better idea. It's time for me to show you how to shape-change.~*

CHAPTER 2

The wolves fled northwest, away from Kilaadi, capital city of the Six Realms of the Monarch.

They found plenty of small game, so they hunted on the move, gulped their food, and continued on again, running as often as they could. Until somewhere north of the northern border of the Six Realms, the best they determined, Aahmes and Namid stumbled to a stop.

Aahmes dropped the small bundle he had carried in his mouth as Namid sank to the ground and closed her eyes against the pain. She hurt everywhere. When she felt a cloak drop over her, she looked up at Aahmes, now back in his real shape and already dressed in his few clothes they had been able to bring.

As he tucked away his weapons, he nodded to her daggers and the small collection of her clothes that sat in a pile near her nose.

"Your turn," he told her, then limped to one of the sparse tall trees and sat down next to it with a sigh.

Namid released the Power, held only by tooth and claw it seemed to her weary thoughts, and returned to her normal shape beneath the cover of the cloak. She dressed in her shirt, tunic, and trousers as quickly as she could manage with limbs that did not seem to want to work right. Putting on her boots was even harder. Too long as a wolf, she guessed. And every movement sent pain shooting through her.

Namid found it difficult to remember how to walk on two legs. She paced to try to regain her balance but soon gave up the effort and instead settled on the ground in the brush next to Aahmes. She set her belt, daggers and few pouches in a pile next to her.

Aahmes draped an arm around her shoulders and pulled her close. She leaned against him, then twisted a little so she could look at him.

She ran one finger along the growth of beard along his jaw. With a crooked smile, he caught her hand and kissed the palm.

"That tickles," he told her.

"So you're ticklish?" she said, with an impish expression as she brushed his neck with a light touch of a finger.

He twitched away with a mock glare, which turned into a yawn.

And, of course, Namid yawned too.

"Something worth investigating further when we're both not bone-tired," she muttered.

She settled against him with a contented sigh. "Are you going to keep it? The beard? It does make you look quite different."

"Don't know," he said as he ran a hand along his jaw. "It's thin. And it itches."

"If only it was so easy for me to look different."

"Grow a beard?" Aahmes said with a chuckle. Namid laughed with him.

"I suppose I could cut my hair short…."

"Don't." Aahmes twined his fingers in her hair and leaned his head against hers. "I like it long."

Namid glanced at him and smiled.

"I'd not expected it to become so much harder, take more and more Power, to hold the shape-change the longer we tried to keep it," she said.

"What's the longest you'd held a shape-change before?"

Namid shrugged. "A couple candle-marks or so is all."

She felt Aahmes nod. "Well, now we know."

Namid yawned again. "Is it possible to be too exhausted to sleep?"

"Hard to relax when you're running from 'gods' and all the people they've tried to send against you."

Namid nodded. "Think they sent their semblance message to everyone in the clans, too? Like Kilaadi and then every single town and village we tried to stop at as we ran.

"Maybe. Although the clans have, by tradition, held themselves apart from the Six Realms and their doings, including their gods. For the most part."

"So maybe no one listened."

"We can hope."

Namid shifted around, trying to find a more comfortable position, and closed her eyes against the ongoing ache in her head.

"Do you decide ahead of time what you'll look like as a wolf?" Aahmes said after several breaths-of-time. His voice sounded like he was half asleep.

"Uh, no. I never thought about it."

"Hmm."

"Hmm, what?"

"Did you notice that as wolves we don't look as much alike as when we're ourselves?"

Namid considered that, her head tilted, and realized that he was right. Their wolf forms, except for the general colors of the fur, looked quite distinct from each other. Unlike they themselves, with their similar facial features, black hair and red-brown skin.

She had never given much thought to how her wolf-shape looked. Now she wondered if she could control its appearance like Aahmes controlled the glamours they had used before.

"Interesting. Think we can change the appearance?" she said.

Only Aahmes' steady breathing answered her. So she settled herself even more comfortably and tried to relax enough to get some much-needed rest.

~ ~ ~

Namid woke all of a sudden, shivering with cold. She lurched upright with an unvoiced groan and looked around. Aahmes was nowhere in sight, but the spot where he had leaned against the tree felt warm to her hand, so he had not been gone too long.

She stumbled around in an attempt to get her limbs working with less stiffness and aching. And also to try to reach the point where walking on two legs felt normal again. Every part of her still hurt, but a little less than before she slept.

She felt moisture on her cheek. Her eyes seemed to be watering. But when she wiped her cheeks, she found blood on her hands. A second swipe with her hands came away clean. And the blood dried and flaked off.

She stared at where the blood had been. What was this? She and Aahmes hadn't blended their Power this time.

While she paced, she laced on her armguards with their sheathed stilettos and buckled on her belt. Then she plaited her long hair into its customary single braid and tied off the braid with a strip of cloth torn from the bottom of her outer tunic. And she reached out, seeking the Wild Power in the area, to see what she might learn.

The main thing she learned was that she was still too drained to do much with Power, although she touched on a lot of it lurking in the vicinity. She closed her eyes against the headache that returned, then looked up at a familiar whistle, a signal that all was well.

She recognized the whistle from her shared time with Aahmes in the Shadowers, that guild of rogues that by now ran the city of Rhadanthus.

Aahmes himself almost immediately followed the whistle as he picked his way through the dense shrubs that comprised most of the plants in the area.

Namid smiled when she saw that he carried a couple of birds.

"I don't think I'll be shape-changing again anytime soon," Aahmes said. "I can barely manage to hold on to my own Power right now. But I managed to bring these two down the non-Powered way, so at least we can eat a little."

They busied themselves getting the birds ready and cooked, then greedily ate them. After they kicked dirt over the remains of the fire and birds, Namid took a slow look around.

"Any idea where we are?" she asked as she turned.

"Somewhat," Aahmes said. "We're definitely in the clans' territory, north of the border with the realm of Denek. These lands used to belong to my clan, before they were killed."

"Who do they belong to now?"

Aahmes shrugged. "Maybe no one. I don't think anyone's nearby. I spotted what used to be a well-traveled road. It looked like it hasn't seen much use anytime recently. Maybe not since around the time I fled sixteen, seventeen winters ago."

"Think we can stop here then? Or should we go further north?"

Aahmes considered that.

"I don't think we want to go too much further north. I remember talk of how bad the winters could get there."

"So you think we'll still be hiding when winter comes?"

He gave her a long look. "I think it's possible. Unless you've got a brilliant idea that you haven't mentioned to get these so-called gods to leave us alone."

Namid shook her head. "Wish I did."

"In that case, shall we find some shelter?" He held a hand out to her.

She took it. "Yeah. And no shape-changing for me either. So still north, at least for a bit?"

He shrugged and they headed the direction that Aahmes picked. "At least roughly, for now. Maybe I can find a landmark I definitely recognize."

"And then?"

"There used to be scattered shelters, small houses in reality, that the clan kept for people to use if they were caught out in one of the sudden storms."

"Like that one we sheltered in before Lann had his clansmates capture us last autumn?"

An expression of distaste crossed Aahmes' features at the mention of his distant cousin but then he smirked. "Better than any of his clan's shelters. *My* clan built its shelters into hills to better keep out the cold. And they also kept them well stocked, from what I remember. Of course, after so long…." He shrugged.

As they traveled, Namid studied her surroundings. She remembered the scattered tall trees of a different part of the clans' territory from the previous autumn, but these trees grew even taller. Their trunks were a deep reddish brown, close to the color of her own skin. Leaves about the size of her hand clung to slender branches, the lowest of which were more than twice her height from the ground.

The brush that grew in large clumps between the sparse trees, and at their bases, reached Namid's height in many places, with many small oval leaves of a pale green. Aahmes picked their path the best he could between the clumps, although often they needed to fight their way through the close-growing branches to continue the direction they wanted. Namid gave little thought to the noise they made – they had seen no signs of anyone nearby.

The afternoon brought Aahmes and Namid to an area of thinner growth and rougher land. As dusk fell, along with rain, they found a somewhat sheltered nook under one tree where it had fallen against another. Small, but not too damp.

Aahmes managed to get another bird with a makeshift sling, so they had hot food. But with no room in the shelter for the fire—it sat out in the rain—after the food was cooked, it seemed more trouble than it was worth to try to keep it going.

Namid considered using Power, as she had to even get it started. But she decided against that when she took stock of her reserve and found it still far too low.

"Anything looking familiar yet?" Namid said as they settled in, huddled together for warmth and to keep from getting dripped on.

"Only in a general sense, so far. But if the trees and tall brush keep thinning, I should be able to get a better idea tomorrow."

After several breaths-of-time of listening to the rain, Namid sighed. "How long have we been fleeing so far? And how are we going to fix this?"

"Somewhat around three weeks, maybe a bit longer, to answer the first," Aahmes said. "I lost track of the days as a wolf, but that's pretty close. The second... well, we could just hide and make our own lives somewhere."

"Nothing to keep them from finding us."

"Which leads to another option. Confront them and battle it out."

Namid considered that. "Would have to be someplace where no one else could get caught up in it. And what damage would we do with a Power battle of that magnitude?"

Aahmes nodded. "Wonder if that concoction of Lann's would work on the 'gods'... the one he made us drink to 'guarantee no magical difficulties', as he put it."

"I remember. Maybe. But how do we get some? And then get them to drink it?" Namid sighed again. "Maybe there's some other way to keep them from using Power."

"Other than the various types of theft the Dark Priests used, of course," Aahmes said.

"Of course."

~ ~ ~

The next morning found them chilled and stiff from trying to fold themselves into the tiny dry space under the tree. But they again had a hot meal, then set out, fighting against fatigue that seemed to drag at them both. Namid suspected it came from their use of so much Power for so long. She hoped it would ease soon.

About midday the trees and tall brush had thinned enough to allow them to see some distance when they came to more-elevated areas. Atop each hill, Aahmes paused for them both to catch their breath while he looked all around before he picked the direction to take to the next hill. Each choice took them more east than north now. After several of these pauses, he turned to Namid with a smug expression.

"Do you see it?"

She gave him a narrow-eyed look, then turned her gaze the direction he had been looking. After studying the hills she saw in the distance, through the ever-thinning plants, she nodded.

"I think so." She pointed to a dark spot near the base of one of the hills. "Over there? That shadow looks too regular in shape."

Aahmes nodded. "Let's take a closer look at it."

He grasped her hand and pulled her toward the hill at a stumbling trot. Neither of them had yet recovered their normal ease of movement and Namid wondered if Aahmes ached as much as she still did.

They both looked all around and even sent out the

tiniest wisps of Power—just about all they could manage—to see if anyone else was near. Although Namid still had trouble sensing non-Powered people that way.

"I don't think anyone's been here for a while," Namid said as they slowed to approach what she could now see was a narrow, rectangular hole in the hill.

Aahmes nodded. "That's how it feels to me, too."

Namid glanced back over her shoulder the way they had come. "Do you think they're following us?"

"Ilenii and Belaraketh? If they are somehow, they're not anywhere close enough to sense. And I don't see how they could be following anyway – we've used so little Power that would be easily detected from a distance."

"Easily detected?"

"Yeah, didn't you notice? The Power we used shape-changing was all contained within. So even running right next to you, I couldn't sense that you used it to hold your wolf shape."

She gave him a startled look. "I *hadn't* noticed."

Aahmes stepped around in front of her to give her a close look. "No wonder. You poured all your Power and concentration into keeping the shape, right? And now you're still drained, aren't you?"

"Pretty much. The Power is trickling back, but not as fast as I've gotten used to. And I hurt."

He nodded. "Yeah, me too. Wonder if it's from being so long in a shape not ours." He shrugged. "My Power is returning slower, too, though I think not as slow as yours. Good thing we've got a place to hole up. Get a chance to rest from running. Should make a difference."

Namid eased into the opening in the hill, and found she needed to turn left to continue. A couple paces long, the narrow passage ended at thick fur hung from the low ceiling.

"Bear skin, I think," Aahmes said as he reached around her and pushed the fur back to reveal the space beyond.

Sidling past her with a rakish grin and a quick kiss in

passing, Aahmes led the way inside and called up a tiny glowing orb of Power for light. Namid followed him and paused just inside the opening.

She inspected the small room they found themselves in. Tucked into the hill, with worked stone walls and ceiling, and a hard dirt floor, it looked not unlike the shelter she had seen before in the clan lands. A brick and mortar hearth sat in the center of the wall to her left and a couple of stone benches flanked it along the wall.

Beyond the end of the farther bench sat a stack of blocks that looked like they were made from dark dirt packed with bits of dried plants. Each block was a little shorter than the length of Namid's forearm with sides a little wider than her handspan.

"Where's the wood for the hearth? I remember that wood's supposed to be precious in the clans' territory, but it seems there are plenty of trees around. That other shelter we used had wood to burn. And what're those?" She waved a hand toward the blocks.

Aahmes chuckled. "Yeah, generally the clans don't burn what wood they have. That shelter was an unusual exception. Most of the wood in the clans' territory is soft, not very useful for making things, and also burns very smoky. There is little that isn't soft and doesn't smoke, and that little is too valuable for trade to just burn for warmth." He crossed the room to the stack of blocks. "These are peat bricks. They come from bogs, in the northern and eastern parts of the clans' territory, if I remember right. They're for burning instead of wood that smokes too much."

With a nod, Namid continued her perusal of the place. In the corner to her right, she spotted two rolls of what looked to be bedding, mats similar to what the Shadowers had used in Rhadanthus while they rebuilt their home. But these mats looked thicker, more truly mattresses.

The mattresses sat beneath several stone shelves that held folded cloth, along with some candles and some earthenware plates and bowls. Next to the bedding and shelves, toward the back corner, hung another fur. A peek behind that revealed a small alcove that held the privy, with a faint sound of rushing water coming up from somewhere below.

Namid returned to the main room and again looked around, standing in the room's center, then smiled at Aahmes. "Might be the most room we've had all to ourselves," she said.

A couple of steps took Aahmes to one of the benches. He brushed his fingertips across the seat. "Plenty of dust. No sign of anyone here recently. And no sign of animals or bugs to worry about either."

Namid studied the hearth and discovered the clever chimney bored through the rock ceiling at an angle. She then looked over the bedding.

"Looks in pretty good condition, despite the dust. And comfortable enough," she said. "A nice change from leaning against trees."

"A bit musty," Aahmes said as he also examined the bedding, "but should still be usable. At least until we can gather fresh materials. It used to be that everything was refreshed in these shelters every couple of summers, I think. Who knows how long it's been for this one."

Namid took a closer look at the items on the shelves.

"Should be some clothes," Aahmes said as he joined her. "Some blankets, too, it looks like."

She nodded as she looked through the clothing items: shirts, tunics, trousers and cloaks. All but the shirts were made of cloth woven in a crossbarred pattern of shades of gray and red.

"Clan Naalin's colors," Aahmes said in response to her questioning look.

"Good to have some new clothes. We didn't exactly pack well for this journey."

Aahmes snorted a short laugh, drew her into his arms and planted a kiss on the side of her neck. She leaned into him, relishing the feel of his arms around her.

"But I finally have you all to myself, anyway," Aahmes murmured by her ear. Then her stomach growled, loudly, and he released her with a chortle.

"And we need to eat. So we should check the state of the root cellar," he said as he turned back toward the doorway that led outside.

"Would anything stored there still be edible?"

"We should find out. Come on."

He led her back outside and off to one side, scuffing his boots through the plant debris on the ground until he hit something that did not sound like dirt and dead leaves.

"Here."

Namid helped him brush away the accumulation of years to reveal a strange wooden door set into the base of the hill at an angle that matched the hill's slope. Namid had not seen anything like it before. Many vertical sticks, longer than she was tall, had been woven together with wires and horizontal sticks to form the door.

They paused to rest before they tackled the old, warped door.

After they wrestled it open, they descended a few debris-coated steps into the ground. Some of the leaves that crunched under their boots gave off a pungent, herbal odor. They followed a short brick-lined passageway to another sticks-and-wires door, this one set upright in a brick and mortar wall built within the cave. Again Aahmes created a small glowing orb and they stepped inside.

Perhaps half the size of the shelter they had just explored, the small room was lined with stone shelves on two walls and large sealed jars of various sizes along the third, along with a few empty buckets. Namid sniffed at the acrid odor that hung in the room, then coughed.

Aahmes nodded. "Yeah, some of it's gone bad. We'll want to clean it out soon. But there." He pointed toward several small sealed jars that sat on a shelf toward the back of the room. "Those should be honey. Should still be good. The rest is probably dried carrots, maybe fruits, corn, some stock, salt, a few spices…. I see some jams, but I think those might be some of what's gone bad. Maybe the fruit, too."

He waved a hand at the largest of the jars. "Should be beans and rolled oats there. Drink in the smaller jars."

"With a bit of extra aging to it," Namid commented.

Aahmes nodded, the corners of his mouth quirked up. "And there'll be a well or stream for water. Maybe further around the hill."

Namid gazed around the room and nodded. "This helps a lot. But let's wait until tomorrow to begin cleaning out."

Aahmes agreed. He pulled a small sealed jar from a shelf near Namid's shoulder—saying it contained stock—and one empty lidless jar, which he filled with oats from one of the large jars. He handed her a few small jars to carry – various spices, he told her. Last, he grabbed one of the buckets.

They returned outside and secured the doors behind them. Aahmes added a touch of Power to seal them against opening for anyone but the two of them.

Back in the house, as Namid was coming to think of the shelter, Aahmes helped her get some peat bricks burning – she managed some blue-white sparks with her Power, but not enough to set the bricks on fire. Then Namid began heating the stock and oats on the hearth, while Aahmes took the bucket and went back outside to find their water source.

After he left, Namid changed into a clean shirt, tunic and trousers from the shelves. Nice to be in fresh clothes, even if mustiness clung to them. When Aahmes returned, he brought a small, sealed jug along with the bucket of water.

"Wine," he said to Namid's questioning look.

He placed another Power seal on the hanging fur and the opening into their shelter, then hauled one of the sleeping mats outside. After she checked on the stock and oats, Namid hauled the second mat out as well and they shook and beat them to get the dust out of them as much as possible.

Aahmes carried the first one back in when it was as dust-free as they could manage. When he returned, he had also changed into clean clothes from the shelves.

"The food looks ready," he said, and they hauled the second mat back inside. For their meal, they used two of the earthenware bowls, along with spoons they found tucked behind them on the shelves.

After they had eaten and cleaned up, Aahmes double-checked his Power seal on the doorway, then collected a couple of candles from the top shelf. He lit them, dripped some melted wax onto one of the benches and stuck the candles there.

"In the winter it'll get cold overnight in here, although this hearth seems to hold the heat well," he said as he helped Namid position the sleeping mats near the hearth. Side by side, the two mats covered most of the floor. With a mischievous expression, Namid drug one of the mats atop the other.

"That will be more comfortable, I think," she said.

She stretched out on the mats with a heartfelt sigh at the relief of lying still. She met Aahmes' gaze with a smile, then watched him heat the wine near the fire as fatigue washed over her and her eyes drifted closed.

~ ~ ~

Namid groaned softly as she woke to the complaints of her numb arm beneath her. She lay on her side, tucked under one of Aahmes' arms and pressed against his side. Her head lay on his shoulder and her other arm rested across his chest, atop the clan shirt he wore. Her own clan clothes had her nice and warm, and blankets covered them both.

And she did not remember getting there – she must have fallen asleep while Aahmes heated the wine. She grimaced at the thought and tried to shift without disturbing him, to relieve the discomfort in her arm.

With her movement, dust and mustiness wafted into her face from the mattresses beneath them and the blankets atop them and she promptly sneezed, shaking both herself and Aahmes. Then his laughter shook them both again.

"Seems like we'd better gather that fresh stuffing for the bed today," Namid said as she rolled over partway so she could better look at him.

With a smile, he pulled her close for a kiss, then quickly turned aside to sneeze. "Guess we'd better," he said.

And so, after they had eaten, after Namid rebraided her hair, catching the strands that had come loose while she slept, Aahmes showed her the grasses and herbs that the clans used to stuff mattresses.

They gathered as much as they could carry in their first trip and returned to the house to tear open a seam on the mattresses and remove the old stuffing. They then rinsed the empty covers with a couple of buckets of water and spread them out to dry in the summer sun. They spent the bulk of the day gathering more grasses and some of the herbs that Aahmes said helped keep bugs away. They moved slowly, still fighting fatigue, and only gathered enough to re-stuff one of the mattresses once the covers dried. They spent some time, too, removing the food that had gone bad from the root cellar.

With the little daylight that was left, Aahmes showed Namid the stream around the side of the hill where he had gotten the water the previous evening. One section of the stream had been widened to form a small pool where they took quick turns getting cleaned up in the cold water.

~ ~ ~

The night had been colder than the previous one, although both had fallen asleep as quickly as Namid had the previous night. Namid found light frost covering everything when she stepped outside that morning. She stretched in the sunshine, pleased to feel less pain this morning, and looked around. Aahmes stepped up behind her and brushed his lips across the side of her neck.

Namid gestured at the frost. "I thought it was still summer for another couple of weeks," she said.

After some thought, Aahmes nodded. "Best I can figure, yeah. Although I think we're in the last weeks of the season now. And winter comes faster in the clans' territory than further south. I can remember one time that it seemed it was summer one day and the dead of winter the next." He frowned. "That was a long winter. We'd better see about gathering redberries while we can, to add to our food stores in case it's a sudden, bad winter."

"And there's still the other mattress to finish."

"We can get that done today and still get some berries, too."

They spent the morning gathering the grasses and herbs for the second mattress, then Aahmes showed Namid how to find the low plants that held redberries, the edible berry that grew native in the clans' territory. After he filled his bucket, he returned to put the mattress back together while Namid stayed to fill her bucket and a third that Aahmes ran out to her.

Several times she glanced over her shoulder as she gathered the berries. Nothing there, and nothing she sensed with the tiny amount of Power she sent out around her. But she could not shake an uneasiness that troubled her, a lingering feeling that they would not have long in this refuge.

As the time approached to head back, Namid found a last hidden cluster of berry plants and stripped them of berries, filling her buckets almost to overflowing. With a glance at the westering sun, she turned back toward their shelter. She kept her attention on her surroundings, as they both had been doing these past weeks, and sent out thin tendrils of Power from time to time to see if anything in the area had changed.

As Namid picked her way through the prickly brush, she considered their food stores. While the berries would help, if they wanted much more than oats and beans for the winter, they might have to brave some village or small settlement where they could get some food without being recognized.

At least so she hoped.

Aahmes had become frustrated with attempts to shape his beard and had shaved it off the day before, so now they both again looked like the semblances the 'gods' Ilenii and Belaraketh had displayed just weeks earlier to try to capture them.

Namid was nearly at the shelter when she stopped. Something *had* changed. Someone else was there.

Chapter 3

Namid eased into some denser brush, using all her skills to try to stay hidden. She scrutinized the hill that held the shelter, and the small glade between it and her location.

Nothing immediately evident.

~*Good, you're back,*~ came Aahmes' voice in her thoughts. ~*It's all right. We just have a couple of unexpected guests.*~

She sheathed her dagger, retrieved her buckets of berries and approached the shelter. Awkward as it was, she held the handles of both buckets in one hand to keep the other hand free. Just in case.

When she was half a pace away, Aahmes stepped out into the glade.

"What is it?" Namid paused, seeing a mix of surprise and consternation in his expression.

"Something I'd never expected," Aahmes said as he took one of the buckets from her. "Two clansmates. But mine, not Lann's. I even remember one of them. Sort of."

"But... how?" What were two clansmates doing there, and so soon after they themselves had come to the shelter?

Aahmes shrugged. "They were just getting to that when

I told them to wait. Whatever this is, I want you to hear it, too."

After a long kiss, he led the way inside.

Namid nodded at the two women seated close together on one of the benches inside the shelter. While she took her time dumping the berries out of her bucket and into several jars, she studied the newcomers with quick glances.

Namid judged the younger woman to be some years older than Aahmes, likely more than a score. Both newcomers had brown skin, lighter than hers and Aahmes'. The younger woman's hair was dark brown and reached just below her shoulders. White streaked the older woman's dark hair, which she wore tied at the nape of her neck. Her face and hands bore a few wrinkles. She caught Namid's gaze and gave her a slight smile.

Namid turned away, suddenly self-conscious as she realized she wore clansmates clothes. And the visitors' clothes both bore the same pattern, the one Namid knew belonged to Aahmes' clan.

The younger woman muttered something in a language Namid did not recognize. Her tone sounded peevish. Aahmes answered her in what sounded like the same language as he set a cup of wine near Namid.

We'll hear what they have to say, he told Namid using the hand-talk they both knew from their time as Shadowers, then took a spot on the second bench.

The woman spoke again – sounded like a complaint to Namid.

"In the tongue of the Six Realms, if you please," Aahmes said in an irritated tone.

Namid glanced over her shoulder at Aahmes to find him frowning at the woman.

The woman huffed a sigh. "Certainly that can wait," she said, her words slightly accented. Her voice was not loud, but Namid got the impression that she did not need to be loud to get what she wanted.

"It won't take long," Aahmes said and grinned at

Namid as she deliberately continued to divide the berries into the jars. When she finished, she brought her cup of wine with her to sit next to him.

With a sharp nod, the younger woman spoke again, her gaze on Aahmes. "As I was saying, you were probably young enough—"

The other woman cleared her throat, interrupting her. "We are guests here, I remind you," she said in a low voice, with a quick squeeze for the other woman's hand. "Have you been so long an Acnald?"

Namid felt Aahmes tense and gave him a questioning look.

"Lann's clan," he said.

The younger woman frowned, with a quick shake of her head for her companion. "No. And no longer. I just don't want to take more time than—" She broke off at the older woman's pointed look.

"As you say," the younger woman said, then looked to Namid. "We had not expected to find anyone using the shelter. Please accept this as our guesting gift." She took a beautiful stamped leather bracelet from her arm and held it out to Namid. The woman wore a similar one on her other arm, and a silvery ring on her left thumb. The other woman wore a similar ring.

Namid glanced at Aahmes, who nodded. She accepted the gift. "Thank you."

The woman gave her an expectant look and seemed to be waiting for something. Namid looked to Aahmes in time to see the hint of a smile cross his lips.

"Namid is not of the clans," he said.

The younger woman started. "No? But certainly—" She stopped when the older woman placed a hand on her arm.

"A word of explanation, then," the older woman said. "Although Aahmestharq has assured us of our welcome here, among our people the home is considered to belong to the eldest woman who lives there, and it is she who determines the welcome for guests. It's clear you have made this your home, even if only intended temporarily."

Namid looked from one to other. "Oh. Ah, yes… you are welcome here." Namid realized then that both their guests had cups of wine sitting next to them on the bench. She took a sip of her own and wondered what came next.

Aahmes gave her arm a quick squeeze and Namid noticed the younger woman's sudden sharp attention at his action.

"I am Taakhanefret Fathnor Ranasdotr, of the clan Naalin," she said and held up a hand to forestall Aahmes' questions. "We'll get to that. My companion is Sanethakht Vithen Kharesdotr, also of the clan Naalin."

"Please, call me Saneth," the older woman said.

"Aahmestharq is already known to us," Taakhanefret said, with a pointed look at Namid.

"I'm Namid, as Aahmes mentioned a short time ago." Something about this woman's manner irritated her and while Namid would welcome her as a guest for Aahmes' sake, she was uncertain she wanted the woman to know much about her.

Aahmes leaned close and spoke for her ears alone. "It's customary to give one's entire name. It really *is* all right."

Namid sighed. "I'm Tanyala Sainamid Shartov," she said, "but I go by Namid."

"Of the ruling family of the Six Realms?" Saneth said.

At Namid's nod, Saneth looked thoughtful.

"I'd heard that the clan Naalin was no more," Namid said.

With a glare for Saneth, Taakhanefret spoke again. "That is what we were just explaining. Aahmestharq—"

"Call me Aahmes."

"Aahmes, then, was probably young enough to be unaware and uninterested in how certain clan customs work. Pledges specifically. Everyone has a rank within their birth clan. When a couple pledges to each other, they both then become part of the clan of whichever of them holds the higher rank within their own clan. So, many who were born into clan Naalin were members of other clans when the massacre was carried out."

"But how do you claim to be of clan Naalin now?" Aahmes said.

"A little-used custom. Until recently, that is," Saneth said. "A death in a clan can change the rank of everyone within that clan, as in the Six Realms, where the death of a queen can make a princess a queen, for example. If a death within one's birth clan changes a person's rank so that they then hold a rank higher than the person they are pledged to, they both can choose to become part of the other clan, even taking any children they might have with them into the other clan."

Namid frowned and pointed at Taakhanefret. "So you were born into clan Naalin, then pledged into clan Acnald, Lann's clan? But with the massacre of clan Naalin, that gives you a higher rank in that clan and so now you're clan Naalin again?"

Taakhanefret nodded.

"And you just drug your families back into clan Naalin with you?"

Both women shook their heads.

"My children are grown and on their own," Taakha said. "My spouse would not leave his clan, so we left each other instead and dissolved our pledge." Under her breath, she added," Good thing, too."

"My spouse died many winters ago," Saneth said in a low voice. "While his clan, Larinaq, has always been welcoming to me, when clan Naalin began to revive, I decided to return. We'd never had children, so the decision was an easy one."

"There are a number of us, enough to restore the clan, although much diminished from what it once was," Taakha said. "And enough to remove Lann, we hope. We need to act before he leads all the clans to ruin. And now that we know you survived, Aahmes...." She leaned toward them. "You could be chieftain."

Aahmes jerked back at her pronouncement. "What? No. My family were advisors, nothing more."

"If the chieftain's line fails, tradition sees the rank pass to one of the advisory families," Saneth said. "The Cohaire."

"And there had already been talk of your mother taking the rank of chieftain next," Taakhanefret said, "as Chieftain Mehtnathor was the last of his family."

"But only talk, Taakhanefret?" Namid said.

"Call me Taakha. And yes, it had not been formalized. But I know that it would've been. Except she was killed."

~*Taakha?*~ Namid asked Aahmes using thought-speech. ~*Don't I know that name?*~

~*My baby sister,*~ Aahmes responded the same way. ~*I think I mentioned her. She was named after this cousin.*~ Aloud he said, "So that's the truth of what was behind the killings?"

"Many believe so," Saneth said. "But no one ever found any definitive proof."

"We got proof enough when Haqareh was the last to see Chieftain Mehtnathor before he succumbed to his illness that night," Taakha said, her tone sharp. "Proof enough when Haqareh claimed he had been named the next chieftain and the remaining Cohaire all acclaimed him as such, then later enjoyed a suspicious glut of luxury goods."

"Haqareh?" Namid muttered aside to Aahmes.

"Lann's father," Aahmes said.

"And Lann has been doing his own culling. Limited, up to this time, at least," Taakha said. "But now that we know the rumors are true, that you live, that you weren't killed, you must return with us, Aahmes. With you to be the next chieftain, we can remove Lann from power and restore clan Naalin's rightful place among the clans!"

From the corner of her eye, Namid saw Aahmes shake his head. She leaned toward Taakha, drawing the other woman's attention.

"You said you hadn't expected to find anyone using the shelter," Namid said, "so, what brought you here, into the clan's former lands? You mentioned rumors about Aahmes being alive. What other rumors have you heard? What sent you here?"

Both Taakha and Saneth gave Namid perplexed looks, then looked to Aahmes.

"We're hunted by some people," he said. "And Lann probably would be one of them, if he knew we were here. Your arrival is... unusual. At best."

"We haven't come hunting you," Taakha said.

"We intend no harm to you or yours," Saneth added.

"No harm? You don't think dragging Aahmes into a clan conflict, a war even, might bring him harm?" Namid demanded. She was not going to lose him again. "And just what *did* bring you out here?"

"A hint, a suggestion," Saneth said. "We didn't know what we would find. We've been traveling the Naalin lands for several weeks now, before we came here."

"What hint?" Aahmes said.

Namid wondered if his thoughts matched hers, that their presence in clan Naalin lands had been anticipated somehow, and now they were found out.

"Lann's Seer spoke with us alone late one night," Taakha said. "She told us we should return to our clan's lands, that we would make a discovery there."

Aahmes and Namid exchanged looks. "With the rarity of Seers, according to Mehratar, what do you wager this one was Wesh's?" Namid said.

"*If* we believe Mehratar, it seems likely the same person," Aahmes said. "Though what that Healer would know of Seers, I'm uncertain."

"I believe Mehratar," Namid said.

Aahmes shrugged.

"If the Seer in fact belongs to this Wesh, perhaps she manipulates Lann, and us, for her own purposes," Saneth said. "Or perhaps at the behest of this Wesh?"

"Wesh is dead," Namid said. "But we know next to nothing about his Seer. Or anyone else's, if they're not one and the same."

"This is beside the point," Taakha said. "We must decide how best to gather the rest of the clan and proclaim Aahmes chieftain. Time is short before travel becomes all but impossible with approaching winter. It looks to be a bad one."

"She's really resolved about that," Namid muttered to Aahmes.

He chuckled, earning a glare from Taakha.

"It's not a matter of levity," she said. "We must act. And it would be wise to have you pledged too, Aahmes, before we proclaim you. Clan Diarmid has always been friends with clan Naalin. Their Cohaire, the ones who would support us, have a few daughters of appropriate age to choose from."

Namid burst out laughing at Aahmes' expression. His amusement at the suitors who had desired her on their stay in Kilaadi the past spring had come home to him now! He glared at her then shook his head at Taakha.

"No."

"Don't be ridiculous," Taakha said. "Of course you two aren't pledged. All to the best, really."

Aahmes caught Namid's hand and held it deliberately in view.

"No, we're not pledged," he said. "We've not yet come close to that discussion. But I've lived longer away from the clans than I did within them. By birth, I'm clan Naalin. But I don't see that I can really claim to be a clansmate any longer, certainly not one to be chieftain. You both are from families of the Cohaire, if I remember those families correctly. Why not one of you? Or I'd think one of the other families has someone most can agree on. Maybe even one of those 'daughters of appropriate age'. If clan Diarmid's Cohaire are such great friends with clan Naalin, that should work well enough, shouldn't it?"

He shot to his feet, released Namid's hand, and stalked outside.

"*That* went well," Saneth muttered, her tone at variance with her words. She took a long drink of her wine and gave Taakha a sidelong look.

"We'll talk with him more," Taakha said. "He'll come around."

"I'm still here," Namid snapped. "And no. I doubt he will."

"You're not a clansmate, nor pledged to one," Taakha snapped back. "You have no say in this."

"You might be surprised," Namid said and followed Aahmes.

CHAPTER 4

Several paces from the shelter, Namid caught up to Aahmes. He slammed his fist against a handy tree and muttered some colorful curses.

Namid leaned against a different tree nearby. "I appreciate the sentiment," she said.

Aahmes nodded. "Yeah. Sorry I found your predicament so amusing this past spring."

Namid chuckled. "I understand. From the outside it does seem rather humorous."

Aahmes growled something under his breath.

Namid sidled up to him, tucked herself in at his side, and wrapped his arm around her shoulder. She bumped his hip with hers. "So, talk to me. I feel I'm missing out on some details here. And Taakha seems to think she can get you to do this."

Aahmes shrugged and gave her shoulder a squeeze. "I'm not sure I've got the whole picture either," he said. "Some of what they said, I think I was vaguely aware of. Maybe."

He sighed. "I'd only seen eleven, twelve winters when I ran from the clans' territory. Much of this held no interest

35

for me, so while I remember the adults and elders speaking about such things, I paid little attention to the details."

Namid nodded.

"So, about this pledging…" she said.

Aahmes groaned.

"Your cousin seems quite determined on that point, too."

Aahmes nodded. "You're familiar with the idea," he said with a crooked smile. "Make sure the heir you're putting forward is safely and appropriately paired."

"Yeah, I might've encountered that idea before," Namid said, her tone wry.

Aahmes' lips quirked up at the corners, which was what she had hoped for.

"But I've no intention of being their heir, their chieftain," Aahmes said. "Those daughters will just have to look elsewhere, if one of them doesn't want to be chieftain herself."

"Good!" Namid said.

Aahmes chuckled at her vehemence and they shared a quick kiss.

"So what can you tell me about this guest gift?" Namid said, indicating the bracelet from Taakha, which she still held. "Do I owe her a gift in return? What would I even give her? We have clothes and food and bedding. Daggers, too."

"As I remember, the guest brings a gift, the host owes the guest a meal and a night's lodging."

"Oh. Well, it won't be anything fancy, but we can do that."

"We can have some of the berries with the meal," Aahmes said. "That will add a little something extra, anyway. I'll get some things from the root cellar."

Namid gave him a mock glare. "And leave me with the pledge-happy cousin of yours."

Aahmes chuckled again. "You could always get some more water," he said. "We could use some. And I'll be back by the time you return."

With a grin, Namid nodded.

~ ~ ~

On her way back from the stream with two buckets of water, an odd, tingling itch grazed Namid's skin. A quick look around showed her nothing different, but she sensed through the Wild Power that something approached.

She dropped to the ground where she stood, the buckets sloshing on either side of her, and sent out a tendril of Power to Aahmes. She found him in the entrance to the root cellar. He linked his Power to hers and together they reached out.

They pulled back hurriedly when they brushed against a wave of Power approaching from the southeast.

Namid drew Wild Power to herself. She sensed an abundance of it around her but was unable to control more than the tiniest bit, still exhausted as she was from the recent shape-changing. Using the technique that she had learned from Mehratar, she created a woven strand of the Power to increase its effectiveness, then built a kind of veneer to cover herself with an impression of no one hiding there.

She tried, and failed, to extend the veneer to blanket the area around her with an impression of no one having been there for years. She felt a brief touch of Wild Power from Aahmes and he built the veneer to blanket the area and joined it to her veneer where they touched. Both pulled their own Power within, close to themselves, so it should not be sensed by anyone who looked for it.

Then they waited.

Slowly Namid turned her head so she could see Aahmes where he also had flattened himself to the ground. Still moving bit by bit, Namid tilted her head and watched through the Wild Power as waves of Power flowed over them, less than a half-pace above the ground.

After the waves had passed, and did not return, Namid let out the breath she had been holding. She and Aahmes dissolved their veneers, then met in the middle of the small glade, again carrying the goods they had been bringing to the shelter.

"Felt like both of them to me," Namid whispered. Probably unnecessary, but it felt appropriate.

Aahmes nodded agreement. "But I think the veneers worked. I didn't get any sense that they discovered us, or even that they noticed anything to catch their attention." He spoke as softly as she did.

"I think they might be searching blindly. Did Belaraketh not know you came from the clans?"

Aahmes gave that some thought. "When I learned about the Power at his temple, I didn't talk about where I came from. And I didn't stay long."

"But they're looking beyond the Six Realms, now," Namid muttered. "Not good."

Aahmes offered no argument.

~ ~ ~

The meal was plain, and they ate mostly in tense silence. Afterward, Saneth left to check on the horses in the stable.

"We have a stable?" Namid said to Aahmes.

He nodded. "Should be tucked into one of the nearby hills, much like this shelter. Since we had no need of it, I didn't even go looking for it."

When Saneth returned, they all settled again on the benches, cups of wine at hand.

And Taakha started in again.

"You must see how we need you," she said to Aahmes. "Surely you remember the high regard everyone had for your family. Even as a child you must have been aware of it. You can do so much for your people—"

"I wasn't raised to be chieftain," Aahmes broke in.

"You can learn," Taakha said.

Aahmes shook his head. "Tell us more about Lann's Seer. And what's happened that made you—and others, I assume—decide *now* that you need to oust Lann?"

"He's never been the chieftain we need," Saneth said. "His father made some effort, at least at first, to try to meet the needs of all the clans. Lann only cares for what he wants, and perhaps what benefits his closest companions. He's cut off most trade and just takes what he wants. He's turned our fighters into raiders. After rumors began about your return, he started silencing anyone who questioned him."

"Silenced as in killed?" Namid said.

"We think so. But we don't know for certain. At least his people have taken away those who questioned him, and no one has seen them again," Saneth said.

"And what of this Seer?" Namid said. "You've seen her – what does she look like? And what part has she played in this?"

"She's always cloaked and hooded, and wears gloves," Saneth said. "She speaks not much louder than a whisper, so it's hard to say what her voice even sounds like. No one I know has seen her face."

Taakha shook her head. "No one," she said. "Probably not even Lann. And I know of no one who has heard any of what she has told him. So we have no knowledge of her part in any of this beyond what she told us. Which we told you earlier."

"Aahmes, even if not as chieftain, we can still use your help," Saneth said. "The rumor of your return sparked us, and others, to action. Your actual return might be what we need to carry us through this. You are still a clansmate, still a member of one of clan Naalin's Cohaire families, but with a different view from your time in the southlands. That might be what we need to carry this off without destroying ourselves."

Aahmes looked uncomfortable. "I don't know what I

can offer—"

"Your magicks, perhaps, when the time is right," Saneth said. "Lann fears them, fears how they could be used against him. Anyone who showed the slightest ability in that area has been taken away."

Namid drained the last of her wine. "If you just want a weapon, I'm sure I know some people…" she said and shared a smirk with Aahmes.

"You must take this seriously!" Taakha almost shouted.

She glared at the hand Saneth put on her arm to calm her.

"Why must we?" Namid challenged. "You show up here, basically strangers, with a good story, but no good explanation for what you're really doing here. You demand Aahmes do as you say and dismiss me like some upstart minion. You're very good at the orders—"

"Namid," Aahmes interjected.

She glared at him but ceased her tirade. She turned her glare on Saneth when she noticed a smile tugging at the corners of the older woman's mouth.

"She might not be clan-born," Saneth said to Aahmes, "but she's got the fire of the clans in her. You're in for an adventure, I'd wager."

She turned to her companion. "And she does have a point, Taakha. Aahmes is no longer the little boy you watched for his mother and ordered around."

Namid shared a glare with Taakha, before they both turned away.

"We understand now what's going on here, in a general sense anyway," Aahmes said, "but really, what do you expect from me, from us? The magic, our Power, is good for some things, but might not be the best thing for this. And we didn't come to Naalin lands to overthrow Lann."

"We came here to be left alone," Namid said.

"You both have this… Power?" Taakha said, her gaze on Namid. "I heard no rumors about anyone other than Aahmes."

Saneth chuckled. "You know Lann has no interest in what the outlanders, the southern folk, do or don't do with magic. But the idea that one of our own clansmates might dabble in such things has him ranting to any and all."

Taakha nodded and looked thoughtful.

"Who hunts you?" Saneth said after several breaths-of-time of silence.

Namid exchanged a look with Aahmes. "First, I've something to ask you," she said, directing her words to their guests. "What are your thoughts about Ilenii and Belaraketh?"

This time Saneth and Taakha exchanged looks. "A couple of the gods of the southerners, aren't they?" Saneth said.

"We don't think of them one way or another," Taakha said. "They're not our gods, so why would we be concerned with them?"

"So you haven't seen them recently?" Namid said.

Saneth shook her head and Taakha frowned. "I wouldn't know them if I saw them," the younger woman said. "I've never traveled south, and we have no likenesses of them in the clans' territory. No statues or paintings."

Namid nodded. One concern at least she could put aside. For some reason, it seemed that the so-called gods who pursued her and Aahmes had not extended their message this far north. Namid brought her attention back to the conversation.

"They are the ones hunting us. And with them after us, any help we might offer might turn out the exact opposite," Aahmes said.

Taakha waved a dismissive hand. "The southern gods are nothing here, you might remember. I'm not worried."

Namid thought Saneth looked somewhat worried, but she kept her observation to herself.

Taakha rose. "We can continue this discussion on the morrow. Our journey today was long."

Aahmes jumped to his feet. "Of course."

He and Namid separated out the mattresses, positioning them as close to the fire as feasible. Taakha and Saneth pulled out some extra blankets from their packs and settled together on one of the mattresses for the night.

After a little more clean-up, Aahmes and Namid also settled on a mattress. Aahmes rolled close to Namid and embraced her. Namid caught sight of Saneth watching them. The older woman smiled at her when she met her gaze, then she rolled over.

~ ~ ~

Namid slept poorly, even tucked tight to Aahmes, and rose when the faintest hint of light seeped in around the hanging fur. Aahmes rose with her. They both grabbed cloaks and stepped outside into the chill dawn air. Aahmes wrapped both arms around Namid's waist and she leaned back into his warmth, her back pressed against his chest.

"I'd had a feeling that this wouldn't last," Namid said.

"This us?"

"What? No! I want this. I mean hiding away here. By ourselves."

She felt him send wisps of Wild Power out around them. "I hadn't paid attention, but yeah. There's something...."

"This thing with the chieftainship, you think?"

"Maybe. Maybe it's part of it. With this Seer involved... I don't know." He shrugged.

"I'm afraid your revived clan is going to want us to throw Power around. 'Make everything right', like Inezha liked to say." She frowned at the memory of the Prazny trying to get them to use their Power that way, a memory that contrasted sharply with other memories of the buoyant woman who had seemed to let little trouble her.

Namid felt Aahmes nod. "That might be what they think they want, what they're expecting. But if we *were* to

42

help topple Lann, we'd do it our way."

Namid nodded, then froze as she sensed a surge of Power coming from the south.

She and Aahmes exchanged worried looks and ducked back inside the shelter.

"That's not just a blind search," Namid said.

Aahmes clasped her hand. He drew on the Wild Power and, following his lead, Namid did the same. They built the veneer again, Aahmes again doing most of it, and sidled up to the opening to look out.

For a breath-of-time, all looked normal. Although the birds had ceased their usual morning songs.

Then the light turned an eerie shade of red.

Aahmes pulled Namid close and poured more Power into their veneer. Together they watched as what looked like red lightning crawled and jumped across the ground.

When it reached the door to the root cellar, it paused, gathered into a ball and sank partway into the door. Then it exploded, tearing the door apart and destroying a good portion of that hill.

The red lightning spread out again and continued its progress across the ground. When it approached them, Namid shrank back, but still watched. She held Wild Power ready to block an attack, but it never came. She shied away from the worry that even the Wild Power might not be able to block such an attack.

The lightning stretched from one side of the opening to the other and worked its way up over them and across the hill that covered their shelter. Namid heard it destroy something toward one side of the hill, a smaller sound of destruction than that of the root cellar. Namid shuddered, awed at the sheer power of the magic while at the same time dismayed at the thought of being unable to counter it if it should come for them directly.

Namid reached out cautiously through the Wild Power and tracked the lightning's progress out and away from them. Periodically it destroyed something else.

"Seems to be other shelters," Aahmes said to her questioning look. "Anything constructed that was at ground-level, or extended even a little above the ground, from what I can tell."

They both jumped at a sound from behind them.

"What was that?" Taakha asked in a voice not much above a whisper. "Did you just do something with your magicks?"

"Sort of," Namid said, her tone one of distraction. Then to Aahmes, "I say we still hold the veneer for now."

He nodded and inclined his head toward the opening. "We'd better check the damage."

"We'll help," Taakha said and started toward the entrance.

Namid blocked her with an outstretched arm. "Not a good idea," she said. "Stay in the shelter for now, so we only have to defend the two of us, if it comes to that."

Taakha glared, but then nodded when Saneth clutched her arm and whispered in her ear.

Senses extended through the Wild Power, Aahmes and Namid eased out of the shelter and hurried to the remnants of the hill that had held the root cellar.

Namid scanned the destruction, then checked the hill above the shelter. The small chimney for the hearth—which had extended out of the ground a couple handspans—had been obliterated.

Aahmes pointed to the hill beyond, which looked untouched. "The stable's under there. Looks like their horses should be fine."

Namid nodded, her thoughts elsewhere, then turned her gaze back to Aahmes.

"What do you wager everything's destroyed?" she said and waved a shaky hand toward the ruined hill that had held the root cellar.

"If not, probably most of it's going to be inedible."

Namid nodded again and turned to look toward the south. Nothing would stop them from sending more of that lightning. Or from coming themselves. Dread took hold of her. She wasn't ready to confront the 'gods'.

"We can't stay here, then," she whispered.

"True."

"Do we go with your cousins, then? Go to help, if we can?"

Aahmes gave her a gentle nudge to get her to turn so they stood facing each other.

"I won't drag you into something—"

"You wouldn't be." She considered his expression a long breath-of-time. "And you do want to help, don't you?"

"I do feel an obligation to my clan."

Namid nodded. "It does go along with what we've talked about before, too. About having this Power and shouldn't we use it to help...."

Aahmes gathered her close. "Time to move on again."

Namid nodded. "But no daughters from the Cohaire for you," she said, trying to lift her mood.

He chuckled.

~ ~ ~

Taakha did not try to hide her satisfaction when Aahmes said they had decided to help clan Naalin. That turned into a frown, however, when he repeated that he would not be chieftain. He deliberately clasped Namid's hand, with a look of challenge for Taakha. Saneth only smiled slightly.

"We need to leave here," Namid said.

"Especially after that," Taakha agreed. She waved a hand in the general direction of the door outside. "Even so, the winter storms will still likely catch us on the way, as it is."

"On the way to where?" Namid said.

"Is that really a good idea?" Aahmes said at the same time.

"The clans all gather at the old hub for most of the winter months," Saneth said to Namid.

"It'll be the best way to garner support. And Lann won't be able to escape," Taakha said.

"We won't be able to escape either, if things go badly," Aahmes said.

Taakha smiled. "They won't go badly for us," she said.

Namid frowned, remembering the underground complex where she had first encountered Lann roughly a year earlier. She was inclined to agree with Aahmes that this did not sound like a good idea.

"If we're going to be joining all the clans in the hub for the winter, we'd probably better put glamours on ourselves again. So Lann's people won't recognize us," Aahmes said to Namid.

"Hope no one there has any ability to sense Power," she muttered.

Aahmes gave the clansmates a brief explanation of what he and Namid planned to do with the glamours, then joined Namid off to the side.

Together they built up a glamour for each of them that changed their features enough so no one would recognize them but kept the essentials of themselves so no discrepancy in something like heights would be noticeable. Taakha and Saneth watched as the glamours slipped over them.

"That will take some getting used to," Taakha muttered. "Are you going to go by different names, too?"

"That will wait," Saneth said.

Namid nodded. "If we're leaving today, we need to gather our things and go. We can decide on details like names as we travel."

The rest of the morning became a scramble to pack everything they thought they would need, while still leaving the shelter useful in case someone needed it over the winter. Namid struggled with the sense that they must get away from that place faster than they were.

Taakha and Saneth had brought only two horses with them. The few extra clothes and food that Namid and Aahmes wanted to bring were packed on them, along with the packs belonging to Taakha and Saneth, and the four of them would walk for the time being.

They set out from the shelter close to midday and headed east, with the two clansmates guiding their path. Saneth and Taakha briefly debated the wisdom of trying to find a road going where they wanted, then decided to just head there directly.

"We're heading straight to the old hub, then?" Namid asked after they had settled that question. "How long of a journey is it?"

"Long enough," Taakha said.

"We travel first to Aghaik, the main settlement in Diarmid lands," Saneth said. "We must pass through their lands anyway, and most of them have come to the idea of opposing Lann's rule. We'll have allies there, and travel companions for the rest of the journey to the hub."

"Maybe we can lose ourselves in with them," Aahmes murmured.

"Assuming the glamour isn't torn from us like before," Namid whispered back.

Aahmes nodded. "I've been thinking about that. What if we use Wild Power for the glamours instead? So far, the clans' territory seems to have a lot of Wild Power, so it wouldn't stand out."

"Makes sense."

Taakha and Saneth slowed so they all walked together.

"I have some ideas regarding names for you," Taakha said. "They shouldn't be ones that are too unusual and stand out too much."

"We'll be getting different clothes, too, right?" Namid said. "I wouldn't think walking in there in clan Naalin clothes—"

"Nothing to worry on that score," Taakha said. "The clan has already been reforming and Lann doesn't care. He believes that those of us who are left are only from the lesser families of the clan and so will just be content to be able to call ourselves a clan again. We'll keep him believing that until we strike."

She shared a fierce look with them and turned the discussion back to names. In the end, they settled on names that were common enough to attract little attention, but not so common as to raise the question of their credibility.

Both Aahmes and Namid would be of lesser families of clan Naalin, families that Taakha assured them would not question their existence. Namid would be known as Nakhtnefre Fathal Tiyesdotr, which she could shorten to Nakht. And Aahmes' name would be Addayris Fathri Qarsson, shortened to Adday. They also settled on a simple history for them both.

"Should our second names be so much like Aahmes' real one?" Namid said. "And like yours, for that matter?" Namid nodded to Taakha.

"Our second names are our family names," Aahmes said. "They're similar because we're of different branches of the family. Yours and mine are two of the most minor branches of the family." Aahmes gave Namid a sly grin. "Although my branch ranks slightly higher within the family than yours."

Namid scrunched her nose at him with a mock glare as her reply.

"We need you to belong to the Cohaire for your involvement in this to carry enough weight," Taakha said, with a frown for their antics. "Especially if we put forth Adday here as possible chieftain."

"We're not putting forth Adday here as possible chieftain," Aahmes said.

"We'll see," Taakha said.

With the names settled, Aahmes and Namid dropped back about a pace to follow the others. Hands clasped, they worked to adjust the glamour to use Wild Power and finally successfully settled it right before Saneth called a halt for the night.

Another day brought them to the settlement Aghaik, a large village of low stone buildings with thick, thatched roofs and hard-packed roads. Every building that Namid saw looked to be constructed of interlocking stones without any mortar to bind them together.

Namid drew a tiny amount of Wild Power to herself and sent tendrils out into the early evening, reaching throughout the village. No sign of any Power that would destroy their glamour. She exchanged a quick smile with Aahmes when she sensed him checking also. Then she frowned at a sudden thought.

~Why isn't this place destroyed?~ she asked Aahmes using thought-speech. *~Doesn't look like that red lightning came through here at all.~*

After a look around, he shrugged. *~Maybe they only went after the isolated places? The places better for us to hide in.~*

~Think they wanted to herd us to a place where we could be seen by others? Maybe spotted by one of their people and then they'd know where to come for us?~

~Could be. At least the glamours are still up. So far, so good.~

"Remember," Saneth murmured to Namid as they followed the wide main street into the center of the village, "your father was from the southlands and you've been living there these many winters after your mother died."

"I remember."

Taakha stopped in front of one of the larger buildings in the village, twice as long as its neighbors and standing three stories tall. She and Saneth watered both horses at a trough there, then hitched them to a low rail in front of the building.

The four of them grabbed their packs from the horses. With a glance over her shoulder at Aahmes and Namid, Taakha led the way through the door.

The interior revealed that the building was a tavern. Or an inn, perhaps, Namid decided. She could believe that the upper floors had rooms to put up guests as lodgers.

Namid followed the others to a round table in one corner and just agreed with what Saneth recommended they get from the server who came to see what they wanted.

"Inar should find us here before we've finished our meal," Taakha murmured.

"The Diarmid clansmate we've been working with," Saneth explained at Namid's questioning look.

Namid and Aahmes exchanged looks, then turned their attention to the drink and food the server brought. Namid had just finished her last bite of food when an older man approached their table.

At a nod from Taakha, he pulled over a chair and sat between her and Saneth, with a quick clasp of their hands in greeting. He ordered a drink from the server, needing to raise his voice almost to a shout to be heard over the noise in the room, which had become crowded while Namid and the others ate.

The newcomer studied Aahmes and Namid until his drink came. Namid studied him in turn. His brown hair had streaks of white in it, more than Saneth's, and his skin was lighter than Saneth's and Taakha's. More weathered, too. He had dark brown eyes, the same as Saneth and Taakha.

After a long pull from his mug, he leaned forward. Taakha and Saneth followed suit.

"This is Inarshen Cathir Bakensson, of clan Diarmid," Taakha introduced the man.

"Inar and Taakha are third cousins, once removed," Saneth told Aahmes and Namid after she had introduced them to Inar.

"Adday and Nakht have joined us and will be helping," Taakha told Inar. "Adday is a fourth cousin, once removed and Nakht a fifth cousin, twice removed."

Inar took another look at Namid and Aahmes. "I don't recognize you. No hint in your faces of any of the Fathir family I know."

Aahmes shrugged. "Not unexpected. I'd be surprised if you knew all the minor offshoots in the clan. My parents left the clans' territory, traveled to the southlands before I was born. Nakht's mother was my mother's good friend and cousin. The story they always told us was that she came to visit, fell in love with one of the caravanners who traded in the town and never returned to the clans."

~*He didn't use the clans' tongue! Unlike Taakha, at first,*~ Namid commented to Aahmes, her thought-speech heavy with surprise.

~*Clan Naalin still taught children our own tongue when I was young here,*~ Aahmes told her. ~*Few of the other clans did. Most favored having children learn only the language of the Six Realms.*~

Inar's gaze shifted to Saneth.

"It's fine," she told him. "They are not any of Lann's."

He gave a sharp nod and drained his mug. "Heading to the hub?"

Taakha nodded. "Need to get a few things, then yes."

"I've got rooms here. Use a couple of them, if you want. We're leaving tomorrow, if you wish to travel with us. Might be good to arrive as part of a group."

With a nod, Taakha accepted for all of them.

CHAPTER 5

The journey from clan Diarmid's settlement of Aghaik to the clan hub, which Namid learned was called Meahan in the clans' language, took more than a week. Several families traveled there together, all of them of clan Diarmid except for Namid and her companions. They brought along several wagons loaded mainly with food.

When they first started out, all of the travelers exchanged names and how they were all related. And Namid spent the rest of the journey relearning it all.

After they heard her story of one parent from the clans but being raised in the southlands, they all but competed with each other to teach her more about her supposed heritage.

Saneth and Taakha seemed to know most of the people they accompanied and spent most of the journey in conversation with first one group, then another. Aahmes stayed close to Namid most of the time, and they both worked to blend in with the clansmates. Although at the first opportunity, Namid changed from her clan Naalin clothes into a plainer tunic and trousers. Many of the clansmates did not wear their clan colors, so she would not look out of place. And she felt less conspicuous in the less distinctive clothing.

As they had the chance, Aahmes and Namid practiced doing small things with their Power while they held it close so no one nearby should be able to sense it. They were careful also to make certain no one in the group might suspect what they were doing. They made a little promising progress, although neither had yet recovered completely from their shape-changing. At least neither experienced any more debilitating pains or inexplicable bleeding.

They worked to improve the Wild Power glamours and managed to form a link so either of them could bolster them – which they needed to do more frequently than Namid liked. They also discovered a way to set the glamours to draw on the ambient Wild Power to help maintain them.

One cold gray afternoon, the group finally came within sight of Meahan: a vast collection of low buildings that flanked a huge mound dotted with a multitude of small chimneys, many of which spewed smoke into the chill air.

"I don't remember it looking like that," Namid muttered, with a questioning look for Aahmes.

He chuckled. "We came from the south when Lann's people hauled us here last autumn," he murmured, his voice low so only she could hear. "This western side has these surface structures. And around to the north, too, I think."

As the group of clansmates wound their way through the structures, Namid scrutinized the buildings. They looked old, and none of them intact. Comprised of broken stones, they all looked deserted.

"None of them have been repaired," Namid murmured as they passed ruin after ruin. "Instead the clans go underground?"

Aahmes shrugged.

Saneth edged closer. "I overheard. It seems you have

forgotten the tales about the surface city," she said to Aahmes.

"Seems so," he admitted.

Saneth nodded. "In short, the city once flourished a couple thousand winters ago, when that season in the clans' territory was not so harsh as now. Then came a time of magical botherations. Strong magicks swept over our lands often and destroyed much, including Meahan-on-the-surface. After that time, the weather in the clans' territory was changed and winters above ground became too dangerous to endure for long. So the clans constructed Meahan as it is now."

She gave them a somber look. "Among the clans, much of the enmity against magic stems from those hard times. Even so many winters later a long-held mistrust lingers in many of the clans, unlike in the southlands. Clan Acnald especially has railed long and loudly against magic in the clans."

She lowered her voice. "Although Clan Naalin has not regarded the magic thus for many winters now, has even used some magic when in their own lands." She gave Aahmes a pointed look. "You might remember seeing some as a child. Still, you'll want to keep your own magic close and secret, I think." She included Namid in that last statement.

Namid and Aahmes exchanged glances and nodded their understanding.

"Of course we will," Aahmes said.

Close to two candle-marks after they entered the ruins, the group came to a wide door set into the side of the mound. Two clansmates stepped up to the door and pushed on it together to swing it open. They all trooped inside, animals and wagons included.

Unlike the entrance Namid remembered, this one had no stairs, just a long slope down. The horses' hooves and the wheels of the wagons on the rock floor created such a din that conversations as they moved further underground were brief and yelled. Candle-lanterns that hung from pegs in the wall every few paces lit the way.

Namid jumped when Aahmes took her arm, then grinned at him. Together they moved to one side of the bulk of the clansmates to join Saneth and Taakha.

"We'll wait until clan Diarmid's gotten inside," Saneth shouted, "then we can make our way to clan Naalin's quarter."

They stood there close to half a candle-mark while the wagons of clan Diarmid trooped past them. Many of the clansmates who walked with the wagons smiled at Namid and her companions and shouted invitations to visit after everyone was settled.

"How many clans are there here?" Namid said when the wagons thinned out, so they only had to speak loudly to be heard. "Do they all come to the hub for the winter?"

Both Saneth and Taakha shook their heads. "There are thirteen clans all told," Saneth said. "And while all of them send at least some of their clansmates to Meahan for the winter—"

"The winter season is when a lot of the governing business is handled," Taakha interjected.

"Yes," Saneth said. "As I was saying, while all of the clans have some of their people here for the season, few send everyone. Only the smaller ones will have all their clansmates in Meahan."

"Like us," Taakha said.

"There just isn't room for *everyone*," Saneth said. "Those who don't come to Meahan have smaller, similar shelters they use in their own lands."

They waited an additional quarter candle-mark until all of clan Diarmid had passed, leaving a ringing silence in its wake. Then Namid and Aahmes followed Saneth and Taakha to a side passage.

"Some of the clan are probably already in clan Naalin's quarter of the hub," Taakha said. "We'll do all the introductions and get you both settled in there. Do you remember the way?" she said to Aahmes.

"Part of it, at least," he said after he gave that some thought.

"Well, ask if you need to."

Aahmes and Namid exchanged looks. "I'm sure we'll be fine," Namid said.

Another quarter candle-mark brought them to a large open room. Walls of red brick helped hide the fact that they were underground. Namid spotted many small holes in the ceiling and realized she had seen them in the passages too. For air, she assumed.

The room held numerous tables, some of metal and others of stone, with a lit candle-lantern placed in the center of each table. The chairs were stools of a design Namid had never seen – a sort of frame made of metal, with cloth seats. In spite of the strangeness of the stools, it looked much like the Shadowers' common room had back in Rhadanthus. Some of Namid's tension bled away at the familiar sight.

A few people had gathered at a few of the tables, several families Namid guessed. That left the bulk of the room empty. Saneth and Taakha led the way to the largest group and the others in the room drifted over as the introductions commenced.

The Naalin clansmates welcomed Namid and Aahmes with smiles and exuberant greetings. They shared several bottles of wine as everyone figured out the family connections the best they could with so much of the clan gone.

After the relationship connections had been settled to everyone's satisfaction, many of the families drifted away, leaving Aahmes and Namid with Saneth and Taakha and two other members of clan Naalin's Cohaire. Namid had learned that two families formed the clan's Cohaire, Fathir and Vithir. The other two people, along with Saneth, were part of the Vithir family. They both seemed close in age to Aahmes and Namid, with darker skin than the two

Shadowers' and hair just as black as theirs. Namid remembered from the introductions that they were Sen and Dyefa, but could not recall their full names. With a mental shrug, she decided she could ask Aahmes later if she really needed to know.

"Are we all there are?" Taakha asked.

"Of the Cohaire? It seems so," Sen said, with a shrug of one of his shoulders. "The highest ranking of our respective branches, anyway."

Dyefa nodded, an action that set her hair's many small braids swinging. "My family came with me, as did Sen's," she said. "And both our branches have a few lesser members who haven't arrived yet."

"It's said that Lann plans to pledge this winter," Sen said.

"Has he picked someone?" Saneth said.

"We'll need to move before then, in that case," Taakha said at the same time.

"It would be easier if he has no heirs yet," Dyefa said. "But so far no one has set forth a possible chieftain that all of us can agree on."

"What of my own cousin, Aahmestharq?" Taakha said, with a quick sidelong look for Aahmes.

Sen nodded. "If he still lives, I could see the families rallying behind him. But after what happened last autumn, how would we even find him. Assuming he does still live."

Taakha leaned toward Aahmes with a smug expression and placed a hand on his arm. "These two know him. They have been with him recently. He still lives."

~*Wonderful!*~ Aahmes observed to Namid through thought-speech.

~*Cleverly maneuvered, though,*~ Namid commented.

When Sen and Dyefa turned questioning looks on Aahmes and Namid, Aahmes returned them with a blank one of his own. But he clasped Namid's hand beneath the table in a tight grip.

"You know him?" Dyefa said, her eagerness clear in

her voice.

Namid nodded. "Yes. But I'm sure he's not looking to be chieftain."

Taakha waved a hand in the air. "I'm sure he'll come around."

"What of the others?" Aahmes said. "I'd think that the other Cohaire who support this action have people who could be chieftain."

"Chieftain Mehtnathor intended for the chieftainship to go to the Fathir family," Taakha snapped. "I told you that."

"But that was how long ago? Approaching a score of winters?" Aahmes said. "Things have changed."

"You haven't even been here!" Taakha said. "What can you know of how things have changed?"

Aahmes pointed at her, his finger right in her face. "Exactly!"

Saneth placed a hand on each of their arms. "Please. We will figure out all of this, but not right now," she said. "When everyone gets here, we can refine our plans. Now I think we'd best get our belongings into our rooms and get settled in." She rose and tugged on Taakha's arm.

After the two women left, heading out a different opening than the one they used to enter, Sen and Dyefa leaned close.

"Since last autumn, Taakha has talked of little else other than her cousin taking over from Lann," Dyefa said. "You know for certain, Nakht, that he would not be chieftain, if it were offered to him?"

Namid resisted looking at Aahmes. "I do know that he doesn't want the chieftainship and hadn't thought to have it."

"So Taakha has already spoken with him about it?" Sen said.

"Yes," Aahmes said. "But as you see, she thinks she can make him see it the way she wants."

"Where is he?" Sen said. "Is he close?"

Namid squelched a smile. "I really can't say right now," she said.

The two clansmates nodded.

"I've not yet heard of any other clansmates from your two family branches," Dyefa said. "I'm sorry. The clan is in such disarray, everyone's taken to claiming their family's sleeping rooms that lie closest to this gathering room, with little regard for the usual family rank claims to specific rooms."

"You can each join the other unpledged men and women in their group quarters, if you don't want to be alone in your family's passages," Sen said.

Namid and Aahmes exchanged looks.

"Perhaps show us our families' rooms and then we can decide," Namid said, when Aahmes just looked at her but did not offer an opinion.

With a nod, Dyefa rose. "Sen, would you please? I should get back to my family and, no doubt, rescue my spouse from our daughters. They do have a way of winding him about their fingers to get what they want." She laughed softly and headed out a different opening.

Sen rose, too. "Bring your belongings along. The first rooms aren't too far and like Dyefa said, you can have your pick. And work it out if you need to with any others of your family branch if they come."

He led them across the room to yet another opening and down the passage there. The same red bricks as in the gathering room lined the walls and Namid spotted many ceiling holes here, too. As elsewhere, candle-lanterns hung from pegs every few paces. Fewer than half of them were lit, though. Sen led them past the first dozen openings, half on each side of the passage, then paused at the next.

"Those first passages were for the highest ranked of the Fathirs, including Aahmes' family. If he joins us, those rooms would be his. Starting here, the next two openings on the left lead to Fathal family rooms and the two on the right lead to the rooms for the Fathri family. No one's here from these family branches. And I fear no one else will come to claim any of these rooms. The Fathir families were all but wiped out, as you know."

Aahmes set his pack on the floor by the first opening on their right. "Our thanks. We don't want to keep you any longer."

Sen looked from one of them to the other, then nodded.

"If you need anything, or want to know where the rooms for the unpledged are, just ask anyone in the gathering room." He left them and returned back the way they had come.

Namid dropped her pack next to Aahmes' and watched Sen walk back down the passage.

"They're very trusting for a group that plans to oust their current leader," Namid said in a quiet voice.

"Yeah. I'm not sure I trust it." Aahmes kept his voice as quiet.

"And I don't want to spend the winter sharing a room with a bunch of other unpledged women," Namid said. "They probably talk too much. And giggle. Had enough of that sort of thing when I was new to the Shadowers."

Aahmes chuckled. "I'm glad to hear it. More secure in a room without strangers."

Namid gave him a sidelong look. He was not looking at her but rather faced the other direction down the passage. He raked his hair back from his face with one hand.

"Aahmes? What is it?"

He seemed to drag himself back from a long way away and turned to her with a sad smile. "What? Oh. Just memories. My brothers and I used to chase each other back and forth along these passages. Until our parents yelled at us to stop. Or all the *other* parents yelled at us to stop."

Namid nodded. "Would you prefer to stay somewhere else?"

He gazed down the passage a long breath-of-time

toward the rooms that had been his family's, then shook his head while brushing his hair back again. "I'll be all right. I hadn't expected so many memories in these passages."

She hugged him to offer what comfort she could. His mention of his brothers reminded her of her own family losses.

Time to change the subject.

"How many rooms are off these side passages? And do you know where that way leads?" She waved a hand the direction away from the Fathir family rooms.

"As many as six or seven rooms each passage," he said. "I think I remember ours had seven when I came here as a boy. That way should lead to the rooms of the lesser families of clan Diarmid, and beyond there to their clan's gathering room."

With a sidelong look, he added, "Of course, we should probably take a look ourselves before too long."

Namid nodded, the corners of her mouth quirked up. "Of course. We wouldn't be proper Shadowers if we didn't poke into everything we can get away with. But it can wait, I think."

Aahmes gave her an absent nod as she hefted her pack. His expression held a hint of sorrow. He grabbed his pack, too.

"Think I'll take the closest of the Fathri rooms just over there," he said and pointed to the entrance to the nearest of the Fathri passageways.

"Then I'll claim the closest of the Fathal rooms," Namid said.

"Sounds good."

Namid watched him until he entered his room, then turned toward her own. A couple of paces brought her to the first doorway in her passage. It was to her right, with a thick woven curtain that acted as a door. The nearest candle-lantern in her passageway hung several paces further in, so in the dimness, she could not distinguish the color of the curtain. With a shrug, she pushed it aside and entered the room beyond.

Within, she found a wide bed atop an elevated section of the floor. A second raised section of the floor formed a table, flanked by thick cushions in clan Naalin colors. Several stone shelves adorned the walls and a couple of hooks flanked the doorway. The back wall of the room held a small hearth similar to the one in the shelter they had come from, with some peat bricks stacked nearby.

After she set her pack atop the table area, Namid got a couple of the bricks burning on the hearth with a small blue-white flame that she created with her Power. She winced at the headache that flared again behind her eyes and watched the flame change to normal yellow-orange as the bricks caught.

The room quickly grew warmer than she expected so she shed her cloak and outer tunics. She hung her cloak from one of the hooks.

Namid used a small amount of Wild Power to seal the curtain so no one but she and Aahmes could move it or go through the doorway. Everything in the room looked clean, no dust lingered from disuse, and the mattress on the low bed had a faint, herbal scent to it, sharp, but not unpleasant. The bed was piled with several pillows and blankets, and Namid resisted its invitation.

She unpacked her meager belongings and placed the clothes on the shelves. Then she plopped down on one of the cushions. It was surprisingly comfortable.

She closed her eyes against the headache, much less than the one that had assaulted her after the shape-changing, at least. She hoped the pain went away completely soon.

An ache had lingered after their time as wolves, but had been decreasing the same amount as her returning Power reserve increased. At least her use of Wild Power had not seemed to make the ache any worse. It had been barely noticeable the past couple of days, but now her head throbbed again from just the small amount of her own Power that she had used.

It felt strange to have time to just sit. The last weeks, ever since she returned to Kilaadi with her brother, it seemed she had been pulled from one thing to another without rest, with preparations for the coronation and all that followed. But in some ways, she had welcomed it. It kept her from thinking too much.

But now her thoughts turned to her father. Images came to her, memories of good times, his smile, his laughter when she outwitted her older brothers at something, the way he always kissed her mother good-bye even if he was only headed to another part of the citadel for the day.

The pain of his loss tore through her again, as sharp as when he had just died. She curled up on her cushion as the tears came.

~ ~ ~

From the look of the gathering room, all the Naalin clansmates seemed to have come there for the evening meal. Namid looked for Aahmes and spotted him at a small table off to the side. The room was less than half full and they would be able to watch everyone from that vantage.

When she sat next to him, Aahmes draped an arm across her shoulders, a concerned expression on his face. He gave her a comforting squeeze. She leaned into his embrace, then sat back when a clansmate brought over a plate of food for her. Aahmes already had one and it looked like he had nibbled at it already.

"Where's the kitchen?" Namid said when they had finished about half their meal.

"If I remember right, it's back the way we came in and off to the right," Aahmes said. "We'll find out, no doubt. Everyone's expected to help out there."

"Like back at Shadow Keep," Namid said. "This feels a lot like back there."

Aahmes nodded.

Namid looked at the table closest to theirs. A man and woman sat there, with three children who had to be theirs – they looked so much like them. Both the man and woman wore fancy rings on their left thumbs and forefingers. Namid studied the rings and judged they would be valuable back in Rhadanthus. If she ever returned there to that life.

At another table nearby, two men were involved in an animated conversation. They both wore simpler rings and just on the thumbs of their left hands. From where she sat, Namid thought the rings looked like they matched each other in design.

Namid glanced at other people nearby and saw that many of them wore rings similar to the man's and woman's. Others wore the plainer rings and only on their thumbs.

Aahmes followed the direction of her gaze and smiled when she turned back to him.

"So tell me about the rings," Namid said.

He nodded toward the closest table.

"See their matching rings? Fancy, and the thumb rings are each attached by a thin chain to a ring on their forefingers on that hand. They're pledged."

"So the plainer rings with no forefinger ring or chain mean…?"

"If you have a chance to get a close look at any of those, you'll see that they also match each other. Those mean that they consider themselves paired, a couple. But they have not yet formally pledged to each other."

"So, being paired is a promise of a sort before the actual pledging?" Namid said. "Might that save you from Taakha's pledging plans for you? Save you from those 'daughters of appropriate age'?"

Aahmes gave her an intent look. "Are you asking me to

pair with you?"

"Ah, well...." Namid felt her face grow warm.

Aahmes chuckled and clasped her hand. He placed a light kiss on the back of it. "Got you with that one," he said with a smile. "And yeah, it might. But I wouldn't want *that* to be the reason we choose to pair."

Namid nodded and held his gaze. "Yeah, me neither."

After a breath-of-time Aahmes added, "It *is* something I have thought—"

"Adday!" Taakha hurried to their table and took a seat across from them.

"Some of the Cohaire from several clans plan to meet tonight," she said in a near whisper, "to talk about getting more supporters and when we'll move against Lann. You should be there, too."

"We can both be there," Namid said.

Taakha frowned, but after a look at Aahmes' expression, she nodded. "Saneth or I will come get you in a couple candle-marks, then."

CHAPTER 6

After the meeting ended, Aahmes and Namid lingered in a nearby passageway and watched until everyone else had disappeared down various other passageways.

"It seems like a good start," Namid said as they sauntered along another passageway, picked at random.

"But it's nothing more than a start. And I'm uncertain we should get too involved," Aahmes muttered.

"At least they found some other claimants for the chieftainship. Although they do still seem to want to pin too much hope on the absent Aahmes," Namid said. She switched to thought-speech. *~Should we even stay?~*

~We're as well hidden here as we can possibly be, I think,~ Aahmes answered the same way.

~What about the attacks on people around you? You were worried about that.~

~And I still am. But as long as we're Adday and Nakht, that should help keep everyone safe. And this could give us time to figure out how to solve our own problem. Maybe we'll even find something here to help. I've sensed no Power here other than ours.~

~Same for me. And we've got ours tightly reined. All right.~ She gave him a mischievous grin. *~Shall we begin our*

explorations of Meahan tonight?~

He nodded in agreement.

They returned to their rooms and changed into their gray Shadower clothes. These would blend particularly well into the shadowy underground areas. Namid left off her usual layered tunics, wearing only her shirt, trousers and boots, with her belt around her waist partly concealed under the shirt. The passageways seemed warm enough that she felt no need for the extra clothing. When they met up, she saw that Aahmes had done the same. And they set out.

They found nothing of interest in the other rooms of the Fathir branch of clan Naalin's quarter. As Sen had said, they were the only ones staying in that section. Namid hoped it stayed that way. Although, the other rooms looked ready for occupants, as theirs had been.

Next they ventured into clan Diarmid's quarter. The passageway that connected to their own led to more empty rooms.

"For a few of the least of Diarmid's families," Aahmes told Namid. "Sen said they stopped coming to Meahan several winters ago after a very public argument with Lann."

"Think he eliminated them?" Namid said.

Aahmes shrugged and led the way further into clan Diarmid's quarter. They prowled around the clan's passageways and poked into the many rooms and storage areas. They discovered little of note. The clan looked to have a number of clansmates more than triple the number of Naalin clansmates staying in Meahan.

Clan Diarmid had plenty of stores, but little that was valuable. No one seemed to be standing guard and no Power warded anyplace they ventured. The few rooms they searched, belonging to leaders of the clan, held minimal valuables. After several candle-marks of this they returned to clan Naalin's passageways.

"Just how big is this place anyway?" Namid asked when

they paused at the passageway that led to her room.

"Maybe bigger than Rhadanthus," Aahmes said with a slight smile. "If we're not to spend all our time here poking around, we'll want to decide on a plan for the best places to search."

"Lann's quarter," Namid said right away with a small smile of her own. "And his clan's. But first I should at least learn the general layout of Meahan."

"Tomorrow will be soon enough to start," Aahmes said. With an intent expression, he pulled her close for a lingering kiss then ran a light finger across her lips. "I'll see you for the morning meal. Sleep well," he said and turned toward the passageway to his room.

Namid stopped him with a light hand on his arm.

"Stay with me?" she said in a quiet voice. "If you want…."

He turned back to her and studied her expression. He leaned close and brushed her cheek with his fingertips, all the while holding her gaze with his own.

She felt that she could look forever into his beautiful gray-brown eyes.

"I do want," he breathed.

With an intent look of her own, Namid clasped both of Aahmes' hands and, backing away from him, led the way to her room and inside.

After the curtain at the door dropped closed behind them, Namid closed the distance between them for a long kiss. She wrapped her arms around him, sliding her hands up his back beneath his shirt. He returned the kiss with a desire and intensity that sent a shivery thrill through her.

She leaned back just far enough to loosen the laces of his shirt. Together they pulled it off and dropped it to the floor.

Aahmes tangled his fingers in her hair and started to unbraid it with a smile at her expression. She took in the sight of his muscular torso and traced the scars there with a fingertip.

"At first, I wasn't very skilled with daggers," Aahmes said, his tone wry.

Namid chuckled and tapped a scar on his upper arm. "I remember this one."

"Yeah. That was the first mark anyone made on me after my early training."

"So you knew then you had to watch out for me?" Namid brushed her lips against the scar she had given him those years ago.

"Something like that. Do you really want to talk about scars?" Aahmes played with her freed hair with one hand. He brushed the side of her neck with the other. She shivered at the half-tickling half-sensual feel of his fingers on her skin.

"Mm, no." Namid ran her hands over his chest and leaned in for another kiss. She had meant it to be quick, but had no complaints that it left her breathless a long time later.

Namid clasped Aahmes' hand and drew him further into the room. As she did so, she renewed the Power around the room to keep anyone else from entering or from hearing anything from within.

"Wait." Aahmes stopped her a step shy of the bed.

Namid felt him do something with a tiny amount of Power – something directed at himself.

"A little something I learned to keep from fathering a child," he said to her quizzical look. "I'm not yet ready to become a father."

Namid chuckled. "I know how to do something like that, too." With a little Power, she used the necessary technique on herself, then wrapped her arms around him.

Aahmes returned the gesture, pressing her body to his. After another ardent kiss he leaned his forehead against hers. They gazed into each other's eyes from a finger-width apart. Then she gave him a teasing kiss, entwined her fingers with his, and tugged him that last step to the bed.

~ ~ ~

Over the next weeks, Aahmes and Namid fell into a pattern of learning as much as they could of Meahan and the clans as quickly as they could, frequently exhausting themselves with long days of activity. Namid used the exhaustion to combat a nagging sense that she needed to be accomplishing more than hiding and exploring.

After their morning meals together, they separated to mingle with the various members of clan Naalin. More clansmates trickled in every day. Everyone went aboveground at least once every couple of days and that let them become familiar with the structures there, and also the structures that housed the horses.

Taakha spoke with them every day, pushing to bring Aahmes to her way of thinking. She developed a unique ability to turn up most often when they found some restful time together alone. Namid found it quite irritating, and Aahmes began to wear a scowl any time they caught sight of Taakha.

As part of their obligation to the clan, Aahmes and Namid helped prepare the midday meals. Aahmes also helped tend the horses. After they felt acquainted with the clansmates of clan Naalin, they ventured further afield and worked at learning the layout of Meahan. That occupied them through most of the autumn.

The entire complex formed a rough circle, with each clan residing in its own smaller complex of rooms and passages that extended from the central area out to the edges, roughly triangular in shape. While called 'quarters', Meahan contained far more than just four clan areas, to accommodate all the clans.

The central quarter was roughly circular and a little smaller than the largest of the clan complexes. It was set aside for the chieftain and his close clansmates and was where most of clan Acnald currently resided. Namid and

Aahmes did not yet venture too close there. Each entry always had at least two Acnald clansmates guarding it every time they checked. And they had yet to find anyone who knew of any other way into that quarter, although a few of the older people they spoke with claimed a hidden way existed.

As they became more familiar with Meahan, they searched for that hidden way after everyone slept. And used the thievery skills they had learned as Shadowers to poke into everything they came across to see what they might learn that could help them solve their problem with the Power, or help with the clans' leadership dilemma.

When any clansmates of clan Acnald were present in the common areas that all the clans shared, Namid and Aahmes worked to stay inconspicuous. Namid noticed that many of the clansmates of the other clans similarly avoided drawing any attention to themselves from the Acnalds.

Namid also learned the clans' colors. The Acnalds always wore theirs – a crossbarred pattern of shades of gray, yellow, red and brown. Other clansmates sometimes wore their own crossbarred colors, and sometimes wore plainer clothes.

The meetings of the Cohaire took place every few days but accomplished little. As time passed, a few more members of the Cohaire joined in, from other clans, but Namid decided they were all waiting for something to compel them to go ahead with their intended ousting of Lann.

One morning many weeks after they had arrived at Meahan, Namid stepped into the Naalin gathering room for the morning meal and found it full of clansmates. As she tried to make her way through the confusion, Aahmes caught her arm. Together they pushed their way to one side.

"The rest of the clansmates have arrived," Aahmes said with a grin.

Namid gave him an exaggerated look of surprise.

"Really? What an amazing thing. I never would have known."

He chuckled. "They traveled all night to make it. The winter storms have arrived, and they weren't even certain they'd get here."

Namid perused the crowd and spotted the newcomers with no difficulty. They all wore haggard expressions, soaked clothes, and looked like they had not slept well for several days.

"It's a bad one?"

"Yeah. It *is* winter. Although just barely, so it's still a little early for a storm this heavy. These clansmates are probably the last to get through for the season."

Namid studied the chaos and soon spotted Saneth and Taakha across the room, trying to organize the clansmates crowded around them. Sen and Dyefa were likewise occupied to their right.

"Think any of these are Cohaire?" Namid said with a wave of her hand at the milling people.

Aahmes shrugged. "Can't tell by sight. They'll probably call a meeting for tonight. We'll find out then."

"Well, as part of the Cohaire ourselves, even if just the lowliest of the members, guess we'd better help with all this." Namid took his arm and pulled him into the crowd.

~ ~ ~

Before time for the evening meal, all the newcomers managed to settle themselves into the appropriate rooms. With the new-come clansmates, clan Naalin had nearly doubled in size from just the day before. The clan was still woefully diminished, from what Namid heard as she helped throughout the day. And everyone thought that this was it; no more clansmates would be found.

She was pleased to discover that no one else would take rooms in the branches she and Aahmes used. But her heart ached at what that meant for Aahmes. He and Taakha were truly the last of that family.

The evening meal was a raucous affair as everyone milled about to get acquainted more than they sat to eat. Namid and Aahmes claimed two of the small seats and pulled them off to a corner to stay out of the way. Still their meal was interrupted several times by newcomers who approached to greet them and find out how they all were related. And when they discovered that Adday and Nakht were of the Fathir family, invariably the clansmates expressed their sympathy at the loss of the rest of the family.

As expected, a meeting of the Cohaire was announced for a candle-mark after everyone had eaten. Unlike previous meetings, this one was to take place right there, in clan Naalin's gathering room.

As the time approached, clansmates streamed out of the room to make room for the Cohaire from other clans. Namid watched all the activity.

"Looks like they're setting watches in the passageways," she commented to Aahmes.

"Not a shabby job about it, either. Notice how they have small groups who seem to just be gossiping."

Namid nodded. "And I saw a few, somewhat-hidden weapons. But are they truly prepared to fight, if this all comes to that?"

Aahmes shrugged and scrutinized the Cohaire who began to arrive.

"I see a few new faces from the other clans. No new ones for Naalin, though."

Together they moved to the center of the room where all the Cohaire gathered. After close to a quarter candle-mark, Taakha called for quiet and everyone found seats. Aahmes and Namid positioned themselves toward the back of the group. From there they could watch everyone. Namid examined the various clan colors she saw. If she correctly remembered the number of clans, fewer than half the clans were represented there.

S. Lynn Helton

"Looks like some clans that Taakha said would be here are missing," Aahmes muttered to her.

After the introductions, the oldest of all the clans' Cohaire, Ethmereneith—a woman with white hair and wrinkled, faded-brown skin—of clan Larinaq, rose to her feet.

"Tonight, we must begin making the decisions," she said. "Lann must go. We all already agree on that. Now that Meahan is closed for the winter, we need to get everything set so we can make that a reality."

"How soon will we act?" demanded a man of about Aahmes' age. He wore crossbarred brown, tan and green. The colors of clan Resaar, Namid had learned.

"Will it come down to actual fighting?" another man asked.

"There's always the chance we'll have to fight," Saneth said. "We hope not to, of course. But from Lann's actions so far, and his father's, I think we need to be prepared for it."

"Any who cannot fight, or wish to remain out of that, should plan to stay back and help protect the families, if needed," Ethmereneith said. "You could still find yourselves in a fight, but the chances are less than for those of us who'll be in the forefront."

"And regarding that forefront, who is to become the new chieftain?" said another woman. Namid judged her to be a few years older than herself.

"Are you thinking it would be yourself, Ofretawe?" a man about the same age challenged the woman.

"I'm thinking why couldn't it be myself, Uarseken!" the woman retorted.

"No reason it couldn't be," Saneth hastened to say, cutting off the start of a potential argument.

"That's what I'd see us decide this night," Ethmereneith said. "We need to support the one who would be our chieftain. All of us. Then we can convince the others, the ones who waver."

"Our next chieftain should be my cousin Aahmestharq," Taakha spoke up from a place to one side. "Chieftain Mehtnathor wanted his mother as the next chieftain. But she's gone and he's the only one who remains from the family."

That led to some mutters as people looked around.

"Is he alive?" someone asked.

"Is he here?" someone else said.

With the quickest glance at Aahmes, Taakha said. "He *is* alive. I've spoken with him."

That set off more muttering.

"So, where is he?" another person demanded.

"He does not want the chieftainship," Aahmes said, loud enough to override the mutters.

"But it's what our last real chieftain wanted," Taakha said.

"We know that it was his wish to see the chieftainship pass to the Fathir family," Ethmereneith said. "But even so, you know how this is done, Taakha. No one is forced to the chieftainship. If your cousin has said he doesn't want it, then that's the end of that topic."

"But—"

"Taakha," Aahmes said, "leave it."

She glared at him but did not continue to protest.

The discussion next turned to the various merits of those of the Cohaire who would be willing to take the position.

Several candle-marks later, after many clansmates drooped with weariness and fought to keep from nodding off, they finally settled on who they would support as claimant: Aahsemerye of clan Resaar, a woman about Namid's age.

"She reminds me of you," Aahmes whispered to Namid, leaning close. "She should do well."

"If she doesn't go crazy first from all the Cohaire wanting to tell her how to go about this."

Aahmes chuckled. "They'll settle down some now, I

think. Well, except perhaps for Taakha." He frowned as his cousin made her way to them through the disintegrating meeting.

"How could you let this happen?" she demanded. "I thought you were going to help us!"

"And we will," Aahmes said with a glare. "But we'll do it our own way."

After she left in a huff, Namid leaned close. "And just exactly how *should* we help? Tempting as it might be in this one instance, we're not assassins, nor do I have any desire to become an assassin."

"Me neither, much as I wouldn't miss Lann. Now that we know our way around, I think we need to do a lot of lurking and listening. See what we can find out. I've a feeling we should be able to come up with something to undermine him."

Namid grinned around a yawn. "Or maybe we can create something that will undermine him. Get even more clansmates wanting to get rid of him."

"Even so."

CHAPTER 7

The next evening, Namid and Aahmes slipped away from the clan Naalin quarter. They followed several passageways to the quarter of clan Naardona, one of the clans that was supposed to have come to the meeting the previous night but failed to attend. Before they reached clan Naardona's more populous area, Namid stopped Aahmes and argued for placing a new glamour atop their current one.

"It'll keep anyone from connecting us to clan Naalin," she said.

So they drew on Wild Power and created a new glamour to make their faces look even more unlike their true faces, and unlike their current look. After they had that set, they pulled a veneer of belonging around themselves and headed into clan Naardona's quarter.

As they sauntered through the passageways, keeping their motion casual, they passed few clansmates. Those they did encounter just gave them slight nods of acknowledgment and continued on their way.

When they heard voices from any of the side openings they came to, Aahmes and Namid paused to listen. They heard nothing of interest until they reached the passageways of the clan's most prominent families. Raised voices came from one side passageway so they headed down that one to see what they might discover.

Few of the candle-lanterns were lit in the passage, and all the curtained rooms they passed were dark and quiet, until they came to the one second from the furthest in. A faint light shone from under the curtain. They positioned themselves in the shadows to one side of the entry to listen.

"…if he doesn't?" a woman's voice was saying. "Others who've been taken haven't returned."

"He took oath," a man's voice said. "We've done as he asked."

"He can't be trusted! That's how we got involved—"

"Doesn't matter now, since he's got Sitkha and Dyaaset."

Aahmes touched Namid's arm to get her attention and tilted his head toward the main passageway. They returned there, making no noise as they moved, and slipped into a shadowed alcove.

"They were probably talking about Lann," Aahmes said in a quiet voice while he kept his attention on the passageway.

"Yeah. Wonder who the others are that have been taken. Where would he hold them? Assuming it *is* him."

"Wager it's not?"

"No."

"The chieftain's quarter is supposed to be much like the clans' quarters, with many rooms. Remember he held us in that one."

Namid nodded. "Think this is why the other clans that were supposed to show at the meeting didn't?"

"Seems likely. And it makes me wonder how much of a secret the plot to overthrow Lann really is."

Namid frowned. "Good point. So time to find a way into the chieftain's quarter."

~ ~ ~

Namid and Aahmes headed deeper into Meahan, toward the chieftain's quarter. They met fewer and fewer people in the passageways as they got closer and the night progressed. They also found fewer candle-lanterns lit in the passages.

After close to a candle-mark, they paused where the side passage in which they stood opened into a wide passageway that Namid recognized. She peered around the corner to study the passageway. Aahmes mimicked her on the other side of their small side passage.

Elaborate lanterns lit the wider passageway and the ornate wood door that stood to their left. Namid remembered that this door set aside the central part of the complex from the rest. Beyond it lay the room in which they had met Lann the previous autumn.

Two large men in leather armor flanked the door. Built much like Haeith, they both stood a full head taller than Namid. They carried sheathed swords at their hips and looked very alert for that late at night.

Namid and Aahmes exchanged looks.

~I still have that poison you gave me,~ Namid said using thought-speech. *~But just the one tiny dagger.~* She tapped the finger-long dagger in its sheath that she wore as a necklace.

~Do you still have any of those needles you would put in your braid?~ Aahmes said the same way.

Namid frowned. *~Should've remembered those....~*

She kept her movements silent as she stepped back from the opening and snaked a finger into a hidden pocket in one of her armguards. She scowled when she found none of her thin needles in their accustomed place.

Right. She had pulled them out when they were in Kilaadi to get more made and had never returned them to their hidden pocket, caught up in other concerns as she had been. So where had she stashed them?

She pawed through her pouches and pockets and found her needles tucked away at the bottom of one of her smallest pouches, almost hidden in the seam. She handed one to Aahmes—both taking care of the sharp points on both ends of the needle—and pulled out the small vial of the sleeping poison to coat her tiny dagger and one end of the needle Aahmes held.

As she returned the vial to her pouch, Aahmes stiffened.

~*Someone's coming.*~ He waved a hand at the passageway opening across from them, then tucked the needle into the small sheath on Namid's necklace. She slid the dagger back into it, too.

~*Time for distractions, then.*~ Namid winked at Aahmes.

With a glance toward the approaching footsteps, she wrapped her arms around him, pulled him against her against the wall and pressed her lips to his.

After a quick startled look, he smiled against her lips and returned the kiss with enthusiasm.

A breath-of-time later they both chuckled as clansmates who passed them offered encouraging comments and suggestions.

After their audience had gone, Namid released Aahmes and spun away as she palmed her tiny dagger and the needle.

~*Follow my lead,*~ she told Aahmes with a playful grin. She whirled out into the cross passageway with a delighted, giddy laugh, in full sight of the two guards.

"Come on," she urged Aahmes and held out a hand to him.

He clasped it and followed her, taking the needle from her at the same time.

She released his hand, spun again in the passage and stopped facing the guards, who watched without expression.

"And what have we here?" she said. "What a beautiful door!"

She whirled back and planted a playful kiss on Aahmes' lips before she skipped toward the guards. They rested their hands on their swords, but otherwise made no move.

"We finally have time alone and you want to look at a door?" Aahmes complained, playing his part. The guard on the left almost smiled. He looked to be the younger of the two. Aahmes shrugged at him.

"You know how much I love wood carvings," Namid said as she slipped between the guards. She pretended to ignore them, but she watched them from the corners of her eyes, ready to dodge if they drew their weapons.

She strode to the door and placed a hand on it, then traced the carvings.

"You should take yourselves somewhere else," the older guard said. "Chieftain Lann will not be pleased if he's disturbed."

Namid stepped closer to that guard and gave him a guileless look. Aahmes eased toward the other guard and shrugged at him again.

"Of course I wouldn't want to disturb the chieftain," Namid said, her voice now a whisper. The guard leaned closer to hear her. She glanced back at Aahmes, clasped the guard's arm, and scratched his skin with her tiny dagger.

At the same time, Aahmes scratched the guard next to him with the needle.

Both guards jerked, their eyes opened wide, and they slumped.

Aahmes was able to catch his man quickly enough to ease him down the wall with little noise. Namid was less successful and looked around to make sure the noise the guard made as he slumped had not attracted any attention. Both guards' breathing was slow and regular, as if they slept.

When it seemed no one was coming to investigate the noise, Aahmes closed the guards' eyes and searched their belt pouches.

"No keys," he muttered as he straightened, empty-handed. "Too bad we didn't bring some wine with us. To make them look drunk."

Namid tried the door. "Not locked anyway," she murmured. She eased the door open enough to peer through. No one waited on the other side and only widely spaced lanterns lit the passage, with its elaborate hangings and smooth wood floor.

"Will they be more obvious outside or inside the door?" Namid said, indicating the guards.

Aahmes shrugged and peered inside. He pointed to a nearby opening off the main passage. "Let's tuck them in there."

It took both of them to drag each large guard into the side room. But the darkness there hid them well.

Aahmes closed the ornate door, with a questioning look for Namid that held a hint of amusement. They both headed down the passage and peered in side openings as they passed but found nothing of interest.

~*So you like wood carvings?*~ Aahmes teased Namid.

Namid just shrugged and gave him a sidelong look. ~*It worked, didn't it? Do you remember the way to the room where they put us?*~

~*Yeah, follow me.*~

Aahmes led the way partway down the passage and turned into a smaller passageway to their left. Another couple of turns into what seemed like just random openings to Namid and they stood outside the room that Lann had used to imprison them and their companions the previous year.

The opening was still blackened, blasted rock.

~*He hasn't replaced the door that you destroyed,*~ Namid observed.

~*Probably wants to have a fancy carved one. And that takes time.*~

~*Before that display, I never suspected you had Power. Certainly not anything like that.*~

Aahmes grinned. *~Before that display, I rarely used my Power, not even for little things like you often do.~*

With a nod, Namid stepped into the opening, Aahmes right there with her. A lantern on a hook to their left provided light. Inside the room stood two tables that held a variety of bowls and cups with several different-colored liquids in them. And off to the side sat bowls with colored powders.

Namid and Aahmes exchanged looks and shrugged.

~Know anyplace else in here where he might hold people?~ Namid asked.

~No place specific. Better just look around as much as we can before we have to leave again.~

They methodically began to check the rooms and passageways of the chieftain's quarter, starting with the path back to the main passageway. When they finished there, they retraced their steps to the ornate door and investigated all the side openings and the short passages they found.

~Even if we do find that Lann's holding people somewhere, that just complicates this whole attempt to oust him,~ Namid commented with a sigh as they walked. *~And I don't see any of this getting us any closer to an answer to our problem with the 'gods'.~*

~No, not so far,~ Aahmes spoke to her second comment. *~But it's been said that wisdom resides with the chieftains. Maybe there's something somewhere in this quarter that might help us. I do know the clans have been in this area a very long time. Maybe long enough to have tucked away some knowledge that we can use.~*

~Hope so.~

They returned to the room that held the hidden guards and found that they had run out of time - the guards were already stirring. Two more scratches of the sleeping-poison settled them back down again, at least temporarily.

~That second dose won't hold them as long,~ Aahmes said.

Aahmes and Namid paused to change their glamour so

they yet again looked different. Just in case the guards might wake and start a hunt for them.

~*I don't know that we should use the poison again tonight, after this,*~ Aahmes added when they finished.

~*We'd better search faster, then.*~

They passed the openings they had already investigated and worked their way deeper into the chieftain's quarter, their pace faster than before.

They still found nothing of use for their purposes. And discovered no rooms that held any prisoners.

That section of the quarter held few people, at least the areas they investigated. The rooms they found were dusty and empty of anything but the barest of furnishings. The few people they did discover—Acnald clansmates from their clothes—were asleep in their rooms.

After they checked the side passages on the way, they came to the entrance to the large audience chamber in which they had first met with Lann.

They peered into the shadowed interior. The chamber held several wood chairs at the far end, all facing the opening where they stood, and no other furniture. Just four candle-lanterns provided light. A few hangings decorated the walls.

After they made certain no one waited in the room, Aahmes and Namid eased inside and followed the wall to their right. Namid thought she remembered glimpses of other openings. Perhaps they would prove more fruitful.

A faded hanging obscured most of the first opening they found. Behind the hanging, a plain wooden door was set in a finger-width from the edges of the opening. It was locked.

~*Promising,*~ Aahmes commented as Namid pulled out her lockpicks.

After Namid made short work of the lock, they stepped through the opened door into the passageway beyond. Namid eased the door closed behind them, which plunged the passageway into darkness.

Namid used Wild Power to call up one of her red glowing orbs for light. And the orb winked right back out.

~*Problem?*~ Aahmes asked.

~*Thought I'd try again using Wild Power for the light. I tried once before, a while back. But that Power's apparently unsuited for it,*~ Namid replied as she drew on her own Power to create the light orb. She winced at the headache that shot behind her eyes and settled there.

With the light floating a handspan above the floor, they headed along the passage. It had no side passages and led them to an opening into a narrow room. Namid fed a little more Power into the light orb to brighten it and tried to ignore the increased headache.

Cluttered stone shelves lined the room and reached from the floor to the ceiling. The center of the room held tall, wooden shelves. With her orb for light, Namid saw a few details of the items on the shelves. It looked like a lot of random items all piled together. But a couple of the shelves to their left held books – those she could see well enough.

Aahmes called up a light orb of his own – and Namid saw him wince as he did so. With the orb following him, he moved to the right into the room and perused what he could see there.

Namid headed to the books. Closer, she saw they all looked somewhat ragged and old. They were of all different sizes and none of the spines contained any writing.

Namid set her light orb on one of the shelves and pulled out books one by one to look inside.

The books held writings of various past chieftains—the best she could tell—some containing what looked like excruciatingly detailed accounts of trade deals and such. After quick looks through a half-shelf of these, Namid decided to see what else the room held. She replaced the book she held, a small thing with a crumbling black leather cover and called her light orb to her.

As she turned to look at the shelves behind her, a book at the end of a shelf that she had not investigated caught her eye. It had an unmarked cover of dark-red leather and sat slightly out of line with the rest of the books.

Namid caught her breath. How could it possibly be?

Aahmes peered around the end of the wooden shelves at her. "What is it?"

She did not answer, only grabbed the book and flipped it over. It certainly looked like it.

When he saw what she held, Aahmes moved closer. "Is that...?"

Namid opened the book. Inside, she found the writings in no language she recognized, as she had expected.

"It is! That book we found in Wesh's tower and gave to Odasoro," Namid murmured.

Aahmes stepped close to look over her shoulder. "But how'd it get here?"

Namid shrugged and moved the light orb closer. The book contained more writing than it had the last time she had looked at it. And she recognized the writing. She squinted, trying to make out what Odasoro had written beneath each line of the older writing.

"What is that?" Aahmes said. "Did the troubadour write that? It looks like nonsense."

"It *is* his writing. But it's not nonsense. It's a code. He taught it to me when I was a child. I hope I can remember how to decipher it."

They both started at a sound from the far side of the room. They drew daggers and doused the light orbs, then waited in the darkness. Namid tucked the book in her tunic while she listened for any movement.

Just when she was ready bring back the light orb, she heard the distinctive sound of a door closing.

~*Time to go,*~ Aahmes said.

Not wanting to risk a light, they felt their way back to the opening through which they had entered and down that passage to the door to the audience chamber.

~*Still unlocked,*~ Namid reported after she tested the door.

Aahmes eased the door open just enough to peek through. Namid bent to peer under his arm. When they found no indication that anyone else was in the room, they stepped out and closed and locked the door behind them.

They hurried back to the ornate door that marked the edge of the chieftain's quarter. But when they approached the room where they had left the unconscious guards, they heard voices.

They exchanged looks and eased close to the doorway to listen.

"—can't just inform him," a harsh whisper was saying. Hard to tell if it was a man's or woman's voice.

"But aren't we supposed to?" That was a different voice, definitely a man's.

"Think!" another voice chided. Namid recognized that one: the older of the two guards. "Don't want to end up like that clansmate who brought him news he didn't like. His family, those who are left, are still mourning him."

"Return to your guarding," the whisper said. "You didn't see anyone enter during your watch. If anyone asks anything, that's all you say. Nothing more. If no one asks, you need say nothing of this."

The voice sounded like its owner was approaching the door. Namid and Aahmes scrambled back in silence and ducked into the nearest doorway.

The footsteps of three people sounded on the wood floor of the passageway. One set, lighter, passed their doorway and headed further into the quarter. The other two sets, booted and louder, headed back toward the quarter's carved door.

After they heard the sound of the door closing, Aahmes and Namid ventured back into the passage. Quick looks both ways assured them that no one lingered nearby.

Exchanging looks, they eased up to the door. Namid reached out with a tendril of Wild Power and Aahmes copied her.

After a breath-of-time, Aahmes shrugged.

~Can't absolutely tell if they're guarding the door again out there,~ Namid said.

~Me neither. But it sounded like that was their plan. Risk it? Or find someplace in this quarter to hole up?~

The sound of footsteps coming from far down the passage toward the audience chamber decided them.

~Someplace to hole up,~ Namid said. *~Might give us a chance to look around better. And keep us from having to keep coming and going.~*

They ducked into one of the side passageways before the owners of the footsteps came close enough to pick them out of the shadows. They followed the passage, then took several turns into additional side passageways to confuse any possible pursuit and avoid others, guards perhaps, who seemed to be half-heartedly looking through the passages.

When they decided they had put enough distance between themselves and potential searchers, they slipped around a ratty woven curtain into a room to catch their breath. The room had clearly been unused for some time, and even the passages nearby had shown signs of disuse.

Namid plopped down on a large dusty cushion and cradled her head in her hands. The headache had not dissipated even the slightest.

"We're going to need to figure out what's up with using our Power, too," she muttered. "And I've a feeling we should warn clan Naalin and the others that their secret attempt to oust Lann might not be such a secret."

Aahmes settled next to her and draped an arm around her shoulders. She leaned against him with a slight smile, followed by a wince as the motion made her head pound.

"There are the other entrances into the chieftain's quarter. We just need to find them from this side," he said. "And then we can warn them."

"That'll work. After some rest, I think."

With a nod, Aahmes drew on some Wild Power to seal the curtain at the room's entrance so no one could try to enter without alerting them. He also placed a veneer on the side that faced the passage to turn aside any interest in what lay in the room. Using Wild Power, Namid placed a shell along the room's walls to keep anyone outside from hearing anything from within. They stretched out on the dusty cushion to try to rest.

CHAPTER 8

Namid woke disoriented and coughing, a taste of blood in her mouth. She wiped her mouth with the back of her hand and her hand came away bloodied. The next breath-of-time the taste of blood vanished. As did the smear of blood on her hand.

Aahmes still lay asleep on the dusty cushion. She watched his steady breathing. At least her coughing fit had not disturbed him, and seemed not to have drawn anyone to their hiding place.

But the blood disturbed her. What did this pain and blood mean, for both of them, when they used their own Power, the Power they carried within them? Their use of the Wild Power did not have the same effect on them.

And the effect was getting worse. Before it had only happened when they linked to do something massive and remarkable. Then when they linked for anything, even something minor. And now most of the time when they used the Power at all.

She reached out to the Wild Power and drew some to herself, not needing to fight it as much as usual. The veneer and shell on the room had begun to slip away so she renewed them. She used her own Power to create a small, dim light orb, and winced at the headache that resulted.

She positioned the orb at her shoulder and took out the thin book. Flipping through its pages, she saw that Odasoro had written on every page that had the other writing on it. Looked like he might have deciphered all of what it said. She began to work her way through the troubadour's coded notes.

~ ~ ~

Namid sat staring at the book with an expression of distaste when Aahmes woke more than a candle-mark later. She felt him reach out with Wild Power to check the veneer and shell. Then he gave her a questioning look.

"I've gotten through some of it," Namid said, keeping her voice quiet. "The more I work with it, the better I'm remembering Das' code."

"And?" Aahmes whispered. He stretched, then renewed their glamours, as the Wild Power had begun to slip away there, too.

"It's disjointed. So far, the first part seems to be notes about the 'gods' and them gathering Power. First what seems to be speculation, followed by sections that read like the writer was watching them. So that would make it extremely old. I poked ahead a little and it looks like it gets into various ways to get blood Power and comparisons of the effectiveness of the different methods."

Aahmes made a face and Namid nodded agreement. She tucked the book back into her tunic.

"Enough of that for now," she said and waved a hand toward the doorway. "Shall we see what else we can find?"

"Like maybe something to eat?" Aahmes said as he headed toward the door.

"That, too." Namid released the Power for the light orb and it vanished. She and Aahmes slipped back out into the passage.

They avoided the areas with people as much as they could. They managed to locate some food. Judging by the activity, Namid guessed it was around midday.

After that, she and Aahmes spent more time exploring the chieftain's quarter. The quarter seemed to hold as few people as the clan Naalin quarter, but everyone there wore high quality clothing and more jewelry than Namid had seen since the citadel in Kilaadi. And the food was exceptional.

After several candle-marks of exploring, renewing their veneer of belonging whenever the Wild Power started to slip away even a little, they had found two other entrances to the quarter. Both were guarded as the first had been, but the doors stood open for the day. They took the opportunity to slip back out of the quarter and head back to clan Naalin. They returned to their clan Naalin glamour halfway there.

When they arrived there, Taakha grabbed their arms before they even stepped into the gathering room.

"There you are! Where have you been?" she demanded with a glare for both of them.

Aahmes shrugged, his expression bland and uncommunicative.

"Just learning where all the clans are," Namid said.

"Ah, well, good. We have to go." She pulled them back down the passage.

Aahmes shrugged his arm free of her grasp as Namid planted her feet to go no further.

"Where?" Namid said.

"We have something important to tell you," Aahmes said at the same time.

As Taakha stopped and looked from one of them to the other, Saneth hurried over to them.

"Good, you found them."

"Lann has called a meet," Taakha said, ignoring Saneth. "Less than a candle-mark from now. We need to be there."

"Lann might already know about your intent to oust him," Namid said in a quiet voice. "The Cohaire need to know this."

Taakha and Saneth exchanged looks. "I'll find the others and tell them," Saneth said and hurried off. "Be careful at the meet," she called back over her shoulder.

"Lann has called for the highest ranked of all the clansmates to attend him," Taakha said. "We need to go."

Aahmes and Namid exchanged astonished looks. "Even after what we've told you?" Namid said.

"It might be a trap," Aahmes said.

"Perhaps," Taakha said, her tone one of disbelief. "But if we don't attend, he will certainly know that something is up. Now he might only just suspect. And we've all taken precautions anyway." She slipped a dagger partway out of her sleeve to show them and hid it again. "Come on."

Namid and Aahmes followed Taakha back through the maze of passageways to the main entrance to the chieftain's quarter, the ornate door. Clansmates from all the clans crowded the passageway and it took them more than a quarter candle-mark to make their way into the audience chamber. Aahmes and Namid made certain they found positions that let them remain near the door that led out while still giving them a view through gaps in the crowd of most of the far end of the chamber.

~Don't seem to be a lot of extra guards,~ Aahmes commented, using thought-speech.

Namid agreed with him as she watched the last clansmates straggle in. While those stragglers eased to spots in the crowd, an older woman stepped up to the front of the room, near the chairs. She wore clothes in clan Acnald colors. When she raised both hands, the room grew quiet.

She sidled to the side, with a bow, when Lann stepped out from behind the row of chairs. Namid shifted her position so she was mostly hidden but could still study him through a small gap between the people in front of her. Even with the glamour concealing her identity, she felt she did not want him to see her.

Lann looked much the same as when she had last seen him, with his pinched face and thin mustache that curved down over the corners of his mouth. This time he did not wear rich furs, but his clothes still exuded wealth and privilege. He peered at the crowd, his eyes narrowed, before he spoke.

"I greet you, clansmates. As the depths of the winter season engulf us, I'm pleased to announce a celebration in two weeks' time, when Sitkhesen and I will be pledged." He held one hand out to the side. A young woman with golden-brown skin and long brown hair stepped out of the shadows and scurried to clasp his hand. She stood next to him, an armlength away, her eyes on her feet and her expression one of misery.

Namid leaned close to Aahmes. "Sitkhesen? Might she be that Sitkha we heard about?"

"I think so."

"No!" a voice shouted out. A young man with very light brown skin and reddish-brown hair shoved his way to the front of the crowd. "She and I promised to each other already."

Lann leaned toward the younger man with a leer. "Why would she take you when she can have the chieftain?" he said. He waved a couple of his guards over. They seized the man's arms and hauled him forward to face Lann.

"You can't do this," the young man shouted as he fought to break free of the guards. "I'm the one she loves."

Lann stared at him a breath-of-time. "So you refuse to relinquish this claim you say you have here?"

"Khaen, don't!" Sitkhesen cried as she struggled in the grip of another guard. "Chieftain, please!"

Lann glanced at her then back to Khaen. "Well?"

"You have no right to—"

Lann pulled out a stiletto and plunged the blade into Khaen's eye. The younger man jerked then slumped. The guards released him and let him fall to the ground.

Sitkhesen screamed and the crowd surged toward the chieftain. They stopped when Lann's guards stepped in front of him, their swords unsheathed.

"Remove this," Lann ordered a couple of his guards with an offhand wave to Khaen's body. "And see Sitkhesen to a safe place."

While the guards followed their orders, murmurs ran through the crowd. But no one else stepped forward. Namid only realized she had drawn a dagger partway when Aahmes tapped her hand.

"He's got more." He waved a hand toward the chieftain.

Lann returned his attention to the crowd.

"Such a shame he couldn't accept the will of his chieftain," he said. "I trust the rest of you will have no such problem. I know all of you will be happy to celebrate with us. And if you hear word of any others who would question my chieftainship, I'm sure you'll uphold your clan's honor by letting us know so we can remove the disruptive element." He waved a hand toward the entrance. "Go your ways now, and return in two weeks to celebrate my pledging."

Namid and Aahmes made certain they were well-concealed in the center of the crowd as everyone hurried to leave the chieftain's quarter.

~In this one special case, I'd consider becoming an assassin,~ Namid fumed.

She clasped Aahmes' hand so they would not get separated in the crowd.

~I can agree,~ Aahmes told her. ~But I think perhaps I know now what we can do here to help. Lann likes so much to take people, presumably hold them somewhere——~

~When he doesn't just kill them in front of family and friends,~ Namid interjected.

~Yes. So, what if he's the one taken?~

He met her gaze and they shared crafty smiles with each other.

~Hold him somewhere until the chieftainship is decided,~ Aahmes continued. *~After that, the new chieftain and advisory families can decide what's to be done with him.~*

Namid glanced back toward where Lann still stood, watching all the clansmates as they filtered through the single doorway. She spotted a shadowy figure standing less than a pace behind him, cloaked and hooded. She could not see the person's face. She called Aahmes' attention to the figure right before they passed though the doorway.

~Think that's the Seer that Taakha mentioned?~

~Fits the description that she gave us,~ Aahmes replied. *~I didn't notice her there earlier. Wonder where she was.~*

They stayed in the thick of the crowd as long as they could, then split off to make their way back to the Naalin quarter.

Namid's hopes of eating a quiet meal with time to talk with Aahmes were dashed when they heard the loud, angry voices coming from the gathering room. Taakha's voice rose over the others. As Aahmes and Namid eased along one wall to claim a table and eat, Taakha admonished the others in the room that they could no longer wait to do something.

Namid looked over the others gathered there. No one that she did not recognize from the various meetings of the Cohaire who supported the change.

"At least I don't spot any possible spies," Aahmes whispered in her ear.

She nodded agreement. "Me neither."

"But how can we be ready to move so quickly?" one older man interrupted Taakha's tirade.

"We still need more time to sway the others to support us," another man added. "We don't have enough—"

"You weren't there," Taakha said. "We can't afford to wait. He killed a man named Khaen in front of everyone and they were all too scared to do anything about it. He'll dare anything, now. We need to show them that we can oppose him! Once the others see something actually being done, they'll lose their fear and join us."

"So what would you have us do?" Inar spoke up.

Namid lost the thread of the discussion as everyone talked at once, trying to have their ideas heard. She watched the confusion while she ate.

They still had not settled on anything when she and Aahmes finished their meal and returned their bowls to the kitchen. Their attempt to ease back through the room to the passageway to their own rooms was thwarted when Taakha spotted them.

"Nakht, Adday, what about you two?" Taakha called everyone's attention to them. "You haven't shared your ideas to help."

Namid exchanged looks with Aahmes.

"Should we bring others into it?" Namid said in a low voice.

Aahmes shrugged. "We'll need someone to help… at least to hold him somewhere," he said and sauntered to where the Cohaire stood together. Namid followed.

"We have an idea," Namid said. She kept her voice low so it would not carry out to any potential listeners who might lurk in the nearby passageways. This forced the gathered clansmates to lean in to hear her.

"What if we were to take Lann," Aahmes said. "Much as he's said to have taken so many clansmates."

"You mean kill him?" one woman said.

"That would be for the new chieftain and the Cohaire to determine," Namid said.

"He should pay for what he's done," Taakha said.

"As Nakht said, they'll decide his fate," Aahmes said. "We suggest capturing him. Hold him away somewhere hidden, until the new chieftain is in charge."

"That won't be easy," Saneth said.

"How could it even be done?" Dyefa said. "He's always

got guards and others nearby."

Namid and Aahmes exchanged looks.

"Nakht and I can get close enough to do it," Aahmes said. "And once he's taken, any guards or other supporters can be controlled by threatening him."

"I'd say Lann won't let anyone do something that will result in us harming him," Namid said with a feral grin.

"But then there needs to be a safe place to hold him," Aahmes said. "With people who can keep him secure as long as needed."

The clansmates fell silent as they considered that.

"Perhaps one of the very old back tunnels?" Sen said. "No one really goes there anymore, and they have fewer ways in and out."

Inar nodded agreement. "But they'd still be easy enough for us to get to, bring food…."

"The two of you can do this?" Taakha said to Namid, doubt and challenge clear in her tone of voice.

Aahmes stepped up next to Namid. "And only the two of us," he said. "We have skills that directly promise success. If anyone else came along, they'd increase the risk too much."

Taakha glared at him, then shrugged as if she did not care and turned away.

"How soon can you be ready, Nakht, Adday?" Inar said while some of the others discussed the who and how of holding Lann in a back tunnel.

"Certainly before he pledges," Aahmes said.

"But not for several days at least," Namid added. "We *will* have to make some preparations."

"Of course," Inar said. "Just let me know how we can help. And let me know when you'll do this – when you know better."

After close to a half candle-mark of assuring the Cohaire they could do this and promising to let them know more later, Aahmes and Namid managed to escape into the passageway that led to their rooms. They walked in silence to the entrance to Namid's room.

"Are you up to talking some before sleeping?" Namid said.

"If you are."

Namid led the way into her room and they both renewed the Power around it to keep anyone else from entering or from hearing anything from within.

After she shed her cloak, Namid plopped down on one of the cushions with a sigh. Aahmes dropped his cloak next to hers and seated himself right next to her. He gathered her into his arms, and she returned the embrace. For many long breaths-of-time, they sat there and just held each other.

Then with another sigh, Namid pulled away a little.

Aahmes leaned close to brush his lips against hers, then scooted back on the cushion.

"Where to start?" Namid said.

Aahmes chuckled. "Where we usually do. What do we have to get done right away, and what is only urgent?"

Namid laughed. "True. Should have grabbed some wine…." She laughed again as Aahmes reached to his cloak and pulled a full skin from one of its pockets.

"Snatched this from the chieftain's quarter," he said. He took a drink and passed it to her.

"Oh, that's good." Namid passed the skin back and pulled out the book.

"I've been feeling an urgency around this. About needing to know what it says," Namid said. "So I want to focus on deciphering the rest of Odasoro's coded writing. It looks like he got all the way through it."

Aahmes picked up the book and flipped through it. "Good, you're not writing the translation in here."

Namid scowled at him. "Of course not. So far, I'm not writing it anywhere. I'd like to teach you the code, too."

Aahmes nodded agreement and handed the book back to her.

"We need to find that hidden passage into the

chieftain's quarter," Aahmes said. "Enough people speak of it that I'm inclined to think it's not just a tale."

"I noticed it's only the older people who seem to know of it. Maybe find the oldest clansmate we can and see if they can give us enough information about it to find it?"

"And connected to that we need to look at the rest of the chieftain's quarter. Get an idea of Lann's habits. You know, the usual information to get in and get out with what we want without getting caught." Aahmes shared a grin with Namid then took another drink.

"Starting tomorrow, then, I'll concentrate on the book. See if I can get all the way through it as quickly as I can."

"And I'll work on hunting down the eldest clansmate. Also maybe slip back in the chieftain's quarter, see what I can learn." Aahmes handed her the wineskin again.

After another drink, Namid opened the book. "So, let's see what we can make of this code."

CHAPTER 9

Late in the morning, Namid stumbled bleary-eyed into clan Naalin's gathering room. She and Aahmes had worked at Odasoro's coded writing long into the night and had finished both the original wineskin and a second one that Aahmes had gotten from the clan Naalin storerooms.

This morning, whirling thoughts plagued her, thoughts of how to oust leaders, hide from the 'gods' or confront them, find a way to fight a threatening Power. She shook her head. So many concerns at once. Maybe too much.

Maybe she just needed to get something to eat.

Namid glanced at the others in the room who lingered over their breakfasts. No one she had not seen before. And also no Aahmes. He had not been in his room, either.

In the kitchen, Namid found enough food still left from the meal to satisfy her hunger but again no Aahmes. She decided he must be out looking for that eldest clansmate.

So she returned to her room, refreshed the fire on her hearth, and picked up where she had left off decoding Odasoro's words.

Many candle-marks later a whistle outside her room

caught Namid's attention. She recognized the Shadower signal and rose stiffly to push back the curtain at her doorway.

Aahmes leaned against the far wall of the passageway. He carried a tray with plates of food and a couple of empty mugs. A wineskin hung from one of his shoulders.

He greeted her with a grin and entered at her gesture.

"You didn't hear me the first couple of times," he said, "so I left you alone. But now it's past time for the evening meal. I'd wager you haven't eaten today."

"Then you'd lose," Namid said as she stretched stiff muscles. She took the tray and set it on her low table area, then pushed the book aside while Aahmes shed his outer tunics in the warmth of the room.

"I ate breakfast," she told him as she snatched a slice of warm bread and took a large bite.

"Ah, well, since you've had food today, shall I just take this back out?"

Namid glared at his teasing and plopped down at the table. "Try and you'll see how practiced I still am with my knives," she said around another bite of bread.

Aahmes laughed. He sat on the cushion on the other side of the table and began sharing out the food more evenly on the two plates.

"I can't help wondering if we should just leave here," Namid murmured. "It sometimes feels too much like we're not accomplishing anything and just sitting waiting for the 'gods' to find us."

"When did you last go above-ground?"

Namid frowned at him, wondering how going above-ground related to her concern. When Aahmes just gave her a bland, infuriating look in return, she considered his question, her head tilted as she tried to remember. "A couple of days ago? Maybe a little longer. The days seem to be running together some."

Aahmes finished dividing the food and poured wine into the two mugs. "Since then, another several handspans of snow have fallen. On top of what was there already. Right now, no one can get to us in here, certainly not from the southlands. And no one's going out anywhere."

Namid scrunched her nose in annoyance then dove into the meal. She spoke between bites, telling him what she had discovered in the book.

"I'm most of the way through it now," she said. "It's still very disjointed, like parts are missing. Maybe there's a second book. Anyway, there's a lot more in there about blood Power, different ways to get it and work with it, how best to get the most. Nasty stuff. Especially the part that said, 'A death provides the richest, most potent blood Power.' That's even written in there twice – for emphasis, I'm sure. Also, the handwriting changes every so often."

"Different people? Or Wesh as different people?" Aahmes said.

"I think the second. The book itself seems very old, but as you get closer to the end, the ink looks less and less faded. But the wording, the way of writing, all seems much the same. Different handwriting aside."

Aahmes refilled her mug.

"Whoever they were, it's pretty clear that they actually did what they wrote about, or at the very least were close observers. But after a while, it changes. It's still about blood Power and gaining more Power in general. But it talks about giving the Power to someone else. Well, really forcing it on them. That's the page the book was open to when we found it."

"Odd. I don't picture Wesh wanting to give anyone else Power."

"It sounds like the thought was to use it to control the other person somehow." Namid shrugged. "Still, someone wrote about things that happened. They managed to force Power on someone else. After many horrific failures. The book doesn't ever name the man that had Power forced on him, but he could do things with that Power. He *could* actually use it. But the important part is what came next."

Namid paused to eat several bites while Aahmes waited her out.

"It's what happened when he used the Power that was forced on him. The book records that strange pains began to plague him, and wounds showed up on his body that had been on the bodies of the people killed to get the blood Power. And the wounds would vanish after a length of time that ranged from a few breaths-of-time to candle-marks."

"The so-called gods gathered Power to themselves," Aahmes whispered.

Namid peered at him, uncertain where he was going with this thought. "Sesaisyd didn't show me how they did it."

"They must have been gathering blood Power. And that's what came to us from him," Aahmes said. "Was forced on us, really." He stared at his hands, lost in thought.

"What happened to him? The one who had blood Power forced on him?" he murmured.

"The more he used the Power, the worse the pain and wounds got. And they were slower and slower to fade."

"It killed him, didn't it?"

Namid reached out to clasp one of Aahmes' hands. "Yeah, it did."

She flipped to a page less than a third of the way from the back of the book. "But here, the writer speculates that it might be possible to reverse it. The blood Power forced on someone could be taken again."

Aahmes squeezed her hand. "How would that even be possible? Blood Power is supposed to come from someone's death, from what I've heard."

"Yeah, according to what was written in here, that's true. Although from some of what the Dark Priests did, I think they, at least, found a way to get some through torture, too. But still the writer thought it would be possible to reverse it. Well, really remove it again from the recipient anyway."

"So does it say how?"

"Not so far. But I haven't finished yet. If it follows the pattern of the earlier writing, it'll describe in great detail all the failed attempts before it tells of any success."

Namid poured herself and Aahmes some more wine, emptying the skin. She leaned back against the wall and closed her eyes. "I want to jump right back into it. Find out what the rest of the books says. But my head is pounding, and my eyes feel scratchy. When you interrupted me, I could hardly focus on the letters to make out what Odasoro's code said."

"Then take a little time away from it. Rest. And finish it tomorrow. We're not going to need that information this night."

"True." She sipped at her wine. "But you haven't told me what you've learned. Did you find the hidden entrance?"

Aahmes shifted on his cushion so he could also lean against the wall.

"Not yet," he said. "But I'm certain now that it exists. It took me a while, and a few changes of glamour, but I eventually met with Bakhtenmaat, an elder of clan Dianchaid. That's the clan the old chieftain's family belonged to."

Namid smiled. "I *was* going to ask the connection."

"Bakhtenmaat might just be the eldest in all the clans. She spoke with me on condition that I would work to stop Lann."

"An easy enough promise to make since we're already planning to."

"Yeah. She wasn't able to give me the location. She claimed she herself had never been there. But she told me something that she said chieftain passed to chieftain. It's a sort of a riddle of directions, I think. 'From the early meeting of five paces sunward feel the breath by one's feet to shift the pebble.' That's what she told me."

"How'd she know this? If it's passed from chieftain to chieftain?"

Aahmes chuckled. "Seems as a young woman, of about your age as she told it, she was something of a trouble-maker. She liked to hide in the chieftain's audience chamber to listen to conversations she wasn't supposed to. And often she heard the old chieftain passing along wisdom to her successor. Bakhtenmaat said she had always remembered this one piece because it was the most interesting thing the chieftain said that day. And she had meant to figure it out, but somehow never did."

"Do you trust her memory?" Namid said.

"I do. As I took my leave of her, she beckoned me close. 'Luck be with you, Aahmestharq. And your secret is safe here,' she whispered to me."

Namid jerked upright and looked at him. "She saw through your glamour? Or did it fail?"

Aahmes shrugged. "It didn't fail."

"Is she the Seer?"

"No. Her legs have failed her, and she no longer can walk. She's been that way for ten winters now. But she saw through my glamour. And without me even knowing until she said something. She told me she had always been able to see through Power-built illusions, even as a child. She had kept it secret because even then the Acnalds were purging the Power-gifted from their clan. She was born Acnald but pledged into Dianchaid and never looked back."

They fell silent as they finished their wine. Then Aahmes rose and gathered up the tray with the dishes and wineskin on it.

"Wait." Namid scooted around the table. She caught his arm to pull him close then kissed him enthusiastically.

When they parted, she grinned at his expression.

"I missed you today," she said. "Sneaking around together."

"When you've finished the book, we'll be back to that.

As for now...." He set the tray down and kissed her again.

~ ~ ~

Namid finished going through the book sometime after midmorning, by her best estimation. After Aahmes had brought her some breakfast earlier, he had headed out to see what he could make of the riddle of the hidden entrance's location.

For many long breaths-of-time, she sat and stared at the closed book, trying to absorb all she had read. She wondered what Odasoro had made of it and wished, with a pang of loss, that she could ask him.

The writer who had tried to take back blood Power that had been forced on someone had not recorded anything that worked. But the writing that had followed had given Namid a few glimmers of ideas, ideas that unfortunately seemed too unworkable when she considered them more closely.

The last portion of the book had concerned itself with the mystery of the cities of Rhadanthus and Corentris, their duplication of each other and how Power in Corentris seemed to affect Rhadanthus, too.

The writer here had not recorded any definitive explanation, but all the possibilities gave Namid plenty to consider. The final writings also detailed some things about the statue known as the Star of Corentris. From the wording, Namid decided Wesh had written those parts, at least, after he became Chendrukhar. They read more like notes intended to serve as reminders of previous thoughts than as thoughts written as they occurred or were tested.

With too much on her mind, Namid tucked the book away, then used Wild Power to bolster her glamour and secure her room. She wandered into the gathering room to see what was going on and interrupted an urgent-seeming discussion off to one side. When the clansmates there spotted her, they beckoned her over.

"Have you seen Adday?" one said.

"Not since earlier," Namid said. "Why?"

"We just heard from clan Diarmid. Lann's people have visited several other clan quarters and have taken people from there."

"Are they coming here, too?" another clansmate said.

"Doesn't seem so," the first said. "Or, at least, they all headed back to the chieftain's quarter."

"Has anyone told Taakha and Saneth yet?"

The clansmates shook their heads.

"Better find them and tell them," Namid said. "I'll see about finding Adday."

She returned to her room, grabbed all her weapons, and secreted them in their usual places, then checked Aahmes' room. Power still secured it and he was not there, so she drew a Wild Power veneer around herself and headed toward the chieftain's quarter.

Once beyond the boundaries of clan Naalin's quarter, Namid ducked into a little-used storeroom and used Wild Power to create a new glamour for herself. It would not last as long as the ones she built with Aahmes' help, but at least she could now hold one herself, for a time.

Then she joined the clansmates that milled in the passageways. Many just stood and complained, but a steady stream headed for the chieftain's quarter. She followed those.

Namid scrutinized the clansmates as she walked and discovered that none were from Lann's clan. She learned where Lann's clansmates were when she reached the main door to the chieftain's quarter. A large crowd had gathered there, and they railed against the Acnald clansmates who blocked the door and a good length of the passageway that led into the chieftain's quarter.

Namid tucked herself off to one side and scanned the crowd. No sign of Aahmes, but she suspected he would have a new glamour, if he was even there. She could look through Power to find him, but decided to wait and see what she could learn.

After about a quarter candle-mark during which she learned nothing new, she moved on to one of the other entrances. She found the same thing there.

The third entrance was the same, but as she turned to leave, she felt a light touch on the back of her hand.

~*Quite the mess, isn't it?*~ came Aahmes' voice in her thoughts.

She glanced at the man next to her and through the Power recognized Aahmes.

~*Very. Any luck with the riddle?*~ she replied.

~*Maybe. Let's find a better place, first.*~

They eased their way out of the crowded passageway and headed into some of the less-used passages well away from the commotion. A small unused room offered a respite from the activity in the passageways.

After they secured the room with Wild Power, after a long kiss of greeting, they settled on the floor by one wall.

"Have you heard how many people Lann's taken?" Namid asked.

Aahmes shook his head. "I did hear they were from several clans, though."

"We need to get Lann soon, then, before this gets any worse."

"Agreed."

"So what have you figured out about that riddle? Have you found the hidden entrance?"

"I've had several thoughts about the riddle," Aahmes said. "I've been trying to break it into parts, while also continuing to check around to see if I can spot anything. Whatever the riddle means, it's got to be something that hasn't changed for many winters."

"Well, there's the 'early meeting'," Namid said. "Do the clans have some regular meeting they hold? Some traditional thing, maybe?"

Aahmes considered that. "Only really gathering here in Meahan," he said. "Otherwise, I don't know of any regular meeting that's been going on long enough to be useful for this."

Namid leaned against his side and pondered the riddle. "Well then, I'd guess early means morning."

"Sounds reasonable."

"What if early goes with sunward. So if early is the time of day, then walk east from wherever this meeting takes place. But meeting of five? Who would that be? Are there five most important clans? Maybe there were five clans to begin with?"

Aahmes leaned back against the wall and closed his eyes. "Meeting of five," he murmured.

Namid watched him and tried to guess the direction his thoughts were taking from the slight changes in his expression. But then she lost her own chain of thoughts in the pleasure of just looking at him.

After several breaths-of-time, he slit his eyes at her.

"What is it?"

Namid felt her face grow warm. "I... uh...."

"Have you noticed that the passageways here always have four directions to go when they cross?" he said with a fleeting grin.

"What?"

He gave her a quick kiss. "While you were admiring me, I was thinking."

"I was thinking, too!"

"But about what?" he said, his expression saucy.

She gave him a mock glare. "So. Four passageways."

"What if it refers to a place where five of them meet?"

"Have you remembered such a place?"

"No. And I've not found one, either. Not yet. But if that's what we need to find, that means there's a relatively small section of Meahan that it can be in."

"So what about the rest of the riddle? Sounds like the pebble acts as some sort of key, maybe, but we're basically in cave system. There must be hundreds of pebbles."

"I'm hoping the rest of the riddle will be clearer when

we find the starting point. Let's finish looking through that last section of Meahan."

Aahmes stood and pulled Namid to her feet. They used Wild Power to refresh their glamour and placed a second over it that changed their appearances yet again. As they left the room, they removed all the Power shells they had placed there. Then they headed into the thick of Meahan, weaving through the many agitated clansmates that milled about in the passageways.

The section of Meahan that they had not yet explored lay on the far side of the chieftain's quarter from clan Naalin's quarter.

In that area, they found far fewer clansmates. And those they saw showed no interest in them.

"This feels somewhat like the Shadowers' ring of Rhadanthus," Namid muttered.

"Chancy, with a good potential for danger?" Aahmes' lips quirked up at the corners.

"Yeah. A little hint of home."

They searched through the area more than a candle-mark before they found a place where five passageways met. The best Namid could tell, it was not far from the edge of the chieftain's quarter.

They waited until they were the only people there then began poking around.

"I'm turned around," Namid said. "Do you know which way is east from here?"

"No."

Namid felt Aahmes reach out to the Wild Power and first send it through all five passageways, then send it straight up through the rock above them.

With a frown, he shook his head. "I let myself get turned around, too. And it's too near midday for me to tell from the sunlight outside right now."

Namid smiled. "Then let's go find something to eat and come back in a candle-mark or so. And I can tell you about what the rest of the book said."

~ ~ ~

After they ate their meal, pilfered from the nearest clan's kitchen area, Namid finished telling Aahmes what the book had to say about blood Power, the cities of Rhadanthus and Corentris and the Star of Corentris. And she shared her thought that perhaps this was only part of the information, based on how disjointed it was. Then they both sat in silence for many long breaths-of-time.

"We're going to have to find a way to get rid of the blood Power that came to us," Namid said. "But I don't know how. If there's another book...."

"If there is, we'll just have to find it. Somehow. But maybe there's a hint in what Sesaisyd showed you about the 'gods' and them gathering Power?" Aahmes said.

"Maybe. I'll have to give that some thought. But for now...."

"Yes." Aahmes' eyes unfocused as he sent Wild Power again through the rock above them. Then he nodded.

"It's been long enough. I can tell the direction now. Come on."

On their way back to the intersection of five passageways, Namid and Aahmes saw few clansmates. And those they did encounter hurried past, deep in their own conversations. That suited Namid just fine.

When they reached the intersection, Aahmes took position right in the middle and sent Wild Power up through the rocks above. This time Namid did likewise, to follow how he sensed the sun's position with the Power.

When they sensed the afternoon angle of the sun, they drew back to themselves in the underground area. Aahmes pointed to the passageway ahead and to the right.

"Should be that one," he said.

With a nod, Namid headed there. After she was in the passageway, she slowed her pace to look all around for anything that might indicate the spot they needed.

The passageway's bricks looked more worn than most of the other areas of Meahan, their edges rounded and many of them broken, leaving small bits at the base of the walls. The mortar in some places was also broken, with pieces missing.

"Too many possible pebbles," Namid said after more than a quarter candle-mark of slow walking and studying the passageway. She waved a hand at the debris by the wall she had been scrutinizing.

"The riddle says to feel the breath by one's feet," Aahmes said as he studied the other wall. "I'm thinking a gap that lets a breeze in somehow."

Namid made a sound of disgust. "So we go crawling along here until we feel the breeze?"

"Could just take off our boots and stockings. Roll up our trousers, like wading in a pond."

Namid glanced over her shoulder at him. "In the middle of winter, on a cold rock floor," she said, but sat to pull off her boots and stockings. Aahmes did the same.

And they continued down the passageway, still examining the walls but now also waiting to feel any breeze on their feet.

Soon the bottoms of Namid's feet felt slightly numb from the cold floor. Then she remembered that technique to warm herself that Aahmes had shown her. She drew a small bit of Wild Power and wrapped it around her feet as he had shown her. She smiled when it worked.

"Hope it's not all the way at the other end," Aahmes said after another quarter candle-mark of traversing the passage at a slow pace.

"Maybe some other clue in the riddle," Namid said.

Aahmes repeated the riddle a couple of times and changed where he paused when saying it to see if that seemed to change anything.

"What if the riddle uses one word for two parts?" Namid said. "We've been saying 'meeting of five'. But what if it's 'five paces sunward' at the same time?" She turned to look back the way they had come. "That's probably in the part we walked before we took off our boots."

Aahmes followed her gaze. "Something else, too. What if this can only be found 'early'? Like in the morning?"

"It's possible. Let's at least see if we feel anything around five paces from the 'meeting of five'."

So they returned to the intersection and each paced out the five paces. They ended at different locations because of the differences in their strides.

Namid stood where she had ended up and closed her eyes to concentrate better on what she might feel. She drew a small amount of Wild Power to herself and tried to sense any air movement with it. Nothing right where she stood. So she sidled a step toward where Aahmes had stopped and repeated what she had done, extending the Wild Power out a little further from her than she had before.

"There!" she said.

"Got it!" Aahmes said at the same time.

They shared a smile, and both moved to a spot between where they had stopped when they paced it out.

"That's a good sign," Namid said. "We both picked the same spot."

Aahmes knelt on the floor and licked a finger to wet it. He held that finger near the wall, close to the bottom, and moved back and forth a bit, then stopped.

"It's here. A slight movement of the air."

Namid repeated his actions and nodded. "I can feel it too."

She touched the wall just above the crack from which they felt the air and placed a tiny spark of Wild Power there to mark the location. Then she sat down to pull on her stockings and boots again.

"So now we just need to 'shift the pebble'," she said and brushed one hand across the pebbles on the ground next to her.

Aahmes finished pulling on his boots and stretched out to look at the pebbles on the floor from a different viewpoint.

Namid saw nothing to choose one pebble over another, so she studied the wall from this lower view.

She started when Aahmes jumped to his feet.

"I don't think it's down there," he said. "The riddle says, 'feel the breath by one's feet' which kind of implies the person is standing."

Namid clambered to her feet. "Sounds right."

They considered the wall again without finding anything.

"Maybe we *do* have to come here early in the day," Namid said. She crossed to the other wall and leaned against it, still studying the first one.

"It's possible," Aahmes said. "But I'm not sure how much sense it makes to have a hidden passage that you can only access at a certain time of day." He stood on tiptoe and ran his hands across the bricks as high as he could reach.

"I don't know." Namid let herself slide partway down the wall as she shook her head. "Maybe this isn't even the right 'meeting of five'. Or it's got some other meaning we haven't even thought of." She slid a little further and gasped.

"What?" Aahmes whirled around, one dagger already half drawn.

"Come here," Namid waved him over. "Slide down and look there." She pointed to a dark line that was just at her eye level now. It seemed to be an area where the mortar was broken out.

Aahmes looked as she directed, then they both hurried to the wall and leaned down to examine that area more closely.

With some trepidation, Namid reached into the gap with one finger. The hole was as deep as her finger was long. She traced the inside of the gap about half the length of the dark line they had spotted, then stopped.

"I think there's a pebble wedged in here," she said.

Aahmes felt along the gap from the other end with a finger and stopped right where she had.

"Feels like it."

Pulling back, he bent over and created a small light orb. Namid saw him wince in its light. From a headache, she assumed, like she suffered now whenever she created one of those orbs.

Aahmes guided the small light to the spot where Namid still held her finger and they both peered into the gap.

"Yeah, a pebble." Namid pulled her finger back out of the gap. "It's wedged in there pretty good. Holding something up, I think."

Aahmes continued to study the pebble. "Hope it's not the rest of the wall," he muttered. "How to shift it without sending it flying across the passage?"

"Use a dagger," Namid suggested. She positioned herself in front of the pebble, hands cupped. "You shift it and I'll catch it if it comes flying this way."

Aahmes gave her a dubious look, then poked one of his daggers in the gap. "I'll try to shift it to the side if possible, but—"

"I'll try to catch it, whichever way it goes."

Aahmes angled the dagger a little behind the pebble to try to pry it out the direction he wanted it to go.

The pebble shot to the side and Namid caught it as it fell from the gap. With a well-muffled screech of metal scraping rock, a thin rod slid down from where the pebble had held it.

The metal rod continued down below the gap in a hole the pebble had hidden, then disappeared. Both Aahmes and Namid heard a faint click and a piece of the wall from the gap to the floor swung out a finger-width into the passage.

CHAPTER 10

Aahmes pulled the door all the way open and they discovered that most of it was wood, with a kind of thick brick facing on it that let it blend with the rest of the wall. The other side of the door showed the mechanism that had unlocked it. The rod that had fallen hit the end of another, tilted it up and lifted a third out of a slot in the floor, which allowed the door to swing open a finger-width. Namid saw how they could lock it again from either side by sliding the metal rod back up and placing the pebble beneath it again with the door closed.

The tunnel beyond the door was no taller than the door. A thick rug, gray with dust, covered the center of the floor. Namid and Aahmes ducked inside and pulled the door closed. Namid replaced the rod and pebble to hold it shut.

Aahmes fed a little more Power to his light orb and they began the crawl down the tunnel. They now saw the far end roughly twenty paces away. Not far from the entrance, the ceiling lifted and gave them enough room to stand upright.

The tunnel now looked more like one of the other

passages in Meahan, right down to hooks along the wall for lanterns. But no lanterns hung there, and the dust on the rug showed no one had traveled that way for a long time.

They saw no side passages branching off, just the tunnel running straight to what looked like another door. Aahmes dimmed his light orb so it provided just enough light to see their immediate vicinity.

"In case there are holes to look through," he said. "Don't want the light to give us away."

Namid nodded agreement as they continued to the other end. There they found a door almost identical to the first one, including the shorter height.

Aahmes dimmed the light to almost nothing and they examined the door and the wall for any eyeholes.

Namid found a small one in the wall above the right corner of the door and they took turns looking through into a dimly lit room on the other side.

"I don't recognize that room," Aahmes said after a long look.

"One of the ones we didn't get to in the chieftain's quarter," Namid said. "Looks like just a sleeping room from here. Do you think risk it now?"

Aahmes nodded. "At least a little better look, I think. Probably everyone's attention is still on the main entrances where all the angry clansmates are."

Namid moved this door's pebble aside and the rods worked the same way to allow the door to open.

She and Aahmes crept into the room and looked it over. Nothing more than a sleeping room, as they had thought. Dim light entered around the edges of the woven curtain that blocked the doorway.

Namid glided to the curtain and moved one edge aside just enough to peek out. Instead of the passageway that she expected, Namid saw another room, with other curtain-blocked openings in the walls. It looked like a small version of the clans' gathering rooms, with two tables and several of those metal and cloth chairs. Aahmes leaned close to look too.

"Continue on?" he said.

Namid leaned out a little further and counted six other openings off the gathering room. She saw nothing to distinguish between them.

~Let's at least see if we can find how this connects to an area we've already seen,~ Namid suggested, switching to the silence of thought-speech.

After they refreshed their glamours and the veneer of belonging, they eased into the larger room. Separating, they each moved a different direction and followed the walls, checking each doorway they came to.

The third doorway Namid checked opened into a passageway, the doorway positioned at the end of the passage. Each of the side walls held two doorways, and a wooden door blocked the end of the passage. She waited there while Aahmes finished checking the other openings.

~All sleeping areas except for this one?~ she said when he joined her.

~Yeah.~ He peered out into the passage and tilted his head toward the door at the end with a questioning look.

Namid nodded and they eased down the passage. When Namid came to the first covered doorway, she moved the curtain aside just a finger-length and peered inside. Another of the small gathering rooms, with other doorways off it. The second doorway that she checked was the same.

~Rooms like the one at the end of the passage,~ she told Aahmes.

She had just turned toward the wooden door at the passage's end when it opened. Both she and Aahmes froze.

A cloaked and hooded figure stood in the doorway, lit from behind.

"Lann returns," the figure said in a harsh whisper. "You should not be here when he gets back."

Then the figure closed the door again.

Namid exchanged a look with Aahmes.

~I think we just 'met' the Seer,~ he commented with a grin and headed back down the passage.

Namid followed close on his heels.

They hurried back through the small gathering room, the sleeping room, and into the hidden passage. Both checked to make sure the door was secured behind them and Aahmes doused his light orb.

They waited at the tiny eyehole, listening and looking through every so often. After less than a quarter candlemark, Namid heard someone barking orders. The voice grew louder and suddenly a bit of light showed through the eyehole. She leaned closer to look.

One of Lann's guards stood at the room's doorway, the curtain pulled to one side. He pushed a young man across the room with a snarl.

"No more of your fussing," he said. "Here's where you'll be staying for now." As he turned away, he added, "All of you."

Namid turned away from the eyehole.

~Let's get out of here,~ she said.

~ ~ ~

On the way back to the clan Naalin quarter, they debated the merits of trying to free the clansmates who now—from what they had witnessed—were being held in the rooms they needed to go through to get to Lann.

"I don't like leaving them there," Namid said. "But freeing them exposes a secret that I'm not sure is ours to share with anyone other than the new chieftain. And taking them out another way is unlikely to work well."

"And going back multiple times is even more unlikely to end well," Aahmes said. "I think we've run out of time. If we're going to do this, I think we must do it as soon as we can."

"Tonight?"

Aahmes nodded. "If possible."

Namid considered what was involved, her head at a slight tilt. "Who knows what part the Seer is playing. I have a feeling she won't betray us, but I don't want to put that to the test."

When they returned to the clan Naalin quarter, Aahmes and Namid separated to find Taakha, Saneth, and Inar. Then they all gathered in one of the unused rooms where Namid and Aahmes explained what they had seen, without revealing the secret of the hidden passageway.

"We need to go after Lann as soon as possible. Tonight, if we can," Aahmes concluded. "Have you decided on a place to hold him and people to guard him?"

"So soon?" Taakha said, her tone hinted that she thought this unwise.

"We haven't yet," Saneth said at the same time.

"We don't think it's wise to wait," Namid said. "He's taken people today. Probably don't want to give him time to take more or do anything else."

Everyone exchanged looks and Inar nodded. "True enough. We'll still need a day to make a place, even if only a temporary one, to hold him at least for a day or two. That will give us time to arrange a better place for holding him longer, if needed. So will tomorrow night do?"

"It'll have to. We'll go after midnight," Aahmes said. "That should still give us enough time to locate him in the quarter. And most people should be sound asleep at that time."

They settled on a place to meet when Aahmes and Namid returned with Lann. Inar, and some others he would choose, would take the chieftain from there.

Namid and Aahmes left the others to make further arrangements and spent a quiet night together. The next day, they kept apart from the Cohaire's preparations to hold Lann and just made certain they had themselves as prepared as possible.

They ate their evening meal early and reviewed their

preparations one last time. Reluctant to leave the book behind but leery of taking it with her when they went after Lann, Namid drew a small bit of Wild Power to create a veneer to help hide the book in her room. With Aahmes' help, she managed one that covered the book with an impression of belonging to her small pile of clothes on one shelf, of being just another shirt at the bottom of the stack. After that was settled to their satisfaction, they tried to get what rest they could.

~ ~ ~

Roughly a quarter candle-mark before midnight, Namid and Aahmes renewed the Power shells and veneers around their rooms and the veneer covering the book, then slipped into the Naalin gathering room. As they headed to the passageway that led toward the outer door and passageways to other clan quarters, they encountered Taakha, Saneth and Inar.

"We'll have a place ready for you when you bring him back," Inar said. "Just meet us where we agreed."

The three clansmates turned one way while Aahmes and Namid headed the other.

After they moved out of sight of the others, Namid drew Wild Power to build a new glamour, with Aahmes' help. She then pulled several of her thin needles from their hidden pocket—she had returned them to their proper hiding place the previous day—and inserted them one by one into her long braid.

"Haven't seen you do that in a long while," Aahmes whispered as he watched her with a grin.

She matched his expression. "Haven't thought I'd need them again until now."

Preparations complete, they renewed their veneer of belonging and made their way back to the hidden passage without encountering any wandering clansmates.

They stopped at the door that led into the sleeping

room to listen and take turns peering through the eyehole. Dim light entered the darkened room from around the curtain at the doorway. Namid thought she saw someone in the bed, but the way the light streamed into the room made it hard for her to be certain.

No matter. This would not be the first time she had needed to cross a room without disturbing a sleeper.

She checked that her tiny dagger had some of the sleeping poison on it, and also her needle that Aahmes had kept. When Aahmes signaled his readiness, they eased the locking mechanism open, catching any parts that might make noise. Then they listened again several long breaths-of-time.

When there were no signs that anyone had heard the few small noises they made, they opened the door and slipped into the room, then closed and secured the door again behind them without a sound. Aahmes added a bit of Wild Power to hold the door against anyone but one of them. A quick look around showed Namid that someone did sleep in the bed.

At the doorway to the outer room, Aahmes held the curtain aside the smallest bit and they peered through the opening.

A single lit candle-lantern sat on one of the tables. A woman sat on one of the chairs there, slumped on the table next to the lantern. Her shoulders shook, like she might be crying.

Aahmes sighed, just loud enough for Namid to hear him. He tapped Namid's dagger necklace and she nodded.

While Aahmes waited at the curtain, Namid crept across the room to the woman at the table, the tiny dagger held ready. Just as she reached her, the woman sat upright and wiped her eyes. She turned toward Namid – perhaps some sense of her presence had alerted her. Namid saw that she was the woman Lann had said he would pledge to. The woman's eyes widened when she saw Namid.

Namid darted to her and clamped her hand on the

woman's mouth to stifle any outcry. Then she stuck her in the arm with the tip of her dagger.

"Sorry about that," Namid murmured in the woman's ear as she lowered her back to slump on the table, now sleeping.

Aahmes joined her there and considered the woman.

~*If we can, when we come back through*——~

~*Bring them all with us? Yes,*~ Namid finished his thought.

At the doorway to the passage, they again peeked through the space next to the hanging curtain before they ventured further. The passageway was empty, with no sounds audible from the other doorways. A single candle-lantern lit it, hung from a hook near the door at the other end.

When they reached the closed door, Aahmes licked his fingers and reached back to snuff the candle. Then he drew a dagger, holding the poisoned needle in his other hand.

They both listened at the door and searched it for any eyeholes. When they found none, Namid grasped the handle and discovered it locked. She drew on the smallest bit of her Power to create a tiny light orb. Still, pain tore through her head, momentarily staggering her. So Aahmes tucked away his dagger and needle and pulled out his lockpicks to open the lock while she tried to quell the pain, even a little.

By the time Aahmes had the lock open, she had managed to push away most of the pain, leaving a slight throbbing behind her eyes that she could probably work around. Aahmes pulled the door open just a crack. Namid doused her light orb and peered through.

~*No one that way,*~ she said.

Aahmes opened the door the rest of the way and they both checked the other direction. No one there, either.

They slipped out the door and eased it closed behind them. Namid looked both directions in the passage they found themselves in. It looked vaguely familiar, which she mentioned to Aahmes using thought-speech.

~*This way, I think,*~ he responded and led the way to the closest end, which another wooden door closed off. He opened it a crack and looked through, then opened it all the way. He beckoned Namid to join him and they stepped through into the audience chamber.

Namid headed toward a door to their right situated behind the chair they had seen Lann use before.

~*I think here,*~ she said.

With a nod, Aahmes joined her and they treated that door the same as the others. It opened to a short passage that ended at a richly woven curtain. A single low candle-lantern lit the passage.

~*No guards,*~ Aahmes commented. ~*I wouldn't think he'd feel so secure even just with his own clan.*~

~*Maybe he's got them cowed that much.*~

~*Could be.*~

With a twist of her wrists, Namid dropped both her stilettos to her hands from their sheaths in her armguards. Aahmes also drew two daggers then closed the door behind them. They eased down the passage to the curtain and paused to listen. Hearing only faint snoring, they each peeked around a side of the curtain.

The room on the other side was richly furnished with a large wooden cabinet to one side and a wooden table and chairs, all decorated with elaborate carvings. Colorful tapestries adorned the walls and a large hearth heated the room. The far wall was taken up by an oversized bed of thick cushions and lush coverings.

Lann lay alone in the bed, but the discarded dress that lay on the floor suggested that he had not been alone earlier. A partly shuttered candle-lantern on the table provided dim light in the room.

Aahmes and Namid exchanged glances and crept to the bed, Aahmes sheathing his daggers on the way. Namid found a sheathed sword and dagger on a belt next to the bed on the side she took. She sheathed one stiletto then eased Lann's weapons away from the bed and placed them behind her.

She and Aahmes again exchanged looks, then lunged for the sleeping man.

In the ensuing scuffle, as Lann woke almost instantly, Aahmes managed to grasp his arms and stuff part of the bedclothes in his mouth to keep him from crying out. Namid tangled his legs in more of the bedclothes and held her stiletto to his throat, nicking him when he did not subside right away. He glared at them both but ceased his struggles.

"Very good," Aahmes said in a quiet voice. "You see how this is going to go."

Namid snatched the belt from the floor and passed it to Aahmes to secure the man's hands. Then she freed Lann's legs and avoided his attempts to kick her.

Aahmes hauled him to his feet. He clamped his hand on Lann's mouth when the bedclothes fell away and the man drew breath to yell. Namid brought her stiletto close and Aahmes pressed one of his daggers to Lann's side. The chieftain wore only his trousers, so the dagger pricked bare skin.

"We don't *have* to take you alive," Aahmes said.

"Try to call for help and we won't," Namid added. "Might simplify things."

When Lann subsided, Aahmes eased his hand away from the chieftain's mouth, but held ready to stifle any attempts to call out.

"Who *are* you? Release me and I can make you both rich. Powerful, too. You can be leaders of your clans," Lann whispered. Namid smirked at this proof that their glamours worked.

"Nice try," Aahmes said.

Namid and Aahmes shifted positions so they were both behind Lann, each slightly to the side. Namid gripped one of Lann's arms while holding her stiletto to Lann's throat.

Aahmes gripped the man's other arm and held his dagger so its point just pricked Lann's side. They shoved Lann toward the door.

"Don't I even get shoes?" Lann protested in a quiet voice.

Namid exchanged a look with Aahmes, who shrugged. So she found a pair of soft indoor shoes half under the bed and dropped them next to Lann's bare feet.

After he put on his shoes, they pushed him in front of them to the door to the audience chamber. As Aahmes reached for the handle, the door opened.

And they came face to face with a startled guard. He immediately reached for his sword.

"Don't." Namid pressed her dagger against Lann's neck, drawing blood.

Lann gave a muted squeak and hastened to add, "Do as they say."

"Leave your sword here and walk with us," Namid ordered. "You know what'll happen if you try to free him or call for help."

The guard looked to Lann, who nodded. "Do it."

The guard took off his sword belt and placed it on the floor. He shifted to one side, a step ahead, to pace them.

Before they reached the door that led to the room with the hidden passage, another of the doors into the audience chamber opened.

The guard took that opportunity to round on Aahmes while Lann tried to break free of Namid. Aahmes ducked the swing of the guard's fist, pulled out his poisoned needle and stabbed it into the man's arm.

Namid kept hold of Lann and spun with him as he tried to reach her. A kick to the back of his knee dropped him and she secured her grip again, blade to his throat. Aahmes gripped Lann's other arm again. Namid then looked to the newcomer. And froze.

"Taakha?"

Aahmes spun around to stare at his cousin, who had

entered the room through the opened door. "What are you doing here?" he said.

"You did it," Taakha said as she closed the door behind her. She glanced at the fallen guard and walked to Aahmes and Namid, her lips curled into a triumphant smile. The smile did not reach her eyes.

"The powder," Lann said.

Taakha nodded as her smile vanished. She lifted a hand, palm upward and blew some reddish dust into their faces. Into Lann's too.

Namid immediately began to cough, so hard she could barely stand. She lost her grip on Lann, and her blade, as the fit continued. And she felt the veneer and the glamours fall away.

Her vision grayed at the edges and her hands and feet went numb. She heard Aahmes coughing, too, but could not even turn to see him.

A roaring haze swept through her. She remembered something like this, but her thoughts felt muddled and the memory eluded her. The room spun and she fell, unable to stop herself, or catch herself.

She reached for her own Power, then for Wild Power, but could not call either to her. She tried to summon the flames of her anger, as she had in Corentris, tried to burn through the effects of the powder.

Nothing.

Namid heard Lann's and Taakha's voices but most of what they said did not penetrate the haze. Something about 'truth' and 'really them'. Then Lann tangled a hand in her fringe of bangs and yanked her head up to peer into her face.

"The powder works just as well as that concoction we used before," he said. "And I don't even have to make you drink anything this time."

The haze thickened around her. One thing Taakha said came clearly to her.

"See, my chieftain, I told you I'd give you Aahmes."

"Why?" Namid managed to croak when she saw Taakha's feet approach through the haze. She heard Lann laugh again and Taakha's feet stumbled out of her line of sight.

"Wait!" Taakha said. "You promised! My son…."

Lann's continued laughter followed Namid into the thick, gray haze. She felt herself being lifted and carried somewhere, her wrists and ankles being tied, but the haziness that engulfed her was too thick for her to see and hear much.

Voices that seemed familiar, yet unfamiliar at the same time, spoke for a breath-of-time, then fell quiet. Whoever carried her, dropped her on the cold floor. Someone kicked her in the side. She gasped and heard Lann laugh again. Footsteps receded, leaving her trapped in the haze.

CHAPTER 11

After an indeterminate length of time, the haze thinned and finally dissipated. Namid blinked to try to make out her surroundings. She lay on a stone floor – she remembered that. A light flickered from somewhere behind her and up. Perhaps one of the candle-lanterns on a hook. Not too far in front of her was a wall, a familiar brick, so she must still be in Meahan.

Her whole body hurt, her side the most. She slowly rolled over and bit back a groan at the increased pain the motion sent through her.

Now she could see the room better, although her loose hair blocked some of her vision. With her wrists bound behind her, she could not do anything about that.

The room, what she saw of it, looked like every one of the sleeping rooms she had seen in Meahan. Except this one was bare of any cushions or blankets for the raised table and bed areas. The small hearth was cold, and a bucket sat in one corner. A single candle-lantern hung on the wall by the door, which had no curtain to cover it. Through the opening, Namid saw part of a passage, better lit than her room, and two armored women who flanked the doorway.

One of the guards turned to watch her but made no other motion. Namid gave the woman a long stare, then looked away. Her throat felt dry, scratchy, and her eyes burned. She wondered how long she had been there and where they had Aahmes.

She wiggled around to try to loosen her bonds, but the ropes were tied tight. The guard just watched her, and smirked when she finally stopped trying to get free.

Namid dozed as she waited for something to happen. She startled when a guard grasped her and hauled her to her feet – she had not noticed the woman approach. While the first guard held her upright, steadying her against dizziness that made her wobble, the second guard untied her ankles.

When the second guard straightened from untying her, she blew more of that powder into her face. Namid tried to hold her breath, but the woman punched her in the abdomen which left her gasping for air. And she inhaled some of the powder again which set off a coughing fit. The haze returned, but thinner this time.

That guard then untied her hands but left a rope still tied to one of Namid's wrists. The guard held the other end. After they let her relieve herself in the bucket, they tied her wrists again.

That was when she realized that she wore only her shirt and trousers. They had taken her outer tunics, boots and stockings. And her weapons, of course. Even her dagger necklace. With her hair loose, she assumed they had also found the needles that had been in her braid.

The guards kept tight hold of her arms and walked her into the passage. There they met two armored men who held Aahmes the same way.

"He's ready for them?" one of Namid's guards said.

One of the others nodded. "Going to make an example of them."

Namid met Aahmes' gaze. From his expression, the

haze engulfed him, too.

She tried to reach Power, any Power. She could sense the Wild Power, but not touch it or call it. So she scrutinized the guards and hoped for a convenient weapon to grab.

The guards marched them along the passage and into the audience chamber.

Namid heard a gasp of surprise when the guards brought her and Aahmes forward to stand next to Lann. She still could not see well, her vision hazy, but it seemed that the room was filled with clansmates.

She tried to move closer to Lann, hoping to somehow get the dagger on his hip, but her guard jerked her back by her hair and held her in place with a painful grip on her arm.

Then Lann's words penetrated the haze.

"And now that these four have been caught, they will be executed for the traitors that they are."

She looked to Aahmes, who looked as confused as she felt. Then guards brought out Taakha and Saneth, also with their hands tied behind them.

A brief hope that Inar had not also been captured, or killed, crossed Namid's thoughts then floated away.

"But I helped you uncover them!" Taakha shouted at Lann. "You promised."

Lann waved a negligent hand her direction. "You would've put this one in my place." He stabbed a finger at Aahmes, who lunged for him. Lann scuttled away as Aahmes' guards seized him and hauled him back.

"Brave as ever, I see," Namid said to Lann, surprised that her voice sounded strong, certainly stronger than she felt.

Lann sneered at her.

"I'd thought I was rid of you an autumn ago." He spat at her. "This time I'll be certain of it."

He turned to the watching, agitated clansmates. "We're taking them to the hill."

Next he turned to the nearby guards and lowered his voice. "Make sure all these line the execution path to witness." He waved a hand at the crowd.

More Acnald guards than Namid had seen to that point herded the crowd out of the room and through the passageway to the outside door.

Lann followed behind, in his heavy, rich furs, and chatted with one of his people who walked with him. Behind him, their guards walked Namid and the others. She realized that the other prisoners, too, wore only their shirts and trousers, and were barefoot. She tried to fight her guard, but the woman only laughed and continued to force her forward, her grip firm.

When Namid spun and bit the guard's arm as hard as she could, the woman still did not let go. With a snarl, the guard slapped her hard which added to her dizziness.

The journey outside passed Namid by in her haze as she fought to stay conscious. She did not know why, just that if she was out, she knew she would be unable to do anything to get out of this.

At least she had not seen anyone carrying an axe. Her brief smile twisted with derision at the thought.

The bitter cold outside sliced right through Namid's thin garments. Hard snow covered the ground. A light snow fell as the guards walked the prisoners along a faint path to the left of the entrance to Meahan.

Namid suspected that it was sometime in the afternoon, but she could not tell for certain. Clansmates lined the path, many engaged in futile struggles against clan Acnald brutes. Before long, Namid was shivering. At first, her feet hurt. Then they went numb.

After she stumbled several times, one of the male guards just picked her up and carried her.

The journey took close to a quarter candle-mark, and Namid shivered violently by the time everyone stopped atop a low hill. Several tall stakes, widely spaced, stood on the bare hilltop.

The guards hauled each of the prisoners to a stake and shoved them to the ground at the base. They secured them to the stakes, looping thick ropes around their chests several times.

During all this, Taakha continued to plead with Lann, who only gazed at her without expression. Namid tried to shake the haziness as fear slipped through the grayness that engulfed her. She fought to pull herself out of it and concentrate on figuring out how to get free.

But for all her desire to fight free, she instead found herself just watching Lann, who lingered after all but one of the guards headed back to Meahan, herding the clansmates ahead of them. Neither Aahmes nor Saneth said anything and Taakha eventually stopped begging.

Lann turned back to Taakha with a smug expression. "I thank you for your help catching these traitors. Know that your son lived when last I saw him," he said. "He was also a help to me. He provided me a tidy sum when I sold him to slave traders who went south with the winter."

He laughed when Taakha shrieked her anger at him. Lann then nodded to the remaining guard.

"Ensure they won't be going anywhere," he said.

The guard hefted a maul that Namid had not noticed before. Lann watched without expression as the man swung it down onto Namid's shin, breaking the bone with an audible crack. Lann smirked at her scream.

The guard moved to each of the others in turn and repeated his action. With each new cry of pain, Lann's smile grew. He laughed at the outraged grimace Namid gave him and, with a casual wave, returned back along the path. The guard propped the maul over his shoulder and followed.

Namid tried to control her shivering, tried to ignore the searing pain so she could concentrate on freeing her hands. But she was already so cold, her hands did not want to move correctly. And she could not wriggle out of the ropes that bound her. Each movement sent new agony shooting up her leg, threatening to knock her out.

She was afraid to look at Aahmes, afraid of what she might see there. But she finally looked at him. He met her gaze wordlessly.

She could not even touch him. She felt a tear slide down her face at his sad smile.

She returned his smile, then frowned. Then anger swept through her.

They were *not* going to end like this! There had to be something they could do. Something she could do.

Aahmes grinned at her change of expression and, with a nod, worked at his bindings.

"Any chance you can call that fire, like in Corentris?" he said. His voice shook with his shivering.

"I'm trying," Namid growled. She fed her anger with images of Lann's self-satisfied face and what she would like to do to that smile of his. She drew upon her anger at Odasoro's death, her father's, and what the Dark Priests had done to her brothers. She reached for the Wild Power, called it, tried to create the whorl of fire as she had before.

But she could not break through the gray haze.

She sagged against her bonds and hung her head. "Maybe when that stuff of Lann's wears off some," she told Aahmes.

"Inar will, no doubt, come free us," Taakha said. "As soon as he can get away with it."

"How did he avoid getting caught, too?" Namid said.

Taakha frowned and glared at Saneth.

"Instead of running, as she was supposed to, as I told her to if anything happened, Saneth attracted the Acnalds' attention," Taakha growled. "Deliberately. To let Inar escape instead."

"Which has left him free to be able to free us in turn," Saneth pointed out.

"Inar shouldn't *have* to come free us," Aahmes said, anger clear in his voice as he directed a glare at Taakha. "What did you think you were doing?"

"Lann had my son!" Taakha said.

"What?" Saneth said. "That wasn't what you told me."

"Lann took him. I couldn't tell anyone, not even you. I had to do what he wanted, or he was going to hurt him!"

"And how'd that end up?" Aahmes snarled. "He's a slave somewhere and we're all going to freeze here."

Taakha started to cry and Aahmes made a sound of disgust. He returned to trying to free himself. After a breath-of-time Namid and Saneth did too.

The more Namid worked at her ropes, the tighter they got. The snow increased, and the slight breeze made it even colder than before. And was the light starting to fade?

Namid shifted position. This was too hard. Her hands did not want to work right and lethargy washed over her. Maybe after a little rest.

She glanced at Aahmes. Looked like he was taking a bit of a rest. She would too. Her eyes did not want to stay open anyway. And why should they? After the recent rough times, she deserved some rest.

She sagged against the ropes that held her.

Where was that blanket? It must have fallen off. No wonder she felt so cold. She reached for it but could not find it.

Oh, well, she would sleep without it. She tucked her face down and to the side, covered by her hair, to try to find some warmth, to try to get more comfortable.

Was that singing?

It sounded like her father's voice, singing to her when she was little. He hadn't done that in such a very long time. His singing soothed her, as it always had. She smiled.

With her eyes closed, she saw Wild Power all around her. Its swirls of green and gold spiraled round and round and formed beautiful patterns. She stretched a hand toward the swirls. If only she could touch them, she'd make such beautiful designs with them.

They swirled closer to her and around her and reached to the snowy sky, sparkling amidst the snowflakes. The gold parts glowed and grew brighter and brighter.

Did she hear voices?

They seemed to be calling for someone. They sounded worried.

She hoped the voices found this Namid they called to....

~ ~ ~

She drifted in the haze. Sometimes it thinned, sometimes thickened. It felt like she was moving, rocking a little from side to side.

Shadows and light passed over her. Their patterns weren't as pretty as the green and gold swirls. Where had those gone?

So very cold. Would she ever be warm again? It seemed impossible.

She heard people talking. A lot.

Why couldn't they just let her sleep, all bundled up and finally starting to feel warm again?

Then the pain came. Fingers and toes. Ears. Her leg.

Make it stop!

~ ~ ~

Someone was talking. The voice sounded familiar but did not belong. She must still be dreaming.

Mehratar could not possibly be talking nearby.

Namid opened her eyes a slit. She saw a stone wall and flickering light, perhaps from a fire. She lay on something soft, with layers of covers on top of her. And she felt almost comfortably warm.

How could that be?

She shifted under the covers and heard footsteps approach. In the short time it took their owner to reach her, she almost drifted off again. Then someone leaned over her.

"Namid?"

That was not the voice she expected.

She tried to focus on the person who spoke, a large bearded man, brown hair with skin a few shades lighter, in a dark tunic, shirt and trousers.

"Haeith?"

He gave her one of his rare smiles. "Indeed. It's good to see you back with us. Mehratar is just seeing to Aahmes and then he'll return."

Namid nodded, then gasped as searing pain shot up both legs and arms. She closed her eyes against the pain and stifled a cry. Even her face hurt.

At a gentle touch on her shoulder she opened her eyes again, just slits.

"This will help." Haeith held a mug.

When she nodded, he slipped an arm behind her back to help her sit. At the sight of her swollen hands with cracked and peeling skin she froze and looked at Haeith.

"Mehratar has been Healing you," Haeith assured her. "It's just going to take some time, he has said. Now drink. It'll help with the pain." He helped her hold the warm mug while she drank the herbal mix within. When she finished it all, he helped her get settled again.

"The herbal mix is stronger this time," he told her. "You should get some relief from the pain soon."

Namid nodded again. As the pain receded, she said, "How are you here? What happened? Is Aahmes all right? And where *is* here, anyway?"

Haeith smiled again, set the mug on the floor, and sat there next to her low bed.

"There's much to tell," he said. "And I wouldn't tire you...."

"Haeith!" Namid said, exasperated. Her voice sounded weaker than she would have liked, but still got the message across.

"Certainly. So, first, yes, Aahmes is all right. Recovering as you are. Then in the order you asked. I'm here through using one of those pendants that the Dark Priests all had. Remember that woman gave us some when we escaped Kilaadi?"

At Namid's nod, he continued. "It's how they could travel far and quickly. Briefly what happened was that we found you where Lann had left you to die and brought you away—"

"We? You and Mehratar, then?"

"And Inezha. She came to Paronia to get us, found us in the capital and showed us how to use the pendants. As to where here is... we're in one of the clans' winter shelters. One of the better ones. And some distance from where Lann left you."

Namid heard more footsteps approaching.

"Haeith? She's awake?" Mehratar said. He appeared from behind Haeith, who shifted aside. Namid saw he wore his customary fine-linen shirt and trousers. His deep brown hair looked more disheveled than Namid recalled ever seeing it before, but his mustache was as neatly trimmed as ever. His expression, which reached his light-brown eyes, was one of relief mixed with satisfaction.

"I'll return when your Healer allows," Haeith said and moved out of Namid's line of sight.

She focused on Mehratar, who sat almost exactly where Haeith had.

"Good, you're awake," he said as he placed a gentle hand on her forehead and sent Healing Power through her. Between Mehratar's Healing and the herbs that dulled her pain, she soon felt better. A little, anyway.

After he finished, Mehratar sat back and studied her with that intense gaze of his. "How much do you remember?" he said.

Namid thought back to what had happened, her expression perplexed.

"We were at the clans' hub, Meahan." She spoke slowly as she worked through her memories, which seemed strangely jumbled. "We captured Lann, to help the clans replace him as chieftain. Then everything went wrong. Aahmes' cousin betrayed us to Lann—"

Namid gave Mehratar a sharp look. "How *is* Aahmes? Where is he?"

Mehratar placed a gentle hand on her shoulder. "He's fine. In much the same shape as you, but you'll both recover. I'll let him in to see you soon. Keep going."

"Uh, well. Lann had something to keep us from using Power. Some kind of powder they kept blowing in our faces. It worked like the concoction he used on us last time we were in the clans' territory. Made everything hazy."

Namid probed her murky memories as she tried to pull out what made some sense from several impressions that did not, like her father singing to her.

"Lann left us tied up outside. In the cold and snow. It was getting dark. And I couldn't use any Power, not my own or the Wild Power.... Wait! What about Saneth and Taakha? They were there, too."

Mehratar's somber expression told her the answer to that even before he spoke.

"I'm sorry," he said. "When we got to you, they were both already too close to death. I tried. But I was unable to save them." He dropped his head.

Namid reached out to pat his arm. She noticed that her hand was less swollen than before, and the skin looked a little better.

After a breath-of-time, Mehratar looked at her again. "Anything else you remember?"

"Some stuff that doesn't make much sense. And other things that aren't clear. People talking, I think. Shadows and light."

"Nothing about sending a stream of green and gold Power shooting into the sky?"

He looked amused when she started.

"Maybe," Namid said. "Sort of. I thought that was something I dreamed."

"It helped us find you in time," Mehratar said. "Inezha

was able to bring us to the edges of Meahan, but she did not know what Lann had done with you and Aahmes. Just that you and he were in danger and that I was needed."

Namid pondered that. "Did Lann's Seer tell her that somehow?"

Mehratar shook his head. "Not exactly." He gave her a long, intent look before he added, "She *is* Lann's Seer."

Namid stared. "What?!"

"Namid?" Aahmes' voice came from somewhere behind Mehratar.

Aahmes hobbled into the room, then he was at her side as he all but shoved the Healer aside in his eagerness to get to her. He reached toward her to gather her in his arms, then shot a questioning look at Mehratar, who chuckled.

"Just be careful," Mehratar said as he took himself further out of the way. "You both are still injured. And I didn't yet say you were ready to get up." He gave Aahmes a mock scowl.

With a gentle touch, Aahmes gathered her close. And she returned his embrace as tightly as she dared. Now she felt everything would be all right.

Too soon, Aahmes released her. He slowly sat back, moving like he hurt. But his smile was wide and relieved.

Mehratar moved back into Namid's view.

"Something you need to know," he said. "Aahmes already knows. Both of you have lost toes to the cold. I couldn't Heal all of them soon enough. So Namid, you might find it feels strange at first when you walk. But that will pass. Also, that damaged leg will need more Healing before you walk on it much." Again he scowled at Aahmes, who only grinned, his expression unrepentant. "After that additional Healing, though, I'll be getting you up to start walking a little. It'll help."

Namid glanced at Aahmes, then examined her hands. And Aahmes'. While both their hands looked bad, they had all their fingers. Aahmes' nose, cheeks and ears looked almost as bad as their hands. Namid gingerly touched her nose and her ears. She smiled in relief to find them intact, just sore, with peeling skin. Her cheeks, too.

She gave Mehratar a questioning look. "How many toes?"

It was Aahmes who answered her. "Two for you and one for me."

"And you should rest again, now," Mehratar told Aahmes as he placed a hand on his shoulder. "And we'll get you both a bit of hot food."

"I'm staying in here now," Aahmes said.

"And that's why I'm dragging all this in here," Haeith said. He carried a bundle of blankets and one of the thick sleeping pads through the door. He and Mehratar arranged the bed next to Namid's and Mehratar ordered Aahmes to rest.

Aahmes eased himself onto the bed and stretched out with a relieved sigh. After Mehratar and Haeith left the room again, he turned toward Namid.

They clasped hands, being careful of their injuries.

"I'm so sorry about Taakha and Saneth," Namid said in a quiet voice. "I was so angry at Taakha… but she didn't deserve this. And Saneth…."

Aahmes nodded, his expression solemn, then he brushed her hand with his lips, choosing the least-injured spot.

"Inezha is Lann's Seer?" Namid said.

"Seems so," Aahmes said. "She knew that Mehratar was going to be needed here, so she left to get him right after Lann took us. There's still a lot she hasn't explained yet, but I've only been awake myself a candle-mark or so longer than you."

"Something to get into more later, then," Namid said as Haeith returned with two steaming bowls that smelled wonderful.

After she and Aahmes ate, propped up with cushions, Haeith carried Namid to and from the privy that sat in the back off the main room which was next to her room.

Mehratar told her and Aahmes that after the next Healing, they both would be ready for a short walk around the whole shelter.

A short, slow walk, he emphasized.

Namid held Aahmes' hand again and drifted off to sleep as Haeith and Mehratar settled her again beneath the blankets on her sleeping pad.

CHAPTER 12

When Namid woke next, she found Aahmes still asleep. But he stirred when Mehratar entered their room, carrying steaming bowls of some kind of stew. Namid's stomach growled and they all grinned at the sound.

While the food cooled enough to eat, Mehratar Healed Namid and Aahmes again, then left saying that they would try a little walking after they finished their meal.

Namid and Aahmes devoured the food in silence. After Namid set her empty bowl on the floor next to her bed, she leaned back with a sigh. Sitting up to eat had been more taxing than she expected.

She smiled when Aahmes reached out and clasped her hand. She rolled far enough to be able to see him without having to twist around.

"Haeith and Mehratar told me some of what happened."

"I heard." He leaned back with a sigh that matched hers.

"Do you know more?"

Aahmes shrugged. "Not much. And I think pieces are still missing." He rolled partway toward her and clasped her hand again.

"Inezha somehow went to Kilaadi to get Mehratar and Haeith. I don't know how," Aahmes said, "but it's clear she has more use of Power than she led us to believe. And she knows how to use those pendants – maybe that's how she got to Kilaadi. I think there's a lot about her that's different from what we thought we knew."

"And where is she?" Namid said.

"She went back to Meahan. To take care of some things, she said."

"She went back? Can we trust that she won't betray us to Lann, too?" Namid struggled back to a sitting position. "Maybe we shouldn't wait for her to return."

"We're not going anywhere for a while," Aahmes said. "A storm moved in after she left. Plus neither of us are particularly mobile. Also, Haeith and I have set Power around us here – no one gets through to us if we don't want them to."

Namid gave him a startled look, then reached out to the Wild Power, and touched her own Power reserve.

"The effects of that powder are gone," she muttered. "How long was I out?"

"Only about a day and a half, I think," Aahmes said. "I was out almost that long, too. Seems the effects of the powder don't last as long as drinking the stuff."

"Ready to try a Healer-approved short walk?" Mehratar poked his head into the room. His hair was no longer disheveled, and his shirt and trousers were even finer than he had worn previously. "Haeith's got Namid."

Mehratar gave them each more Healing after which Haeith gave them his concoction for pain. With help and support from Haeith and Mehratar, Namid and Aahmes struggled to their feet and hobbled through the three rooms of their shelter. It was an underground shelter like the one Namid and Aahmes had used before, but this one had a main room with four stone benches and a cooking hearth, and two side rooms for sleeping, plus the small privy room at the back. A large stack of peat bricks sat next to the hearth.

The opening that led outside looked like it was also much like in the shelter Namid and Aahmes had used. But Haeith steered Namid away from there.

"You'll feel the cold much more than before. For a while at least, according to Mehratar," Haeith told her. "No reason to cause you even more discomfort."

As Mehratar had warned her, Namid found that walking felt strange. And the damaged leg was no help. Haeith told her she had lost the smallest toe on each foot to the cold. From the random shooting pains in her feet, it felt like they were still there. Then the pain from her shin eclipsed those other pains, even with the herbs Haeith had given her to help.

After Haeith helped her through a single trip around the shelter, Namid was more than ready to rest again.

When she was settled again on her bed, Mehratar let her see her wounded leg and feet. She had not really believed him about the toes until she saw for herself.

The others left mugs of water next to her bed and Aahmes' and returned to the outer room. Namid looked at Aahmes and found that he had already drifted off to sleep again.

She settled herself into a more comfortable position and sleep claimed her again, too.

~ ~ ~

Healing sessions, walking and long periods of rest filled the days that followed. Namid learned that the others had found her and Aahmes late that night after Lann had left them in the cold. That had been almost two days before Namid first woke.

She also learned that this shelter had a root cellar in which nothing had gone bad. Its door was just a couple of paces from the shelter's door, and it contained a well for water, too. A stable situated further along the hill held the horses that Haeith and Mehratar had brought with them.

Every Healing session saw the damaged skin looking healthier. The constant pain of the first several days diminished to rare random instances. Namid slept a lot and saw nothing of Inezha.

Neither Haeith nor Mehratar could tell Namid more about Inezha's involvement or how she knew about how to use the pendants from the Dark Priests. But they were able to tell her about happenings in Kilaadi after she and Aahmes had fled.

Most of the dignitaries who had come for Talorisin's coronation left soon after. Namid's and Tal's mother had spent much of her time helping Tal's wife learn about her new position as Lady Royal. Yokana was now known as the Matriarch Royal. Cameni and Enric had lingered in Kilaadi for several days after the coronation before they left. To travel to Enric's family, Mehratar thought.

When Namid asked why Haeith had not gone with them, he gave a slight shrug and said that Cameni's father had released him from his service to their family in favor of service to Tal's. And while he and the Monarch had an agreement that he would help guard the family and teach the children weapons, Tal had all but ordered him to go with Mehratar when Inezha had arrived in Kilaadi to get the Healer.

Tal had begun to settle into his new role as Monarch. And Yokana seemed to enjoy continuing to get to know her grandchildren. Beyond that, neither Mehratar nor Haeith had more to tell her.

Close to a week after Namid woke, Inezha returned. She looked much the same as the last time Namid saw her, although her very curly dark hair had grown, and seemed even darker, nearly the color of her dark skin now.

After Inezha peeled off her warm outer clothes, Namid saw the other woman wore a pale green vest that laced down the front with an embroidered shirt of an even paler green. Her trousers and boots were both of nearly the same shade as the vest.

She brought with her two bundles that held Namid's and Aahmes' things, the rest of their clothes and their weapons that had been with them when they were taken. In her bundle, Namid also discovered some of the clothing that had been in her room in the clan Naalin quarter, along with the leather bracelet that Taakha had given her.

She brushed her fingers over the worked leather as she remembered Saneth and Taakha with a pang of sorrow at their fate. With a slight frown, she shook herself free of her melancholy and tucked the bracelet back with the rest of her clothes. She wanted to wear it, but *after* her skin had healed more.

Aahmes and Namid had managed to walk short distances without assistance at that point and so they joined the others in the main room for the evening meal.

After the first bite, Namid pointed her spoon at Inezha. "Talk," she said.

Inezha's surprised expression faded as she met the others' stern gazes.

"All right. I suppose I owe you something."

"Something…" Aahmes muttered, with a scowl for the Prazny.

"Where to start," Inezha said.

"Power," Namid said. "And how do you know how to use those pendants from the Dark Priests?"

Inezha chortled. "That's an easy one. I long ago learned how to conceal the little Power I have. Until those annoying shells of Power you and Aahmes like to put up, anyway. And I used to work with the Dark Priests."

Namid lurched back and wished she had her daggers at hand. "What?"

Aahmes caught her when she lost her balance and steadied her. Namid felt him draw Wild Power and she did the same.

Inezha just sat there and gazed at them, her smile

lessened but not gone.

"You've no need to worry. I worked with them only for my own purposes, not as part of all that business with the sword Akavos and the attack of Sy'shythys."

Haeith met Namid's gaze as he adjusted his position so he could more easily reach his sword. "And what are these purposes of yours?" he said.

Inezha shrugged and took a bite while they waited on her. "I have several things going on right now," she said. "I'm just fighting to make everything come out right."

"Everything? And that includes giving us to Lann so he could try to kill us?" Aahmes said.

Inezha gave him a wide-eyed look. "No, not at all! All that I knew was that those two clansmates needed to return to their clan's lands, that they would find something important there. I didn't know it was you! And I didn't know Lann would do that! But I did know later that Mehratar needed to come to the clans' territory, that you were in danger. That should count for something."

Namid turned back to her meal, not sure what to say.

"Perhaps if you told it all from the beginning," Haeith said to Inezha. "I suspect this could become confusing otherwise."

Namid glanced at the others. Aahmes shrugged and Mehratar's attention was on his food. Inezha met her gaze with a bland expression.

"Yes, do tell us, Lann's Seer," Namid said.

Inezha frowned at the title. "Others like to call me this person's or that person's Seer, but I'm not theirs," she muttered. She took a few more bites of her meal and looked at each of them in turn.

"All right. But there's a lot. I'll shorten it as I can."

"Without leaving out anything important," Aahmes said.

"Even so," she said and smiled at him. "To start, to answer Haeith, my purpose is simply to restore to the Prazny people what is rightfully ours: our city and our standing. Everything is in support of that."

"Your city?" Mehratar said.

"You think to restore Nazextas?" Namid said.

Haeith gave her a surprised look. "The Spirit-City was the Praznies' city?"

"Yes," Inezha said, making it clear she answered all three questions. "Ever since our city's destruction, we have been cursed to wander, scorned by most we encounter. It's not right."

"And how will you restore that city?" Aahmes said.

"That's where you and she come in," Inezha said as she pointed to Namid. "Since all that Power came to you from the dead god, it should be a simple matter for you."

Namid and Aahmes exchanged looks. "We'll restore this Spirit-City?" Namid said, her disbelief clear in her tone. Then she laughed. "Sorry to have to tell you—"

"I'm certain that you two are the ones who can do this," Inezha broke in. "You *will* do this. You just needed to be ready." She gave a firm nod, as if that explained it all.

Aahmes glared at her. "'Needed to be ready'," he repeated. He leaned toward her and Namid recognized the dangerous look in his eyes. "What exactly does that mean?"

Inezha leaned back a handspan from the menace in his voice and glanced at each of them. "Much as Mehratar described it when we traveled together the past spring, I Saw what actions would best lead to my goal and I took them. And I Saw you both gathering great Power and using it."

"What actions? What have you done toward ensuring we were *ready*?" Aahmes' tone had grown even colder.

Namid huddled in on herself. She had the sudden feeling that this was going to be very bad. Aahmes had half-drawn one of his daggers and held enough Power to make her feel twitchy sitting next to him. Although she still held Power, too.

Inezha looked at her hands as if studying them, then

looked up at Aahmes with a slight smile, her head still tilted. She glanced at Namid.

"Set events in motion that made sure you could be there at the right time to get Sesaisyd's Power," she said. "Events to save Tal's life and for you to find him. Events to keep either of you from getting caught up in others' intentions for you to rule your respective peoples."

With a slight shake of her head, Namid glanced at Aahmes, who seemed frozen in place staring at Inezha.

How was this all possible?

"You're *Wesh's* Seer too?" Namid said after a breath-of-time.

Inezha smirked.

"Events," Aahmes repeated and his stare turned into an angry grimace. "Like the massacre of my clan?!" He lunged at the Prazny, a dagger reaching for her throat.

"No!" Inezha yelled as she scrambled away. Namid caught Aahmes' arm and tried to hold him back. Mehratar and Haeith moved away to either side of the room. Mehratar watched them all, his expression intent, and Haeith's hand rested on his sword's hilt, but he had not yet drawn it.

"Wait!" Inezha said. "Let me explain."

Aahmes stopped trying to free himself from Namid's grip. But she still felt the tension in him.

"*Try* to explain, then," he ordered.

Inezha put her back to one wall. "All I knew, all that I told Lann's father, was that clan Naalin should not have the chieftainship. I didn't tell him to kill everyone! Or anyone!"

Namid studied Inezha. While her expression looked concerned, she saw something in the Prazny's eyes that did not fit. She had the sudden impression that Inezha did not care that the clan had been murdered. However it had happened, it meant that Aahmes had left the clans' territory. If he had stayed, likely they would never have met. And escaped Rhadanthus together. And....

Namid released Aahmes. She sank back on the bench and held her head in her hands. Mehratar hurried to her, but she waved him away.

"Not something Healing can help with," she muttered.

When she looked up again, Aahmes still stood in the same position. He gripped his dagger so hard his knuckles were white. But he watched her with concern.

Namid turned her attention to Inezha.

"Are you the Seer who told my parents to send me away?"

Inezha nodded, still keeping an eye on Aahmes.

"Have you steered all the events of our lives?" Namid shouted. "Made sure we'd become what you decided you needed so you'd get your precious city back?"

"I've done what I needed to for my people!" Inezha shouted back. "And remember, without that, you two wouldn't have all this Power. You wouldn't find yourselves probably the most Powerful people alive right now."

"Wouldn't be hunted by the 'gods'!" Namid yelled. "Chased across the realms."

"Just how long have you been Seeing and acting on events?" Haeith asked in a low voice.

For the first time, Namid saw real concern in Inezha's expression. She stared at Haeith and licked her lips. Then she met Namid's gaze and as quickly looked away.

"I was there when the disaster took Nazextas," she said. Her gaze fixed on a far memory and she avoided meeting anyone else's. "My brother, Boudra, was the one who attacked the Dark Priests' army with Power. Well, not my brother by birth. We were raised together and so considered ourselves brother and sister. He was the one whose Power became part of what happened to Nazextas. You saw that when you were in the city, right?" She glanced at Aahmes, Namid and Haeith just long enough to see their nods.

"But... wasn't that...." Namid paused to better gather her thoughts. "When we were in the Spirit-City, I got a feeling that those events that I saw happened a very long time ago," she said.

"Yes," Inezha said.

"Just *how* long ago?" Aahmes said.

Inezha gave that some thought. "Something over a couple thousand years, I think. After a while, the years blend together."

"More than four thousand years, in reality," Mehratar said.

Namid stared at him. At the edges of her vision she saw the others staring also.

"How could you know that?" Inezha said.

Mehratar ducked his head and shrugged with one shoulder. When he looked at them again, his expression was a mixture of resolve and discomfiture.

"Very easily," he said with a deep sigh. "I also was around at that time. My father is Jelth."

CHAPTER 13

Namid stood outside the shelter on a clear patch of ground beneath a tree and leaned against the trunk to take her weight off her injured leg. She had needed to get away from the others, needed some time to think about what they had learned. And if she was being honest, worry about what they hadn't learned yet. She had a feeling that there was more.

She was as bundled up as she could manage and still walk, but she did feel the cold much more than before, in her hands and feet mostly. Just as Mehratar had warned. Although the technique of warming oneself that Aahmes had taught her alleviated that a lot. After she fought the Wild Power to make it work.

She leaned her back against the thick tree trunk and closed her eyes. A few flakes of snow brushed her cheeks and the setting sun provided light but no warmth.

Hard to believe. Both Mehratar and Inezha had seen several thousand years. At least. And Mehratar was the son of the so-called god of Healers. No wonder he was a Master Healer.

Namid glanced back over a shoulder at the sound of

footsteps in the snow. When Aahmes joined her, she wrapped an arm around his waist and leaned against his side, his arm around her shoulders. They stood like that, in silence, for many long breaths-of-time. Then Aahmes shifted slightly.

"A navn for your thoughts?" he said.

Namid smiled as she pictured him offering her one of the gold coins of the Six Realms of the Monarch. "Not sure my thoughts are worth that much right now," she said. "I feel all twisted around. And like I want to destroy something."

Aahmes nodded. "Or someone," he said in a low voice.

"Well, yeah. But we're still not assassins."

"Well, yeah," he imitated her.

"Part of me wants to just run again. Far away. Maybe if we went as far as where Haeith is from no one would find us."

"Sounds good to me. But?"

"Well, first, there's this Seer who it seems has been after us our entire lives."

"True."

"And there's the problems with our Power. From all we know, it's not going to improve on its own."

"I agree. But maybe something in that book can help us. On a second reading, maybe it'll give us an idea of what to do to fix this."

"The book!" Namid whipped around to stare at Aahmes. "How could I have forgotten it?"

"Perhaps a few other things had your attention," Aahmes murmured.

"But I don't have it!" Namid said with a frown. "It's still back in Meahan."

"It wasn't in with everything Inezha brought back?"

Namid gave him a worried look. "No."

Aahmes pulled her close and brushed a hand over her hair. "Then when we're back to ourselves, Healed, we'll just sneak back in and grab it."

Namid nodded against his chest and hugged him closer. She delighted in his touch, even through the layers keeping her warm. She told her worries they needed to take a rest for a time, leave her alone so she could enjoy the moment.

When they both felt the cold too much, they headed back inside.

In the main room, they found an interesting tableau. Each of their companions sat on one of the benches. By themselves. Haeith occupied the bench closest to the outer door and he sat there running a whetstone along one edge of his great-sword. Mehratar and Inezha both seemed almost mesmerized watching him.

Aahmes and Namid exchanged amused glances and sat on the empty bench to Haeith's left.

"Good, you're back," Inezha said. "We need to talk about this. I think it holds the key." She pulled out Odasoro's book and held it up. "Oh, and here are these back." She held out two of the circular, green-gray metal pendants they had gotten from Dark Priests seasons ago in Kilaadi.

Namid snatched the book from her and gingerly accepted the pendants. She handed one to Aahmes.

"They're great for travel, as long as you can wait a day or more after using one," Inezha said. "These should be ready to use again now."

Namid scrutinized her pendant, then tucked it in her pouch. She would ask more about it later.

"How'd you get the book?" she asked Inezha.

The Prazny gave her a bright smile. "I grabbed it from your room in Meahan when I got your other things. Your shells had faded so it was easy to find. Originally, I got it from Odasoro. He wasn't needing it any more at that point."

Inezha must have taken it from Odasoro after he had fallen to Andrin's Power in the Monarch's great hall. This time Namid lunged at Inezha, and Aahmes held her back.

"He lay there dying and you stole a *book*!" Namid shouted. "I thought you'd gone to try to help him!"

Inezha shrugged. "He was already dead. Nothing to be done to help him. And I didn't want Andrin to get the book."

Namid glared for a breath-of-time longer before she let Aahmes urge her back to their bench.

"Not that it helped me, any," Inezha continued. "I couldn't read the original writing. And what I assume was the bard's translation... well, he'd written it in some sort of code, it looks like. Have you been able to read it? What's it say?"

Namid only answered with a scowl.

"It's got something we can use to restore Nazextas, doesn't it?" Inezha said.

Namid shrugged this time and tucked the book in her outer tunic. "Not that I can tell. It talks a lot about blood Power."

Inezha's expression turned thoughtful.

"How are the two of you more than four thousand years old?" Namid said into the silence. "You're not really two more 'gods', are you?"

Both Inezha and Mehratar shook their heads.

"It's blood Power," Mehratar said. "You know that's how the so-called gods gathered their Power, right?"

"We suspected," Aahmes said.

"That's how they did it," Mehratar confirmed. "And they found a way to use it to extend their lives. And then they used it on a few others to extend their lives, also. Like me. I was the last of my father's children. All the others died while he gathered Power, like the other 'gods'. He claimed he could not bear to see me die, too. So he used blood Power on me to give me long life."

"You yourself, then, don't have blood Power? Or use it?" Inezha said.

"Absolutely not!"

"But Jelth did? The god of Healers?" Aahmes said.

Mehratar seemed to shrink within himself. "I've always been a better Healer than him. He set himself up as that god. But the real Healing work was mine. It's pretty much always been mine."

"But you have to use blood Power again to stay alive," Inezha said. "Do you just run to your father for that?"

Mehratar turned his intent gaze on her. "Jelth used the blood Power on me just the one time," he said, his voice flat. "No more has ever been needed. Who kept you alive?"

Inezha looked at her feet. "No god, that's for certain. It was Wesh. Seers have always been rare. When Wesh found me, he decided to keep me around. He didn't want to risk the chance of never finding another one if I died. 'I can't lose you,' he told me. But he had to use the Power to keep me alive every few hundred years or so. Now that he's gone...."

"Must the 'gods' also renew their own lives from time to time?" Haeith said to Mehratar.

"Not that I'm aware of. But I've tried to have as little to do with them as I can. However it is that they are still alive, it seems more like what Jelth did to me. Not that it means they don't want to gather more Power. They've never really stopped that."

"Do you know where Jelth is?" Namid said. "Is he likely to join the hunt for us, too?"

"He probably would, if he was around," Mehratar said. "Assuming he hasn't changed. But I haven't seen him since a few hundred years after he gave me long life. That was not too long after the disaster at Nazextas."

"One less to worry about anyway," Aahmes muttered in Namid's ear.

"What makes you think that the book has something that can help restore Nazextas?" Namid said to Inezha, bringing them back to the earlier topic.

"Wesh kept that book. He scribbled madly in it whenever he took another's Power and essence."

Namid nodded. "I remember something about that... about him learning to extend his own life - but not the way the gods did. He discovered that way to take a person's essence and Power. And so that's the path he took."

"He was there at Nazextas," Inezha said. "He's the one who pulled me from the city right before the Power took it, and everyone who was left within the walls."

"So you'd use some technique from this book to restore your city?" Aahmes said. "Using blood Power?"

Inezha shook her head. "No. Maybe. I'm not sure. What made it into the Spirit-City—the best I could tell— was these 'gods' tearing blood Power from all the people of the city and grabbing at my brother's Power. But it's not me who'll restore the city. You two are the ones who must restore Nazextas." She looked from Aahmes to Namid. "Restore the city and bring all the Praznies there to live. Gather my people there, free them from the scattered existence they've suffered all these years."

"But what if they don't want to go there to live?" Namid challenged her.

"Of course they do! And any who are uncertain, you can just make them happy there. Who wouldn't want to be happy?" Inezha said.

"We've talked about this before," Namid growled. "We'll not be using the Power to *make* anyone anything."

Inezha shrugged, her expression unconcerned. "You'll restore the city."

"And why would we want to do that?" Namid snapped. "You've done your best to make us do what you want, be what you want. At a cost neither of us would have been willing to pay, had we even been consulted. Why should we restore the city?"

Inezha's eyes widened. "You would deny me this? After I made sure you both got all that Power, after I saved Tal." She turned away. "Fine. At least share what the book has to say. I'll find others somehow who'll not hoard their Power to themselves."

159

Namid felt a sudden surge of Wild Power in the room. It came to her, to Aahmes. And through it she sensed his anger, a match for her own. Both Mehratar and Haeith gave them concerned looks but held themselves still.

Aahmes clasped Namid's hand as he rose to his feet. A look at his expression told her all she needed to know about how close he held his anger. She felt much the same.

Inezha jumped to her feet. She held her gaze bland, but Namid thought her expression also held more than a hint of panic. Without a word, the Prazny wrapped up in her cloak and left the shelter.

Namid squeezed Aahmes' hand but said nothing. She did not know what to say.

She felt Mehratar send out a thin wave of his Power.

After several long breaths-of-time, the Healer leaned his elbows on his knees, dropped his head to his hands and rubbed his temples with his fingertips. "She's settled down in the stables," he told them. "Probably for the night."

With a squeeze for Namid's hand, Aahmes pulled his hand free and began to pace. She watched him limp around the room.

"What is it this book holds?" Haeith asked after Aahmes had circled the room a couple of times.

Namid sighed. "Disjointed writings. About the 'gods' and Power. About ways to gain blood Power. In unfortunate detail. Some information about forcing blood Power on another, and some ideas about how to reverse that, but nothing that seemed to have worked."

"Would it be a bad move to restore the city?" Mehratar said. He leaned away when Aahmes rounded on him in anger. "I just ask. Might it not be a good thing? It was certainly a horror that gripped all those people."

"Restoring the city doesn't mean restoring the people, does it?" Namid said. "How could it? You're the strongest Healer I've encountered. Is that something you could do?"

"No."

"Reverse the taking of blood Power..." Haeith said, his

tone thoughtful. "If the so-called gods got blood Power from the city, would restoring the city take that Power back from them?"

Aahmes and Namid exchanged glances. "Could that be the answer?" Namid murmured.

Haeith looked from one of them to the other. "There is more, is there not?" he said. "I see something in your expressions."

"When I broke Akavos, that Power that came to Namid and me – that was Sesaisyd's," Aahmes said. "His own Power... *and* the blood Power he had gathered."

"Blood Power forced on you both," Mehratar murmured. "I'd not heard of such a thing. I feel that it's not a good thing."

"It's not," Namid said. "The book speaks of strange pains and wounds for the one who had the blood Power forced on him. He could use the Power, but the more he did, the worse the pain and wounds got."

"You've both been experiencing such things, haven't you?" Mehratar said. "I remember an injury that I couldn't Heal. That was many weeks ago, after we brought Tal's family and their fellow villagers away from that fire." Mehratar turned his intent gaze on Namid.

She only nodded.

"Might I see the book?" Haeith said.

Namid handed it over and watched him open it.

"Power here," he said and glanced at her.

Aahmes returned to sit next to Namid and claimed her hand again. They all watched Haeith while he flipped through the book. After he reached the back of the book, he closed it and flipped it over, so the back looked like the front now. Then he opened it again and paged through the first few pages.

"Something here," he muttered. "A holding Power to preserve the pages, the writing. But something more. Similar to a semblance...."

Namid leaned closer when he trailed off. She glimpsed

part of the pages inside the book, but they only looked as she expected... right-side up to her, and so upside-down to Haeith.

"What is it?" Aahmes said.

"Might I borrow a dagger?" Haeith said without looking up. "Mine's still in a pack in the stable."

"What are you going to do?" Mehratar demanded.

"Nothing dire, I assure you," Haeith said. He took the dagger Aahmes handed him and nicked the side of his finger with the tip. He let a tiny bit of blood drip onto one corner of one of the pages, then pressed against the slight injury with his thumb while he returned the dagger. He sent a thin stream of Power to the page.

For a breath-of-time, nothing changed. Then, bit by bit, more writing became visible, while the writing that had been there faded away, even Odasoro's writing. The new writing looked similar to the old. After the old writing had faded to invisibility behind the new writing, the drop of Haeith's blood also faded away.

Haeith gave Namid a slight smile. "There seems to be a bit more in the book. Perhaps something here of use." He handed the book back to her.

She flipped through the pages and saw that they all held the new writing now.

"Odasoro was the one who figured out what the writing said," Aahmes said. "Can we still see the previous writings to use what he wrote to help decipher this new writing."

Namid sent a tendril of Wild Power into the book. Nothing changed. So she sent the thinnest tendril of her own Power into the book. And the writing changed back again.

A drop of blood fell from under one of her fingernails onto the page. Some of it promptly faded away. She moved her hand away to avoid getting any more blood on the page. Blood rimmed all of the fingernails on that hand, but no more dripped. Namid met Mehratar's gaze.

"From using my own Power," she said. "This is what it does. But the Wild Power didn't work for this."

"We can't keep switching the writing back and forth, then," Aahmes said. "We need to copy the new writing and compare it to what Odasoro figured out. I hope much of it will be readable that way."

"I am willing to switch the writing as needed," Haeith said. "It's only a tiny wound."

"No. I don't trust it," Namid said. "This was Wesh's. Let's not use more blood Power on it than we have to."

She sent another tendril of Power into the book to change the writing back to the new writing again. As it changed, the last of her blood on the page disappeared.

"Once more after we copy this, then," Haeith said.

"Of course, we'll need pen and ink and something to write on," Namid said. "I don't suppose such things might be stored in the root cellar?" She gave Aahmes a questioning look.

"Not usually," Aahmes said with a shake of his head.

Mehratar cleared his throat, with an abashed look directed at Namid. "I happen to have those things," he said. "They're still out in the stable, in one of my bags, because I had no idea why we'd need them. Inezha told me to be certain to bring them with us when left Kilaadi."

"Well, that's convenient," Aahmes muttered. His expression displayed his disquiet.

"And more than a touch unnerving," Namid said as she matched Aahmes' frown.

Haeith grabbed his cloak. "I'll get them."

"But tomorrow's soon enough to begin the copying," Mehratar admonished Namid, giving her one of his intense looks. "After a good night's rest."

CHAPTER 14

Over the next several days, the four of them took turns copying the newly revealed writing from Wesh's book into the blank book that Mehratar had brought with him. Inezha kept to herself but watched with great interest whenever anyone worked on copying from the book.

When neither of them was copying pages, Namid and Aahmes continued their less than inspiring walks around the shelter as they worked to get their strength and balance back. Outside storm after storm blanketed the clans' territory and kept everyone close to the shelter.

The day that Haeith copied the last of the new writing was the same day that Mehratar told Aahmes and Namid that they could try their sparring sessions again, if they wished. Namid's mood brightened after she wore herself out in a too-short bout with daggers against Aahmes.

They found they were both much clumsier than before and would need a lot of work to get back to their former level of skill. But they both enjoyed the challenge and found a way to laugh at their fumbles.

And Mehratar was pleased that neither needed any Healing when they finished sparring for the day.

The next day, Haeith brought back the original writing in the book. He needed to use two drops of blood that time to make it work. When she saw that, Namid was relieved that they had decided to make a copy. A need for more and more blood each time to switch the writing seemed ominous.

Interspersed with as much sparring as Mehratar would allow, Namid and Aahmes began the task of seeing what words they could figure out from the work Odasoro had already done. Inezha hovered nearby while they worked. She made a face at Namid when the latter wrote what they were deciphering in the same code that Odasoro had used. When it became clear that they were not going to share what they deciphered, the Prazny wandered off.

"She doesn't seem happy with that," Aahmes said as he wrote a word in the bard's code.

Namid shrugged. "I don't feel I can trust her. And I don't feel comfortable putting whatever is in here in a form that just anyone can pick up and read."

Aahmes nodded his agreement. "Perhaps Haeith, though? Teach him the bard's code so it's not just the two of us who can read this."

"Seems reasonable."

Over the next few days, they and Haeith worked on the book, filling in the words that they could easily and teaching Haeith the code. The afternoon of the fourth day after they had started, Namid paused at a sudden realization. She had just filled in perhaps half that page.

"I don't think this part is talking about blood Power," she said. "I think this word is statue." She pointed to a word that they had not yet converted to the bard's code. She flipped through the original book to a page near the back and pointed to that same word, with the coded word for statue beneath it.

"This section of the first writings is about the Star of Corentris," Namid said. "And the new writings seem to be more on that. I remember something about Wesh,

Chendrukhar probably at that point, wanting to keep the Star out of Rhadanthus."

"Let me see." Aahmes pulled the book over in front of him – they were using a bench as a table and sitting on the floor. Namid watched him work his way through the coded words Odasoro had written on those pages. Haeith leaned close, sometimes asking about one of the coded words.

After he reread that section, Aahmes looked up from the book. He exchanged glances with Haeith and Namid.

"Have I read this rightly?" Haeith said. "Wesh wrapped the Star in his Power to alert him if the statue was ever in a city, so he could remove it again from there?"

"That's how I read it, too," Namid said. "Especially combining what was in the hidden writings with what was in the first ones. I'd thought the first ones were just random notes. But it looks like he deliberately put some things there and the rest in the hidden writing."

"Why is it significant that he wanted to keep the Star out of Rhadanthus?" Haeith said.

Namid shrugged. "I hope he wrote that down in here, too. We Shadowers just thought the Power on it was a way for him to recover it if it was stolen. It's valuable, not counting whatever its connection is to Corentris."

"I wonder how that story even got started in Rhadanthus," Aahmes said. "About him being able to tell its exact location after a half-day. He didn't seem the kind to spread stories like that."

Namid glanced at Inezha. The Prazny sat far enough away that she likely could not hear them. She had her eyes closed but Namid doubted she slept. "Could be someone else spread it around, for her own purposes."

Aahmes followed her gaze. "Could be."

Haeith tapped the book. "Back to this," he said. "What does the statue have to do with blood Power? Most of the book is concerned with that. But then he writes about the statue and keeping it out of a city. We need to decipher the rest of the writing."

Namid nodded and stretched. "We do, but later. I need to do something else for a while. My eyes and head ache."

"I'd like to look back over what we have already," Haeith said, "if you'll trust me to keep both books for a time?"

"Of course."

Aahmes rose when Namid did. "I don't feel up to more sparring today," he said.

"No, me neither."

Inezha opened her eyes. "Have you finished yet?" she said. "Found what we need?"

"I'm not certain that there is a *we*," Namid said.

Inezha shrugged. "You're the only ones who can do this. You can't really think it's good to leave a ghostly city wandering about. Drawing people in who never escape?"

Aahmes glared at her. With a huff of irritation, he caught up the cloaks he and Namid had claimed from the shelter's stash of clothing.

"Let's get outside a bit," he invited Namid over his shoulder.

She caught up to him a couple of paces from the shelter and he wrapped her in her cloak. They ambled along the path that led to the stable, avoiding the snow piled on either side.

"She's not wrong," Aahmes said when they were well out of earshot of the anyone at the shelter.

"Not about some things, anyway," Namid agreed. "But I'm just not seeing anything in this book that's going to help us get the 'gods' to leave us alone and get rid of this blood Power."

"And now the Star of Corentris is in his writings. Could all of this be connected?"

"Spirit-City, Star, blood Power. I suppose. But how?"

Aahmes shrugged. "I don't see it. At least not yet. Suppose we do restore the city. Is there harm in that?"

Namid frowned. "I don't like being made to do

something…."

"Agreed. But we can choose to do it, even with everything she's done to get us to do this."

Namid nodded. "Well, I'd think it'd take a lot of Power. Would we be able to use the Wild Power to do it? If not, what will that do to us? Or if we can get rid of the blood Power first, would we still be able to bring back this city? Do we know for sure it even *can* be brought back?"

"And here are some more questions. Where does the city belong? If we bring it back, would we be dropping a whole city on a place people already live? Do we have to be where the city was originally to bring it back?"

"I wouldn't mind dropping a city on Lann," Namid muttered.

Aahmes chuckled. "No argument there."

They walked in silence then.

"Another storm's coming," Aahmes said when they reached the stable.

Namid glanced at the bright sun. The air was frigid, but she saw no clouds. "How soon?"

"Tonight, from the feel of it."

Inside the stable they found Mehratar perched on an overturned half-barrel where he worked on some tack. He smiled when they entered.

"Another storm, you said?"

Aahmes nodded. "Feels like a bad one again. Thought we'd take the horses out for maybe a candle-mark, while we still can."

Mehratar studied them both and Namid felt the lightest touch of his Power.

"Don't overdo it," he said. "I just got you both Healed."

Aahmes and Namid tacked up two of the horses and put a lead on the third – three had been how many horses the others managed to bring with them from Kilaadi. They led the horses outside and mounted.

Aahmes led the way among the snowy trees, picking a

path that was not too deeply covered in snow. Namid followed with the third horse and basked in the bright afternoon.

They rode only a half candle-mark before they turned back. This time Aahmes found a path that let them ride side by side.

Namid felt his gaze on her and drew her own back from the sparkling snow on the trees around them.

"What?" she said, the corners of her mouth quirking up.

"I could wish for much more of this," Aahmes said. "Peaceful time alone. Just us."

Namid nodded. "We do seem to keep running from one thing to another. Perhaps we need to make an oath or something that when we get this blood Power problem of ours solved, we'll let everyone and everything else fend for themselves for a while. Maybe even go somewhere far away for a while. Someplace we can't be found."

Aahmes reached out and clasped her hand. "I so swear," he said.

Namid laughed. "I so swear," she repeated.

~ ~ ~

After they settled the horses again in the stable, they struggled back to the shelter, fighting against the rising wind, peppered with hard pellets of snow. They were soaked through and shivering when they stumbled inside.

"Get out of those wet clothes right away," Mehratar ordered them.

Namid scurried into the side room she had been using for sleeping and worked at getting her cold, soaked clothing off. But she was so cold, and her hands, feet and leg ached so much, she made little headway.

Then Inezha joined her. She helped Namid peel away the sodden clothes then enveloped her in a warm blanket. She found some thick, soft socks and made Namid sit so she could ease them on her feet.

"My thanks," Namid said in a quiet voice.

"Of course," Inezha said. "I'm not like Lann, you know. Or the Dark Priests. *Really*, I'm not. I've just done what I had to."

"But at what harm to others? Couldn't you have prevented it and found another way?"

Inezha looked away, shrugging. "Can't change it now."

"And what of Staehw?" Namid said.

Inezha looked up sharply. "What of him? I would've thought you'd be happy to be well rid of him."

"It's true I didn't like him," Namid said. "And I certainly have no wish to encounter him again. But it seems odd that he was chasing us, chasing Akavos so greedily. And then he wasn't. Was he just another obstacle, too?"

"No, not really an obstacle. Just an annoyance, really. He's fine. Off with another Prazny van. And not inclined to chase you anymore."

Namid glared at Inezha. "What did you do to him?"

"*I* did nothing to him! But Wesh owed me. And Staehw was getting involved in things he shouldn't. So Wesh took away a few select memories of his."

Namid rose unsteadily. When Inezha reached out to help, she batted the other woman's hand away. "Just like you urged me and Aahmes to do to people. Make them do what we want. Make them forget what we want. Just stay away from me."

Namid hobbled back into the main room and sat where Mehratar indicated she should, on a bench close to the fire, near Aahmes. The Healer handed her a warm mug and she drank the hot broth within, grateful for the warmth that spread through her.

Inezha joined them in the room and again sat far away from the rest of them. But she met Namid's gaze without hesitation and even smiled at her. Namid shuddered at her unconcerned expression.

Aahmes scooted closer to Namid and draped an arm around her shoulders.

"What's that about?" he murmured in her ear.

Namid placed her hand atop one of his. Both bore numerous thin white scars, the remnants of their ordeal in the cold. Using thought-speech, she told him what she had learned about Staehw's fate.

Aahmes frowned when she finished and directed a disapproving look at Inezha. The Prazny only returned the same unconcerned gaze, with a slight smile.

~*Don't know if I'd be happier if she could go somewhere else for a while, or worried about what she'd be doing that we can't see,*~ Namid commented.

~*Yeah,*~ Aahmes said.

Haeith stumbled in from outside, his arms full of what looked like goods from the root cellar. Mehratar told Aahmes and Namid to stay put by the fire and he and Inezha helped Haeith place everything around the walls.

"That ought to hold us," Haeith said when they finished. "Looks like this storm might be the worst yet."

Aahmes drew some Wild Power to himself and sent it out into the storm. "Seems likely," he said after a breath-of-time.

"Good," Inezha said. "Then after we eat, I'll head back out."

"What?" Mehratar said.

"Where are you going?" Namid said at the same time.

Inezha grinned at them all. "Storms are the best time for me to come and go from Meahan. Keeps them all guessing."

"And just why do you want to return there?" Aahmes said. "What do you plan to do?"

"Oh, nothing you need worry about," Inezha said with a sweet smile. "I just want to see what Lann's up to. Make sure no one's looking for you two anywhere close to where we actually are. This should be the last time I need go there. From what I can tell."

"You can't take the horses out in this," Aahmes said.

"You shouldn't go out in it yourself," Mehratar said.

Inezha laughed. "Of course not. My pendant is ready to use now. And by the time the storm is finished, it'll be ready to bring me back."

With nothing to say to that, they finished their meal. Inezha invited Aahmes and Namid to watch through Power when she used the pendant, so they could learn to use it too. After they edged closer, she placed one hand atop the pendant on her chest and sent a thin tendril of Power into the thing. And vanished.

"Not much different from the step technique you taught me," Namid said to Haeith.

He gave a slight nod. "But something in the pendant amplifies it. The range is much further."

"So shall we leave now, too?" Namid said to Aahmes, aware of the surprised looks from the other two men.

Aahmes shrugged. "We could. But I can think of many reasons not to, not least of which is that we're unlikely to find another shelter as good as this one. Also, I don't know exactly where we are. I haven't been in this part of the clans' territory before."

"We traveled east from where we found you, but not in a straight path," Haeith said.

"So this is probably clan Acpher's territory. Or clan Retheim's. Still, we need to know where we'd be coming from to best go where we want," Aahmes said.

Namid glanced at the clothing stacked on shelves in the main room. "No cross-barred clothing in clan colors to tell us whose shelter this is," she said.

"Not in the other rooms, either," Aahmes said.

"You two still have recovering to do before you should even consider traveling," Mehratar said. "Best to do that hidden away, anyway."

After she gave that some thought, Namid nodded agreement. She pulled out the books, pen and ink again. "Then let's get this finished up."

CHAPTER 15

The storm lasted through the next day, giving Namid and Aahmes time to spar—at least as much as Mehratar allowed them—and still finish deciphering the last of the writing in the book.

"Still seems somewhat disjointed," Namid said as Aahmes wrote the last few words in Odasoro's code.

"From the parts you've read aloud, it sounds most like it's this Wesh's notes to himself to help him remember," Mehratar said. He poured Namid some more wine and settled on a bench near the fire.

Aahmes wiped the pen clean of ink and capped the ink bottle. "So what do we have?"

"The notes cover various topics," Haeith said.

"I don't know that they are all connected either," Namid said. "Not really."

"Perhaps not as he wrote them," Mehratar said. "But we might be able to connect them in ways he couldn't. Many times new ways to use the Power have been created or discovered that way."

Namid gave him a thoughtful look. "Possibly."

"We know we need to find a way to halt the damage

from the blood Power that came to us," Aahmes said. "I think that means taking it from us somehow."

"Taking it…" Haeith murmured. "In all the notes, it speaks of 'taking it' from someone else. Maybe something in there that didn't work to take it from that man would let you remove it from yourself."

Namid tilted her head as she considered that. "That's true. Wesh didn't try to remove blood Power from himself. Or at least he never wrote anything about trying it. He was always trying, and failing, to remove it from that other person."

"How does that tie in with restoring Nazextas?" Mehratar said. "Are you even going to try to restore the city?"

Namid and Aahmes exchanged looks.

"Maybe," Namid said. "I don't know. I don't really know what it'll accomplish."

"I've been considering that," Aahmes said. "And I might have an unwelcome thought on it."

He raised a hand to Namid's questioning look, asking her to wait as he poured himself more wine.

"Some of what I saw in the Spirit-City did not come from my memories, my past," Aahmes said as he took a seat at Namid's side. "As Inezha said, I saw some of what had to have been the city's past. And I saw a lot of people. Spirits." He turned to look at Namid. "What if they're trapped somehow, in a way similar to how you told us the Dark Priests had trapped your brothers' spirits?"

"It's entirely possible the 'gods' are still drawing Power from them," Mehratar murmured.

Namid gave them a horrified look. "I'd hope you're wrong."

"But you don't think we are," Aahmes said.

Namid shook her head. "No, I don't. It makes too much sense. But how? Even if we knew where the city once stood, there wouldn't be any bodies to burn, like I did for my brothers. And that still doesn't get the blood

Power out of *us*."

"I've seen you drain yourself of the Power you carry," Haeith said. "Perhaps if you draw on only the blood Power and drain it from yourself?"

"Possibly," Namid said with a frown.

"But still, what to do with the Power?" Aahmes said. "The book has a little to say about what happened to Nazextas. It reads most like a description of what he saw from a distance. And I didn't notice anything that looked like something that we could reverse to undo the disaster."

"Where was Nazextas originally?" Namid asked Mehratar. "When it was a real city? Do you remember?"

Mehratar sipped his wine and gave that some thought. "Of course at that time the 'Six Realms of the Monarch' didn't exist as such," he said. "The city was in an area of low hills. It had one main river that ran through it, and a few smaller ones that joined the main one nearby, but not within the city. As I remember, that main river was not overly large. The area was forested."

"Any idea where it was in relation to anyplace we know now?" Namid said. "Was it far south?"

"Thinking perhaps above the cavern that held Corentris?" Aahmes said.

"Possibly." Namid nodded and sipped some wine.

Mehratar shook his head. "I feel that it was further south than we are now, but remember nothing more definite than that."

"Perhaps Inezha will remember," Haeith said. "She was there, and is determined on this, so it seems likely."

Namid nodded. "If we can't even find the physical city, I don't see how this can be accomplished."

"I remember that old Prazny said something about the Spirit-City appearing to us again," Aahmes said. "Wonder if he meant more than just that second time."

Namid shuddered. "Great. More of this prophesy 'you're fated' drivel."

Aahmes chuckled. "Not sure I really care if we're

supposed to be fated or not. I'll just be happy to be rid of the blood Power."

"If we could enter the Spirit-City again, perhaps you two could guide its travels to its original location," Haeith said.

Namid studied him as her thoughts jumped to something else. "You aren't like him, are you?" She cocked a thumb at Mehratar. "Also much older than you seem?"

Haeith treated them to one of his rare smiles. "I'm not. I have but two score and a few years. And some random, cryptic knowledge and ideas I've picked up in my travels."

Namid matched his smile.

"So I suppose we'll wait for Inezha and see what she can tell us. Instead of getting away from her while we can," Namid muttered.

Aahmes laid a hand on her arm. "We have a good shelter here. No guarantee we'd find another to take us through the rest of the winter."

Namid nodded. "True enough." She frowned. "Not that I like it."

Aahmes gave her arm a gentle squeeze.

She smiled at him, then looked to the other two. "Well, that's the city then, for now. What's next?"

"Maybe, in a limited fashion, we could see if safer variations of any of the techniques for removing the blood Power might work on ourselves," Aahmes said.

Namid frowned again. "I suppose we could try some things," she said. "But I don't have a good feeling about any of them."

Mehratar shook his head. "The ones I've picked up on from what you've said sound dangerous and uncontrollable. I think harm is almost a certainty."

"But you can Heal us," Aahmes challenged.

Mehratar nodded. "I can," he said. "But not if you kill yourself."

That squelched the conversation for many long breaths-of-time. After they all had refilled their drinks,

Namid sprawled on a bench and leaned back against the wall.

"And what are the so-called gods plotting while we're snowed in here?" she said. "Before you came to the clans' territory did you have word of anything? Anything about the theomachy?"

"Some messengers did bring news to the Monarch," Haeith said. "And he shared it with us."

"The 'gods'"—Mehratar practically spit the word—"seem to be concentrating on their temples. For now, anyway. I doubt there's one left intact. And woe to anyone who was there at the time."

"We know that Ilenii, Belaraketh and Roivah-neheb are all involved. It was unclear, before we left anyway, if others have joined in," Haeith said.

"Ilenii and Belaraketh are out of control," Mehratar said. "They've repeatedly demanded that you two be handed over to them." He inclined his head toward Aahmes and Namid.

They exchanged looks. "Can we afford to wait out the winter here?" Namid said.

"You don't really have much choice," Mehratar said. "You're not even close to recovered enough to be ready to face them, with any hope of victory. And we need to figure out what's to be done to resolve this blood Power trouble."

"We," Aahmes repeated.

Mehratar gave a vigorous nod. "Yes, we. I've seen a lot in the years I've been alive, travelling and Healing. Something must work."

Aahmes just shook his head and leaned back next to Namid. "Back to throwing Power around tomorrow, I suppose."

Namid leaned her head on his shoulder. "So what's different?" she muttered.

~ ~ ~

The storm petered out sometime overnight which gave them a bright, clear sunrise the next morning. After their morning meal, instead of sparring or working with Power, Namid and Aahmes decided to explore the area around their shelter. Perhaps even see if Aahmes could figure out better where they actually were.

They packed some food and water with them, in case they stayed out through the midday meal. And they layered on warm clothes; the sun was bright, but the air was still frigid. Haeith gave them a few packets of his herbal concoction.

"Just in case you push yourselves," he said with the hint of a smile.

Mehratar just shook his head at them and warned them not to overtax themselves in their explorations.

They ambled away from the small glade in front of the shelter, heading roughly west. Although the storm had left surprisingly little snow, they still sometimes struggled through drifts as they traversed low hill after low hill.

The climb up a steeper, wooded hill that they came to several candle-marks from the shelter was more taxing than Namid expected, and they stopped atop it to look around. Namid leaned against a tree to ease her leg, which had started to ache.

They were in an area of heavy forest which made seeing much at any distance problematic. Through the trees Namid thought she spotted more hills like the one they stood on. The snow held some animal tracks.

"Have a better idea where we are?" Namid asked Aahmes after they both studied their surroundings.

"Only somewhat. The forest here confirms what Haeith told us, that we are east of Meahan. But no telling how far. At least not right now." He slapped a hand against the green-gray trunk of the short tree next to him. "This type of tree grows nowhere else in the clans' territory, so I know this is the Kheill forest. From what I remember, it covers much of the eastern portion of the clans' territory. So that puts us definitely in lands that belong to either clan Acpher or clan Retheim."

"At least it's not clan Acnald lands," Namid murmured and took a drink from her waterskin.

"Yeah. Those lie north of Meahan."

A faint sound came from the direction they had been heading. They both dropped to the ground and crawled toward that side of the hill, trying to stay hidden.

~*A horse?*~ Namid said to Aahmes through thought-speech. She drew a dagger as they found a spot near the edge of the hill in some underbrush.

~*Sounded like,*~ Aahmes answered her the same way.

They eased further along the hill, and Namid drew a small bit of Wild Power to herself to reach out and see if she sensed anything. Before she could, she heard a crazed yell from behind them. Something seized her foot and hauled her roughly back, away from Aahmes.

With a snarl of anger, she kicked out with her other foot and hit something. Whatever gripped her foot released it and she scrambled to stand with a wince for the renewed pain in her injured leg and now both feet.

Before she could see what she faced, something hit her from the side. It knocked her flat again.

"This time I'll finish it right," snarled a voice she recognized.

Somehow Lann had found them.

Aahmes scrambled past her as she again fought her way back to her feet.

She gathered more Wild Power, but hesitated as Aahmes and Lann struggled together, each holding the other's dagger away with a free hand. They moved so much that Namid feared to hit Aahmes if she sent a bolt of Power at Lann.

With a sudden burst of strength, Lann broke free of Aahmes' grasp and kicked him in his injured leg, dropping him. Namid lunged for the clansmate, but before she reached him, Lann dipped a hand into a pouch then withdrew it and blew the powder he held into Aahmes' face.

Aahmes dropped back as he coughed and tried to wipe his eyes clear.

Namid pounced on Lann and gracelessly tried to reach any part of him she could with her knife. When Lann tried to blow the powder in her face, too, she managed to duck away and so caught only a little of it, just enough to make her feel a slight unsteadiness. Then she was back, two daggers out now. She slashed at him and drove him back from Aahmes.

Lann aimed a kick at Namid's bad leg, but she managed to avoid it, only to twist too far and have the leg collapse under her. She rolled away from Lann's frenzied dagger strikes, but a couple of them clipped her arm.

Then Aahmes lunged at Lann, although Namid was not sure how well he saw through swollen, reddened eyes. Namid scrambled away and formed the Wild Power into a narrow attack, ready to unleash it on Lann the first chance she saw.

A sound to her left drew her attention, and she almost loosed the Power there before she recognized three other clansmates: Dyefa, Sen and Inar. They ran past her, sliding in the snow, and joined the scuffle with Lann.

After some vicious struggling, the four managed to subdue and tie Lann, not without injuries to all involved.

When Lann began to scream at Aahmes and Namid, Aahmes tore a piece of cloth from the chieftain's shirt and stuffed it into the man's mouth.

Aahmes shared a satisfied grin with Namid then dropped clumsily to sit on the ground. He gathered up some snow and wiped his eyes with it.

After a critical look at Lann's bonds, Namid joined him. The clansmates gathered around them, each clasping their hands in turn and exclaiming their relief and happiness that Namid and Aahmes lived.

"How did you find us?" Namid said when everyone settled on the ground in places from which they could keep an eye on Lann, who mumbled incoherently behind his gag and glared his anger and hatred at all of them.

"We were after him," Dyefa said and waved a hand at Lann.

"But…." Namid glared at Lann. How could *he* have found them?

"After Lann took the four of you to the hill, we knew we dared wait no longer," Sen said. "That same night, most of the clans rose against him and his people. But it's taken almost this long to finally overcome all of them. And then we discovered that Lann was no longer in the chieftain's quarter, that he had left to seek out 'the two who had escaped', as he had raved about since he discovered you were gone."

"But even so, there've been several storms since then. There shouldn't have been any way to track us," Namid said.

"All true," Inar said. "We learned that he had seen some tracks leading roughly east from the hill after it was discovered the next morning that you two had not perished with Saneth and Taakha. So we started there."

"And visited the shelters that lay that direction," Dyefa said. "We figured that's what *he* was doing, and eventually found signs that it was so."

"And then, this morning, we finally picked up his actual trail," Sen said. "He must've been moving again almost as soon as the storm blew itself out. We knew we were close and so hurried to catch up to him."

"At a good time for us," Aahmes said.

"But what of you two?" Inar said. "How did you survive when the others didn't?" His tone held a hint of accusation in it.

"We wouldn't have," Namid said, "except we had some help. Although they came too late to save Saneth and Taakha. I'm sorry."

Inar studied her expression, then nodded.

"So will you return with us?" Dyefa said. "Meahan is safe now, with Lann captured and his people incapacitated and cowed. We'd welcome you."

Namid dared to look at Aahmes' expression as she wondered if he would want to return to his people now that it seemed he could. He met her gaze and shook his head.

"Someday, yes, I'd like to return," he told Dyefa. "But we're tangled in some difficulties of our own that we need to resolve. And we wouldn't bring them to Meahan."

Dyefa looked crestfallen but nodded her acceptance. "Then someday it will be," she said.

Sen and Inar seized Lann's arms and hauled him to his feet. Namid jumped up as she remembered the powder. Without explanation, she snatched the pouch from Lann's belt and checked inside to make sure it was the right one. She tucked it into one of her own pouches.

"Something he used against us that we might have need of," she said to the clansmates' quizzical looks.

With waves of farewell, the three clansmates hiked their captive down the hill headed west. Before they passed from sight into the forest, all but Lann looked back and raised hands again in gestures of farewell.

Namid sank to the ground next to Aahmes and scrutinized his face. His eyes looked better but had a slightly dazed look to them.

"I'll be fine," he assured her with a slight smile. "I didn't catch the whole dose. My eyes just still burn, but not too badly. And I wouldn't trust that I can control any Power right now."

Namid nodded and dug out the packets of Haeith's herbal concoction. She passed one to Aahmes.

"If your injuries feel anything like mine, we'll both need all he sent with us to make it back." She gave him a sidelong look. "Unless you'd like to explore some more."

Aahmes' chuckle was half cough. He pulled out his

waterskin. "I only want to get back to our shelter and lie down. Perhaps for a very long time. Days even," he said and tipped the herbs into his mouth, swallowing them with a long drink of the water.

Namid also swallowed some of the herbs, then laboriously stood again.

"That sounds perfect to me. Let's go."

CHAPTER 16

The journey back to their shelter took them close to twice as long as their journey out, even with Namid using the step technique of travel. Once. While they learned they could use Wild Power for it, Namid was unable to step them as far as she had the previous spring when she used her own Power. And the pain from her injuries kept her from the control she needed to repeat its use.

They used all the herbs Haeth had sent with them just to be able to stumble back later that afternoon, in the rising winds and colder air that heralded another storm.

Mehratar met them at the shelter's entrance, his expression intense. He Healed them while they shared what had happened that day, then ordered them to stay off their feet until morning, at least.

This latest storm lasted most of the next day and Inezha returned the following day. Namid managed to corner her when she returned, when the others were out tending to the horses.

"We need a few answers," she told the Prazny.

"About what?"

"First, what is it you're playing at with Lann?"

Inezha widened her eyes. "Nothing. I'm done with him. I didn't even see him this time. What the rest of the clansmates will do with him, though, I can't say."

"Anything else with the clans?"

"A few suspect that you and Aahmes still live," Inezha confided, "since, of course, your frozen bodies weren't at the execution site the next morning. But I've said nothing." She met Namid's gaze with an earnest one of her own.

Namid studied her expression. "All right. Then, about your city—"

"You'll help? That's wonderful!"

"We've been discussing it, but nothing's decided," Namid said. "Do you know what needs to be done to restore the city? How would that work?"

Inezha plopped down on a bench. "The book doesn't tell you? I'd thought it would be in there."

"It doesn't have a section on how to restore Power-blasted cities, no. There is some information that might contribute to a solution, but nothing definite yet."

Inezha's expression fell.

"One thing we think might help is knowing the location of Nazextas. The original location when it was a normal city."

Inezha gave her a sharp look.

Namid frowned back at her. "What?"

The Prazny shook her head. "You truly don't know?"

"Know what? What is it?"

"Your city of Rhadanthus currently stands where Nazextas did. It's curious. You've been living in the very spot these many years."

Mehratar's arrival cut short further discussion as Inezha jumped up and left the shelter when he appeared in the entrance.

Mehratar and Namid watched her in silence and the Healer took a seat on a bench across from Namid.

"You're pushing your recovery too much," he said with

a stern look for her.

Namid shrugged with one shoulder. "Perhaps. But I feel that it's necessary. What if spring arrives early? We need to be ready."

"Not at the risk of setbacks and further injury," Mehratar admonished.

Namid shrugged again and the silence stretched between them.

"I feel that I don't really know you, in spite of traveling with you all those weeks this past spring," Namid finally spoke up. "What's it like having lived for around four thousand years?"

This time Mehratar shrugged. "A mix, just like a life of any length, I'd expect. Interesting, sometimes tedious. Sad, too."

"So you rode circuit Healing? Was that so no one would guess?"

"In part. I also wanted to keep moving, too, to avoid Jelth and the others, if I could. After a number of years, I'd turn over the Healing to an apprentice. Then I'd move on to a different circuit for some years. After I'd been away from an area for many years, I'd be back again, but as my own grandson or great-nephew, named after a grandfather or great-uncle and following in his footsteps."

"You must have seen so much in that time," Namid said.

"A few things," he said with a slight smile. "And some concerning things, too. There are fewer and fewer people with a lot of Power than there were when I was young."

"The 'gods'? Getting their blood Power from those who held the most Power of their own?"

Mehratar shrugged and nodded at the same time.

"Were you there, too, when Nazextas fell?" Namid said.

He shook his head. "No, I was far across the lands that have become the Six Realms. I felt it, though. I think everyone with Power felt it. I didn't learn until later what had happened. Or at least what we were told happened. It didn't quite match what Inezha told us."

"The 'gods' do seem to like their own versions of events," Namid muttered, and Mehratar chuckled.

Aahmes and Haeith joined them and they set about preparing the evening meal. Mehratar ordered Aahmes and Namid to rest more so they perched on a bench while Namid shared what Inezha had told her about Nazextas and Rhadanthus. Inezha returned in time for the meal.

After everyone ate, after they separated for their own pursuits, Namid and Aahmes chatted about the two cities sharing the same location.

"Things falling into place just like that autumn with Akavos," Aahmes commented with a shake of his head.

"Yeah," Namid said. "But now we know a lot of it has to do with Wesh 'steering events' as he told us and Inezha doing much the same."

"True. Still...." He shook his head again. "So back to Rhadanthus in the spring?"

"I think so," Namid said. "At least we can claim that's the plan for now. And if we learn something to change that, then we will."

~ ~ ~

Aahmes plopped down next to Namid when Mehratar called a break in their sparring. They had been fighting two against one with Haeith, and Namid noted with satisfaction that Haeith looked ready for the break, too. He wiped sweat from his eyes and gave her a slight nod.

The Healer had insisted they stop so he would not have to re-Heal Aahmes' and Namid's damaged legs, so he said. And if she was inclined to admit anything, Namid was ready for a break, too. Her leg ached every time she moved it even the slightest.

Three weeks of storm after storm had kept everyone close to the shelter and given her and Aahmes plenty of time to work on regaining their skills. They had worked some again with Wild Power, too, but being within the shelter limited how much they could do.

Namid took a drink from the water skin Mehratar handed her and passed it to Aahmes while the Healer looked him over with his Power.

"So once we get to Rhadanthus again, what then?" Aahmes said as he unwound the tight wrap that Mehratar had insisted he wear around his damaged leg when they sparred. Namid wore one, too.

"A good question," Mehratar murmured.

"Assuming that's where we have to do this – whatever it is we end up doing," Namid said. "I think we have to expect that the 'gods' will find us there. We'll have to clear the city. Get everyone out. Maybe to Tower Hold for the time we need."

"I'd think you'd *need* to have the 'gods' find you there," Inezha said as she lifted her head from where she lay on a bench near the fire. "How else can you take back the Power they stole?"

"We don't know that we can do any such thing," Namid said. "So far we're just guessing at all this. We don't even know about finding the Spirit-City. Maybe we need to be there instead to do this."

"You haven't yet tried any of the ways the book talks about to maybe get the blood Power out of you," Inezha said. "Don't you need to figure out which will work?"

"We've still got almost half the winter before we can consider any real traveling," Aahmes said. "Plenty of time to figure this all out." He nodded to Mehratar when the Healer finished using his Power to ease the damaged leg.

Mehratar turned his attention to Namid.

"Is there any change?" she said when he finished.

"Some for the better. But it's to be expected that it's slow, even with my help. The damage was extensive, and the cold didn't help."

Namid frowned but nodded.

"What is there to figure out?" Inezha demanded. "Use all that Power you two have, even the blood Power, and restore the city. Should be simple."

Namid stared at her. "Simple? I know how to make defensive shells with Power, move things, throw fire around and do some different illusions. I don't see where any of that becomes recreating a city from a ghostly version of it. We don't even know how much Power it'll take. A lot, I'd think. Could be more than we've got."

"Wouldn't it just pull from the Power that the 'gods' stole?" Inezha said. "I'd think it should."

"Maybe," Aahmes said. "But we don't know that."

"And if it does, that'll bring the 'gods' down on us. No doubt about that."

Inezha shrugged. "So pull more Power from the surroundings, Wild Power, too. You've done that before."

"We don't even know that Wild Power would be suited for this," Namid said. "We've encountered several things we do with our own Power that don't work well, or at all, using Wild Power."

"Pulling in Power," Haeith murmured. "The book said something like that. About that statue."

Aahmes gave him a sharp look. "The Star of Corentris. Yeah, in those hidden notes." He started to stand, then sank back with a grimace.

"I'll get the book," Haeith said as Mehratar again looked at Aahmes' injury.

After a breath-of-time, the Healer shook his head. "You're pushing too hard," he told Aahmes. "Even after Healing, bones take time to regain their original strength." He shared his glare with Namid. "Both of you. You need to ease up on the sparring."

Namid wrinkled her nose in displeasure but nodded under Mehratar's intent gaze. Aahmes imitated her, then quirked a quick smile at her.

Haeith brought the two books to where Namid and Aahmes sat and joined them. Inezha sat up so she could see but stayed on her bench.

Haeith flipped through the original book, then handed it to Aahmes, open to a certain page. He did the same with the second book that contained their copy of the hidden writings.

"Yes, if you put these two parts together"—he pointed to lines in each book—"then it reads that when the statue was in the city it pulled Power to itself. He didn't know to what purpose, nor how much it would pull if left to do so, and apparently didn't investigate further. Only decided to keep the statue out of the city."

"Wonder if he did investigate but didn't write it down," Inezha said.

"It seems likely it was Wesh as Chendrukhar writing this from Chendrukhar's memories. Maybe Wesh didn't get all his memories when he took his Power and essence," Aahmes said.

"Star of Corentris," Namid said. "Is that city also tied into this somehow?"

"Mention of that city has brought to mind this," Haeith said and reached into his pouch. "I've carried it with me since Corentris, although tucked away until I remembered it this day." He held out a golden shepherd's pipe, etched with a design of leaves and vines.

"The golden pipe," Inezha murmured. "I remember mention of that."

Mehratar leaned close to study the pipe as Haeith passed it to Namid.

"I'd forgotten about this," Namid said. "Could it be part of this, too? Can you still play it?"

Haeith shrugged then shook his head. "I've been unable to get even a single note from it since that autumn. Although I haven't tried in recent weeks."

Namid put it to her lips, but her attempt to play it resulted in only silence. The others each tried in turn, with no better success.

With a shrug, Mehratar handed it back to Haeith. "I

sense a subtle Power about it, but it's not anything I've encountered before," he said.

"I've not seen the thing before," Inezha said. "But it's pretty. It was part of the events with Akavos?"

Namid nodded. "But seems it's no help now."

Haeith tucked it away again. "Disappointing. I'd hoped it might be of help. Still, I'll keep it safe. Perhaps it yet has a part in this. Just not with any of us. I have the music still, too. No good unless someone can play the pipe, though."

Namid nodded absently as she reread the parts of the books Haeith had pointed out.

"So *is* the city of Corentris part of this?" Namid murmured.

"It's destroyed and buried," Inezha said. "How could it be?"

"It had some kind of Power connection to Rhadanthus," Namid said. "We know that."

"The connection need not relate to the Praznies' city," Mehratar said. "It *has* been several thousand years. It's just as likely something the Dark Priests set up on their own, for their own purposes."

Aahmes and Namid exchanged looks.

"Maybe," Namid said.

"That doesn't matter," Inezha said. "If this Star can draw Power, just get it and use it to get all the Power you need to restore my city."

Aahmes and Namid exchanged looks again. Then Namid laughed.

"Get to steal the thing again, I guess," she said.

CHAPTER 17

Aahmes and Namid kept their sparring sessions shorter and more moderate the next few days. They worked again with Power, cautiously and always beneath protective shells of Power to keep anyone else from sensing their activities, so they hoped.

The random wounds and bleeding continued to plague them whenever they tried using their own Power but grew no worse. And they spent long candle-marks walking near their shelter, staying within the concealing trees.

On one such walk, something that had lurked in the back of Namid's thoughts suddenly jumped out at her. She stopped with a soft exclamation.

Aahmes gave her a concerned look.

"I just remembered... we don't have to wait until spring to travel," Namid said. "The Dark Priests' pendants."

Aahmes eyes widened and he nodded. "The others used them to get to the clans' territory from Kilaadi, so they work over a long distance."

"Maybe they could get us to Rhadanthus, then."

"Maybe. We know we're east of Meahan. And perhaps

a little south, best I can tell. So that would put Rhadanthus quite a bit further away than Kilaadi."

Namid grinned at Aahmes. "Best you can tell? I thought you always knew where you were," she teased.

He caught her around the waist and pulled her close. "As I've told you, I've never been in this part of the clans' territory before. So I have only a rough idea where we are, based on memories of talk about the lands." He stole a kiss, but his expression was serious.

"I think we should go alone," he said. "Leave the others for their own safety. We don't know what the 'gods' have been doing while we've been hidden, but I wouldn't be surprised if we draw their attention as soon as we return south."

After giving that some thought, Namid nodded. "I'm glad of the others' help, but I have to agree. How soon should we leave then?"

"I haven't yet used one of the pendants. I'd like to at least try them out, maybe a couple of times. Short distances, to get a feel for them."

"Makes sense. How about now? Back to the shelter?"

"I don't have mine with me."

Namid frowned. "Well, the others brought themselves and a horse each. Maybe one pendant could bring two people?"

"Or together we could use one pendant. That might be safer."

"Relatively, anyway. Link or blend the Power?"

"Let's try linking first. And see if the Wild Power might work for this. I'm getting tired of bleeding."

They clasped hands, drew Wild Power to themselves, and linked to each other.

But when they tried to use it as Inezha had shown them, both holding a picture of the outside of their shelter in their thoughts and directing the Power to Namid's pendant, nothing at all happened. Not even the slightest hint that the pendant could do anything with Power, let alone let them travel a distance.

So they linked their own Power and repeated their actions.

They felt a sluggish response from the pendant. Then with a snap they both felt, their Power blended and poured into the pendant. And they stood outside the shelter. Both squeezed their noses against the bleeding and sat together on a rock in the meager winter sunshine.

"It works," Namid muttered after the bleeding stopped.

Aahmes nodded. "Not something to do a lot of, though."

A rustle from behind them drew their attention. Haeith stepped out and let the heavy fur that formed the shelter's door fall back behind him. He joined them, crouching next to their rock.

"That Power use extended beyond the shells," he said in a soft voice. "No one is near, so no one should have sensed it."

Namid and Aahmes exchanged guilty looks. "We've gotten too complacent," Namid said.

"Keeping high vigilance for a long period is difficult," Haeith said. "It's understandable."

"Maybe. But not acceptable," Namid said. "Thank you for the reminder."

Haeith nodded, then rose and headed to the stable.

After he was out of earshot, Namid leaned close to Aahmes. "We need to go. Just us two. Find a way to get this blood Power gone. And I think we need to know what the 'gods' have been up to."

"How soon?"

"I'm not sure yet. Certainly not before my pendant is ready for use again. And we'll need to take some things with us. A few days?"

Aahmes nodded. "Before then, we should at least test some of the least horrific ways to remove the blood Power. See if any show even a chance that they'll work on ourselves. While we still have the Master Healer nearby."

Namid made a face but nodded. "I know we need to. I'm not looking forward to it, though."

Aahmes clasped her hand. "Me neither."

~ ~ ~

That afternoon, Aahmes and Namid took themselves a short distance from the shelter to see what they could learn about removing the blood Power. The others joined them.

While Namid reread the sections of Wesh's notes that discussed trying to remove blood Power from someone, Haeith and Aahmes set up additional layers of protective Power shells.

After she read several of the descriptions, Namid set the book aside with a sigh.

"Reading them again, I just don't know about *any* of these," she said. "They all sound too extreme and too likely to kill us."

Mehratar gave her an intent look. "I'd wondered about that when you said you wanted to see if any would work on yourselves."

"The sword, Akavos, took the Power from Sesaisyd," Haeith said. "Only as it killed him, granted, but perhaps there would be something like it to take the blood Power from you."

"It took *all* his Power," Aahmes said.

"And shattered when you hit the stone table with it," Haeith said. "Odd in itself. That should not have caused a blade of that quality to shatter."

"There's something I learned from the Dark Priests," Namid said. She spoke slowly as she tried to remember. "Akavos was forged with Wild Power. It was intended to bind Sesaisyd. But sometime later, someone changed that purpose. Made it into an imperative to kill him and bind his Power."

"Forged with Wild Power," Aahmes said. "How would that even work?"

"Maybe the reverse of what we did with those Powerful bits we took from Chendrukhar's towers and melted down?" Namid said.

"Maybe."

"Something else odd," Mehratar said. "I've been trying to remember what I've seen and know about blood Power. Precious little. But that you two seem to hold this Power is not something I've heard of before. The times *I* saw the 'gods' work with blood Power, they always gathered it and used it right away."

"But we talked of them gathering Power to themselves," Inezha said. "What's the use of becoming more Powerful if you don't hold on to it? If it only lasts a short time?"

"So the 'gods' probably have some way to hold their gathered blood Power," Namid said. "Neither of us did anything to be able to do that."

"The Power that came to you might have done that, too," Haeith said.

Namid started to pace. "So we're stuck with this blood Power? But others who use blood Power, like the Dark Priests, don't have it to draw on again. They have to get more."

"Makes Haeith's suggestion of depleting ourselves sound more like it would work," Aahmes said

"And *that* we can try," Namid said.

"But you'll need all the Power you've got to bring back Nazextas," Inezha protested.

"Holding on to that Power won't do us any good to bring back the city if it kills us before we can do that," Namid said.

Inezha frowned, but then nodded slightly. She moved to the edge of the glade and leaned against a tree, arms folded, her expression unhappy.

"So try to make something to draw the Power from us

or see if the blood Power can be depleted?" Namid said.

"We have no forge or smith," Inezha said.

"Aahmes can shape metals," Namid said.

"Small things," Aahmes said. "And it takes some time. Also, of course, the metal to work with."

Namid nodded. "Depleting the Power it is, then. Which leaves us with the question of what to do with it?"

"Won't that draw the attention of the 'gods'?" Inezha said. "Anything likely to take that much Power? You'd do better to save it for the restoration of the city, when drawing their attention would actually be useful."

"Are you saying this as the Seer?" Aahmes said.

Everyone looked at Inezha and Namid thought she would say yes, even if untrue. But the Prazny shook her head.

"No. I haven't Seen anything about that."

"That's what I'll use the Power for," Namid said. "To look out around us as far as I can manage. Something useful and less noticeable."

She could tell from his closed expression that Aahmes did not like the idea, but he said nothing. Instead he scuffed a place to sit near the center of the glade and held a hand out to her.

She did not reach for it. "I think only one of us should try this at first."

"Agreed," he said. "But I'll be right here in case you need support or more Power. Or rescuing." He grinned.

With an exasperated look for him, Namid took Aahmes' hand and settled next to him. Haeith hovered nearby, but still a pace away. Inezha stayed where she was. Mehratar settled within reach.

"Being so close might not be a good idea," Aahmes warned the Healer.

"Being so close might save her life, or both your lives, if this goes badly," Mehratar countered.

Aahmes frowned but raised no further objection.

Namid shifted around to find a comfortable position

and pulled out a dagger. Before she could think further about it, she made a small slice in the side of her left thumb and let the blood drip steadily into a tiny puddle at her side. Mehratar hovered, his attention on the wound, but held back from Healing. Aahmes took the dagger and cleaned it, then clasped her other hand so their skin touched, but held his Power back, away from her.

Namid briefly met everyone's gazes, then she stared down at the blood while she reached for her own Power. She concentrated on drawing out only the slippery Power, entwined with her own, that she associated with blood Power.

For a breath-of-time, she felt Aahmes' Power flow to her too, but then he managed to halt it.

She reached out to the puddle and tried to send her Power through her blood, hoping that was the way to do it. She closed her eyes and used that Power to reach out around them through the forest. Searching and sensing. Seeing what she might learn of their surroundings as she had done before with her own Power and even the Wild Power.

She drew heavily on the blood Power, now able to distinguish it by feel from her own, and reached further and further.

Her head began to pound, but she still reached out. She was vaguely aware that someone clamped down on the cut she had made and wrapped her finger with a cloth. But still she reached out.

Trees and wintered grasses, hills and rocks. She touched on Meahan, several leagues to their west, she thought. And further. She reached southward now.

Vague impressions of people – none with Power so she could only guess at their presence and their numbers. But she felt strife. Further south, villages tucked away for the winter. Then a blot.

She paused, exploring. Old Power there, but burned. Burned buildings. Death. Jelth's destroyed temple.

She reached further, working to disregard the stabbing pain in her eyes.

Could she reach Kilaadi? Would that drain enough blood Power?

Impressions of forests and fields, people and animals. Roads. Buildings. A town she did not recognize.

Then a Power. Strong.

And alarm tore through her.

She shunted her Power away from her. Diffusing its sense, she hoped, as she fled back to the north as fast as she could manage.

Some Power followed, its intent hostile, and she threw Wild Power at it as she dove back to their hidden refuge, flinging Power out wide to confound any attempt to follow it to her and her companions.

Then she was back in the glade, staring at Aahmes.

"Hide us with Wild Power," she said. "Quick!"

He drew Wild Power and blanketed it over them, atop their defensive and concealing shells of Power and atop the hills that held their shelter and the stables. Namid smiled when she realized it felt similar to the Wild Power concealments they had found in the mountains far to the east.

While Namid squeezed her nose with one hand to try to stop the bleeding, Haeith and Mehratar pulled her under the trees near Inezha. Aahmes joined them there and they all ran for the shelter.

When Namid stumbled as her legs gave out beneath her, Aahmes wrapped an arm around her and helped her along.

They reached the shelter and ducked inside ahead of the Power that flowed toward them from the south. Everyone huddled at the doorway and watched.

As Aahmes and Namid had seen before, red lightning crackled across the ground, filtered through the trees. It was denser than before, the branches closer together.

It touched on everything it encountered but seemed to

do nothing else.

When it reached their shelter and the hill that hid the stable, it flowed up and over them, a finger-width or two above the ground. As it continued further north and east, Aahmes grinned at Namid.

"It worked!"

"What did you do?" Mehratar said. "I sensed that lightning, but nothing else. Something with Wild Power?"

"It felt like the hidden pockets of Wild Power we found in the Arinsk Mountains," Namid said as she slid down the wall to rest on the floor.

"Yes," Aahmes said. "I used those as a guide and created something similar here. No one else seems able to sense the Wild Power, so this area just looks undisturbed to anyone looking. No one's here."

He held a hand out to her. "Let's get further inside."

She grasped his hand with a nod, glad for his help to get into their shelter and to a bench. Then Mehratar crouched next to her and his Power flowed around her.

"What did you see using the blood Power?" Haeith asked as he handed Namid a cup of cool water.

"Nothing particularly useful," she said after she drank several swallows. "I pushed it, trying to drain the blood Power—"

"Which it feels that you have," Mehratar interjected.

Namid shared a quick, pleased look with Aahmes. "Good!" she said. "That wasn't too bad. I saw Meahan, then several villages, far away from here. Everywhere it felt that things are disturbed. Uneasy, at best. A lot of strife."

"Likely from the theomachy," Haeith said.

Namid sighed in relief as Mehratar's Healing eased her aching head. She finished the water and set the cup next to her on the bench.

"Are they still destroying each other's temples?" Inezha said.

Namid shrugged. "I didn't sense anything like that. But I also wasn't looking for it. I didn't reach as far as Kilaadi.

It felt like the 'gods' have their Power spread out across the land to the south, waiting to sense something. Us, I'm sure."

"Good," Inezha said. "Then they'll come when you work to restore the city. And we can pull that stolen Power from them!"

CHAPTER 18

Namid sat bolt upright, wide awake and uncertain why. Her motion disturbed Aahmes and he sat up too, giving her a concerned look.

She shrugged back at him while she reached out with the tiniest amount of Wild Power. "I don't know."

She felt him send out Wild Power, too.

"I don't sense anything," he said in a soft voice.

She sent the Power out a little further and stopped with a frown as her head began to hurt again. She pulled the covers around her shoulders and grabbed a waterskin that lay next to her sleeping pad.

But she held it without drinking from it when she realized what woke her.

"The blood Power is back," she told Aahmes. "Restored. Refreshed just like my own Power does after I've used a lot and then rest."

The lightest touch of Aahmes' Power brushed her, and she sensed when he turned it back to himself, too. He frowned.

"So entwined with our own Power that it can act the same, somehow," he muttered as he scooted over from his sleeping pad to sit next to her.

Namid leaned against him for comfort and smiled when he wrapped his arms around her.

"How are we going to get rid of all of it?"

She did not expect him to answer, but he did.

"We know it's possible to burn yourself out – be unable to use *any* Power anymore."

"You'd give up the Power?"

He pulled her even closer. "To be able to live? Have time with you. No question."

She ducked her head and held him tight. She realized she felt the same.

"Me too," she told him.

Much as she enjoyed having Power, being able to do the extraordinary things others could not, she would too.

After several long breaths-of-time, she wriggled free and took a long drink of water.

"So it looks like we've got our solution. Use up all of our Power, pull the so-called gods' Power too if we can, and bring back Inezha's city."

Namid saw Aahmes' grin in the faint light that came from the low fire in the outer room. "But later," he said, and kissed her.

~ ~ ~

Over the next several days both Aahmes and Namid gathered items they wanted to take with them and stashed them in a back corner of the stable. They kept the small pile hidden with Wild Power.

The day before they planned to leave a strong storm blew in and everyone spent the afternoon and evening in the warmer main room of the shelter, with the fire burning high. They amused themselves with games Haeith had shown them and shared several skins of wine. Talk was limited mostly to aspects of whichever game they played at the time and comments on the raging storm outside.

Inezha jumped up after one particularly loud howl of wind faded away.

"We needn't wait for spring to arrive to travel!" she announced. "We can use the pendants. We have enough of them to take all of us, and the horses, too. We could be somewhere warmer right now. We could be working to restore Nazextas instead of sitting around playing soldiers' games."

Namid and Aahmes exchanged quick glances.

"Can these take us all the way to the city?" Mehratar said. "Rhadanthus, right?"

Inezha shrugged, unconcerned. "If not, we can still hole up somewhere warmer for the couple of days or so that we'd need to wait before we can use the pendants again."

"Are you certain that it's Rhadanthus that we must travel to?" Haeith said. "What of the Spirit-City? It seems tied most closely to the original Prazny city. Might it be better to attempt this from within it?"

"How would we even find the city again?" Namid said. "If that's even where we'd need to be to do this."

She looked up startled at the silence that followed her question and found the others looking at Inezha.

"We have a Seer with us," Mehratar said.

"Can you See where the Spirit-City will be?" Namid said to Inezha. "See where we can find it again?"

"It doesn't work that way," Inezha said with a frown.

"Then how does it work?" Aahmes said.

"An image or vision just comes to me. Most often when I've been concentrating on a goal or problem. But sometimes nothing comes to me. And sometimes, in very rare instances, I've been able to concentrate on wanting to See something specific and have actually Seen something related to that."

"So do that," Aahmes said. "Or better yet, maybe you can See something that will help us get rid of this blood Power before it kills us."

Inezha shrugged, her expression inscrutable. "I can try. Don't disturb me." She headed into the side room she had been using for sleeping.

The others exchanged looks.

"Think she'll See anything useful?" Aahmes said.

Namid shrugged. "And will she tell us the truth about it, or tell us about it in a way to get us to do what she wants?"

Aahmes frowned at that and passed the dice to Mehratar. "Your turn."

And so they passed more time.

Inezha returned several candle-marks later, after the others had finished their evening meal. Shadows lurked in the skin beneath her eyes. She grabbed a bowl of stew and a mug of wine. She drained the wine, refilled the mug and sat near the fire.

After she wolfed down almost half her meal, she looked up to meet the others' gazes.

"Well?" Aahmes said. "What have you Seen? What sage wisdom do you have to impart to us?" His voice sounded much as it had when he had been at his worst in the Shadowers. Namid glanced at him, but he would not meet her gaze.

"Much that was random and unclear," Inezha said. "That's not unusual. I did See you and Namid in the Spirit-City. A glimpse."

"None of the rest of us?" Mehratar said.

Inezha shook her head. "No, but it was just a glimpse. Everything I Saw this time was only glimpses. Glimpses of Power and people in city streets, glimpses of the 'gods', blood."

"So maybe we find the Spirit-City again, or maybe you Saw what has already happened," Aahmes said. He waved a dismissive hand in the air and met Namid's gaze. "Doesn't sound like anything to change the plan."

"Still travel to Rhadanthus, then," Mehratar said. "But the pendants will make that journey much easier. A day to gather whatever we need to take, and we can be gone from this place."

After more discussion about plans to leave the shelter in two days, they all separated to get some sleep. Inezha returned to the side room and Haeith and Mehratar settled near the low fire in the center room.

After they wished the others a good night, Aahmes and Namid retreated to the other side room and went through the motions of preparing for sleep, although Namid did not unbraid her hair as she usually did at night and neither of them shed their outer tunics.

After they settled under the covers, Aahmes clasped Namid's hand.

His voice came to her in her thoughts. *~As soon as they sleep.~*

She nodded agreement and they waited.

After close to a quarter candle-mark, Namid slid out of bed. At Aahmes' questioning look, she placed her hand atop his.

~Forgot something,~ she told him.

While Aahmes watched, Namid pulled out the book Mehratar had brought from Kilaadi, and the pen and ink. She tore an unused page from the back of the book, making as little noise as she could manage, then wrote a short note to leave for the others that told them that she and Aahmes had decided they needed to investigate some things on their own.

She handed the note to Aahmes, who nodded his agreement after he read it. Namid returned the book, ink and pen to their concealment within her bundle of clothes and placed the note on the floor in the doorway to the other room, off to the side but still clearly visible.

Then they waited some more, until the sounds from the center room indicated the two men there slept.

Moving silently, as they had learned as Shadowers, Namid and Aahmes collected their meager bundles of clothes from under their bedcovers and slipped into the shelter's middle room. They wrapped Wild Power around themselves as they went, to help hide them.

Mehratar and Haeith both lay near the fire atop their sleeping pads. As Aahmes and Namid eased through the room to the outer door, Haeith stirred and rolled over. Namid thought she caught a glint of reflected firelight from his eyes, then she and Aahmes stood in the entry area, poised before the heavy hanging fur that covered the opening to outside.

They slipped around the fur, letting in only the tiniest bit of cold air, and hurried to the stable.

Aahmes stuffed his clothes in his pack in the corner and hefted it and the two packs of food they had stashed there. Namid stuffed her clothes in her own pack and pulled out the pendant. She grasped Aahmes' arm between his sleeve and glove, skin to skin. She carried her own gloves tucked in her belt.

"I think we should go straight to the ghost city," she whispered. "That way we won't have to chase it around the countryside."

Aahmes looked surprised. After a breath-of-time, he nodded. "Assuming the pendant can take us there," he said. "Worth a try."

"Let's try for that square where the five roads met," Namid said. She showed him the image of the place in their thoughts. They linked their Power and together fed it into the pendant with the intent of travel to the square they pictured.

A sound at the stable entrance caught Namid's attention and she thought she saw Haeith enter and open his mouth to say something. Then the stable winked out of sight.

~ ~ ~

Namid had expected the pain. She hurt all over, her head more than anywhere else, and her eyes the worst part of that. But why couldn't she see anything?

"Namid?" Aahmes' voice.

"I'm here," she said, and tasted blood. Sensations other than pain returned. She lay on something cool and hard. Felt like stone. And she still gripped her pack and Aahmes' arm.

"Did we make it?" Aahmes said. "I can't see anything."

"I don't know. It's dark for me, too."

She felt Aahmes shift. He groaned. Still keeping hold of his arm, Namid sat up, with a groan of her own. Warmth ran down her cheeks and she tasted more blood. But then the darkness lightened.

"I think I'm starting to see something," Aahmes said.

Namid waited for her sight to clear further then looked around.

She and Aahmes sat in the square in the ghost city. It looked much as she remembered, although the streets and buildings looked more transparent than before. And the shadowy blue-white glow seemed dulled, more blue-gray.

When she looked at Aahmes, Namid could not suppress a gasp of dismay. Blood ran down his cheeks like tears. She touched a hand to her own face, and it came away streaked with blood. She must look as bad as he did. The pain continued to ease, slower than she wished, except for her headache and a lingering, burning ache behind her eyes.

Aahmes met her gaze. Namid wondered if her eyes were as bloodshot as his.

"We're quite the sight," Namid said.

He grinned, then winced. "Wonder where the city is right now." He dug in one of the food packs and pulled out a waterskin. He poured a little water into his cupped hand and rinsed the blood from his face first, then both hands.

Namid shrugged. "Since this worked, it probably doesn't really matter." She shifted around to reach the other pack and also cleaned off blood, then took a drink before she repacked the skin.

Aahmes struggled to his feet, clutching the handles of his pack and one of the food packs in one hand. He stood there wobbling and looked around.

Namid pulled her few remaining needles from their hidden pocket and slipped them into her braid. Then she joined him, likewise holding the handles of two packs in one hand. Aahmes clasped her free hand in his.

"Does it feel colder than before?" Namid said.

Aahmes nodded. "And the light's dimmer."

"When we were here before, the city, or the people maybe, did react somewhat to things I said or thought about. Maybe a way to learn what we need...."

"Maybe learn what it is we need to learn," Aahmes said with an amused expression. "I'm still not too sure about what we need to know."

Namid nodded her agreement. She shifted the straps of her packs in her hand, then set the packs down again and gave them a good long look. Under Aahmes' quizzical gaze, she pulled her hand from his and worked to stuff her too-small pack of clothes into the pack of food. It fit well enough. She hefted the single pack and slipped one arm through each handle to carry the pack on her back.

"Seems better to have free hands," she told Aahmes.

With a nod, he followed her example. Then she clasped his hand again.

"Free hands?" he said with a hint of a dangerous expression.

She chuckled. "To some extent. I hope if we hold on to each other we won't get separated here. Like happened before."

He squeezed her hand gently. "Works for me. So where do we go? Or shall we just ask questions of the air?"

"Questions..." a whisper in the air said.

Aahmes looked startled.

Namid laughed. "That's what they did to me last time. Didn't those whispers talk to you, too?"

"No."

She waved a hand in the air. "So, try a question. They seem to want to talk to you now."

Aahmes shrugged, his expression skeptical. "All right." He turned his gaze out away from Namid. "How do we get rid of the blood Power that infects us without dying from it?"

After a breath-of-time of complete silence, a flood of whispers whirled around them, too many to make out individual voices or words.

"That's not helpful," Namid said.

The whispers stopped and Aahmes gave Namid a quizzical look, eyebrows raised. She shrugged.

"Dying…" said a whisper.

"Yeah, that's what we want to *not* do," Namid said.

"Maybe we need to go to a specific place within the city," Aahmes whispered after they had waited in silence.

"Worth a try," Namid said. "Maybe try for the central tower. Did you see that before?"

"The top, I think. From a distance. This way?" Aahmes headed across the small square.

After only a couple of steps, Namid halted at a tug on her free hand – from something or someone unseen. Aahmes halted with her.

"Did you feel that?" Aahmes said.

Namid looked the direction the tug had come from. "A tug off that way?" she said.

"Yeah." Aahmes grinned. "That way, then."

Together they followed the narrow roadway to their left and headed deeper into the city.

CHAPTER 19

The gentle tugging guided them through many twists and turns. More than a candle-mark after they had arrived in the city, Aahmes and Namid stepped out of a last side-street into the open plaza that surrounded the tall, crystal tower that dominated the city center.

Aahmes pulled Namid to a stop at the edge of the open space. He gazed up at the tower and his mouth fell open.

Namid chuckled. "You didn't see it before."

Aahmes shook his head. "Not like this."

"I saw it a couple of times. I kept getting pulled to different parts of the city. Once I even stood on that balcony with Boudra. I think right before he cast that spell that caused all this."

"Not the cause…" a whisper said.

"Only a piece…" said another.

"Priests, gods, Boudra, all were part…"

Namid and Aahmes exchanged glances.

"Think we can guide the Power here to learn what we need?" Aahmes said.

"Maybe. When we were all here before, it felt to me like the whole city was Power." She looked around. "I just wonder where everyone is. I often saw a lot of people about when the city flicked me here and there."

"Dying…" a whisper said.

A strong tug on Namid's free hand pulled both her and Aahmes forward. The city darkened and she saw what looked like a deep-red mesh emerge from the gloom.

Aahmes shook his free hand and Namid could see some of the red mesh attached to it. "What is this webbing?"

As the mesh grew more visible, Namid saw that it connected to *both* her and Aahmes. It seemed to stretch throughout the city. And she began to see the people… a few at first, then more appeared. They were faint, still ghost-like, not nearly as visible as they had been when she and her companions had been in the city before.

The red mesh went through everybody she saw.

"I'm going to try something," she told Aahmes. "Hold your Power away from mine again, just in case."

"Wait—"

But Namid had already plunged her awareness deep into her Power, specifically into the blood Power twined with her own. She sent the tiniest tendril of the Power out into the city and the entire red mesh vibrated with it. As if from a great distance, she heard Aahmes say her name, but she disregarded him for the time being.

She lifted her free hand and examined the red strands that connected her to the mesh – some strands as thin as threads and others as thick as her fingers. With a frown, she reached for the mesh and felt it resonate in the blood Power she carried. And the longer she concentrated on the webbing, the more she actually felt it against her skin. She shuddered and returned her awareness to her surroundings.

"And just exactly what was that?" Aahmes demanded. He held up his free hand to show Namid the blood that dripped from around his fingernails. Her own hand was the same.

She nodded toward the still-visible mesh.

"Blood Power," she said. "All of it. Connecting the city and connecting us to it. And connecting everyone here. All the people. Or spirits. Whatever they are."

They both jumped as a tremor flowed through them from the mesh.

"And I wager connecting the 'gods' too," Aahmes said with a frown.

"Now we know how to get them to come to the city's restoration," Namid said.

"They feed…" a whisper said.

"Holding us…" another said.

"And what if they're coming right now?" Aahmes said to Namid, ignoring the whispers. "What if they felt that?"

"Wager we can find out," Namid said and challenged him with a look.

He sighed and pulled her down to sit next to him on the ground. "Let's see what we can see, then."

They linked their Power, blended it, and reached out together through the mesh. As Namid had thought, it touched on every part of the ghost city and connected it all together. Namid cringed as the sliminess wrapped around her, but she found she sensed more clearly through the mesh, sensed even more of the Power.

A few strands of the mesh extended beyond the city walls. She felt blood Power pulsing through them as it was pulled from the city. One strand had a familiar feel to it. When she followed it, far beyond the city walls, she found Ilenii.

At her start of surprise and apprehension, Aahmes drew them both back to themselves.

"Did she notice us?" Aahmes said.

"Didn't seem like it."

"Good."

The city flickered around them, a deep bell tolled and the ground shook. Then all was still.

"So that's where they draw the Power from," Aahmes

said in a low voice, his eyes closed against the blood that ran from them again.

Namid stretched out on one side on the ground to wait for the agony in her head to subside, the pain and bleeding from her tongue to stop.

~*Wager that's how the blood Power returns, too,?*~ she said through thought-speech.

~*Must be.*~ Aahmes agreed. ~*Without having to kill more, anyway.*~

~*At least they're very far away,*~ Namid commented.

"And I think the city moved," Aahmes said aloud, then grimaced when his stomach growled. "With the way time is different here, I don't think we can stay here too long."

Namid looked up at him, watched him pull out a waterskin and some food. He handed her the food while he again rinsed away blood. She handed the food back and accepted the waterskin he held out when he had finished with it. After she rinsed the blood from her mouth, she took back some of the food and ate, taking small bites, cautious of her still-swollen tongue.

"I didn't sense that any of the 'gods' noticed us near," Aahmes said.

Namid shook her head. "Me neither. For Ilenii anyway, it felt like she just pulls on the blood Power but otherwise pays it little attention."

"A few thousand winters of doing that," Aahmes said. "They probably don't even think about it."

"Blood…" a whisper said.

"Oh, good. They're back," Aahmes said as he stood and helped Namid to her feet. His tone sounded less than pleased.

"What about blood?" Namid asked the whispers. "Can the blood Power restore Nazextas?"

"Can we survive using it to do that?" Aahmes added.

An unexpected footstep sounded from their left but when Namid turned, she only glimpsed a bit of pale blue cloth as it disappeared around the corner of a nearby building.

"There's someone else here?" Aahmes said as he drew a dagger.

Namid tilted her head the direction she had seen the cloth.

~*Didn't look ghostly,*~ Namid said.

She grabbed the packs and joined Aahmes as he crept toward the corner. They paused when they reached it, then leaned around for a quick look.

They jumped back just as quickly, as their look had put them no more than a handspan away from a thin man who looked back at them.

He chuckled and came around the corner.

"Nice to know you're both more cautious now," he said.

Aahmes and Namid exchanged glances.

"Come," the man beckoned them toward the tower and headed that direction himself. "It will be less disorienting if we're inside. Also, perhaps you'll find out what you need."

After exchanging another look, Namid and Aahmes followed the stranger.

"Who are you?" Namid called to him. The man did not look like he was moving very fast, but he stayed a pace ahead of them. He did not answer her.

The man led them partway around the tower's base, then pushed open a door in the side and urged them within.

"Not sure this is a good idea," Namid muttered.

Aahmes nodded his agreement, then paused. "Did you feel that?"

Namid paused too and closed her eyes to better concentrate on the faint vibration that thrummed through the blood Power mesh.

"It's the others! Get inside," the man insisted. "They'll not sense us in there."

With simultaneous shrugs, they followed him into the

tower. He pushed the door shut behind them and leaned against it.

The walls inside gave off a faint glow, enough for them to see they stood in a large, circular room, barren of any furnishings. A staircase wound its way up along the wall and disappeared through a hole in the ceiling a couple of paces above them.

Namid set the packs on the floor at her feet and studied the stranger.

He stood a few finger-widths shorter than Namid and had the same golden-brown skin, dark eyes, and straight, white hair that the Shadower Keizha had. But this man looked older. Although he had moved sprightly enough, Namid judged by the wrinkles in the skin of his face and hands that he was well beyond a couple score years older than herself. He wore a simple, pale-blue robe, long enough that it brushed the floor.

When she became aware the man studied her in return, she looked away.

The man chuckled again.

"You don't remember me," he said.

Namid looked back at him. "Should I?"

The man shrugged. "I suppose not. You were not at your best. And injured. It was when you were in the city before."

Namid glanced at Aahmes, who shrugged. She turned her thoughts back to the first time she had been in Nazextas and, after several long breaths-of-time, the memory came to her.

"It was after the Power slammed me into the wall," Namid said. "I only saw the bottom of your robe and your shoe, and wasn't even certain I had actually seen those."

They all looked down as the man stuck one white-clad shoe out from beneath his robe.

"Not surprising. Let's at least be a little comfortable."

He nodded to a spot behind Aahmes and Namid, where three chairs now stood.

The man led the way to them, muttering as he did so. "Just hope we have the time."

When they had all seated themselves, he folded his hands in his lap and gave each of them a small smile.

"To answer you from earlier, my name is Vlatas."

Aahmes groaned and dropped his head to his hands. "The *'god'* Vlatas?" he mumbled.

The man shrugged. "Well, yes. Although not nearly as much of a god as I had intended those many long years ago. I've been trapped in the city since this all happened to it. And you two are descended from another of the 'gods'. Sesaisyd."

Namid nodded.

"And some of the others hunt you and you've somehow gotten caught in the blood Power mesh that entangles Nazextas," Vlatas said. "Something went wrong when Sesaisyd's Power came to you. This"—he waved a hand at them—"is *not* what should have happened."

"Wonderful," Aahmes muttered, his tone sarcastic. "So what is it that *should* have happened?"

"You would have gotten his ability to sense and use Wild Power," Vlatas said brightly. "Always. Not just when the moons are all dark."

Namid and Aahmes exchanged glances.

"And you did, I can see. But how did the rest come to you?"

"What does that matter?" Namid said. "We need to find a way to get rid of it before it kills us."

"Assuredly. But how you got it might lead to a solution."

"Nothing came to us at all until I broke the sword to keep the Dark Priests from claiming the Power it took from Sesaisyd," Aahmes said.

"Sword?" Vlatas voice rose in his astonishment. "Akavos? You broke Akavos?"

At their nods, he looked troubled.

"But how can that be? That's not what he made the

sword to do."

"What who made it to do?" Namid said.

"What was it supposed to do?" Aahmes asked at the same time.

Vlatas shook his head in consternation and stood up. "I think it best if you see for yourselves. Come along. And bring your things, just in case."

He led the way to the staircase, but around underneath it to stairs that led down. He called up a light orb similar to those Aahmes and Namid used and spoke as they headed down.

"Sesaisyd is the one who created the sword Akavos. He pulled Wild Power into its forging. Made it hard for any of the rest of us to sense. He had come to believe that we should not have been stealing the Power we had been from people of lesser Power. The sword was supposed to pull the stolen Power from us."

"But I learned from the Dark Priests that the blade had been forged to *bind* Sesaisyd. And sometime later, someone had distorted that into an imperative to kill him but bind his Power," Namid said.

With a thoughtful look, Vlatas shrugged.

"That's untrue about the original purpose. But I can see some of the others changing the blade to turn it against Sesaisyd. At first none of us wanted to give up that Power. And such a thing in his hands didn't make him any friends among us."

"At first?"

"Since then, I've come to believe as he did," Vlatas said. "So many hundreds of years of nothing much to do but ponder can change a person's view."

He stared into the distance, then pulled his gaze back to them with a start.

"Anyway, Sesaisyd hid the finished blade in this city and, to get it and destroy it, the rest of us banded together. That was one of the very few times we did such a thing."

"Again, not the story we heard," Namid said. "Even

the whispers here last time said the Dark Priests came for Akavos."

Vlatas nodded, his expression grim. "Yes, that's what we led the people here to believe. So they would oppose Sesaisyd and keep him from whisking the blade away from us to another hiding place."

"But something went wrong here, too," Aahmes said.

"Horribly wrong. Here we are." Vlatas stopped at a door on their right and touched it with a small bit of Power. It swung open away from them and he led the way into the small room beyond.

As the light from his orb spread through the room a slender shape hanging upright in the exact middle caught it and reflected it back to them, then began to glow on its own. Vlatas brightened the orb and stepped to one side to let them approach.

"Akavos?" Namid blurted.

CHAPTER 20

Namid stared at the sword that she had last seen shattered into bits.

"How can that be here?" Aahmes breathed. He took a step toward it, one hand stretched out to clasp the hilt.

"It's no good," Vlatas warned. "This is only an echo of Akavos. From the time before the destruction of Nazextas."

Aahmes gave him an enigmatic look. He clasped the hilt and hefted the glowing sword.

"How? I don't believe it!" Vlatas said.

Aahmes shrugged. "It feels a little different from the one I broke," he said. "Lighter. And I can feel the Wild Power in it. I didn't in Corentris."

"But that shouldn't be possible," Vlatas stammered.

Aahmes shrugged again. "Maybe because of the Wild Power heritage from Sesaisyd...."

Vlatas looked from Aahmes to Namid and back. "I suppose that could explain it. It still might exist only within these walls, though."

"So even though this is extraordinary, it still might be no help for us," Namid said.

"I didn't say that," Vlatas said. "Let's return upstairs."

He continued speaking as they climbed the stairs. "You need to sever the hold, the connection the blood Power has on you, on your own Power. Perhaps Akavos is exactly what you need to do that. That speaks very much to its original purpose. Perhaps this echo of the sword retains that original purpose."

"And how do we use it?" Aahmes said.

"That I don't know," Vlatas admitted. "When I came here with the others, we'd planned to wrest the sword from Sesaisyd so he couldn't take all our Power to himself. I never learned how it was supposed to have worked. We thought he might even have meant to kill us all. It fit the way we all usually interacted."

"Maybe much like other uses of Power," Namid said. "Directed Power and intent?"

"Maybe," Vlatas said.

When they reached the main level again, the chairs were gone, the room again empty. Namid caught a glimpse of a large, rough-surfaced floor covering that looked oddly like a map. It filled the room. Then it vanished. The others did not seem to have seen it.

"So if you were here to grab the sword," Aahmes said, "does that mean Sesaisyd and his followers were here to stop you? And what happened to cause this? We've heard several different versions."

"An unfortunate and unlikely convergence of Power," Vlatas said. "Boudra trying to defend the city against the wrong people. Sesaisyd and his followers defending themselves. And the rest of us throwing Power around to try to find the sword and hamper each other, trying to get the sword first even though we'd said we'd work together."

"So trying to pull the blood Power from ourselves now wouldn't cause something similar," Namid said.

"I wouldn't think so," Vlatas said. "But I doubt it'll work. The blood Power in you is tied to all of it around us,

221

including me, all the spirits of the city, and the remaining 'gods'. I don't think you can just pull away one part."

Aahmes got a stubborn look on his face and shared a look with Namid. "Maybe not, but I think we have to try."

Namid dropped down to sit on the floor, suddenly tired. "Maybe rest first?"

Vlatas sighed. "You can rest here a breath-of-time, but you shouldn't sleep. If you do, you risk becoming trapped in the city as I am. And being part of the city as it is, you might not be able to get the sword to work for you. I've certainly been unable to get anything of significance to work."

"Wonderful," Namid muttered. She slipped her pack off her back and stood again. She reached toward the sword. "Then let's see what we can do with this."

With a nod, Aahmes set his pack on the ground next to hers and together they clasped the hilt of the sword, standing in the center of the room. Vlatas hurried away to stand by the wall.

When nothing immediately happened, Namid grinned. "That's a good start, anyway. Nothing happening without our intention."

Aahmes matched her expression and held out his other hand for her clasp. "I think try directing Wild Power into the sword first," he said. "Together but without blending it."

Namid nodded and reached out to draw Wild Power to herself. But no matter how hard she tried, she still was unable to reach any.

A questioning look to Aahmes got a shake of his head in response.

"I'd wondered whether you could even call on any Wild Power from within Nazextas," Vlatas said.

Aahmes shrugged. "So we see if we can do anything with our own Power," he said.

Namid frowned, but nodded her agreement and they linked for that. With the familiar snap, their Power blended. Under their direction, it flowed to the sword. Namid felt the usual headache building but kept her attention on guiding the sword to sever the ties the blood Power had to them.

Concentrating, they used their Power to direct the sword's Power to the blood Power tethers that linked them to the city and tried to slice through. But the different Powers balked a short distance from each other. The harder they tried to push with their own Power, the more resistance they met.

As Namid's headache screamed through her head, she reluctantly pulled the Power back. Aahmes did likewise.

And they both sank to the ground, in agony and bleeding again – both from a multitude of slices on their arms this time.

A breath-of-time Vlatas stood and studied them, then retrieved waterskins from their packs and a couple of old shirts and helped them clean up.

"You're going to have to do this from outside Nazextas," he said as they finished. "It's clear this won't work from here."

"But can we even take the sword with us?" Namid said.

"Unlikely," Vlatas said. "You said it was destroyed out there." He waved a hand vaguely away from them.

"And this one is only an echo," Namid murmured. She turned her gaze to Aahmes. "So now what?"

"Easy," Vlatas said. "You'll have to restore the city. Make it so it's no longer the Spirit-City."

"Of course," Aahmes said. "Simple as that."

Namid chuckled.

"Perhaps not simple," Vlatas said with a frown. "But I think it can work. I've had some time to consider this, among other things…."

He held his hand out for the sword, but as Aahmes passed it to him, it slipped from their grasp and shattered on the floor, in eerie silence, into shards much like those they had seen when Aahmes shattered the real sword.

These shards sparkled as they dissipated into the air. One small shard was left behind in Aahmes' hand. He closed his fist around it before Namid caught more than a glimpse of it. Before Vlatas seemed aware of it at all, Aahmes tucked it into a pouch on his belt.

"Which reminds me," Namid said, "you claim to have been captive here all this time, and yet the stories say you were one of the 'gods' who confronted and defeated Sesaisyd. So how much can you reach beyond this captivity? And what can you really do?"

Vlatas studied her, then slowly shook his head. "Your stories are wrong. I was never there. I've been here since all this happened." He waved both arms at the faintly glowing walls around them. "Must've been one of the others taking my place."

Namid shuddered at the animosity in Vlatas' voice, especially because his expression showed no sign of it. The look Vlatas gave her was serene but with a hint of puzzlement.

"I've been able to sort of keep track of events out there. A little. But it's a long time. Nothing much has caught my attention after they felled Sesaisyd and turned him over to those people who called themselves his Priests. Power-grubbing little mages – worse than we ever were."

Aahmes and Namid exchanged looks and gathered up their packs.

Their actions did not escape Vlatas' notice. He gave them an approving smile. "Too right. You mustn't linger. Too long in the city and you'll not be able to stay awake. And then you'll be trapped here, too."

He pushed them toward the door with surprising strength. "And besides, you must find the key to draw the city back together."

Aahmes resisted his push. "Now there's a key, too? What key?"

Then Vlatas had them out the door of the tower and

back in the courtyard. The pressure against her back ceased and Namid turned to question Vlatas further.

But he was gone.

Aahmes grumbled something under his breath but did not repeat it at Namid's questioning look.

"Well," she said.

Aahmes looked around at the deserted city. "I think I hate that about this place," he muttered. He met her gaze. "Want to try getting the whispers to give us any further cryptic hints?" he said.

Namid shrugged her pack onto her shoulders. "Like what?"

Aahmes looked back at the tower. Namid followed his gaze and saw that the door had vanished now, too. "Do we even believe anything he said?" she muttered.

Aahmes shrugged and headed toward one of the streets that led out of the courtyard. "Who knows. He sounded a little... off there at the end."

Namid nodded her agreement. "So, some key," she said.

"Key to draw the city back together..." a whisper said, sliding past her in a breath of air.

"Yeah, thanks," Aahmes said. "Not very useful."

"Think we need to return to Corentris and see if we can somehow call Akavos back into existence?" Namid said

Aahmes snorted. "Right. How? As I remember, the shards it broke into flew into us. Seems like doing that would be much what we need to get rid of the blood Power and if we could do that, we wouldn't have the problem."

Namid growled a soft curse.

They walked several long breaths-of-time in silence. Namid found it harder and harder to put one foot in front of the other as fatigue swept over her and tried to drop her in her tracks. She stumbled several times as she tried to keep to her feet and struggled to keep her eyes from closing.

"This came on us fast," Aahmes said after he stumbled a couple of times, too. With their free arms around each other's waists, they supported each other. "I didn't think we'd been here that long."

"Maybe while we were in the tower the city moved and we just didn't feel it," Namid said. "It seemed like each move was a real day for us before. I assume that wouldn't have changed."

"Got to get out of here."

"Which way?"

"Here." Aahmes guided Namid through several twists and turns until they found themselves back in the small square where they had arrived.

Namid slumped against a wall but forced herself to stay upright to keep from falling asleep.

"If it's been a couple of days or more, think the amulets'll work again."

Aahmes gave her a perplexed look. After some thought, he seemed to realize what she meant.

"Maybe. Wouldn't want to risk it, though. Can't concentrate." Even standing against the wall, his eyes drifted shut. With a start he snapped them open again and pushed away from the wall. He wrapped an arm around Namid's waist again.

"Got to keep moving," he mumbled. "Only way to get out."

Afterward, Namid was uncertain how they managed it, but she and Aahmes stumbled through more streets and found the city wall and a gate.

A toll of the now-familiar bell, the bright light, and the ground shook, knocking them from their feet. It was all Namid could do to crawl the last bit to the gate, Aahmes right next to her.

The gate swung open as they neared, and they fell through.

CHAPTER 21

Aahmes and Namid fell only a short distance but landed hard on damp, cold ground. Before she got her bearings, Namid began to slide down a steep slope, scraping through the moist earth and over rocks and low brush. Sudden fear of sliding off some cliff cleared the fog of fatigue from her wits and she grabbed wildly for anything to stop her slide.

Before she could grasp anything more substantial than grasses that tore free in her hands, her side slammed into a large rock. The impact knocked the breath out of her, but she stopped sliding.

"Aahmes?" she called when she caught her breath. She heard no other sounds in the night and feared to move too much and possibly dislodge the rock she lay against. Nazextas stood further up the steep slope from where she lay. The city gave off little light. The gate stood closed.

"I'm here," Aahmes said from somewhere behind Namid. "Hold there for now. That rock looks a little loose from you hitting it."

Namid concentrated on trying to breathe better around the pain in her side rather than on how loose the rock might be. She looked around as much as she could without moving from where she lay.

Her path down the slope was clear to see – a scraped area in the dirt and grasses. To one side, above her in her current position, she could just make out the trunks of some trees in the dim moonlight. The air was cold, but she saw no snow in the limited view she had.

Scuffling sounds near her feet caught her attention.

"I'm here," Aahmes said. "Grab my hands."

Namid shifted to be able to see, and yelped as the rock shifted with her. Then Aahmes lunged for her and she met him and clasped him close.

The rock that had caught her tumbled down the slope, crashing through brush and small trees in its path.

Aahmes and Namid began to slide again but managed to stop themselves after a few paces by digging the heels of their boots into the dirt downhill from them.

"I'm awake now," Namid quipped.

Aahmes clasped her tightly a breath-of-time longer and chuckled softly, then eased his grip. He still kept hold of her though, as they worked their way sideways to a nearby tree to prop themselves against.

Namid looked up the hill again in time to see Nazextas contract into a vaporous swirl and disappear. She scrutinized their surroundings then.

They stood braced against a pine tree on a steep, rocky slope. Other pines grew scattered across the parts of the hill she could see. Otherwise, low grasses and shrubs dominated the area, all dried and leafless for the winter. The dirt was dark, gritty and damp at the same time. Namid twisted to look down the slope and nearly knocked them both loose.

They clutched the tree trunk, heedless of the rough bark, and held on as they worked to get their feet under them again.

But Namid did get a glimpse further downhill.

After many paces, the trees grew thicker and it looked

like the slope eased off. But how to get there without further injury?

Aahmes followed her gaze. "I just know this is going to be enjoyable," he said. His tone indicated anything but.

Namid continued to study what she could see in the dim moonlight and tried to pick a pathway down.

"Any idea where we might be now?" she said. "The trees and grasses, even the dirt, don't look like anything I've seen before. This doesn't look like the Arinsk Mountains."

"Damp, no snow – at least not right now," Aahmes muttered. "Maybe we're in Denek. Or northern Yiruny, possibly. I don't think I've been to this area, but these trees look like ones I remember from traveling through that area many winters ago."

"Hmm, all right. I think I see a way we can get down without too much damage to ourselves." She pointed to one side, where at least the hill had several less-steep areas between their level and the trees.

Together they struggled across the slope and down. They slipped many times but managed to keep from falling, or sliding too much. They paused within the thicker grove of trees to take stock.

Dirt covered both of them, with twigs and bits of leaves mixed in. Their clothes were torn, and they sported several scrapes. But nothing worse.

Namid sat on a relatively level spot and tried to fight a yawn. "Need to find a place to hole up," she mumbled around further yawns that would not be suppressed. "That surge of energy's going fast."

Aahmes nodded and stifled a yawn of his own while he looked around.

"Maybe something over there." He pointed to their left. "I think I see larger rocks, so maybe a cave. Otherwise, we might have to climb a tree."

Namid shook her head as she drug herself back to her feet. "Not climbing a tree. I'd probably fall right back out

– if I even made it up to begin with."

Helping each other, they stumbled through the trees, bleary-eyed and fighting to stay awake long enough to find shelter.

At first, the rocks Aahmes had spotted looked less promising as they approached. But when they eased around them, they found a small hollow on the other side – big enough to give them shelter on three sides.

With a groan, Namid crawled in. Aahmes followed on her heels and together they drew on Wild Power to create a defensive shell across the opening. Namid just managed to pull her arms from the straps of her pack before she fell into a deep slumber.

~ ~ ~

Her side hurt, also one foot and her head. And her arm was numb.

With a soft groan, Namid tried to roll over, but could not. She could barely move. Had she been locked away somewhere?

She pushed frantically against a weight pressed against her and heard a familiar groan. Aahmes.

With a deep breath to help calm herself, she curled close to him. He wrapped an arm around her and buried his face in her hair.

"All right?" he murmured.

She nodded. "Mostly. Sore, though. And I'll need to get up soon. Find a handy bush."

He chuckled into her hair. "Yeah, me too. But I'd rather stay like this."

"Yeah, me too."

But all too soon they did have to pull themselves from their shelter. Namid had no idea how long they had slept. A thin layer of snow covered everything, and gray light filtered through thick clouds. Daytime, at least, but she was not even sure what time of day.

They set up a rough camp and tended their injuries the best they could. Then they dug out some food from their packs and huddled together in their shelter with a small fire at the opening.

After she had silenced the grumbling of her stomach, Namid shifted around to look at Aahmes.

"All right, let me see the shard," she said.

Aahmes' confused expression dissolved as he figured out what she meant. He reached into a pouch and pulled out the piece of the sword he had kept. When he dropped it into her hand, Namid saw that it was not truly a shard of the sword itself, but rather of—

"The black jewel?"

"Seems so," Aahmes said. "Or an echo of it that is somehow solid."

Namid studied the shard of the jewel in her palm. It was still roughly oval-shaped, a little shorter than the length of her thumb. Parts of it looked chipped away, forming sharp edges without marring the overall oval shape. She returned it to Aahmes when he held his hand out for it and noticed a hint of Wild Power from it as she did so.

"Did you sense that?" Aahmes said.

Namid nodded. "Maybe this jewel-shard is what holds the Wild Power for the sword? Could explain why it's still here when the rest isn't."

"Maybe." He tucked it away again.

Namid pulled one of his arms around her shoulder and snuggled close.

"If I wanted to live in a cave, I'd say let's just stay here. Barring the blood Power, of course."

Aahmes nodded agreement then he twisted around so he could look at her. "Wherever you want to stay, or go, I'd be with you."

Namid considered his expression, then leaned close for a long kiss.

"And I want you to," she said when they parted, both a

little breathless.

Slowly Aahmes smiled, as if not quite sure he believed what he heard. He drew her into his arms. She leaned against him with a smile. For several breaths-of-time they just sat there and watched the fire.

"I would build you a home that you wouldn't get chased out of," Aahmes murmured. Then he laughed softly.

"What?" Namid said.

"Although I imagine you'd want to have a hand in the building of it," he said.

And Namid laughed with him. "Of course." She turned in his arms to look up at him. "Are you actually offering?"

He met her gaze with a serious expression. Then his gaze slid away from hers and he brushed his hair back from his face with one hand.

"This is not how I'd thought to do this," he muttered as he dug something out of one of his pouches. "And they're still rougher than I had hoped. But I don't think I want to risk waiting...."

He held out one hand to her. In his palm rested two silvery-blue rings, one larger than the other but otherwise matching in style, shiny, with a faint design that looked etched into the metal. Namid picked up the smaller one and looked closer. The design was stars mixed with what looked like swords or daggers.

She looked up to find Aahmes studying her from little more than a finger-length away. "I don't know the formal way this works – I've never been there for it or been told what to say. And I have *no* idea what the tradition is in the Six Realms.... But, will you have me? To be paired?" he said, his voice cracked a little, betraying his nervousness.

Namid did not trust her voice so she only nodded. Aahmes treated her to the largest smile she had ever seen from him and swept her into his arms.

She held him tightly a breath-of-time, then pushed him back a handspan. When he released her with a question in his expression, she only grinned.

"I want to put it on before I drop it," she said. "Or are you supposed to put it on my finger?"

Aahmes looked chagrined while still smiling at the same time. "I don't know."

"Well, then…" Namid snagged the larger ring from Aahmes' hand and slipped it onto his left thumb. She held the smaller ring out to him. "Your turn."

With a diffident smile, Aahmes took the ring and eased it onto Namid's thumb. All the while he held her gaze with his own.

She vaguely noticed the light getting brighter – the clouds must be breaking up. That was nice.

Namid continued to hold Aahmes' gaze as she leaned close for a good, long kiss, losing herself in the sensation.

The bluish light that seeped into the alcove grew in intensity. That seemed off, somehow.

Namid reluctantly pulled away from Aahmes, squinting in the glare.

Just outside the opening of their hollow, two small indistinctly shaped glowing figures hovered a finger-width above the ground. The bluish glow that surrounded them was almost too bright to look at. She groaned as she recognized the creatures: they indicated the so-called gods' special attention, whether for good or ill. She doubted in their case that it was good.

Aahmes cursed under his breath and scrambled to gather their stuff. Namid helped, dousing the fire and grabbing her own pack when Aahmes finished. They stepped around the creatures and tried to ignore how they turned to follow their every move.

"Think they were watching Nazextas somehow?" Namid said.

"Could be. Can you step us out of here?"

With a nod, Namid reached for the Wild Power in the area and found it with no effort. She held it ready as she searched around them for a good place to step to. She heard Aahmes suggest they do many shorter steps, if that would be faster, so she settled on the first likely spot she sensed. She also sensed Aahmes drawing on Wild Power to give them the veneer of nothingness.

"Won't last long," he muttered. "But should give us what we need."

"Ready?"

They both gave the area a last look to make sure they had not missed anything, then Namid took Aahmes' hand and stepped them away.

CHAPTER 22

As she had done the previous spring when Aahmes had been wounded, Namid looked through the Power for another good location and stepped again. After several more of these search-and-steps, Namid sank to the ground in a thick copse of trees.

"I don't think I can do another one right now," she said.

Aahmes reached out to the Wild Power around them to see what he could sense while Namid dug out a waterskin and drank.

"I think we're clear of them," Aahmes said several long breaths-of-time later. He took the skin that Namid held out to him and settled next to her.

"After we rest some, I think we should go further," Namid said as she leaned against his shoulder.

"I think I can do a few steps," Aahmes said. "I've done it before, just not as far as you've brought us."

"It's harder to do with the Wild Power," Namid said.

Aahmes shrugged. "The travel technique isn't something we can use in these forested mountains, so I'll take what I can get."

Namid wrapped her arms around his closest arm and looked up at him. "I didn't get to ask earlier… is there a certain, customary amount of time after a couple becomes a pair that they must wait before they pledge to each other?"

Aahmes' surprised look gave way to a smile. "If there is, I don't know of it. But don't you nobles of the Six Realms have rules about that sort of thing? Aren't you supposed to wait a long time to come to know each other better?"

"I'm sure there *are* some rules. But I don't know them. And none of those rule-bound nobles are here right now." She gave him a sidelong look. "And how long have we known each other?"

"Good point," Aahmes admitted. "Ten winters, maybe a bit longer."

"Exactly. Plenty long. I'd pledge to you – now." She gave him another sidelong look. "I'll wager you've been working on the other rings, the pledge rings, too. Although when you've found the time…."

Aahmes grinned. "I *have* been working on the others, the pledge rings. But they're not yet done."

He reached into the same pouch and pulled out two more rings. Made of the same metal, these two were elaborate filigrees of stars and daggers to harmonize with the plainer thumb rings. Attached to each was a fine chain of the same metal. As she looked closer, Namid saw that some areas of the filigree were less detailed and rougher than others. Still….

"Beautiful," she breathed.

Aahmes ducked his head. "I find I like working with the metal. And I've even been able to use the Wild Power to do it. Just need to attach the chain to the thumb ring."

He plopped down on the ground beneath one of the trees and pulled his ring from his thumb. Namid sat next to him to watch as he used the thinnest tendril of Wild Power to fuse the last link of the chain to the right spot on his thumb ring.

He spoke while he worked.

"You do know, of course, that you'll not get out of the big celebration and all the fuss by doing this? I'm sure your mother will insist on something large and fancy to formally tie us together as far as the Six Realms nobility are concerned."

Namid laughed. "I don't doubt it at all. I can survive it if you can."

"It'll make her happy, I think."

"Yeah, no doubt about that. And what of the clans? Won't we have to go through some ceremony or celebratory fuss with them, too?"

"Possibly," Aahmes said after he had considered that. "It would probably depend on the new chieftain. And if we choose to allow them any say."

"The clans don't require approval from someone in authority within the clan to be recognized as pledged?"

"I'm not sure. I think it varies from clan to clan. But because of my perceived position within our clan, it would only be the chieftain's say, if anyone's."

Aahmes handed her his now-joined rings in exchange for her thumb ring. He repeated the process with hers, then held a hand out for her hand.

"Again, I don't know the proper, official way this is done. But I do remember one part that I heard as a boy, mostly uninterested in the whole thing at the time." He eased the two rings onto the thumb and first finger of her left hand.

"I am yours, my beloved, and you are mine," he said in a low voice. He looked at Namid to see her reaction and gave her a relieved smile when she nodded and smiled.

She held her hand out for his and placed his rings on his thumb and finger.

"I'm yours, my beloved. And you are mine."

For a long breath-of-time, they gazed at each other then, with smiles, shared a deep, long kiss.

"We need to find someplace to hole up for a while," Aahmes murmured against her lips.

Namid readily agreed.

~ ~ ~

The cave they found two more steps away served them well for the time they spent there to recover from their visit to Nazextas and hurried departure. Another reason they lingered was to take some time to just be alone together.

Early their third day there, something woke Namid from a sound sleep. She held herself still as she tried to figure out what woke her. From the pale light that came in the cave entrance, she judged it was only a little after dawn.

She shifted and Aahmes tightened his arm around her.

"It woke you, too," he said.

"Yeah, but what?"

"I haven't sensed anything specific. Another one of those vague feelings. I think we need to move again."

Namid raised herself on one arm, with a small gasp at the cold air that hit her bare skin as the covers slid off. She scooted up to give Aahmes a quick kiss, then hauled the covers back over them both.

"Yeah, that's what it feels like to me, too. Maybe in a little bit?"

Aahmes smiled and pulled her close to lie atop him. "I think we have some time."

~ ~ ~

Later Aahmes renewed the veneer of nothingness he had been holding over them any time they were not in some sort of shelter. They repacked everything they had hauled out while they stayed at the cave and scattered the evidence of their fire.

Namid reached out to the Wild Power but sensed no

threat nearby. Next she called up a memory of the map she had studied many years ago that showed the Six Realms of the Monarch. Paronia sat in the center of the six realms. The realm of Denek sat to the north and north-west, north of Yiruny which sat west of Paronia.

"So, assuming we're in Denek, we need to go south, at least," she said. "Maybe east."

"You're thinking to head to Rhadanthus?"

"Or Corentris. They should both be roughly south of where we are now."

Aahmes looked thoughtful. "You think perhaps this key is somewhere in Corentris, maybe?"

Namid shoved the last of the things into her pack and straightened. "I'm not sure what to think about the key at all. Could Vlatas have been trying to mislead us?"

Aahmes pondered that while he shouldered his pack. "So many have, it's certainly possible." He paused and his gaze grew distant. Then he turned back to Namid.

"Better take a look at the blood Power strands," he told her.

She turned her attention to her own Power, entwined with the blood Power as it was, and looked through it to the blood mesh they had discovered in Nazextas. Bit by bit, the mesh became visible in the sunshine, with even more blood-red strands that reached out from her into the distance. Too many to follow. And a great many that tied her and Aahmes together. These were a deep, dark red, almost black. Something about them made her even more uneasy than she had been before.

As she tried to figure out what it was, a quiver ran through the mesh. The unpleasant pull on her Power seemed familiar.

Namid reached out with a small bit of Power and extended her senses along the mesh, trying to learn more.

When she came out of the Power, she shared a worried look with Aahmes.

"The so-called gods are drawing heavily on the blood

Power," she said.

He nodded his agreement. "I couldn't tell who, though. I think three of them. Maybe four."

"I couldn't tell where they are, either," Namid added. "Which I hope means they can't use this thing," she flapped a hand in the air, indicating the mesh, "to tell where we are, either. All I sensed is that they are nowhere nearby."

She narrowed her eyes and examined the mesh a breath-of-time longer through the Power while she toyed with some ideas.

"What is it?" Aahmes said.

Namid released the last little bit of Power she held and shrugged. "Maybe nothing. A couple of ideas of something to try. But let's find a new place, first. Just in case."

With a nod, Aahmes shouldered his pack and clasped her hand. "I'll take us south-east. That should be at least close to the direction we want, no matter where we end up going."

Namid hefted her pack and they stepped.

~ ~ ~

Two steps away from where they began the day, they found another cave alcove to shelter in. It sat low on the north side of one of the mountains, which put the bulk of the mountain between them and where they suspected any of the 'gods' might be. The cave opening was small, but the inside was wide, and tall enough for Aahmes to stand upright. Barely. Namid wondered fleetingly why no animal sheltered there for the winter. They did that, didn't they?

"Let's wait to set up a camp," Namid said, "in case this attracts attention."

"And just what is the 'this'?"

Namid dropped her pack to the side of the cave opening, tucked it in with some rocks and indicated for Aahmes to do the same, then led him further into the cave.

"A couple of things I thought of," Namid said. "First I want to see if maybe we can use Wild Power to cut a strand of this." She waved a hand and watched the blood mesh ripple with her motion.

"All right. I can see where this could draw their attention."

"Maybe. Who knows? Would you please set up the defense shell?"

Aahmes used Wild Power to enclose them within the cave in a shell designed to make it seem that no one was there and also contain any loose Power. Then Namid drew on Wild Power.

"I'll try it alone first," she said.

She formed the Wild Power into a sort of blade and tried to slice through one of the strands that connected her to Aahmes. The Power met some slight resistance, then passed through as if neither Power touched the other.

"Together, then?" Aahmes said.

They both gathered Wild Power and linked together and repeated what Namid had tried. With the same result. They tried to seize one of the blood strands with Wild Power with no different result.

Aahmes frowned, then pulled the small black shard from a pouch. "Maybe try with this?"

So they tried drawing on the tiny amount of Power in the shard, tried feeding Wild Power into it, tried reaching through the shard with Power to grasp the strands. They even tried variations on who took the lead on guiding the Power. Nothing.

They grabbed waterskins for drinks and settled at the cave opening to rest.

Aahmes leaned back against the wall and closed his eyes. "I hate to suggest it…."

"Try next with our own Power?"

"And the blood Power, too."

Namid frowned but nodded. "Exhaust all the possibilities we can think of."

"Especially before we encounter any of the 'gods' again. I'd rather not be trying to peel the blood Power away from us while fighting them at the same time."

Namid dug another waterskin out of her pack and the already bloodied shirt she had used to clean up in Nazextas. With a nod, Aahmes pulled the same from his pack.

"Ready?"

"As much as I think I can be. I suggest we try with the smallest amount of Power we can manage, though. Might keep the wounding to a minimum."

Aahmes gave her a skeptical look, then agreed. So they repeated their attempts to cut a strand of the blood mesh. First, they used their own Power while they held the twined blood Power separate as much as they could, then they used the two together, then they tried only the blood Power.

Namid daubed at the blood that dropped from her nose and sighed.

"Not even a hint that we might be on the right track," she muttered. "Although I think the blood Power at least touched the strand. Maybe stuck to it a little. And at least no sign we're drawing any unwanted attention."

Aahmes leaned back against the cave wall with his eyes closed, a dampened sleeve of his shirt over his face to catch the blood from his eyes.

"I can think of one more thing we might try, but I think even if it works, we're likely to have even worse wounding than we've had to this point."

"Well, *that* doesn't sound good."

Aahmes grinned. "No. But I have a feeling it just might work. We use blood Power alone and instead of trying to slice one of the strands, we try to break it. Pull on it until it gives way."

Namid considered that, her head tilted. "I agree," she said finally. "But we have no way to predict how badly this might injure us. Maybe we should have brought the others after all."

"Do you want to go back for them?"

"No, I don't think so. I still think our reasons for leaving them behind are valid. And Mehratar hasn't been able to help much at all with the wounds from the Power anyway. Let's just prepare the best we can for this."

She pulled out their blankets and the last full waterskin. And Aahmes pulled out a couple of the parchment packets that contained the herbs from Haeith. He also spread out their blankets, cushioning the floor as much as he could. Namid looked at what they had and sighed. It looked like so little to deal with potentially too much.

She met Aahmes' gaze. "Let's try it."

Together they drew on the Wild Power and renewed their protective shells. Then they stretched out on their blankets, clasped hands and twined their Power together, focusing on using the blood Power. The blood Power they carried blended. With it, they clutched opposite ends of one of the dark strands that linked them and pulled.

Namid sensed a tremor ripple through the other strands that joined her to Aahmes, but it did not extend beyond them. The strand she grasped writhed and seemed to be trying to slip from the Power she wrapped around it. She pulled harder and the strand stretched taut between her and Aahmes. Something tugged painfully within her, but she also felt something give slightly.

She pulled harder.

Without warning, the blood strand snapped. The loose ends whipped back on both of them. And the sudden release of tension threw them physically away from each other.

Breathless, Namid lay where she fell. Again, she could not see, and she felt blood running down her face like tears. Her hands and feet burned and the half-healed slashes on her arms felt like they had all split open again. Her head pounded in time with her heartbeat and she could not seem to catch her breath.

Someone groaned, but she did not know if it was her or Aahmes. Another groan, and she knew that one was him. At least he could groan.

After lying there to gather her strength, Namid rolled toward the sound of Aahmes' voice and pulled herself across the floor toward where she thought their bedding lay.

"That was a surprise," Aahmes said from somewhere ahead of her. She could barely hear him. He sounded in as much pain as she was.

"I can't see again," he continued. "It sounds like you're getting close."

"I can't see, either," Namid said. "Do you have the cloths and waterskin?"

"Not yet." She heard some rustling then.

She continued toward the blankets, so she hoped anyway, pausing frequently for the agony from moving to ease enough that she could start up again. After too long, she felt the bedding under her arms. Then she bumped into Aahmes.

By feel, she took the waterskin he handed her and some cloth and one of the herb packets. His hands were already wet.

Namid dumped the herbs from the packet into her mouth and swallowed them with a sip of water. Then, heedless of the water that fell onto the bedding, she wet the cloth and worked at cleaning the blood from her face and arms. The skin on her hands felt hot and stiff and was painful to the touch and to move, but she did not let that stop her. She could not move well enough to pull off her boots to see to her feet. She hoped they were not too bad.

After an interminable time, her vision finally cleared. By then some of the pain had eased, too. She met Aahmes' gaze.

"It worked," she said with a wry grin.

"Not something I want to repeat," he said and pulled her close to his side. They leaned back against the cave wall.

"Not something I think we *should* repeat," Namid said. She stretched out her fingers and considered the damaged skin in the dim light that made its way to them from the cave entrance. "The wounds are getting worse and taking longer to heal. I think we're going to have to stop using anything other than the Wild Power. At least until we pull the city back."

Aahmes nodded. "Going to be a long trip back to where we need to be, then. We can't use the amulets."

"True. Not sure I really want to keep using something that was the Dark Priests' anyway." Namid twisted, with a muffled groan, to look at Aahmes.

"I'm beginning to think it was a foolish idea to leave the others behind. Well, Haeith and Mehratar, anyway. Still not comfortable with Inezha."

"I don't trust her," Aahmes said, then shared a wry look with her. "We should have at least brought horses."

Namid chuckled and winced at the twinge the motion caused her. "So shall we rest up and heal up, and then begin stepping our way to someplace we can get horses?"

"Now there's an idea I like."

Namid chuckled again, and winced again. "Ow. Don't make me do that."

~ ~ ~

Namid and Aahmes stayed several days at their cave to rest and heal. At the base of the hill, they found a small stream to replenish their water. It also served to let them clean up better. Aahmes even managed to get a few birds, which gave them something else to eat.

The fourth night at their shelter, they felt recovered enough to plan their next move. After they decided they would leave the next morning, they settled next to their fire to enjoy its warmth and the luxury of not running from or to something. Aahmes sat with his back against a rock, his arms wrapped around Namid sitting in front of him. Namid leaned against his chest and idly watched the flames in front of them, relishing his closeness. She was considering whether she even wanted to move to their bedding further inside the cave to sleep when she remembered the pouch she had taken from Lann.

She twisted around trying to find the pouch at her belt that held the one from Lann.

After a few breaths-of-time of this, Aahmes tightened his embrace to hold her still.

"If you keep doing that, we'll soon be doing something that's not what I think you're planning right now," he whispered. His breath tickled her ear and sent delicious thrills through her.

She paused and leaned back against his chest, twisting just enough to brush her lips along his jaw. "While I certainly wouldn't object," she murmured, "this is something I've been needing to remember to share with you."

With a sigh, Aahmes released her. She scooted a little away from him and dug in the last pouch to find what she was looking for.

"I remember. You took that from Lann."

With a nod, Namid opened it and peered inside, tilting it to get light from the fire to help her see. Aahmes leaned close and looked also.

"It's that powder he used on you, and Taakha used on us both back at Meahan," Namid said. "Thought it might be of use. And I didn't want to leave it with him, anyway."

Aahmes reached into the pouch and pulled out a pinch of the reddish powder. He dropped it into the palm of his other hand and moved it around with a finger.

"Doesn't look like much, for all the trouble it causes."

Namid nodded absently and sniffed at the pouch. "I think it's what he also used in the wine, when I first met him," she said. "It kind of smells like the aftertaste tasted. Judging from what we've seen of blowing it into someone's face, it doesn't seem to take a lot. I think we should both carry some. Do you have a pouch I can dump some in?"

With an absent nod, Aahmes dumped the powder in his hand back in the pouch. He rose, dug in his pack and pulled out a pouch slightly smaller than the one Namid held.

Together, they poured half the powder into Aahmes' pouch. He tied it and tucked it in one of the larger pouches on his belt. Namid copied his actions, then without even needing to consult on it, they both wiped their hands well with the snow that sat in patches on the ground nearby.

Then they settled back in their spot near the fire.

Aahmes pulled Namid close and brushed her neck with his lips. "Now, where were we…?"

~ ~ ~

The next morning, they packed up everything—their food stores quite depleted even with Aahmes hunting for birds—and prepared to move on.

They continued to move southeast, alternating doing the search-and-step technique. By mutual agreement, they each controlled steps only three times each day, then they found someplace to rest and spend the night.

Three days they traveled like this and the fourth day found them in drier, less vegetated hills.

"This area seems like those hills we crossed from Paronia into Yiruny," Namid said when they paused around midday to eat.

Aahmes agreed. "I'm hoping we're getting close to someplace we've actually been before. This is similar, but still not anyplace I truly recognize."

Namid shook her head. "Certainly not me. Do you want to try to reach Foroughi?" She named the city that they had visited once with Enric, the city where his friend

247

Baron Zelimir lived.

"Possibly. Although, I think we're still a fair distance north of there. And we could even be east of there, now, too."

"Might be worth doubling back a little, if we are further east. We'd be able to get horses there."

"Let's at least see if we can sense it," Namid added.

After they finished their meager meal, they drew on Wild Power and linked. Together, they cast out with their senses to the south and south-east. They hoped to at least find some town or village, if not Foroughi itself.

Just at the edge of their reach to the southeast, Namid sensed a knot of Power.

She and Aahmes jerked back from it and let the Wild Power go.

"That wasn't Foroughi," Namid said.

Aahmes raked his hair back from his face. "No, but I think I know that place. Although it feels different."

Namid tapped his arm when he did not continue. "So tell me already."

"I think that was Belaraketh's temple complex. But it didn't feel right. Not like I remember from when I learned there."

Namid considered that. "If it *is* his complex, that at least gives us a much better idea of where we are."

Aahmes nodded his agreement. "The temple complex is located in northern Yiruny, near the point where the realms of Paronia, Denek and Yiruny all meet. If we push the search-and-step a bit today, I think we can reach there this evening."

"Why would you want to?"

"It felt to me like it had been attacked. I sensed other Power there, and the sense of Belaraketh's Power was much less than before. We might be able to learn something. And perhaps scrounge up some food. Maybe even find horses, too, if any escaped the attack."

CHAPTER 23

Twilight found Namid and Aahmes lying flat atop a hill that overlooked the destroyed temple complex. Large rocks and small leafless shrubs helped conceal them and they both renewed a concealing shell of Wild Power around them as needed.

Namid scrutinized the scene below, trying to guess what might have happened. Fire, certainly. It had raged through the entire complex, which was the size of a small town. And the stones that had been walls for the buildings looked melted similar to what had happened to the village where they first met Mehratar. The gate and wall that she saw on the nearer side of the place looked to have been pulled out and down. Or maybe blasted out from within.

She drew more Wild Power to herself and reached out to the destruction.

"I sense only remnants of Power there," Aahmes murmured.

"There's no one alive there with Power," Namid said. "Can't really tell if there might be someone without Power."

"Haven't seen any movement."

"Me neither. I doubt we'll find horses here. Maybe some unruined food stores, though."

Aahmes pointed to the side. "I think we can approach from around there. I'll surround us with the nothingness veneer as we get closer."

They edged back out of sight of the complex, then made their way down and around the hill. The area Aahmes had indicated was a rough path. Before they stepped out where they could possibly be seen from the ruin, Aahmes built the nothingness veneer and Namid renewed the shell around them and added a defensive shell to it, all with Wild Power.

A couple of the moons were near full and provided adequate light for them to follow the path as twilight faded.

Namid drew a dagger and held tight to as much Wild Power as she could. This place did not give her a good feeling.

Side by side, she and Aahmes approached the blasted gate and the remnants of the encircling wall. Without needing to consult, they paused at the rubble-strewn opening and both crouched there.

From their concealment, they looked into the complex. Nothing moved. The only sound was the rustling of some dried twigs in the slight breeze. Little remained to identify anything within the walled area.

Namid stretched out again with the Wild Power and sent it flowing through the compound. She discovered nothing new.

With a slight gesture to proceed, Aahmes led the way inside.

~*This area was housing for the students – the more advanced ones getting the better, less crowded buildings. And there were fields to grow food,*~ Aahmes told Namid through thought-speech as they slipped through the ruins.

As at Mehratar's village, Namid saw no bodies. And everything looked undisturbed since the destruction.

While Aahmes poked through a few of the more-intact structures, Namid reached out with the Wild Power to see if any of the Power remnants felt familiar.

It was a jumbled mess. Much of the Power felt meager and half conceived. Perhaps the students?

After long breaths-of-time, she found some hints of Power that felt familiar. Both Belaraketh and Ilenii had been there at some point not too long before their own arrival. Within the current season, Namid thought.

~I can't sense exactly how recently this happened. You?~ Namid decided to continue using thought-speech in the hope of remaining as hidden as possible.

Aahmes shrugged. *~Everything's cold. But it so far doesn't look like any wild animals have moved in. Although why they haven't, I don't know. Maybe a few weeks?~*

~There's a Power here that doesn't feel familiar,~ he added. *~Not counting what feels like Belaraketh's people.~*

~Whoever did this, I'd wager.~

~Yeah.~

With cautious steps, they continued further into the compound. As they walked, Aahmes named the buildings they encountered: stables, Power practice area, studies, housing for the initiated and higher-ups, dining hall. All reduced to unrecognizable rubble.

In one corner of what had been the dining hall, Aahmes uncovered stairs that led down.

~Used to be food storage down here,~ he told Namid and led the way down.

The stairs descended perhaps the height of a story to a small landing and continued further down to the right. Namid drew on the Wild Power to help her see in the dark and smiled when it was both easier and more effective than using her own Power, as she used to.

Aahmes dug in his pack and pulled out a candle and lit it with Power.

Namid squinted and made a sound of complaint.

Aahmes laughed softly. *~Sorry about that. Power's never*

been much use helping me see in the dark, and the Wild Power hasn't made a difference.~

~Could've warned me,~ Namid griped.

Aahmes just laughed again. *~If there's any food to be found, it'll be down here.~*

They resumed their descent, then Namid froze at the sound of rocks hitting rocks nearby. She and Aahmes exchanged looks as Aahmes snuffed the candle. They eased back up the stairs, moving as silently as they ever had as Shadowers.

Together they peeked over the edge of the floor. The remnants of the walls blocked much of the surroundings, but Namid did not see anything out of place.

Namid and Aahmes split up as they eased toward what had been the front outer wall of the dining hall and around opposite ends. Namid reached cut with the Wild Power to keep track of Aahmes. She could no longer see him in the midst of the destruction.

"Who's there?" A woman's contralto voice pierced the silence of the ruined compound. "No need to hide. Come on out and let's get to know each other."

Namid scuttled around some rocks headed toward the voice, then paused when a wave of Power washed over her. It had a familiar slimy feel to it, and she felt a tug on the blood Power mesh.

~We need to get out of here,~ she told Aahmes. She hoped he was close enough to hear her, as she eased back toward the compound's outer wall.

~Agreed,~ came his faint reply.

"I can hear you sharing whispers," the woman said. And Namid heard her moving through the ruins. "What are you whispering to each other, I wonder?"

Namid frowned as she remembered another time someone had been able to hear their thought-speech to each other. Seemed it was not as private a way to converse as she had thought.

Namid continued to move and tried to hurry without

making any noise. Then an eerie sound came out of the night. A beautiful sound. The woman was singing. No words, just tones of music. Flawless.

And Namid paused to listen to the entrancing melody. She had never heard the like before. Another voice intruded in her thoughts – she vaguely thought she should listen. But the voice could not break through the soothing spell the music wove through her.

This seemed familiar....

A wisp of Wild Power touched her, jolted her attention. She reached out to it and the Wild Power she held linked to it with a snap. The haziness in her thoughts cleared and she sensed Aahmes struggling to free himself as well.

She sent a surge of Wild Power through the link to help him unravel the last strands of the Power that wrapped around him from the music.

A cry of rage rang out through the ruins and the next instant thick ropes of red Power whipped through the area, reaching and striking out randomly. Namid threw herself on the ground to avoid them. After the ropes had passed, she stood again and ran for the wall. Through the Wild Power, she sensed that Aahmes headed for the same spot.

Twice more she dropped to avoid the woman's Power, then she reached the ruined gateway. A breath-of-time later, Aahmes joined her.

More of the ropes of Power reached for them and they twisted to avoid them. Then one caught Namid's ankle. Another caught Aahmes' wrist.

"And there you are!" the woman said, still hidden somewhere in the destroyed complex.

The rope around Namid's ankle slithered up her leg as if alive and twined the blood Power mesh with it as it wrapped further around her. Namid sliced at the rope with Wild Power and writhed to try to keep it from binding her. More of the ropes came out of the night and caught her arms and trapped them tight to her body. The ropes began to pull her back from the gap in the wall, back again further into the complex. She spared a glance for Aahmes and saw that he was similarly caught.

"Defenses," she said and began to build the firestorm, constructed entirely of Wild Power.

Aahmes slammed a stronger defense shell around them both and linked to her with Wild Power to lend his strength to the firestorm.

The firestorm raged around the two of them as the blue-white flames ate away at the red ropes. A hint of music slipped into Namid's concentration. It slid over her skin and thrummed in the blood mesh. Something tugged on the mesh, tugged on her own Power. The music urged her to relax, stop fighting.

A woman approached, fastidiously picking her way through the rubble with the long skirt of her silky gown held up to avoid touching anything, her nose wrinkled as if she smelled something unpleasant. The light from the fire gave a glow to the woman's auburn hair and pale, freckled skin. She smiled when she saw Aahmes and Namid.

"It *is* you two!" she said. "This will show Ilenii—"

Namid did not wait to hear what this would show Ilenii. She yanked at all the Wild Power she could reach, twined some around Aahmes. At the same time, he also yanked at Wild Power and sent it coursing through the black jewel-shard from Akavos that he now held in one hand.

Aahmes' effort sheared through the ropes. The broken ends flailed in the air and struck all of them. Namid grasped his hand, reached out with the Wild Power as far away as she could and stepped.

She stifled a scream as the blood Power mesh constricted around her, cut into her, and yanked hard on her own Power. She held on to Aahmes and the Wild Power and strained to complete the step.

Something snapped and she and Aahmes dropped into normal night.

Aahmes grasped her to keep her from falling and held her tight. One or both of them trembled from the strain.

Namid pushed gently against Aahmes' chest to get him to ease his grip.

"Can you handle another step or two?" Her voice sounded weak to her.

"Not really any choice, I think," he replied. "Together? Since we're already linked."

Namid nodded her agreement. Together they renewed their shells of concealment and defense. Then they reached out through the Wild Power to find another place to step to, as far away as they could manage. And from there, they stepped once more.

They picked a random direction to seek shelter and jogged to gain some distance without wearing themselves out too much. They kept half their attention on where they jogged as they reached out around them with Wild Power to see if they sensed the woman following them.

Close to a candle-mark they traveled this way, until both stumbled with exhaustion. They found a clump of rocks that offered a meager sheltering alcove and crawled within to rest and eat and drink a little. They still kept their senses extended through the Wild Power.

"So much for getting more food," Namid mumbled.

"Think she was waiting for us?"

Namid shrugged. "I think we would have sensed her if she had been. Maybe we tripped some trap that we didn't sense and then she came for us."

"Or maybe they have some way to track us down through that blood Power mesh."

"I think the trap is more likely," Namid said. "Otherwise, wouldn't they have come after us as soon as we left Nazextas?"

"Maybe they just didn't want to travel that far. Probably figured we'd head back to more familiar places."

Namid groaned. "Now there's a lovely thought."

Aahmes held her close. Namid snuggled in even tighter.

"I'd wager that was the 'god' Shiara," she muttered.

"Only female god we haven't encountered before," Aahmes said. "At least of the main eight. Hope the minor 'gods' aren't in on this, too."

Namid yawned, then Aahmes did, too. "Try to sleep," Aahmes encouraged her. "I'll watch for a while and wake you later."

Namid nodded. She hauled out some blankets and settled in better, still close to Aahmes. As she drifted off, she felt him building the Wild Power concealment screen that resembled the ones in the Arinsk Mountains.

Namid's watch came far too soon. Hadn't she just closed her eyes?

Aahmes told her he had sensed nothing worrisome, and no one, through the Power. With a grin and a long kiss, he stole the warm blankets from her and settled in to sleep.

Now chilled, Namid pulled her cloak closer and paced to the opening to their alcove. Three of the moons provided some light so she could look over their surroundings. The area reminded her of the area near where she and Aahmes and Enric had first met Inezha. For a breath-of-time, she lost herself in the pleasant aspects of her memories of that first meeting and the feasts with the Praznies.

Returning to the task at hand, she reached out with her senses to get a better idea of where they were. A few night creatures around, although none nearby. Further and she touched on what seemed to be a small group camping. No one with Power there, so she could not be certain. But a small gathering of horses and the sense of a fire banked for the night. Probably a road near that spot, she decided.

She reached further and found another clump of Power, much smaller than the one that had been at Belaraketh's temple complex. And beyond that a second one. And further yet, a third.

Small towns or large villages. All demolished.

CHAPTER 24

Midmorning, Namid and Aahmes looked over the first devasted town from their spot hidden within Wild Power and concealed by a clump of bushes for good measure.

The town was as destroyed as Belaraketh's temple complex. And nothing moved within it except a wisp of smoke that drifted skyward from one of the buildings. Namid imagined she felt heat from the melted stones of the closest buildings.

"They're not just going after each other," Aahmes murmured.

"Followers of one or another of them?" Namid said.

"Seems likely. And that reminds me, did you notice the secondary mesh at Belaraketh's temple?"

Namid gave him a surprised look and shook her head. "Secondary mesh?"

"Yeah. Something like this blood Power one we're entangled with." He flapped one hand in the air. "But the one at Belaraketh's temple was all but disintegrated. And it wasn't blood Power. It felt most like his own Power."

Namid considered that. "Think he had all his followers linked together? Like everyone in Nazextas is with the

257

blood Power. Including us."

"It's what it looked like."

"So he was drawing Power from his followers," Namid murmured. "Maybe that's the true purpose of those tattoos that we got at the temple complexes. Not to track us, but so our '*gods*'"—she sneered at that last word—"could steal Power from us to make themselves even more Powerful."

"And so naturally the others would want to eliminate the followers. Try to decrease their rivals' Power."

Namid shook her head. "Amazing. What they'll do for more and more Power." Then she chuckled. "Wager Ilenii and Belaraketh are cursing themselves over that moment of pique that made them burn off our tattoos to cast us out? If they hadn't done that, we might not have noticed and severed the links they had to us, probably to our Power. At least not as soon as we did."

Aahmes chuckled too and nodded his agreement.

She returned her attention to the ruined town and sent Wild Power through it once more, probing for any hint of Power left that might be set to let someone know another Powerful person was there.

"I think I found something like what might have tripped us up at Belaraketh's temple," Aahmes said. "You have to follow the mesh, though. The blood one, I mean. Belaraketh's is here, too, but falling apart."

With a grimace of distaste, Namid reached out to the blood Power mesh and stretched her senses through it. When she touched on what Aahmes was talking about, she withdrew from that Power.

"We can avoid that easily," she said. "Now that we know it's there. Just not sure it's worth even bothering." She waved a hand in the direction of the town. "Doesn't seem that we'll find any food there."

With a frown, Aahmes agreed. "We need to find something soon, though. We didn't bring enough for such an extended journey."

Namid nodded as she idly watched the town. She started at a hint of motion.

"Did you see that?"

Aahmes shook his head and looked where Namid indicated. They watched several long breaths-of-time before they saw another hint of motion.

Namid placed her fingers on the back of Aahmes' hand to keep their thought-speech between just the two of them. She hoped.

~Leave or look into it?~

~I don't sense anyone,~ Aahmes replied the same way. *~No sense of Power either.~*

~Its headed for that knot of Power that will alert someone.~

~Let's see if it does that, then.~

They settled back further in their clump of bushes and renewed their defense and concealment from the Wild Power they held. Namid slowly drew more to herself from her surroundings until she could hold no more.

The whatever-it-was seemed to be sneaking through the ruins of the town, darting here and there but always hidden. They did not catch more than a glimpse of its movement. After it reached the spot where they sensed the trap, they saw no further movement.

~Is it gone somehow?~ Namid wondered.

~I think it stopped——~

They both jumped as the sensation of a clanging bell pulsed through the blood Power mesh. Aahmes added another layer of defense around them and they both crept through the foliage near the town, trying to find a spot from which they could see the source of the alarm that continued to inaudibly jangle them.

They had just reached another large clump of bushes when the alarm stopped.

"Aahmes? Namid?" A voice called out over the dead town.

Namid exchanged looks with Aahmes and mouthed "Inezha?"

Inezha continued, "Might as well come out. You won't take any harm here this day."

Aahmes lightly clasped Namid's wrist. *~Think she's just saying that? Or has she Seen this?~*

~Since she's here right when we are, I've a feeling it's the second.~

~Yeah. Me too.~

"So you've Seen that, have you?" Aahmes called out. He tightened his grip on Namid's wrist and stepped them to the far side of the town.

"That I have," came Inezha's voice, now fainter, either further away from them or she faced the other direction.

Namid gave Aahmes a questioning look. He just shrugged, with a wry grin, and began working up something with the Wild Power.

Namid felt him tense as a quiver ran through the blood Power mesh. They both crouched even lower. Namid again sent Wild Power out and touched on Aahmes doing the same.

~Gathering quite the crowd,~ Namid commented when she sensed, then spotted, Belaraketh and Ilenii standing some distance away in the ruined village. And even further away, the woman they believed was Shiara. None of the three stood close to where Inezha had been. Namid felt the faintest hint of Power that she thought might be Inezha, now in a different location in the ruined town.

"Stay out of this, Shiara," Ilenii's voice called through the town.

Aahmes and Namid exchanged a glance. They had rightly guessed her identity.

"I *told* you I could find them," Shiara called back, a hint of a whine in her voice. "I almost had them."

"Almost being the important word," Ilenii yelled. "You're always just almost—"

"You think you're so much better! I can sense through the mesh, too," Shiara yelled back. "And… I've got them now!"

Namid felt a slight tremor in the mesh and Shiara stepped out of a shimmer of air directly in front of her and Aahmes, the red Power ropes whipping toward them. Aahmes held up the hand with the shard from Akavos and pulled on their twined Wild Power.

Green-tinged flames flared out from the jewel-shard and attached themselves to the ropes, eating at them and following them to the 'god'. With a shriek she lost hold of her Power and disappeared through an air shimmer.

Laughter came from their right, then, and red lightning jumped through the ruins. Namid twisted their defense shell to deflect the lightning away from them and Aahmes again shot out some fire as the ropes came at them from another direction. More of the lightning came from a different direction.

The Power converged around Aahmes and Namid, battered at their defenses and blinded them with bright flashes as all the attacks clashed. Aahmes turned to Namid and clasped both her hands, one holding the shard between them.

~*Firestorm together this time,*~ he told her.

With a nod, Namid built up the blue-white firestorm around them and Aahmes added a twist to it to send the attacking Power bouncing back toward their attackers. Even through their defense shells, Namid felt the heat of all the Power. And the din from it was deafening.

Aahmes tilted his head toward where they could now see the attacking 'gods' and pushed against the whirling firestorm. He split it into three and sent those smaller whorls flying at their attackers.

The fires raged toward the 'gods'. They flowed faster than a horse could run, and left smooth, burned paths in their wake. They struck the so-called gods' defenses and flung them far back into the ruins, then winked out.

Aahmes sagged against Namid and they both slipped to the ground. She bolstered their defenses, but worried how much more they could do if the 'gods' recovered from that faster than they did.

A different Power flowed through the town, one Namid had not felt before. With it came a voice only somewhat like Inezha's but with a subtle difference Namid could not define.

"Flee this place while you yet can, lest destruction overtake you here," the voice said. Somehow Namid knew the message was not directed to them.

"It's that Seer," Belaraketh yelled from somewhere in the destruction. "The one kept by that pretender."

Namid shared a glance with Aahmes, then felt three odd, distinct pings through the blood Power mesh. And the sense of the three 'gods' left the town.

Namid ignored the discomfort it caused as she tried to sense where they were through the blood mesh. All she could determine was that they were nowhere nearby. Nor was anyone else who was bound into the mesh.

Namid daubed at the blood that dripped from her nose and struggled to her feet, helping Aahmes up, too. They strengthened their defense shell and turned toward the sound of footsteps approaching. That strange Power still lingered in the town.

Inezha emerged from the dust and smoke left behind from all the Power that had been flung about. She stopped where she was just visible. Namid sensed that the Power flowed from her. Inezha tilted her head and studied the two of them, then shook her head slightly.

"You're safe enough here, now," she said. Her voice sounded completely normal again. But Namid could feel the Power that swirled around all of them and even passed through their defenses to brush her skin.

"What are you even doing here?" she said.

Inezha chuckled. "After you left us, Mehratar and Haeith were determined to follow you. The Healer, at least, was extremely unhappy that you had left them behind. They used the amulets to travel to Rhadanthus, as we had discussed. But I suddenly knew that I needed to come to this place. So I came here instead. Now they're probably wondering where I am, too." She laughed. "I've been waiting too long to learn why I was supposed to come here. I'd say that we now know why."

She sat on a broken rock close by and calmly emptied some pebbles from her boots.

"I'm glad you finally decided to show up. The waiting was getting tedious. Now I can move on—" She stiffened and Namid felt a surge in the Power that drifted around them. Then Inezha spoke again in that other voice, her face turned toward them, her pupils wide but her eyes unfocused, not seeming to actually see them.

"First to the tower, then the city," she said.

And the strange Power vanished as if it had never been. Even when she reached out with Wild Power, Namid sensed no Power about Inezha, just as usual.

With a pat on her shoulder, Aahmes dropped to sit on the ground.

"That's pretty impressive," he said to Inezha. "Did the people your van accosted find it entertaining? What tower and what city are we talking about here?"

Inezha scowled at him. "Tower? City? Oh, you finally got your Seeing! Well, I've no idea. That's the joy of being a Seer. You utter all these impressive, ominous things that you have no idea about, often don't even remember saying."

She replaced her boots and rose. "Whatever it was, you get the pleasure of figuring it out on your own. I can't help."

"Need to be somewhere else, now?" Namid said.

Inezha gave her an enigmatic look and shrugged. "I just know I'm not supposed to be with you two right now."

She turned away and began picking her way through the ruins. "I think one of the cellars might have some edible food still in it," she called back over her shoulder.

Namid sank down to sit next to Aahmes. "Well, then."

He draped an arm around her shoulders. "I don't think

I could have said it better," he said with a laugh.

Namid chuckled a little, then sobered. "That's three of them we know for certain now. After us, I mean."

"And not getting along too well with each other, either. Maybe something we can use against them."

"Maybe." Then her stomach growled, and she had to laugh again.

Aahmes struggled back to his feet and held out a hand to help her up. "But first, my beloved, let's find that food, then get out of this place."

"I like hearing that," Namid said in a soft voice.

Aahmes' startled look dissolved into a grin. "Food?" he said, and his grin widened.

Namid gave him a mock frown that slowly morphed into a grin to match his. "Beloved. And you know it!" She stepped close for a long kiss, then bounced out of his arms and away into the town. "Now let's find something to eat."

~ ~ ~

It took longer than Namid would have preferred but, as Inezha had suggested, they found some food tucked away in some cellars of the ruined buildings. By midday they had gathered enough to hold them for several days, at least. And they had eaten their fill for the first time in many days.

Much as she would have liked to rest, Namid agreed with Aahmes when he muttered that they should probably step away from the town.

They linked with the Wild Power to do the stepping together. Two long steps was all they managed before they wearily decided they needed to find a place to recover from the confrontation with the 'gods'.

They sheltered in an abandoned hut tucked away in a small, hidden vale within the rock-strewn hills. Some herder's hut, Aahmes speculated. Late the next day, they moved on again.

CHAPTER 25

"Tower first, then the city," Aahmes muttered as he and Namid clambered over and around rocks, trying to find a way down from the hills. They now traveled south as much as they could, with many detours around large clumps of rocks they could not clamber over.

"The city is probably Rhadanthus," Namid said.

"Or maybe Corentris," she added after a breath-of-time.

"Could be Nazextas," Aahmes said as he helped Namid over one of the larger rocks.

"I hope not. I don't think I want to go there ever again."

Aahmes chuckled. "I won't argue. But what about the tower? There's one in Nazextas, but we can't really go there before the city, since it's right in the middle of the city."

"Unless we stepped to the inside of the tower. Or used the pendants," Namid said.

"I don't think I can picture the interior well enough to trust either way to get there," Aahmes said.

After she thought about that, Namid nodded

agreement.

"It's possible that she means Tower Hold," she said. "The Star seems to be involved in this somehow. And it's still there, I would think."

"I don't see Thes keeping it anywhere else," Aahmes agreed. "I'm tired of all these rocks. Ready to step again?"

Namid paused and looked around, then looked within to judge her control of the Wild Power. "I think I'm recovered enough from our encounter," she said. "Now that we're sure they're close, though, I want to avoid wearing ourselves out with just travel uses of Power."

"Agreed," Aahmes said with a quick nod. "But also now that we're sure they're close, I think we need speed, too. Now it *is* a race again. Especially if they have any idea the Star is involved. Thes and the Shadowers won't be a match for these 'gods'."

Namid frowned. "Too true." After some thought, she plopped down on a convenient rock. "Let's take some extra time, then, to see if we can tell exactly where we are. Figure the most direct way to get to Rhadanthus instead of just heading that general direction. I think it'll be a good use of Power, even if it means we can't step again right away."

Aahmes considered that, then settled close to her on the rock. He clasped one of her hands and brought it to his lips with an impish glint in his expression. Then he clasped her other hand, too.

"Let's see how far we can reach together, linked with the Wild Power."

Namid nodded. "But if we're doing that, let's find a place to camp, in case we're too drained after reaching so far."

Aahmes agreed. They hunted nearby for more than a quarter candle-mark before they found a good, rocky alcove that would do. They set up a quick, rough camp then settled atop their bedding against one of the large rocks that ringed their alcove and again clasped hands.

They drew to themselves as much of the Wild Power as they could hold, and linked to each other.

Together, they reached out with the Wild Power, concentrating on areas south of them first. They moved slowly and took the time to get more than just an impression of the areas they touched. After a candle-mark of this, when their control and concentration faltered, they pulled back to their alcove.

Namid groaned when her senses cleared. She reached for a waterskin and took a long drink before she met Aahmes' gaze.

"Nothing felt like any city I know in that direction," she said.

Aahmes shook his head and winced. Namid wondered if his head ached as much as hers did.

"Me neither," he said as he pulled out some food and shared it with her.

"Could we be that far off?" Namid said. "Further west than we thought?"

Aahmes shrugged. "Possibly. We'll figure it out. Try again after we've eaten and maybe rested a bit."

And so they did. This time, they reached to the southeast and Aahmes pulled the small shard with its Wild Power into their link. Just as she was about ready to quit for the night, Namid sensed something at the edge of their range.

~Yes,~ came Aahmes' voice in her thoughts. ~I feel it too. Think you can stretch with me just a little bit further to get a better sense of it?~

~I'm with you.~ And she sensed amusement and a wave of love from him.

They reached further and narrowed the Wild Power to a thin tendril to stretch it even further.

Namid started in surprise when they touched what they had barely sensed.

~That's Wild Power!~

~I think it's the Star,~ Aahmes commented.

Namid felt a strange warmth from the distant Power, and a sense of welcoming. Then she was back in their alcove staring at the glowing jewel-shard in the palm of Aahmes' hand.

Their gazes met and Aahmes shrugged.

"Well, then…" he said.

"Yeah."

The glow faded and Aahmes put the shard back in his pouch.

"We're still further north than I expected. But at least we now know where Rhadanthus is."

"We're not going to cross that distance in just a couple of steps," Aahmes said. He twisted around and arranged their bedding better for the night.

"Think we should use the pendants? If they can reach that far, then it would just be the one last time that we'd need to use our Power with the entwined blood Power."

Aahmes drew her under the covers with him and shook his head.

"I don't think we can risk it. Who knows what condition that would leave us in. At least with the stepping, we can control how much we exhaust ourselves. And no random wounds."

Namid scooted herself close and looked up at him from a distance of only a few finger-widths. With a grin, she brushed his lips with hers.

"For tonight, let's do something else that might exhaust us."

Aahmes returned her grin and kiss. He pulled her even closer and twined his fingers through her hair to unbraid it.

~ ~ ~

Much later, as Namid was drifting off to sleep, Aahmes startled, jerking upright.

Namid drew Wild Power in alarm and gave him a quizzical look.

"What is it?"

For a long breath-of-time he didn't answer. Then his attention returned from what seemed a great distance. His expression was sheepish as he wrapped his arms around her.

"Sorry about that. I just figured out what's been bothering me about that destroyed town. Before everyone showed up, bringing their various Powers, the only Power I sensed there was Belaraketh's."

Namid considered that and frowned. "Well, we think it was a town of his followers, right?"

"Yes, but that's not the issue. I should have sensed the Power of whoever destroyed the town. But the *only* Power there, other than that ever-present blood mesh, was Belaraketh's."

Namid shook her head as she tried to deny what that meant. "He killed his own people," she murmured.

"Looks that way."

And Namid remembered something she had read in that book. She shivered at the sudden chill her thoughts gave her.

"Wesh wrote, 'A death provides the richest, most potent blood Power.' So, many deaths means that much more Power. They're gathering even more Power."

"And quickly. All at once."

Namid shook her head again. "This is bad. Even more than before." She slumped and covered her face with her hands.

"I do wish we could just go far away from all this."

Aahmes tightened his arms around her.

"Say the word and we'll go as far as you want."

Namid chuckled and raised her head. "Oh, how I wish. But I actually think we can do this, even beyond Inezha's firm belief that we're the ones to do it. Free those trapped spirits in Nazextas, cut off the blood Power from everyone attached to the mesh. Destroy the mesh. Probably restore the city – won't that be a surprise to some! We can help, can do this, where others probably can't. So, I think we have to."

With a gentle touch, Aahmes turned her to face him and gave her a long kiss.

"Then that's what we'll do," he said.

~ ~ ~

The next two days, they again pushed the search-and-step technique as much as they could without draining themselves too badly. Again each of them controlled it three times each day, stretching out as far as they dared.

The evening of the second day found them close enough to Rhadanthus that they thought they would arrive the next day with only a couple of search-and-steps. They found a deep hollow, well-hidden by the scrub bushes that grew in the area, and made a cold camp.

As they tried to settle into sleep that night, concerns plagued Namid.

"And what is it?" came Aahmes' voice in the darkness as she shifted position for the fifth time.

Namid sighed. "Think we'll find the 'gods' there tomorrow?" she said. "I just have to think they must know we'd be going there."

She felt him shrug. "Possibly. But we haven't felt them near. Even through the blood mesh. I have a feeling we won't see them again until we actually try this... whatever exactly we're going to try."

Namid laughed in spite of herself. "The whole restore an ancient ghostly-city while draining the blood Power that was forced on us and also draining the blood Power from the 'gods' at the same time?"

Aahmes laughed, too. "Yeah, that."

"I hope so." Namid was lost in her thoughts for several long breaths-of-time before she spoke up again. "So you think we need to do this from Rhadanthus and not Corentris?"

"I do," Aahmes said. "But I also think we might get a better idea of things once we have the Star of Corentris in our hands. These Powerful objects seem to have a way of doing that, from what we've seen."

"I sense Haeith and Mehratar both near the Star," Namid said.

Aahmes nodded. "Can't tell if Inezha's anywhere nearby, though."

"I wager she'll show up as soon as we start anything, if she's not there already."

"Probably. So, anything else? Or can I get some sleep?"

Namid rolled over partway to punch him lightly in the shoulder. "Is that all you can think of?"

"We're as ready as we can be for tomorrow," he said. "What else should I think of?"

Namid tucked herself against his side, with his arm around her shoulders.

"That's actually also bothering me. Have we forgotten something?"

Aahmes sighed and gave her shoulders a squeeze. "I'm sure we'll find out soon enough, if we have. Now sleep. It would be a shame if I had to drag you half-awake to this amazing Power display we're planning."

Namid chuckled and tried to focus on soothing thoughts to help sleep come.

~ ~ ~

Neither of them slept well that night and so they rose as the first hint of dawn lit the sky. After a quick morning meal, Aahmes used the search-and-step technique to take them to a hill a short distance from Rhadanthus.

They squirmed their way on their bellies to the top to get a look at the city. Namid used a touch of Wild Power to help her see in the dim light.

Ahead of them lay the North Gate, closed. But Namid saw no Warders at the gate. Had any of the Warders even survived Sy'shythys a couple of autumns ago? She did not remember having seen any of them the last time she was in the city.

The road that led toward their hill from the North Gate looked overgrown, like it had not seen much use the past year. Not too surprising, Namid thought. Most of the trade ran east and west through the city. And with probably so few people still making the city their home, likely the north road had not been traveled much.

She next turned her attention to Tower Hold, standing east of Rhadanthus. From where they lay, Namid could see the tops of the three towers, but no movement there.

She suddenly felt very exposed.

"We don't exactly blend into the grass here," she whispered. "Probably still too dark, now, but won't they see—"

"I've got the Wild Power blanketing us, like before," Aahmes broke in.

"Oh, good. Guess I'm not really awake yet."

"Do you want to wait to do this? Rest a bit more?"

Namid considered that. "Not really. Think we can just ask Thes for the Star?"

Aahmes gave her a sidelong look. "Where's the fun in that? I figured we'd test Tower Hold's defenses and watchfulness. See if we can slip in, grab it, and get back out. It's a good time for it – few Shadowers are usually awake at this time of day."

Now it was Namid's turn to give a sidelong look. "I do see the appeal."

"He did send us away," Aahmes said.

"He didn't really have a choice, remember."

Aahmes shrugged. "Let's try some thievery. Don't want to lose those hard-earned skills."

Namid sighed but met his grin with one of her own. "It would be the easiest way to keep from involving the Shadowers. Hopefully keep them safe from this. But what about getting everyone out of Rhadanthus? I'd assumed they'd go to Tower Hold while we throw Power around."

"They still can. We'll just see to that after we've got what we came for. It'll give Thes something to do other than be annoyed with us."

Namid chortled. "All right then. Step to the Tower Hold gates?"

"Why not right to the room holding the Star? You brought everyone out from someplace. Shouldn't that mean we can step into someplace? You even suggested that for that tower in the Spirit-City."

Namid shrugged and smiled. "Yeah, I did, didn't I? Seems like it should work. Although it feels somewhat like cheating." She shared an amused look with Aahmes and reached out to clasp his hand, then paused.

He gave her a quizzical look.

"Vlatas said we must find the key to draw the city back together," Namid said, drawing out her words. "I just remembered – and maybe it's that something I was thinking we'd forgotten. There *is* a key… that one that Dar left for me. Its bow is shaped like the statue."

Aahmes stared off into the distance, then met her gaze. "I remember it. Is there anything special about the key?"

Namid shook her head. "Dar left me its impression. Remember I told you? I had one of the Shadowers help me make it. So it's just a copy, probably not even the best metal."

Aahmes frowned. "Still. Odd that Dar had left that for you. And that it's got the same shape as the statue."

"But the only things I know it opens are the gates to Tower Hold and a couple of the inside doors."

"Could we have missed someplace else? Another lock it opens. When we were looking through there a winter ago?"

Namid sighed. "It's certainly possible. But I thought we were thorough. I wouldn't even know where else to look."

Aahmes laughed. "It will be the best bit of thievery ever. We'll just look again through all of Tower Hold for a door we missed. Without any Shadower catching us."

Namid grinned. "More of a Trial than any either of us had to do to prove we belonged with the Shadowers," she said. "Let's get the Star early in our search, though. Oh, and we'll have to start with my room."

"Why?"

"I don't have the key with me. I never thought I might need it when Thes sent us away. So I left it in my room."

Aahmes' frown quickly morphed into an expression of amusement. "Then we'll start there."

He reached out to her. "Together to step?"

They clasped hands and drew on the Wild Power, linking to it and to each other. Namid pictured her room in Lord Tower, the tallest of the three towers that comprised Tower Hold. She shared the image in Aahmes' thoughts. And they stepped.

~ ~ ~

Namid's room looked no different from the last time she saw it. Not much there. A few items of clothing even still lay atop her bed where she had tossed them. Dust lay over everything… the bed and clothes, her small table, and the lid of the chest at the foot of the bed.

"I'm surprised," Namid murmured. "No one's moved in here."

"Maybe afraid to steal the room belonging to one of Lord Thes' mages," Aahmes said with a soft laugh.

Namid snorted and opened the chest. "I left the key in here."

She rummaged around, then straightened with a frown. "It's not here." She dumped the clothes from the bed into the chest and closed the lid. "I suppose it's reasonable to think that Thes would've wanted to have the key."

"Perfect," Aahmes said with a wide grin. "Now we get to skulk through his room, too. This is getting better all the time."

Namid gave him a sharp look, then matched his grin when she saw that he meant what he said.

"I've never heard of any Shadower who managed to get away with something from the leader's own room," Namid said and used a bit of Wild Power to wrap just a hint of a veneer of belonging around them.

"Exactly!"

Their path from Namid's room to Thes' was an easy one. Just up the stairs and down a short hall. They encountered no one on the way.

~*A little too easy,*~ Aahmes commented through thought-speech.

Namid nodded and tested Thes' door. It was unlocked.

She reached out through the door with a tendril of Wild Power to see if she could sense anything and listened at the door as well. After a breath-of-time, she looked at Aahmes.

Anything? she asked Aahmes using the Shadowers' hand-talk.

Aahmes shook his head and eased the door open. Together they slipped inside. Namid pushed the door closed behind them.

This room looked little different from when it had been the mage Chendrukhar's. Namid and Aahmes went opposite directions around the large bed headed for the two wardrobes. But they both paused on either side of the bed, first.

The bed had one occupant, Keizha. But the older Shadower slept to one side of the bed, leaving the other half open. It was rumpled, showing someone else had been there.

Aahmes rested his hand there.

Still a little warm, he told Namid through hand-talk.

They both scanned the rest of the room, but no one else was there.

Quickly then, Namid said with hand-talk and headed toward the wardrobe closest to her.

They each looked through the wardrobe they had chosen with the speed and thoroughness learned as Shadowers. Then back to the door and back out to the hallway. Aahmes led the way to his room, not far from Namid's. It was as dusty and unused as Namid's. They paused inside.

"He must have it with him," Namid whispered as they both leaned against the door. "Or maybe he's given it to one of the others."

"Let's just get the Star, then. After we have that, we can hunt through the whole stronghold to find Thes, if we need," Aahmes whispered back. "Or if we run into him, we can see if he's got the key. And be on the watch for any locked door we missed before."

"Unless someone else already found and opened it," Namid muttered.

Aahmes shrugged. "If they did, makes it easier for us. Still might want to look for any we don't remember, anyway."

"Sounds good."

They eased back out the door and headed down the stairs to the room that held the Star of Corentris. Along the way, they did pass a couple of Shadowers, neither of whom noticed them, tucked within their Power veneer as they were.

~*Surprised more mages don't take up thievery,*~ Aahmes commented. ~*This is almost too easy.*~

Namid stifled a laugh. ~*Laziness, maybe. This* is *too easy, but I imagine it's even easier to awe everyone and have them falling all over themselves to avoid offending you lest you use your Power against them.*~

This time it was Aahmes who stifled a laugh.

They paused on the landing with the door that led to the room the Star had been in and reached out through the Wild Power.

~*I don't sense the Star,*~ Namid said.

Aahmes shook his head. ~*Me neither. Better take a look.*~

He opened the door and they slipped into the room, closing the door again behind them.

The room looked much as Namid remembered it. The long, narrow table stood against the wall to their right and the door in the wall to their left was closed. A single candle burned low on the table, at the end opposite them, but otherwise, the table was empty. No Star of Corentris.

The door to their left swung open. Both Aahmes and Namid jumped to the sides, daggers in hand. But they relaxed when they recognized the gray-haired and bearded man with weathered skin.

"And look who I'm findin' wanderin' around the tower," Thes said as he entered the room and closed the door behind him. "They said you'd be comin' for the Star." He gave them both the familiar stern look, but Namid had a feeling that something was off. However, she could not pinpoint what.

Namid sheathed her daggers. "Who said? Haeith and Mehratar?"

For the shortest breath-of-time, Thes got a confused look on his face, the expression not obvious behind his gray tangle of beard. And it disappeared so quickly that Namid felt she must have imagined it. "Aye, that it was."

Namid shared a glance with Aahmes. Something was definitely off here, but she was still uncertain what. And she could not tell from his expression if Aahmes felt the same. He sheathed his daggers as Namid had and stepped closer to Thes, but off to the side.

"Since you knew we'd be coming for the Star, you just moved it to make it harder for us?" Aahmes said, a slight edge to his tone.

Thes gave a bark of a laugh. "Aye, o' course."

Namid shifted to place Thes even more between herself and Aahmes. She reached out with a sliver of Wild Power. She felt no glamour, semblance or veneer around him, so it *should* be Thes. She cursed to herself that she found it so difficult to sense people who did not have

Power themselves. But yes, there was something….

"So can we borrow the Star?" Namid said. "We just need to see something. Oh, and the gate key, too."

Thes turned to look at her, just a touch too slowly, his movements a little too stilted. "Aye, we can be doin' that." He opened the door behind him. "This way."

He snagged the candle and led the way through the door, down the stairs in the next room and out to the hallway to the next tower.

Once there, Thes headed down the next set of stairs. Namid followed, with Aahmes behind her. He slipped his hand into hers. It made walking down the stairs a little awkward, but she had no complaint.

~I don't sense the Star anywhere,~ he told her. *~And I don't sense Haeith or Mehratar, either.~*

~Me, neither,~ Namid answered the same way after she sent Wild Power sweeping out through Tower Hold. *~Do we believe Inezha that they were actually coming here?~*

She received an impression of a shrug in her thoughts.

"So you're not keeping the Star in your warded chamber?" Aahmes said aloud.

"Naw, found a better place."

They followed Thes through the halls on the ground floor. Aahmes still clasped Namid's hand, but again held a dagger in his other. She felt that he held as much Wild Power as he could. She drew more to herself.

~Do you think continue along with this? Or get out of here and return later?~ Aahmes asked Namid.

Namid twisted her wrist to drop a stiletto into her free hand from its wrist-sheath. *~Pretty sure it's a trap of some sort. Thes acts much like the people under the Dark Priests' control used to. But I think follow along for now. Don't want to give them any more time to set up something even nastier.~*

~True,~ Aahmes replied, with a hint of a chuckle.

Namid strengthened her link to the Wild Power and to Aahmes and they both bolstered their defensive shells. Then they followed Thes through the Guest Tower kitchen area to the stairs that led down to storerooms underground.

When Namid paused at the top of the stairs, Thes gave her a quizzical look.

"The storerooms?" she said. "Really?"

It looked like Thes listened to something inaudible to them. Then he gave them a half-smile. "Not quite. Found a better place for hidin' it. Come on."

While they followed the older Shadower, Namid sent out a wave of Wild Power, both at ground level and down the two levels she knew the storerooms reached. Nothing nearby. She extended her reach through the tunnel system she and Aahmes had explored the previous winter. Nothing different there.

Until she touched on the hidden Power cavern.

She could not sense within the cavern, of course, but the edges of its Power felt disturbed. Through thought-speech, she told Aahmes what she had found. He shared a grim look with her when she glanced at him over her shoulder.

~Let's get the firestorm ready, as much as possible, without unleashing it,~ she suggested.

Aahmes gave her a slight nod. So they continued to follow Thes, through the storerooms to the tunnel that led to Rhadanthus and through the tunnel system. At the same time, Aahmes and Namid concentrated on twining the Wild Power, then weaving it as Mehratar had shown them to get the most effect from the least use of Power. They built the firestorm to the point they could unleash it without any delay. Namid took the primary control of it, while Aahmes also prepared some bolts of Power and held them poised to unleash.

Their underground journey was mostly silent. Namid could not think of anything to say to the probably controlled Thes. And he did not volunteer any conversation. It made for a long candle-mark of walking.

When Thes brought them to the junction that led to

the trapdoor in the old Keep, but instead turned down the tunnel to their practice cavern—the tunnel that was supposed to be hidden with Power—Aahmes and Namid exchanged grim looks.

They slowed and let Thes draw ahead of them a half-pace. His candle flickered in a slight breeze that came from ahead and caused their shadows to dance wildly. Further ahead, the tunnel was not as dark as it should have been. A faint glow came from some light that direction.

Aahmes and Namid dropped their grip on each other and each drew another blade. They eased up to the entrance to the practice cavern, each hugging one wall of the tunnel, as Thes walked a couple of paces into the space and stopped.

From their vantage, only part of the cavern was visible. The light came from somewhere to the right. Together, Namid and Aahmes sent a tendril of Wild Power into the cavern, now able to reach within. They recoiled at what they found.

And the next instant, they both leapt into the cavern, clearing a distance of more than a pace from the entrance in case some unpleasant surprise had been set there for them. As they moved, Namid released the beginnings of the firestorm, sending a stream of fire to their right.

Directly at their friends.

CHAPTER 26

Namid gaped in horror and yanked the Wild Power back to herself, hauling it away from the several figures who stood near the wall in the light of a couple of floating Power orbs. Behind Haeith and Mehratar, and Cameni and Enric, stood three other figures. The way the light orbs hovered, Namid could not tell who they were, but a touch with a tendril of Wild Power revealed their identities.

"Told you they'd be fast enough to stop their attack," Shiara said.

Both Belaraketh and Ilenii sneered at her before they turned their attention to Aahmes and Namid. Ilenii gave a casual wave of one hand and Thes walked toward Enric and stopped next to him. The others looked unconscious, but standing, caught in something like the Power Andrin had used to freeze people for a short time, leaving them unaware of events. But this time, their eyes were closed. When Thes stopped walking, he seemed caught just as the others were, and his eyes closed.

And now that she was looking and not just reacting, Namid saw that a Power shell encased them. It would probably have kept them safe from her firestorm. She was glad she had not tested that, though.

"And what is this?" Aahmes said after everyone who was able to had stared at each other for a breath-of-time. Namid sensed that he still held Power bolts ready.

Ilenii stepped out from behind the captives and held her hands out to the side. Empty. But Namid felt a quiver in the blood Power mesh that joined them all. What was the 'god' up to?

"This is simply an incentive to do things the easy way," Ilenii said with a feral grin for both Namid and Aahmes. "It's quite simple. You two give us your Power, pass along the Wild Power ability that you claimed from Sesaisyd, and your friends will live through this. You two might even, too."

Namid sensed Aahmes' surprise through their link.

"Give you our Power?" Namid said. "What jest is this?"

Shiara giggled but sobered at a glare from Ilenii.

"I can assure you that we don't jest," Ilenii said. She took a step closer. "Of course, if you'd rather, we can just tear the Power from you. But if we're forced to do that, the chances of you surviving decrease to almost nothing."

"The incentive part," Belaraketh said.

Ilenii smirked. "Of course. Incentive." She waved a hand back toward the captives who stood near Belaraketh and Namid felt a sudden surge of Power. The captives all stiffened in apparent agony, mouths open in screams, but with no sound.

"Stop!" Namid shouted.

The captives all relaxed into their previous positions. Ilenii gave Namid an expectant look.

Namid shared a glance with Aahmes. He turned slightly toward her and with the hand on his side away from the 'gods' tapped one of the pouches at his waist. Confused at first, Namid realized it was the pouch that held the powder from Lann.

She sheathed one of the blades she held, dropped that

hand to her side, and held it slightly behind her leg to hide it from Ilenii's view. She made the Shadower hand-talk sign for agreement, followed by the one for readiness.

Aahmes sheathed the dagger he still held in the hand he had used to tap his pouch, then loosened the top of the pouch.

Namid edged to the side and hoped her movement would help hold the so-called gods' attention.

"Say we agree—"

"It's amusing that you think you have a choice," Ilenii interjected.

"Which method of transferring the Power do you wish to use?" Namid continued, as if Ilenii's interruption had not happened. She held her tone to one of confidence to hide the lie in her question and smiled at the confused expressions the three 'gods' wore.

"There's more than one method?" Shiara said.

Ilenii made a cutting motion with her hand at the other woman. "She's just stalling."

Namid suppressed a smile at that. Of course she was doing just that, but only to pull at least Shiara and Ilenii toward her and to let Aahmes draw closer to the 'gods'. She sheathed her second blade, palming some of the powder from her own pouch in her other hand at the same time. Then she let her arms hang at her sides, to imply a lack of threat.

"I'm just asking," Namid said with a deliberate hint of complaint in her tone. "Some of the methods I've come across require a lot of preparation, others can get very messy." She directed a pointed look at Shiara. "Do you really want to get blood splatters all over that lovely gown you're wearing?"

Shiara looked horrified and smoothed her pale silk gown with her hands.

"But I did come across one interesting method," Namid continued. She sidled closer to the other two women and dropped her voice almost to a whisper to draw them in. She smiled to herself when they leaned toward her. "Probably something you haven't seen yet. It's supposed to make sharing Power, or giving it away, easy and smooth. It does require touch." Namid held up her empty hand and gestured the two even closer.

"How does it work?" Shiara breathed.

Working to keep her expression bland, Namid raised her other hand, opened her fist and blew all the powder in her hand into their faces before she jumped away. Aahmes followed her action with his own, adding a second large dose of the Powder. He jumped back too, and they threw a defensive shell of Wild Power around their helpless friends.

Shiara shrieked and clawed at her eyes. "What is this stuff?!"

Ilenii lurched back and swiped at her eyes, cursing.

Then Namid realized their error. While she and Aahmes had maneuvered around to get Ilenii and Shiara between them, that meant they had allowed themselves to get separated. Belaraketh slammed Aahmes with bolts of Power that sent him further back as the 'god' grabbed at Namid. He managed to catch her arm as she tried to dart away too late.

He threw his weight back and tried to drag her to Ilenii while she fought him. A twist of her other arm brought her stiletto from that armguard into her hand. She turned and slashed at him.

He ducked just enough that she missed and threw bright sparks of Power in her face.

The defense she and Aahmes held saved her from that attack, but sparkles from the glare interfered with her vision.

Namid cursed and stomped hard on Belaraketh's foot, then slashed at him again. He twisted out of the way again and this time seized her long braid.

She grinned at his howl of pain as the needles concealed within pierced his palm and fingers from the force of his grip.

Another twist and she drove the stiletto into the arm that held her.

With another cry of pain, he let go.

Namid and Aahmes both dashed toward their captive friends but collided with an unseen barrier. They spun around at the sound of Ilenii's laugher and just managed to strengthen their defenses in time to block the bolts of Power that both Ilenii and Belaraketh threw at them. Behind the sibling 'gods', Shiara crouched and tried to wipe the powder from her eyes.

With a sneer that was half snarl, Ilenii somehow drew the blood mesh into visibility and interwove her Power through it.

One handed, Belaraketh rained bolt after bolt of Power on Aahmes and Namid, seemingly unconcerned with the blood that ran from the wound in his other arm from Namid's blade.

Aahmes held their defenses, while Namid directed the Wild Power at the barrier that kept them from their friends. She built the firestorm in a confined space and used it to burn a hole through.

She ran the last few steps to Thes and Enric, touched their shoulders and sent them away from there, similar to the way she had snatched everyone's packs from the collapse of Corentris. She repeated this with the rest of their friends while Aahmes followed close behind and held their defenses, reflecting Power bolts back at the 'gods'.

Ilenii shrieked in anger as Namid sent the last captive to safety. She snaked blood Power through the blood mesh to entangle Namid and Aahmes, right through their defense, then pulled on their blood Power. Namid fought the sudden wave of dizziness that threatened to overwhelm her.

Aahmes clasped Namid's hand.

"Follow my lead?" he shouted over the noise of the Power battle.

When she nodded agreement, he twined all the Wild Power that they held together and did something that duplicated the blending they achieved with their own Power. And she felt him draw from that Wild Power shard he carried.

Namid struggled to breathe as the blood mesh tightened around her and the blood Power pulled at her. "What are you doing?" she shouted at him.

"Step!" he shouted back as he clutched her hand and threw the Power at the three 'gods'.

Namid stared at him dully. But as his attack exploded in the cavern—centered on the 'gods'—and swept toward them, she drew the last bit of Wild Power they had and stepped them away.

~ ~ ~

Namid stumbled and fell to her hands and knees, gasping for air and trembling from the aftermath of searing pain that stepping through the bound blood mesh sent through her. Aahmes was in much the same condition.

Namid struggled to fight off the darkness that threatened at the edge of her vision then took in their surroundings.

Yes, they had made it.

Their five friends still stood locked in the Power as they had been in the cavern beneath Rhadanthus. But now they were all in a hidden hollow at the base of the north side of the hill Aahmes and Namid had used earlier to study the city. While smaller, this hollow was otherwise much like the one where the two had spent the previous night.

Namid collapsed the rest of the way to the ground, unable to hold herself up any longer. She felt Aahmes place the Wild Power concealment over their hollow, then he collapsed next to her.

After a long breath-of-time, Namid rolled over so she

could see their frozen companions. She drew just a little Wild Power to herself—all she thought she could manage just then—and scrutinized them through the Power.

She felt Aahmes draw some Wild Power, too. He seemed to be directing his to the blood mesh, which had gone quiet again, something Namid was thankful for.

"Is it like the hold that Andrin did?" Aahmes asked.

"Somewhat," Namid said as she continued to study the Power that held their friends. "It's also somewhat like when Mehratar would make someone sleep."

"Hope we don't need a Healer to break it," Aahmes muttered.

Namid released the Wild Power and studied each of their companions to reassure herself that they were all breathing and were not in any distress. Then she rolled onto her back, pushed her pack to one side, and stared at the sky.

"That could have gone better," she said.

"And it could have gone worse," Aahmes said. "From what I can tell in the blood mesh, they've moved further away."

"The powder didn't affect Ilenii," Namid murmured.

"Didn't look like. But I think it did affect Shiara, at least."

"If all the 'gods' come when we do this, how are we going to stand against them?"

Aahmes was silent, with a thoughtful expression.

"I don't know," he said finally. "We're going to have to figure something out."

Namid sighed and rolled over to dig a waterskin out of her pack. After she drank, she slowly sat up and again studied their frozen companions.

"Wonder what Enric and Cameni are doing here. I wouldn't have expected to see them paying a social call on the Shadowers."

Aahmes chuckled and took a drink from the waterskin. "Thes *is* Lord of Rhadanthus now. Your brother even confirmed it."

"Though who knows if the official proclamation has made its way to the city yet," Namid said.

"True. But Enric's father's holdings are not that far away. Maybe he was sent to pay a visit to the new Lord."

Namid nodded absently. "Maybe. Or maybe Inezha brought them here, too, as part of her plans."

Aahmes nodded, his expression thoughtful. "I could see that, too, although what part they might have in this…." He shrugged as Namid turned her attention back to the Power that held their friends.

"I might see a way to free them," she said. "But it looks like they used blood Power."

She shared a dispirited look with Aahmes.

"So we probably have to use that to free them," he finished the thought. "I'm not yet up for that."

Namid shook her head. "Me neither. Maybe after some food and a bit more rest."

With a nod of agreement, Aahmes helped dig out the food they had scrounged from the devastated town a couple of days earlier. And he pulled out the one wineskin they had rescued.

Namid nibbled at the food while she hobbled around their frozen friends. She touched the back of Cameni's hand. Her skin felt cooler than Namid expected. With a slight shake of her head as she wondered what to make of that, Namid pushed down on Cameni's shoulder. The other woman sank to the ground, not really sitting, more like her knees folded under her. But otherwise she made no movement.

Namid glanced at Aahmes and he joined her to ease the others to seated positions on the ground. They all felt cool to the touch, but otherwise still looked only deeply asleep. While sitting up.

With a shared shake of their heads, Namid and Aahmes returned to their meal.

"Think it might end on its own, like Andrin's spell?"

Aahmes said after they finished eating and again studied their friends.

Namid shrugged. "I'd like to think so, but doubt we should plan on it."

"Yeah, that's what I was thinking. Ready to see if we can break this... whatever it is?"

Namid frowned. "Maybe." She drew some Wild Power to herself and reached out to the Power that held their friends.

It felt much like the blood Power mesh that she and Aahmes were connected to. But none of their friends should be part of that.

She drew more Power, while trying to ignore her growing headache, and gently shifted the mesh around Haeith, trying to see what the 'gods' had done. She managed to move it aside, but then it slid back right away.

One brighter strand of the mesh caught her attention and she followed it through the twistings and turnings of the mesh's weave. After a long breath-of-time, she found similar strands around each of the others, one to each person. She drew back to look through the Power at the mesh as a whole.

With a groan, she released the Wild Power and sank back on the ground, cradling her head.

She was aware of Aahmes sitting still next to her and felt him release Power. With a groan of his own, he clambered to his feet and approached Haeith.

"Did you see the brighter strands?" he said.

"Yeah. Looks like the 'gods' drew blood Power from them to ensnare them."

"And to hold the snare," Aahmes said. He lifted first one of Haeith's hands, then the other. He did the same for each of their friends, then returned to plop next to Namid.

"A small cut," he said. "On the side of one finger for each of them. It looks recent."

"So hopefully they haven't been like this long." Namid sighed and frowned. She wanted to free them, but her headache had grown worse. And exhaustion washed over her. "I don't think I can do anything further right now. Maybe after a bit of sleep."

Aahmes gave her a concerned look, hauled out some of their blankets, and helped her get settled.

"I'll strengthen our defenses and see what more I can learn about this." He waved a hand at their frozen friends.

Namid barely acknowledged him as sleep claimed her.

Chapter 27

Namid fought against bonds that encased her, crushing her. Not chains, something else. Slippery, sticky. Bindings that surrounded and smothered, bindings to keep her in the dark.

With a gasp, she lurched upright out of sleep. Aahmes sat next to her, one hand clasping one of hers.

She stared at him, disoriented. Then she remembered. And realized the source of what she had thought a dream. "Were you able to break all the bonds?" Namid said.

"I think so. You'd already half-broken most of them, as it was. And I think we'll now be able to break the hold they have on the others. After seeing what this was."

Namid frowned. "When could they have bound me?" she muttered.

Aahmes shrugged. "It was sloppy, too. If I'd been more alert earlier, we could have eliminated it then." Then he added, "They caught me, too, but with bonds not nearly as tight as yours."

"This just keeps getting better," Namid muttered.

Aahmes barked out a laugh and planted a kiss on her lips. "So who shall we free first?"

"I'd like to say whichever of them can help us free the rest, but I'm not sure that would be any of them."

"I'd say Mehratar or Haeith first. Perhaps one of them might know something helpful. Or at least they're the most practiced with the Power."

Namid nodded. "Mehratar, I think. Since this 'spell' sort of resembles what he does to make someone sleep."

Aahmes nodded his agreement. "Also good if anyone needs Healing. They don't look well."

Namid studied their friends and spotted what Aahmes meant. They all looked wan and the skin around their closed eyes looked bruised.

"How long did I sleep?" Namid asked in alarm. "How long was I caught up in that binding?" She looked to the sky and tried to judge the time of day by the light. The gray clouds made that impossible. All she could tell was that it was day.

"Not long," Aahmes assured her. "It's perhaps midafternoon."

With a nod, Namid rose and walked to Mehratar. She crouched in front of him and just watched him breathe. Then she sat next to him, within reach. Aahmes joined her.

"Want to take the lead on this?" Namid asked him.

"I can, if you want."

Namid shrugged. "I suppose it doesn't really matter which of us does. It's likely to be bad, no matter what."

Aahmes gave her shoulder a squeeze, then drew one of his daggers. He made a small slice on the side of his thumb and passed the blade to Namid, who emulated him. They let several drops of blood fall to the ground in a single spot between them and the captive Healer, then each clamped a hand around their wound to stop the bleeding.

With a shared glance, they reached out to their own Power and the blood Power mesh, and each touched the small puddle with a fingertip.

The mesh blazed into view. Namid scanned it and spotted the brighter strand that extended from the wound on Mehratar's finger. She also noticed something she had missed before.

"It's not really our mesh," she muttered. "The one tying us to them and to Nazextas. Somehow, they created something like it, but just wrapped around these five."

Aahmes pointed to a less dense section. "Here, I think. We can break this from the others and then more easily unravel the part around Mehratar."

Namid sniffed against the blood that had started to run from her nose and nodded.

She followed Aahmes' lead and they did much as he had described, working as fast as they dared as they raced against the reaction that built within them.

With a final snap, none too soon, the binding around Mehratar broke and fell away. He slumped to the ground, but almost immediately struggled back upright.

One hand squeezing her nose to stop the bleeding, Namid took the cloth Aahmes handed her and wrapped it around her forearm to help staunch the blood from multiple slices there. A glance at Aahmes showed him also squeezing his nose. With his other hand, he held a second bundle of cloth to his neck and upper chest. When he met her gaze, he gave her a slight shake of his head.

Mehratar stared at the two of them, seemingly trying to focus. "Wha—?"

"You were held in a binding," Namid told him. "We don't know how long."

Mehratar blinked a couple of times, then looked from each of them to the other with a frown.

"Not again," he muttered. He snagged the cloth from Namid and wrapped her arm much better than she had. Next he checked Aahmes, and repositioned his hand holding the cloth to his throat and chest.

Only then did the Healer look around at the hollow and the others who were still held.

"Do you know how long?" he asked. "Oh, you said you didn't. How about where are we, then?" He took a long drink from a waterskin that he found propped against Namid's pack.

Namid shook her head. "We might be able to figure out how long—with your help—if you think we need to. As for where, we're north and perhaps a bit west of Rhadanthus. Hidden from the 'gods'."

"We hope," Aahmes added.

Mehratar nodded absently and scrutinized the others who were still bound. Namid felt his Power reach out to them, but it felt much more subdued than normal. And he staggered a little when he finished, then sat down abruptly.

"We need to free them as soon as we can," he told Namid and Aahmes. "Best I can tell, it's been a bit longer than a day, but the binding draws on them to sustain itself. The longer it's in place, the weaker they'll get. Pretty much the nature of using blood Power."

Namid sighed and reached for her pack. "After a little food, I think I'll be up for doing it again."

With a nod of agreement, Aahmes also pulled out some food and they shared with Mehratar. The Healer seemed better than when he had been bound, but he still looked haggard.

After about a quarter candle-mark, Namid indicated she was ready. Mehratar gave her a skeptical look but did not say anything.

"Let's see if we can get rid of all the bindings at once, this time," Namid said. "And then treat ourselves to a good long recovery."

"If we get one," Aahmes muttered.

They decided they had no need to make another slice in their fingers. Since they both still bled from their use of blood Power, Aahmes and Namid planned to just use the blood from their wounds.

Aahmes clasped Namid's hand and linked his Power to hers. When their Power blended, they directed it to the remaining bonds that held their friends.

Many long breaths-of-time passed as they poured more

Power into their efforts, then finally drew on the blood mesh that connected them to Nazextas. That last let them break through whatever the 'gods' had set to hold the bonds in place. The bonds snapped away from all four remaining captives.

The snap of Power tore through Aahmes and Namid and flattened them. Then Mehratar knelt at their sides offering water and bandaging the new wounds that he could. Next he moved on to the freed captives.

Namid lay where she had fallen, eyes closed, and breathed through the pain. She hoped that once Haeith had recovered some from the bonds he might have some more of those herbs that dulled pain. A light touch on her arm drew her attention and she slowly turned her head and squinted at Aahmes, who looked as bad as she felt. Still, he smiled when their gazes met.

Then he closed his eyes, asleep.

Namid listened to Mehratar tending the others and hoped they would all be all right.

The next she knew, Haeith gently shook her awake and offered a waterskin and one of his herbal packets. He slid an arm behind her back to prop her up so she could drink. She downed it and gave him a nod of thanks.

He eased her back to the ground and placed a blanket over her. She turned to check on Aahmes and found him gazing at her.

"Only one last time of this," he murmured. "To get rid of it by bringing back that cursed city. Then we're done with it."

She nodded agreement and hoped that would be true.

~ ~ ~

Namid heard the murmur of voices. Sounded like the sharing of tales to catch up on what everyone had been doing. A gentle hand touched her arm, then her cheek. A blanket was tucked around her. She decided she did not need to fully wake yet.

Some time later, Namid coughed herself awake. She sat up trying to catch her breath and coughed harder, but tried to keep quiet about it. She tasted blood. Someone handed her a waterskin and she drank.

Namid woke to a stream of sunshine on her face. She rolled over and came face to face with Aahmes. He greeted her with a smile and a kiss, then sat up and passed her a waterskin. She sat up and looked around.

Cameni and Enric huddled together in the center of the hollow by a low fire, really not much more than glowing coals. They gave her nods of acknowledgement but stayed where they sat. They both looked better than they had when held by the so-called gods' binding, but not completely well. The bruises under their eyes stood out starkly against their pale skin. And Cameni looked worried.

Neither looked like they belonged outside in a hollow by a campfire. Both wore richly embroidered clothes, Cameni's gown a pale purple and Enric's doublet and trousers blue. Cameni wore her long red-gold hair in two braids, decorated with silk ribbons that matched her gown. Enric's light brown hair looked like it needed a trim. Or perhaps he was letting it grow so he could tie it in a queue, Namid speculated. That style had been popular in Kilaadi for Tal's coronation.

Mehratar rose from where he had been sitting near Enric and Cameni and approached. He looked better than the other two, but not completely well himself.

An effect of the so-called gods' bonds, Namid decided. Looked like it hit Enric harder than the others. Maybe because he had no Power of his own.

Namid returned the waterskin to Aahmes and tried to stand, but her legs would not hold her. She dropped back to lean against Aahmes. Everything ached.

"How long?" she croaked to Aahmes.

"A bit more than a day," he told her.

Mehratar knelt next to her and clasped both her hands

as his Power washed over her. Some of the aches faded.

He looked down at her left hand then, where he held it, then looked at Aahmes' left hand.

"I see congratulations are in order," he said with a smile.

Namid could not contain her smile. She and Aahmes murmured their thanks.

"Where are Haeith and Thes?" Namid asked.

"Just off getting a few things for us," Aahmes said.

"We'll be here another few days, at the very least," Mehratar said and motioned to Cameni to help Namid get herself sorted out. Cameni spoke little, just kept giving Namid worried looks until they joined the others at the fire.

There Aahmes handed Namid a small bowl of hot stew and settled next to her.

Enric studied her, then gave her a smile.

"You're looking much better," he said. "And you have our thanks for freeing us." Cameni shuddered. He draped an arm around her shoulder and pulled her close.

"How do you come to be here?" Namid asked around bites of food. "How did the 'gods' take you?"

"As Aahmes said you guessed, we were visiting Lord Thes," Cameni said. "We'd really just arrived."

"We were speaking with Lord Thes—" Enric began.

"He met us right in his stronghold's courtyard!" Cameni exclaimed. Namid could not tell if she was surprised or affronted. Maybe a bit of both. Probably not something usually done in Navele.

"Yes," Enric said. "Most kind of him. As I said, we were speaking, just the normal introductions and greetings sorts of things when there was a flash of light."

"It hurt, and quite blinded us," Cameni said.

"And after that, I only remember snippets," Enric continued. He glanced at his cut finger, now wrapped. "Some pain. Someone talking, sounded like giving instructions or orders. Walking."

"And then we woke up here," Cameni said as she looked around the hollow with an expression of not-quite disgust, betraying her opinion that her surroundings fell short of what they should be.

Mehratar took up the narrative then.

"You and Aahmes were in bad shape. Use of the blood Power, and your own Power, too, I'd say. Is that correct?"

Namid nodded.

"Something similar with these cuts," Mehratar said as he held up his own sliced finger, wrapped in a strip of cloth. "I could not Heal them, just as I could not Heal any of those wounds you two take from the blood Power. The slices have a similar feel to them."

"The 'gods' used blood Power for their binding," Aahmes said.

"But the most extraordinary thing," Cameni gushed. "Mehratar here knows a Healing sleep. And he's shown me how to do it."

"She's proven better than most at learning it, certainly she shows promise," Mehratar said. "It doesn't Heal those wounds, but puts your bodies in a state that enhances their ability to heal on their own. I used it before, to help Heal you, your legs in particular, after we found you near Meahan."

Cameni gave him a quizzical look at that.

"We'll give you the whole story later," Aahmes murmured to her.

Namid looked from Mehratar to Cameni. "That's wonderful! Thank you."

The two inclined their heads in almost identical gestures. Namid stifled a laugh.

"Thes and Haeith returned to Tower Hold to get us some more supplies," Aahmes told Namid as he leaned close. "Not sure Thes will return with Haeith."

"Was he angered at us?" Namid said.

Aahmes grinned. "Angered, yes. 'How dare these so-called gods be messin' wi' the Shadowers!'"

Namid chortled at Aahmes' imitation of Thes, then winced as that woke a number of aches again.

Aahmes gave her shoulder a gentle squeeze. "Angered at us? Not this time. But he did give me the definite impression that he expects us to straighten this matter out, so such a thing doesn't happen again." He shared a wry look with her.

"Of course he does. Well, soon—"

"Not too soon," Mehratar interrupted her. He pointed first at her, then Aahmes. "You two cannot succeed at your task, not as you are right now. We are this close. You will be as Healed as possible before you finish this."

Namid stared at him, then exchanged glances with Aahmes. "Yes sir," she said to Mehratar, but with a slight grin to take any sting out of it.

Then she gave him a questioning look and glanced to Cameni and Enric. "Our task...."

"We know what he refers to," Cameni said.

"Everyone just thought we should not speak too openly of what we are about," Aahmes said.

"Ah," Namid said with a nod. She finished her meal and set the bowl aside to deal with later. Aahmes brought over another blanket and settled in next to her, wrapping the blanket around them both. The sun had some warmth to it, but the air still held the chill of winter. As she thought about it, Namid realized it must be near the start of spring.

For a breath-of-time Namid stared into the glowing coals of the dying fire and mostly ignored the low murmur of conversation among the others. As her thoughts cleared, she startled.

"What about the St— statue and the key?" she said, turning to Aahmes and only just remembering to speak circumspectly.

A laugh went around the small circle. Enric pulled something from his belt pouch and reached across the fire ring to hand it to Aahmes.

"You were right," he said.

Namid directed a look at Aahmes that was half curiosity and half glower. "Whatever you wagered about me, I get half," she said.

Aahmes leaned close and whispered in her ear. "Everything I have is yours." He pressed the navn and gem from Enric into her hand and closed her fingers around them as he brushed her cheek with his lips.

Then in a normal voice he said, "I knew it wouldn't take you long to remember those items."

"Here's one of the items you asked about," Mehratar said as he pulled the Star of Corentris from a bag that sat under a blanket. He passed it to Namid. "No sign of any Power about it that I can sense," he said. "Haeith had it tied to his belt under his cloak when the 'gods' took us, and they did not seem to notice it at all."

"And no sign of any Power from it, or any Power gathering while it was in that cavern, either," Aahmes told her.

Namid turned the Star over in her hands, admiring again the distorted star-shaped statue and the valuable jewel set into the center of one side. The jewel was a smoky, silver-gray color and one she had seen nowhere else. She tapped it with a fingernail as she tried to get her thoughts into some semblance of order.

"Wait to use any Power," Mehratar warned even before she had considered it. "You are still wounded enough and weakened enough that you might be unable to control it. And would most certainly do yourself more harm, in any case."

Namid squinted at him, then glanced around the hollow before she realized she could not see the Wild Power shell that Aahmes had set over them.

"It's still there," he told her. "Earlier, before we both fell unconscious, I managed to link that shard we found to the shell. So it's holding it for us right now."

"Because he is also forbidden to use Power for now,"

Mehratar said with an intense, stern look for Aahmes. "Any Power."

"What did you do?" Namid asked, trying not to smile.

Aahmes gave her a stern look, then chuckled. "Tried to draw Wild Power right after I woke from that sleep of his and knocked myself right back out."

"And it could have been much worse," Cameni said.

A hint of movement to her left caught Namid's attention. Haeith eased his way through the surrounding bushes and joined them. He carried two stuffed packs, which he set down before he sat.

"Enough food to hold us for several days," he said. "Should be long enough?" He directed that to Mehratar.

Namid felt a hint of Mehratar's Power wash over her. "I believe so," the Healer said.

"Thes?" Namid asked Haeith.

"He chose to stay in Tower Hold. That upper room of the tallest tower has defenses that should even foil the so-called gods," Haeith said. "At least for a time. He and his Lady plan to stay there 'until those two miscreants finish fixin' all this'. His words, not mine."

Haeith gave Namid one of his rare smiles. "He's got his people working on getting everyone out of the city and into Tower Hold. I added some defenses to the Hold and a warning, so we'll know if they need help."

"They'll fit everyone from the whole city into Lord Thes' Hold?" Cameni said, disbelief clear in her tone.

"You haven't yet had a chance to look over the city, Lady Cameni," Haeith said. "Few yet live there and all but a small portion of the city itself still lies in ruins from the Dark Priests' attack over a year ago."

"You do still plan to complete the task in the city, correct?" Mehratar said.

Namid nodded. "The only other option is an even more-ruined city buried under who knows how much dirt and rock. I'd rather not have to try to figure out how to make that work."

She turned to Aahmes. "And what of the key?"

He waved a hand at the statue she still held. "Do you still think we need it, now that we have this?"

Namid shrugged. "I really don't know. But I'd rather have it and find we don't need it than the other way around."

Aahmes nodded. "I did mention it to Thes before he and Haeith left earlier. He said he'd dig it out for us."

"I'll return to retrieve it, probably after sunset today," Haeith said. Namid nodded and leaned against Aahmes, her energy suddenly draining away. He gave her a concerned look and she smiled at him.

"You'll both benefit from more sleep today," Cameni said.

"Normal sleep," Mehratar added, "not the Power-effected one I used on you earlier." He turned his intent gaze on Cameni. "That is one to use sparingly," he instructed her.

She nodded her understanding.

Aahmes and Namid helped each other back to Namid's nest of blankets and settled in together.

"Now we've got two of them to harp at us," Aahmes murmured, but grinned.

Chapter 28

Darkness. Namid opened her eyes and it was still dark, only a little moonlight. She rolled just far enough to see Aahmes lying asleep next to her. She tried not to disturb him as she untangled herself from the blankets, then grabbed one again to wrap around herself against the night's chill.

A sense of Haeith's Power came to her from outside the Wild Power shell that lay over the hollow, then Haeith stepped inside, with Thes behind him. Mehratar rose from where he had huddled close to the coals of the fire. Namid joined them. Thes startled her by pulling her into a fierce hug. He slipped the key shaped like the Star into her hand as he let her go.

"I'd been worryin' about you. Glad to see you gettin' up and about."

Namid patted Thes' arm in thanks. She felt Mehratar's Power sweep across her and gave him a questioning look.

"Much better," he assured her. "You should be feeling it, too. I'll allow you to draw a small bit of your Wild Power to see if Aahmes' shell needs to be bolstered. And you may bolster it, too, if it does."

Namid stiffened when he said he would allow her, then forced herself to relax under his intent, knowing gaze. She still felt the lightest touch of his Power, she suspected to monitor that she did herself no further harm.

She brushed away some rocks and sat near the coals. With some hesitation, she reached out to draw Wild Power to herself. It was slow in coming, but when she finally grasped some, it brought her no discomfort.

Tentatively she reached out to the Wild Power concealment that Aahmes had placed over their hidden hollow. It needed no bolstering and she took the opportunity to scrutinize it through the Power. As he had said earlier, Aahmes had done something different for this one. It drew Wild Power steadily from the small shard, which seemed to steadily draw Wild Power from around them, just a trickle to maintain the shell. Namid had not known a person could set up something like this.

"You could at least warn a fellow."

Namid jumped at Aahmes' voice right next to ear and the Wild Power she held slipped away again. Aahmes turned her around and planted a solid kiss on her lips.

When she could breathe again, Namid gave him a wry grin. "Had it set to warn you if someone poked at it, did you?"

Aahmes tried to frown at her, but the corners of his mouth kept quirking up. "Of course. Might be the only warning we'd get."

"And you set it to pull Wild Power on its own?"

Aahmes pulled the small black shard from a pouch and held it up. "Not too difficult once I figured a way to link it to this," he said.

"Is that...?" Haeith rose from where he had crouched near the coals warming his hands.

"In a sense," Aahmes said and let him take it. "We got that from an echo of *that sword* in the ghostly city." Namid smiled at Aahmes' adherence to speaking vaguely.

He glanced at her. "Thinking about it, I believe this

shard is the true Power that was within that sword."

Namid considered that but could not see an argument to refute that. Haeith returned it to Aahmes who tucked it away again.

"Brought more food for the lot o' you," Thes said as he set down a full pack. He looked from Namid to Mehratar. "How much longer 'til we're seein' the end o' this fuss?"

"A couple more days?" Namid said, her gaze on Mehratar.

The Healer nodded thoughtfully. "I think so. You and Aahmes are healing much better than I had reason to believe you would. But—"

"But we need to make sure we're ready to do this the first time," Aahmes broke in. "I certainly don't want to have to try to do it again."

"Judging by the wounds you took from this most recent use of your Power, you might not get a chance to do it again."

Namid plopped down next to the coals. "Wonderful," she muttered. She had suspected such a thing, the idea buried deep inside her, but hearing it aloud made it that much worse.

Aahmes squeezed her shoulder. "We've got this," he told her, confidence clear in his tone. "But for now, I'm going back to sleep." He returned to the blankets.

When Namid did not follow him, Mehratar sat next to her. Haeith and Thes wandered toward the edge of the hollow as they spoke in low voices. From the little Namid heard, it sounded like they were finalizing plans to get everyone temporarily settled in Tower Hold.

She sighed and hoped that would be enough to keep them safe.

"I worry that waiting will only give the 'gods' more time for more destruction," Namid murmured.

"But not waiting is almost certainly asking for failure," Mehratar said. "If you feel up to it, I don't see why you couldn't reach out carefully to see what they are up to, if you can."

"Did Aahmes tell you of the blood Power mesh we discovered while we were in the ghostly city?" Namid lowered her voice almost to a whisper.

"He did. It explains a lot."

"I can try to sense through that, but to do so I'll need to use a little blood Power myself."

Mehratar studied her, then shook his head. "You need to *not* use your own Power or the blood Power it's twined with. You'll need that for your task. But here." Before she could object, Mehratar pulled out a small blade and sliced the side of one finger. He grasped her hand and dripped several drops of blood into it. "Use that," he instructed as he Healed the small slice.

With a nod of thanks, Namid touched a finger to the drops of blood and reached out in the same way she would reach for Wild Power. The blood Power was there, more potent than she expected. She took hold of it and reached through the mesh to see if she could determine anything about the so-called gods' activity, or even their locations.

Less than a quarter candle-mark later, she came out of the Power and sagged.

"All I can tell for certain is that they are not nearby. Nowhere near us or the city over there right now."

Mehratar helped her to her feet and, after they cleaned the blood from her hand, steered her to her blankets. "That's good, then. Now rest. Sleep some more. It'll see you ready that much sooner."

Namid willingly snuggled back into the warmth at Aahmes' side and drifted off again.

~ ~ ~

When Namid woke next, it was bright day. The others had gathered around the small fire and she smelled something wonderful cooking.

She stumbled the few steps to join the others and they greeted her with smiles. Aahmes handed her a bowl of hot food and mug of hot drink.

As she ate, she looked over everyone seated there. Thes was gone again, she assumed back to Tower Hold. She hoped he was safe there. Haeith returned her regard with a solemn expression but did not say anything. He did nod at her food when she failed to take another bite right away.

Cameni and Enric had their heads together talking in low voices as they ate. While everyone looked much better, much recovered from their captivity, Enric looked less so.

Perhaps the binding from the so-called gods affected those with no Power of their own worse than it did others. No doubt Cameni would see him back to health.

Mehratar looked tense, but otherwise fine. When Namid met his gaze, she felt his Power wash over her. And he gave her a slight smile.

Aahmes looked much better than a few candle-marks earlier. He squeezed her hand when their gazes met, then went back to his own meal.

"Something that's bothered me," Cameni broke the silence a breath-of-time later, "what brought the 'gods' here? To this city? Could they have followed one or more of us? Is there a chance they can find us that easily again?"

"They did have a way to keep track of us when we were looking for that sword of Enric's," Namid said.

Enric's head came up sharply at that.

"How?" he said.

Namid lifted the bangs off her forehead to show the scar at her hairline where the tattoo from Ilenii's temple had been. "Both Aahmes and I received tattoos when we learned about Power at the temples. Did you?" She directed the query to Cameni, who exchanged a glance with Enric then shook her head.

"Probably that means they can't find you, then," Namid said. They both looked relieved.

"I sense no connection from her to the mesh, or

307

anything else, so I think we're safe," Aahmes murmured, studying Cameni. Namid felt the faint brush of Wild Power as he then turned to study Enric, Haeith and Mehratar in turn. "No," he said and released the small bit of Power he held. "Nothing connecting anyone else, either."

Namid sagged in relief at the easing of a worry she had not even acknowledged until then.

"And I didn't sense any Power from the statue, either," Aahmes added with a glare for the bag that held the Star.

"The book said in the city," Namid mused. "So far, the statue's only been *under* it." She leaned over, grabbed the bag, and grinned at Mehratar's aborted attempt to stop her. "I know. Nothing yet. I just want to see something."

She pulled the Star from its bag, held it up in a shaft of sunlight, and turned it around and over, examining it from all sides. She tried to slide a fingernail between the edge of the jewel in the statue's center and the surrounding metal. She flipped the statue over and studied the underside of the base, running her fingers across the smooth metal. She could not see it at first, but her fingers discovered an interesting depression. She held the statue up to eye-level and could just make out the slight concavity her fingers had found.

Feeling the others watching her, Namid pulled the key with the star-shaped bow from the pouch where she had stashed it and held it to the depression without touching the two. She turned the statue and key to show the others. The key seemed a perfect match to the depression. The very tip of its bow looked like it would fit a small notch that Namid just then noticed at the edge of the base. Comparing the key and notch, Namid guessed that the key's tip would extend the slightest bit beyond the edge of the statue's base if the key was placed into the depression.

"Something else to try when we get into the city," she said and smiled at the astonished looks she got.

"Where did the key come from?" Cameni asked as

Namid put away both statue and key.

Namid told the story of how the previous leader of the Shadowers had left her the key's impression and she had the key made. When she finished, Mehratar again admonished her and Aahmes to rest to be ready for their task.

And so the rest of that day, and the next, Namid spent her time doing mostly nothing and growing ever more restless with the inactivity. But it was worth it.

When she rose shortly after dawn the morning of the third day—after having been under Mehratar's Power-effected sleep the night before—she felt almost normal. She still had lingering aches, but nothing that she thought would interfere with what they had to do that day. She roamed around their hollow to try to ease some of those aches even further.

Soon everyone was awake. They ate a hurried breakfast and cleared the hollow of signs of their presence.

Over objections from both Mehratar and Cameni, Namid told them she and Aahmes would step everyone to Tower Hold, then only they two would go into Rhadanthus.

"Should you perhaps wait until nightfall?" Enric asked.

Namid glanced at Aahmes and saw no preference in his expression.

She shrugged. "Don't see what difference it would make. We'll go as soon as all of you are safe in Thes' tower room."

Of course, it did not go that smoothly.

Namid and Aahmes found they could not step directly into the tower room, which had been Namid's preference, so they stepped to Namid's room. Aahmes held a Wild Power shell around them similar to the one he had placed on the hollow. They decided to dispense with any other shells, so when they left Namid's room and headed for the top tower room, they caused quite a fuss among the Shadowers.

After too much time, they finally made it into the top room of the tower. There, Thes awaited them, looking noble in some fine clothes. Keizha hovered nearby, also wearing fine clothes. Both greeted them warmly as Haeith took up a position at the door.

"And we must go," Namid said, breaking away from the greetings.

"Aye," Thes said. "But you come back after you're done fixin' this."

"We'll watch as we can from the window," Keizha added, with a wave of her hand to indicate the wide window that faced Rhadanthus.

"Just don't step outside these walls until it's done," Aahmes warned.

Keizha gave him a motherly pat on the arm. "We know. Don't you be worryin' about us."

Namid and Aahmes took their weapons, the Star and the key, and food and water for the day. Everything else they left piled near the door. On the way past Haeith, they met the warrior's gaze. With a nod of acknowledgement, he unsheathed his sword.

Mehratar followed them as they stepped out of the room, giving Namid a slight smile in answer to her quizzical look. He closed the door behind him and Namid felt him send a wave of his Power out and around them and into the nearby city.

He nodded to Namid as his Power dissipated. "The city's empty. No one's there now – not even any animals."

After he favored both Aahmes and Namid with one of his intent looks, but said nothing further, he returned to the tower room. The door closed, leaving them alone in the hall to make their step into the city.

Aahmes clasped Namid's hand and gave her a quick kiss. Needing no words, they drew Wild Power to themselves, fortified their defenses, and stepped into the ruined city of Rhadanthus.

CHAPTER 29

Namid found the silence of the city disconcerting. She had not really noticed before how many sounds there were, even when it had been peopled by only the few survivors of Sy'shythys.

She and Aahmes stood at the edge of the blasted depression that marred the center of the city. After a quick look around, they hurried to shelter in a nearby ruin that still had a partial roof. Aahmes placed the Wild Power shell around the ruin to hide them while Namid pulled out the Star. She set it on the ground, already sensing it drawing Power to itself.

"Wonder how long it needs to draw the Power," she murmured.

With a shrug, Aahmes pulled out the jewel-shard from Akavos and worked to link them through it to the Star so they could draw on its Power.

"Assuming it'll let us link," Aahmes said. "Don't know what it's drawing Power for."

Namid nodded and pulled out the key. "Place this now or wait?"

Aahmes shrugged.

"You're no help," Namid grumped but grinned at him. She tipped the Star over and fit the key into the depression on the bottom with an audible snap. As she had guessed, the tip of the key's bow extended just beyond the edge of the statue's base. Hardly noticeable, but she wondered at the purpose that served.

They both peered at the Star and waited for something to happen. When nothing obvious did, Namid shrugged, set the Star back on the ground, and sat next to it. Aahmes joined her and wrapped an arm around her shoulders.

Namid sent a thin tendril of her own Power into the blood Power mesh. She had gotten better at spotting the 'gods' within the mesh, but could only guess most of the time at which was which, except for Belaraketh and Ilenii. Still, they were not close, none of them.

After she told Aahmes that, they settled in to wait, sharing some food and drink and talking of random things, such as ideas of what they would do after they cleansed themselves of the blood Power.

In the midst of describing an improbable journey, Namid bolted upright at a sudden thought.

"The warning!"

Aahmes gave her a perplexed look. "What?"

"That spell or whatever it was that Chendrukhar placed on the Star—"

Aahmes rose with a curse and reached out with Power to the Star. Namid joined him and they easily found the Power Chendrukhar had placed on it. Namid wished that they had time to study it more, figure out how it was there and yet they had not sensed it, but they had already been in Rhadanthus several candle-marks. The spell had been set to go off after the Star had been in the city half a day, to warn the mage to remove it. Or so they believed. Namid hoped it was still that long.

"If that spell goes off…" she muttered as she tried to discover a way to remove it. "A great, bright beacon shooting up into the sky—"

"I remember," Aahmes said. "It'll be perfect to draw the 'gods' to us. But sooner than we'll want, I think."

They clasped hands and spent close to a quarter candle-mark trying various things with their Power to dismantle the warning.

When they still had not figured out anything, they paused to drink and consider the problem.

"I don't want to use blood Power," Namid said.

"Agreed. Maybe this." Aahmes held out the small jewel-shard.

Namid studied it and noticed a faint glow within it. "Worth a try."

So they settled themselves again, all too aware that time was slipping away from them. They drew Wild Power, linked to each other and the jewel-shard, and again poked at the Power warning on the Star.

This time, a faint glow appeared within the jewel on the Star. It matched the glow in the shard.

"There's a tug on the shard," Aahmes said. He brought it closer to the Star. With a bright flash, the shard leapt from his hand to the jewel on the Star and sank into it, merging with it.

And they were able to discern how the mage had wrapped his spell around the statue. Hurrying as much as they dared, while taking care to avoid anything that would make matters worse, they unwound the coils and knots of Chendrukhar's spell one by one.

When they finished, the sun stood high in the sky. With sighs of relief, they sank back into a shaded area and pulled out a little more food and a waterskin.

Namid kept part of her attention on the statue, though, just in case they had somehow missed something. From time to time, she also touched on the Power it was pulling to itself.

After they ate, she and Aahmes swept all around them with Wild Power and checked the blood mesh, too. No one was nearby. Namid felt a slight tremor in the mesh, but it did not affect them, so she disregarded it. They dozed in turns in the afternoon sun while they waited for the Star to finish gathering Power.

As late afternoon shadows stretched through the ruins, Namid shook Aahmes awake.

"It's stopped," she told him. "And hasn't done anything else. Just sits there holding all that Power."

He yawned and stretched, then looked toward the setting sun.

"Guess we're doing this in the dark after all."

Namid grinned at him. "Shadowers' time of day."

With a matching expression, he caught up the Star.

"Ready then?"

Namid took a breath-of-time to study his face and filled her mind with thoughts of him, of being together with him after this was over. After a long kiss, she nodded.

"I think right in the city's center," she said and waved an arm toward the gaping depression where the heart of Rhadanthus had been. "That's where the tower is in the ghost city."

With a nod of agreement, Aahmes bolstered their defensive shells and led the way from their shelter.

Namid followed and caught his hand in her own. He turned back slightly to brush her fingers with his lips, and they made their way down into the hole.

The footing was difficult. Ice still lay in patches and loose rubble lay elsewhere. The bottom of the depression lay a few handspans lower than the line of lighter-colored stones embedded in the wall of the hole that Namid had spotted when Thes had first shown her this destruction. From within the hole, she saw that the layer extended all the way around.

She and Aahmes hiked to the center of the depression and stopped.

"Here?" Aahmes said.

Namid looked around. "Looks good."

Aahmes set the Star on the ground then shifted it back

and forth a little on the loose rubble to get it to sit straight.

"Links still feel steady?" he asked as he settled to one side of the Star.

Namid checked all the Power links, hers to Aahmes, to the statue's Power, to the Wild Power, and to the blood mesh.

With a nod, she sat across from him, on the other side of the statue, facing him. She drew a dagger and made a small slice on the side on her thumb as Aahmes mirrored her action. They dripped a few drops of blood onto the ground between them to make a tiny puddle of their combined blood. Each touched a finger to the small puddle and reached for the blood Power that had come to them. It leapt eagerly to them and they drew it into all the Power links they had forged.

Namid clasped both Aahmes' hands and smiled when he gave them a squeeze. She gazed at their rings, on their left hands, then looked up to meet his gaze.

"Ready?" she said.

"Yeah. Any thoughts about how to pull the ghost city?"

"A possibility. Here…." Namid closed her eyes and reached out to Aahmes in her thoughts. She led him into the mesh, following a particular strand.

~*I've noticed some differences in the strands of the mesh,*~ Namid told him, switching to thought-speech. ~*There are these.*~ She indicated several thick strands.

~*Connected to our friends the so-called gods,*~ Aahmes observed.

~*Yes. And these others.*~ She indicated the bulk of the rest of the strands, thinner and somehow sickly looking.

~*Those who are trapped in Nazextas?*~ Aahmes guessed.

~*I believe so. And then this one,*~ Namid indicated a thick strand that looked sickly.

~*Similar to both,*~ Aahmes mused. ~*You think that's Vlatas?*~

~*I do,*~ she gave an impression of a nod. ~*And I think we can follow his strand to get close enough to Nazextas to draw it back with us.~*

She sensed Aahmes' attention moving through the mesh and received a sense of agreement from him.

Together they drew on their own Power, now blended, lightly attached a tendril of it to the mesh strand they believed was Vlatas and followed it through all the twists and tangles of the blood mesh. Sooner than Namid expected, they reached a node on that strand, in a heavy cluster of other nodes from the sickly looking strands.

~I'll follow your lead,~ Aahmes told Namid.

~You assume I know what I'm doing,~ Namid countered with an impression of amusement.

~Or at least have an idea to begin with,~ Aahmes retorted. His own amusement colored the thought.

Namid reached out through their blended Power and blood Power to the cluster of nodes and strands. She pictured Nazextas, the ghostly buildings and streets, and remembered the people she had seen walking those streets. A hazy impression of the city formed around the cluster.

Aahmes channeled more Power into Namid's effort and added his own memories of the city. A faint quiver ran through the mesh and out away from the cluster.

Next Namid presented a sensation of movement, of drawing the city, the cluster, away from where it was and toward her own location. Aahmes stayed right with her and lent his own strength to the effort.

A hint of movement and she increased her efforts as she tried to set aside the pain that built behind her eyes. Her senses sharpened within the flood of Power.

Another quiver rippled through the blood mesh, but this time coming toward the cluster. Agony shot into Namid from the mesh strands that connected her to the rest. Pain from Aahmes tore through her, too.

She lost her hold on the images of the city and people and the cluster halted. Desperately, she and Aahmes built a shell around themselves within the mesh. But the attack along the strands slid right through.

Then Aahmes twisted the Power of the shell just a bit, similar to what he had done during the attack from Belaraketh and Ilenii a year earlier. The next attack that flowed along the strands bounced away from them before it reached them. More Power flowed into the attack and it bounced back, piled up, and abruptly ran back the directions it had come. Namid felt a sense of surprise and alarm through the mesh.

She shared a sense of thanks and love with Aahmes, colored with a hint of amusement at their attackers' alarm, then returned her attention to Nazextas.

While her effort had seemed to be working, they needed something faster. She could already feel the pounding in her head and pain pricking at other parts of her body. How long before they could no longer control the Power?

She decided on a different approach. She drew more Wild Power to herself, pulling it through the Star, and wove it with the blended Power, hoping it would strengthen her efforts. She pictured the city and people again, but this time added the desire for home and peace to the mix.

She poured her own desire for a home she was not torn away from, sent away from, and the sudden realization that Rhadanthus felt most like the home where she belonged.

A strong tremor in the mesh shook them both, giving warning of the attack that followed.

Waves of Power ran along the blood mesh and slammed into Aahmes and Namid from multiple directions. The Power knocked them over and sent innumerable needles of agony tearing through them. And that was after their defense shells blocked at least half of the combined attack and sent half of the rest surging back to where it came from.

Namid managed to keep her grip on Aahmes and this time held the images of Nazextas and its people. To that she added the image of Rhadanthus and drew them together, picturing Nazextas overlying the ruined Rhadanthus and merging with it.

A surge of Power from the Star tore through her, through Aahmes, and enveloped the cluster and the image of Nazextas. The entire blood mesh trembled as the cluster rushed toward Rhadanthus. It engulfed Namid and Aahmes and threw them back to themselves as it landed in the depression in the center of Rhadanthus.

Namid opened her eyes and attempted to stifle her groan at the pain that coursed through her body. Even without looking through Power, she could see the mesh and the faint image of Nazextas. Both expanded and stretched out across the ruined city, until they filled it completely. And everything felt sharper, more vivid, faint sounds louder and colors brighter than they should have been. Almost painfully so.

A sudden surge of Power hit Aahmes and Namid, but this time their shells held, and the Power flowed around them. Namid's ears popped as one by one, distortions formed in the air nearby, positioned in a rough circle surrounding them.

Namid and Aahmes helped each other to their feet and stood back to back, leaning together to stay upright, hands clasped, with the Star held together in Namid's right hand, Aahmes' left. Together, they poured what Power they could into a defensive shell, but Namid felt their blended Power, with the blood Power that had come to them, too, draining into the blood mesh that now filled Rhadanthus.

After they each stepped out of one of the distortions, Belaraketh, Ilenii and Shiara gathered together and built a defensive shell around themselves. A tall woman with dark brown skin, pale green-gray eyes, and black hair worn in many thin braids appeared directly in front of Namid: the god Narqir. She held Namid's gaze for a breath-of-time, then gave her a slight bow and backed up toward the edge of the depression.

A man Namid had never seen before stepped out of

the air to her left. He jumped back away from the center of the depression and threw Power at the three who stood within their defense shell. After studying him, Namid detected a resemblance to Mehratar in the shape of the man's eyes and jaw, and his light-brown skin and dark brown hair were both the same shade as Mehratar's. He must be Jelth.

Streams of Power came from behind Namid to strike at both the three and Jelth. A quick look over her shoulder and Namid saw another man she did not know, with golden-brown skin and black hair. The 'god' Roivahneheb, she assumed.

Vlatas was the last to arrive. He looked around with an incredulous expression and raised his arms to the starry sky overhead as he drew in a deep breath. He stepped close to Aahmes and Namid, with a glare for Shiara and her companions. He built a second shell around the shell Aahmes and Namid held just as Power struck at them from all sides.

"I'll hold them off as long as I can," he shouted over his shoulder. Namid could barely hear him over the noise from all the Power being thrown around. "Finish with your work here. Restore the city."

Aahmes gave her hands a squeeze, which she returned, and they again turned their Power to the cities.

Nazextas now filled the entire area within Rhadanthus' walls, and the buildings looked a little more solid than before.

The Star in their hands suddenly flared with light and sent a brilliant beam reaching high into the sky. Namid felt an answering surge to the south.

"Corentris?" Aahmes shouted.

"They *have* been connected," Namid shouted back. She ducked as something large flew toward her, then past her and into the city. It had looked like part of a building.

She felt a tug on the blood Power she carried, and it flowed out faster. And more pieces of structures flew by, coming from the south. The ground beneath their feet shook, a shiver sort of motion and dirt and rubble sifted into the depression, filling it under their feet somehow and lifting them higher.

Ilenii shrieked what sounded like a denial and poured more Power into her attack. A bit of her Power attack made it past Vlatas and staggered Aahmes and Namid.

Namid reached out through the blood mesh and tangled herself in it like tangling her fingers in a mess of yarn. She fed her purpose of seeing the city whole into it and pulled it into her purpose.

Several of the 'gods' cried out and left off attacking each other to concentrate on Aahmes and Namid. With each new attack, more and more of their Power leaked through, shooting pain through Namid and Aahmes.

More and more pieces of buildings came from the south, trailing globs of dirt that fell to the ground behind them. Namid could not see where the pieces of buildings went through the near-constant flashes of Power around her and Aahmes. But she sensed that they formed a massive whorl around the central depression, much like when she formed the firestorm.

And that gave her an idea.

She sent Aahmes a quick thought-image of the firestorm and felt his support and agreement. He poured more of their blended Power, backed by Wild Power, into the effort of putting the city back together, freeing her for the firestorm.

She called more Wild Power, shouted aloud for it, and drew it with her will, with every part of her being. For a breath-of-time, it seemed everything halted and sudden silence fell.

Then the Wild Power roared into her, through her, swirled around her outside and within Vlatas' crumbling defense. She felt Narqir's Power join with Vlatas'. Then Namid noticed nothing but the blue-white fire.

CHAPTER 30

With howls and shrieks, Power raged through the city, roiled around everyone in the city's center.

Namid's flames spiraled around her, the outer edge of the maelstrom at the edge of the depression, a hungry blue-white blaze. She squinted into the blinding light, flames filling her vision.

Power thundered through her, no longer clearly blood, or Wild, or her own. And Power flashed around her, her flames, the so-called gods' desperate attempts to rip the Power from her and Aahmes, or to stop them. She no longer knew which.

The 'gods' yelled, screamed with their efforts, their voices blending into the cacophony.

Fear suddenly stabbed through Namid when she realized she could not sense Aahmes. Her hands heated, burning with her firestorm. Did she still clasp his?

A quick sense of his presence reassured her, with the squeeze from his hands still holding hers helping even more.

Then her attention was caught by the blood.

The mesh around them, whipping in and around the

firestorm, alternately yanked on them and plunged through them. Each yank brought with it a burning pang; each pang worse than the previous. Gold-green swirls twined around and through the mesh and blue-white flames danced across it. And the blood from her sliced thumb slowly, slowly dripped to the ground as it drained vitality and blood Power from her at the same time.

Drip....

She drew more on the blood Power, felt Aahmes right there with her. Together, they impressed the idea of one city from two on the Power that roared through them. They ripped at the blood mesh to recreate the city.

And the blood mesh ripped at them.

Some of the luster cleared from Namid's vision. She saw the pieces of the city join the chaos, flying past and whirling around to snap into their places from long ago.

The so-called gods' Power battered her and Aahmes. It raced along the blood mesh to tear at what they were doing, to try to tear their Power away.

White paving stones flew into the center of the storm, under Aahmes' feet, under Namid's, and lifted them up to form a floor. More of their Power, more of the blood Power, was ripped from them to build the city anew.

Drip....

The blood mesh flared into visibility; the strands connected to the 'gods' forming the brightest parts. Those strands writhed in the air like they were alive and homed in on Namid and Aahmes, diving at them and into them.

Namid screamed as searing pain tore her, tore through her. She heard Aahmes scream, too.

She clung to Aahmes' hands and clung to the Power they directed, although it felt like pieces of her were being torn away, shredded by the blood mesh and the 'gods'.

Waves of fatigue broke over her and tried to draw her into the deceptive peace of no longer fighting.

Drip....

Bit by bit, the lower part of the firestorm changed,

turned white and formed into stones, then a stone wall, almost too bright to look at. The central tower grew up from the ground, surrounding them.

Namid heard a shriek of rage and other shouts from outside the tower. The shriek sounded like Ilenii's voice.

With a snap that Namid felt all through her body, she sensed the last pieces of the city fall into their places. A flare of red-gold light blinded Namid, then she found herself outside the tower, hands holding only Aahmes' hands – the statue gone. She and Aahmes stood only because they held each other upright. Barely.

Drip....

In the confusion of whirling, slowly diminishing Power, Namid could make out little except for the wall of the tower. But through the din the Power made, also diminishing, another sound came to her.

Voices. Coming from all around.

But she saw no one.

Chanting, but she could not understand the words.

The rhythm of the words resonated deep within her somehow – and she realized that the rhythm matched the rhythm of her heartbeat. As the Power whirled slower and slower, the chanting grew louder and the speed increased, drawing her in.

Pain tore through her again, tore Power from her.

Drip....

"I Saw that it would take death to bring back my magnificent city," Inezha's voice crooned in her ear. "Send all your Power into the city. Make it right. And don't worry yourself. I've Seen that there will be death, but it won't be your dear Aahmes. I'll take good care of him. He'll not long miss you."

But when Namid looked, Inezha was not there.

The last of the Power swirled away and claimed the last of her strength with it. She could tell Aahmes was near but lacked the strength to even turn to look for him. His hands no longer clasped hers.

As she sank to the ground, the city filled with voices, exclamations of surprise and joy. Her sight cleared and Namid saw all the people from Nazextas, gathering, laughing.

Real.

She no longer saw the blood mesh, nor felt it. And she felt separate, apart from the city somehow. Watching, but not belonging to what she saw.

Drip....

In among the milling people of Nazextas, Namid spotted several people slumped to the ground. The so-called gods.

As she watched, Ilenii, Belaraketh and Shiara helped each other to their feet. They looked haggard and angry, frightened and older than before. When they caught sight of Namid, noticed that she watched them, they clutched each other, their expressions panicked.

Through senses still painfully heightened, Power-burned, Namid saw that the 'gods' were at least as drained as she felt. And completely drained of blood Power. None of that Power was anywhere in sight.

The three 'gods' managed to create one of those shimmers in the air that they used to travel somehow. It was clear to Namid that they could barely manage such Power, even with the three of them working together. All three stepped into it and vanished.

Jelth staggered past, not even looking at Namid. He met with Roivah-Neheb. They looked as bad as the other three. They too only barely managed to create one of those shimmers and disappear into it.

A soft chuckle nearby drew Namid's attention. Vlatas sat propped against the tower, slightly to her right, and watched all the activity. When he caught her gaze, he gave her a nod of acknowledgement and a smile with a touch of sadness to it.

As she watched, he slowly became more and more transparent.

His voice came to her just before he faded away completely. "Time to go."

Drip....

Namid discovered she could move, could turn a little, and found Aahmes there with her on the ground. She shared a stricken look with him and clasped his hand, clutching it tightly. All around them, the people of Nazextas—just returned from their shadowy existence in the ghost city—began to fade.

A cry of delight rang out over the murmur of voices and Inezha hurled herself into the plaza that surrounded the tower. A young man with black hair and red-brown skin much like Namid's own separated from the crowd and caught Inezha in his arms. Namid recognized the mage Boudra, the man Inezha called brother.

A breath-of-time later, Inezha gave a cry of dismay as her arms passed through her brother and Boudra began to fade.

"No!" she screamed as she, too, began to fade.

Boudra placed his hands on her shoulders. "It's as it should be," he said. His voice came clearly to Namid and Aahmes. "You don't belong here anymore either."

And Namid remembered what Wesh's book had said: 'A death provides the richest, most potent blood Power.'

"But we have to bring all the Praznies back home," Inezha said.

"We can't force them," Boudra said. "If they want to return, they'll find their way here."

"We'll let them know," Namid called to them. She hoped Inezha heard her as she faded away.

Boudra inclined his head to her and then he was gone, too.

Namid gripped Aahmes' hand. Tears ran down her face as all around them the former citizens of Nazextas finally, truly died.

Then the light around her died too.

CHAPTER 31

The city stood restored and its pale-gray stones gleamed in the early-spring sunshine. Where new structures had been erected after the devastation of the killing mist, the Power had transformed them to match the rest of the city, but otherwise left them unchanged. A gleaming white tower now occupied the center of the city.

And all the ruins were gone.

Lord Thes had decided that his city was new enough it needed a new name. He favored calling it Rhazextris but had not yet officially declared it so.

When Inezha had appeared out of nowhere between the east gate of the city and Tower Hold, as the Power swirled and rebuilt the city, Haeith and Mehratar had spotted her from the top of Lord Tower. When she headed toward the city gate, they both ran down the stairs of the tower and out, to follow her into the city.

Before they reached the gate from the tower, they had lost sight of her, but decided that the city center was the most likely place for her to go. They arrived there in time to see Namid and Aahmes collapse in a blood-soaked heap just outside the door to the shining tower in the city's center.

Before he moved either of them, Mehratar drew them both into the Power sleep. Then he and Haeith carried them to one of the small buildings that rimmed the plaza around the tower.

That was where Namid woke days later, bruised and battered and with a strange sense of lightness. Before long, well-wishers and people who wanted to talk about what had happened swamped her and Aahmes.

When Thes finally arrived, he managed to shoo the well-wishers away, something neither Haeith nor Mehratar had accomplished. After a quick look at Aahmes and Namid, his expression one of concern and assessment of their condition, Thes told them there was something they needed to see.

Mehratar warned that they should not overdo it and Thes assured him they were only going across the plaza to the tower. He led the way, uncharacteristically silent in the face of their inquiries.

Haeith and Mehratar followed.

Inside the tower door, Thes stepped aside and waved his hand with a flourish at the main room.

"What are you makin' o' this?" he said.

Namid exchanged glances with Aahmes and shook her head at the sight of the floor of the main level. A translucent image that looked like some sort of map covered the entire floor. Namid picked out hills and rivers and right in the center, in what looked like a city, sat the Star of Corentris.

Cameni and Enric joined them from where they had been looking at the far side of the map.

"Isn't it wondrous?" Cameni breathed.

"And you two look much better," Enric said with a quick side glance at Cameni.

She flushed, then grinned. "And yes, of course, you look much better. How are you feeling?"

"Sore, tired," Aahmes said.

"Drained," Namid added, then made a small sound of surprise. "It worked!"

She grasped Aahmes in a tight hug that made them both ache, and almost topple over, but he did not complain. "The blood Power's gone."

"Along with much of that Power that came to us from Sesaisyd, it feels like," Aahmes said.

Namid shrugged and tentatively reached out with her own Power, diminished but still there. "I can still sense the Wild Power," she said with a smile.

Aahmes nodded. "Me too." He suddenly lost his balance and had to steady himself with a grip on Namid's arm.

"And it's back to rest for you two," Mehratar said.

~ ~ ~

Aahmes and Namid spent many long days resting and recovering in the small building. When Mehratar allowed, they did their best to answer the questions Thes had about his new city. He and Keizha visited often and kept them apprised of how everyone was settling into the new buildings.

Namid saw less of Haeith, but he did visit at least once every couple of days, sharing his own observations on how the city fared. And when he left from those visits, Namid was certain she heard Narqir's voice greet him outside the building, heard her and Haeith engaged in energetic discussion as they walked off.

Narqir herself only visited once, alone, to tell them the 'gods' had taken themselves somewhere far away. "And the excess Power is gone," she said. "It hasn't returned. I'm back to what I was before all the craziness those thousands of years ago. I'm sure the others are, too."

She seemed happy with the outcome. Namid wondered about the others.

Close to four weeks after the restoration of the city,

Cameni and Enric took their leave saying they needed to return to Enric's family, that they had obligations they needed to tend to. But they promised to return as soon as they could and, of course, make sure Namid and Aahmes did not miss their wedding, once they set a date.

The next day, Mehratar released Aahmes and Namid from his care and his ordered period of rest, but told them to find him if they started to feel worse again. And he instructed them to still spend more time resting than being too active for another week or two. Walking around the city would be fine, but no sparring. They both grinned at him.

Then Thes collected them and took them back to the tower in the center of the city.

He opened the door, ushered them inside with a flourish, a bow, and a self-satisfied smile. Then he closed the door behind them, leaving them alone.

When Namid gave Aahmes a confused look he smiled at her. He clasped her hand and drew her further into the tower, walking through the translucent map that still covered the floor.

"Lord Thes has formally offered us this tower. For our home," Aahmes said, his voice solemn with ceremony but the corners of his mouth kept quirking up. "If you approve of the place, of course. He also asks that we accept positions as his advisors and court mages." Aahmes winked at her. "He's completely serious about it this time, unlike the first time he mentioned it seasons ago. He assures me that the duties won't be too demanding most of the time."

Namid looked around the room with its enigmatic map and statue, and the staircase curving up to floors above.

"He's just giving us the tower?"

"Right now, everyone's able and allowed to pick their homes from the new buildings. So why not us, too? If you want to stay here, that is."

Namid met his hopeful gaze with a cautiously pleased

one of her own. Was there a downside to this that she wasn't seeing?

As if he knew her thoughts, Aahmes chuckled. "No one else seems to want to live in an ancient mage's tower," he told her. "But Thes decided that, if that ancient mage might happen to still be around somehow—"

"He's not," Namid interjected.

Aahmes nodded in agreement. "But even so. Were he to come back, he'd likely not object if his tower went to the two of us." He gestured expansively around them. "It's ours. If you want."

Namid caught him close. "I do want," she murmured.

Aahmes grinned, then kissed her.

"Welcome home, beloved."

~

NOTES AND PRONUNCIATIONS

A week is eight days long.

A "candle-mark" is roughly equivalent to an hour.

A "breath-of-time" is an indeterminate short amount of time, roughly seconds to a few minutes.

A "pace" is the length of a double step (roughly five feet).

Aahmes -- AH mehz
Aahmestharq -- AH mehz thahrk
Aahsemerye -- ah seh MEH ryuh
Acnald -- AHK nahld
Acpher -- AHK fur
Adday -- AH day
Addayris -- ah DAY rihss
Aghaik -- AHG ayk
Akavos -- ah kah VOHSS
Andrin -- AN drihn
Arinsk -- AHR ihnsk

Bakensson -- BAH kehn suhn
Bakhtenmaat -- bahk TEHN mah aht
Belaraketh -- bel AHR uh kehth
Boudra -- BOO druh

Cameni -- KAM uh nee
Cathir -- KAH theer
Chendrukhar -- CHEHN droo kahr
Cohaire -- koh HAY ruh
Corentris -- kohr EHN trihss

Dar -- DAHR
Das -- DAHSS
Denek -- deh NEHK

Dianchaid -- DYAHN chayd
Diarmid -- DYAHR mihd
Dyaaset -- DYAH ah seht
Dyefa -- dee EHF uh

Enric -- EN rihk
Ethmereneith -- ehth meh reh NAYTH

Fathal -- fah THAHL
Fathir -- fah THEER
Fathnor -- FAHTH nohr
Fathri -- FAH three
Foroughi -- FOHR oh ee

Haeith -- HAY ihth
Haqareh -- huh KAHR eh

Ilenii -- ihl EHN ee
Inar -- ih NAHR
Inarshen -- ih NAHR shuhn
Inezha -- ihn EH zhuh

Jelth -- JELTH

Keizha -- KAY zhuh
Khaen -- kah EHN
Kharesdotr -- KAH rehss doh ter
Kheill -- KAYL
Kilaadi -- kih LAH dee
Krendl -- KREHN duhl

Lann -- LAN
Larinaq -- LAHR ih nak
Levil -- LEH vuhl

Meahan -- MEE uhn
Mehratar -- MEH ruh tahr

Mehtnathor -- meht NAH thohr

Naalin -- NAH leen
Naardona -- nahr DOH nuh
Nakht -- NAHKT
Nakhtnefre -- NAHKT nehf ruh
Namid -- NAH meed
Narqir -- nahr KEER
Navele -- nuh VEEL
Nazextas -- naz EHKSS tuhss
navn -- NAH vuhn

Odasoro -- oh DAHSS oh roh
Ofretawe -- OH freh tah weh
Ordra -- OHR druh

Paronia -- puh ROHN yuh
Prazny -- PRAHZ nee

Qarsson -- KAHRZ suhn

Ranasdotr -- RAH nahss doh ter
Resaar -- reh SAHR
Retheim -- reh THAYM
Rhadanthus -- ruh DAN thuhss
Rhazextris -- ruh ZEX trihss
Roivah-neheb -- ROI vuh NEH hehb

Sainamid -- sah EE nah meed
Saneth -- SAH neth
Sanethakht -- sah neh THAHKT
Sen -- SEHN
Sesaisyd -- seh SAY sihd
Shartov -- SHAHR toff
Sitkha -- SIHT kuh
Sitkhesen -- siht KEH sehn
Staehw -- STAY oo

Sy'shythys -- sih SHIH thihss

Taakha -- tah AH kuh
Taakhanefret -- tah AH kuh neh freht
Talorisin -- tal OHR ih sihn
Tal -- TAL
Tanyala -- tahn YAH lah
Thes -- THEHSS
Tiyesdotr -- TEE yuhss doh ter

Uarseken -- oo AHR seh kehn

Vithen -- VIH thuhn
Vithir -- vih THEER

Wesh -- WEHSH

Yokana -- yoh KAH nuh

Zelimir -- ZEL uh meer

~

AUTHOR'S NOTE

Thank you for reading my book. I hope you enjoyed it!

Please consider leaving an honest review on the book's
product page at your favorite online bookstore
and on Goodreads. Reviews from readers like you are
powerful and greatly help other readers
discover books they might enjoy.

-Lynn

ABOUT THE AUTHOR

S. Lynn Helton lives in the foothills of the Rocky
Mountains, U.S.A., with her family and a couple of crazy
cats. Lynn enjoys camping and hiking, playing games,
crafting, reading (a lot) and, of course, writing.

Read more about her books on her website:
www.slynnhelton.com